TALLEYMAN
IN THE ICE

Also by John James
TALLEYMAN

TALLEYMAN
IN THE ICE

John James

Futura

A Futura Book

Typeset by Selectmove Ltd
Reproduced, printed and bound in Great Britain by
BPCC Hazell Books Ltd
Member of BPCC Ltd
Aylesbury, Bucks, England

Futura Publications
A Division of
Macdonald & Co (Publishers) Ltd
66–73 Shoe Lane
London EC4P 4AB

A member of Maxwell Pergamon Publishing Corporation plc

DRAMATIS PERSONAE

IN *FLAMINGO*

Captain
Paxton Only, an ambitious man.

Wardroom Officers
Lieutenants:
Henry Sherwin, a veteran.
Thomas Talleyman, a frustrated potato farmer.
Andrew Longville, a devoted seaman.
Frederick Orton, an interrupted barrister.

Paymaster Oliver Biddell.
Captain Michael Fincham, Royal Marines.
Surgeon: Robert Thacker.
Chaplain: Arthur Dincombe, Fellow of St Tibb's College, Cambridge.
Chief Engineer: Charles Craddock, a temporary officer.

Gunroom Officers
Gunner: Matthew Wasely, a devout man.
Boatswain: John Harris.
Carpenter: Walter Hook.
Mate Andrew Cricklade
Mate Charles Sladen.
Mate Will Neve.
Cadets Fox, Dyke, Pritchard, Chessil.

Marines

Sergeant Madden; Corporal Keary, Corporal Egan; Marines Garvey,
Hurley, Driscoll, and others.

Seamen

Ten-year-men: Abel, Silverwright, Sterling, Orme, and others.
Volunteers: Nussey, Calne, Moulton, Smales, and others.

Other Officers

Lieutenant (Fat Jack) Pither, an emaciated officer.
Major Esteron, an official of the Honourable East India Company.
Lieutenant Willy Little, a sapper.

Civilians

Josiah Talleyman (father of Thomas), a reformed ironfounder.

Richard Talleyman, his second son, a financier.

Mr Bolton, Secretary of the Agapanthus Club.

Baron Krabbe, a.k.a. Count Rakoff, a Baltic baron in the foreign service of the Tsar

Dushan Rakoff, his son, a political prisoner.

Mr Strand, a Brazilian gentleman from Acushnet.

Lord Dunscore, a magnate from Tenby.

Lord Denain (Philip Suttle), a young peer.

Arabella Talleyman, sister to Thomas.

Harriet Talleyman, wife to Thomas.

Albert and Edward Talleyman, sons to Thomas and Harriet.

Doctor Wormset, a society physician.

Young Doctor Wormset, his son.

New Doctor Wormset, his grandson.

Real People

Dean Llewellyn Llewellin.

Admiral Price.

Captain Burridge, RN.

Captain Sir James Nicholas, RN.

Admiral Fevrier des Pointes, a French sea-officer.

Rear Admiral Zavioko, Governor of Kamchatka.

Author's Note

This is a novel. Except for a few persons who are in the public domain, like Admiral Price and Dean Llewellyn Llewellin, the characters exist entirely in the author's imagination. Nevertheless, it is time an attempt was made to answer a number of questions about the Russian War of 1854, which was not fought entirely in the Crimea. Aficionados will recognize in *Flamingo* the lines of *Chaa-Sze* and the upper works of Dupuy de Lome's *Audacieux*. The chess match of pp303–308 was played in 1851 between Mr Staunton and Mr Williams in London: incidentally, White won. The Agapanthus Club was founded by Mr W.M. Thackeray.

Mate at this period was the rank title used for the men later called sublieutenants.

Prologue

All this happened when Talleyman went to the Russian war in HMS *Flamingo*. The Flaming Oh, the sailors called her, or the Flaming Ooh, or the Flaming Ah, sometimes modifying the first word for the sake of euphony or of emotional expression. But mostly they called her the Old Oh: frequently they spat, although whether this was to express emotion of some kind or to ward off an evil eye, or merely out of habit no one could rightly explain.

Flamingo was an odd ship in many ways. She was laid down on the Tyne, in 1848, without much fuss and a certain confusion about her cost in the Navy estimates. When the *Illustrated* were told they might send someone to draw her on the stocks, the day given turned out to be a week after she had been quietly slipped into the water and towed away to have her engines set up.

After that there were occasional notes in the press about her being taken down to Portsmouth for her trials and proving so badly trimmed that she had to be taken back to Newcastle to have a full poop added to her flush deck with its eighteen guns: although there were rumours that this was only done to give the Captain, if she ever got one, a more luxurious suite. Then, finished, she was laid up in ordinary in Portsmouth with no one in her except the Boatswain and the Carpenter and the Gunner, and a few of their minions.

When the Russian war began to threaten, the yards were far too busy getting the big wooden three-deckers, with their hundred and odd guns and their new-fitted engines that might give them four knots if they worked and coal enough for three days, ready for the great expedition into the Baltic, for anyone to think of taking *Flamingo* off the mud. In any case it seemed that their Lordships could think of nothing to do with her. But eventually the Board of Admiralty were prodded by another agency of the Government into bringing her out for some unspecified use. Unspecified, that is, to the press. And after some consideration, seeing he was just back from Canada, they offered her to Commander Paxton Only.

Only had only come home at the end of April, when the rush for posts was long over and the Guards had gone off for the great campaign along the Danube and Admiral Napier had sailed on the secret expedition to attack St Petersburg, as was reported weekly in the *Illustrated*. Only listened to what he was supposed to do, and considered. He then talked very plain to their Lordships, mostly by letter, keeping one copy for himself. He argued from the size of the vessel, nearly as long as *Victory*, where the engines had meant reducing the number of guns, rather than from the number of men she was said to need. He hinted that there was no one else competent to do this job, considering where he had spent the last three years. At last, because their Lordships were under pressure from other interested parties to get the ship under way, they agreed that *Flamingo* needed a Captain and not a Commander, so Only moved up out of turn to the Captain's list and saw the certainty of an Admiral's Flag and pay before he died. Then he went down to Portsmouth and looked at the ship. And he cried.

He found that the original Boatswain had exchanged into a liner and had been replaced by an older and harder man, John Harris. At the start of the war, the Gunner had asked to go on shore on the grounds of age and infirmity and had been replaced by one Matthew Wasely. Mr Wasely himself had been on shore for some years, and was in private life the minister of a dissenting chapel in Southsea. The Carpenter, Walter Hook, had at least been in the ship since she was handed over, and had kept her moderately sound and watertight.

Only had agreed to sail without a Master, since these were hard to find when the big ships had been satisfied, and he himself was qualified as a navigator. The Board of Admiralty gave Only a very aged First Lieutenant, a man called Sherwin who had been on shore for many many years: but he had, like Only, been at Navarino, which was twenty-six years in the past and the last time the Navy had fought a battle. He had been pestering his Member of Parliament to get him a post, thinking perhaps he might be given a berth in a hulk or guard ship and so release a younger man for sea duty. Their Lordships decided that if they took Sherwin they would release a younger man from *Flamingo* to go into some hulk or guard ship.

Their Lordships told Only they could find him three Mates, who had just passed from midshipmen, and one of them had done the course at HMS *Excellent* and was therefore qualified in gunnery and steam. He could appoint one cadet, as was his right, but they would also give him three more, thirteen years old and straight from school, the war having made the Navy suddenly a popular profession in the eyes of some parents. They could find him a Chief Engineer, and luckily one Charles Craddock had offered his services because he had worked for Messrs Nasmyth and helped to set up the engines.

They could provide a new-promoted Lieutenant of Royal Marines, to rank as a Captain at sea, and thirty or so Marines, new recruited. Out of the depot at Portsmouth, and from *Excellent*, they could find him eighty regular sailors, ten-year men, mostly lately joined. Only noted that seventeen of these were able seamen, and counted himself lucky: most of the big liners which had gone to the Baltic had fewer than that among a thousand complement.

3

The rest of the crew Only would have to find himself. He needed no more than three more lieutenants, a paymaster, a chaplain and about a hundred men. He left Sherwin to get the ship ready for sea, and went off to find the rest of his crew. And one of those he went to ask was Thomas Talleyman.

I

The Fens

1

Only found Talleyman in Hurrell's iron foundry in Cambridge, down the river end of Bridge Street, between the roadway and St John's. Talleyman was watching the casting of a four-foot gear wheel. The molten iron ran into the sand mould. Talleyman had thrown down with his frock coat somewhere, his shirt and cravat were streaked with coal dust and his trousers were powdered with ashes. He was sweating. His broken nose glowed of its own, fit, Only thought, to melt the iron by itself, in a face browned by land weather, not by sea winds. He asked, by way of greeting,

'What are you doing here?'

'I have,' said Only, 'been trying to find a chaplain. I was told that you were here, and that has saved me the journey out to Fen Dilney. But what is all this?'

'It is gearing. For a pump. The link between the steam engine and the pump. I want it by the end of the summer. We can spend the autumn and winter draining Dilney Fen. At least the first two hundred acres. One moment – ' He walked across and spat on the iron, watched the spittle break into globules and sizzle on the cooling surface – 'Six hours. For practical purposes, tomorrow. Before we start filing. And cleaning.'

'When you have drained your two hundred acres?' Only asked, with the interest of one farmer in another's problems.

'Potatoes.'

'You have a market?'

'Liverpool. The Irish immigrants will eat nothing else if they can buy potatoes. I have an Irish gang arranged to clear the ground. And for planting.'

7

'Is there somewhere we can talk?'

'I have no more to do today. I cannot take you to the Mitre. Not in working clothes. People will think you strange in the Baron of Beef. You are too well dressed. I have a room at the Pickerel. It is across the bridge. If you are not ashamed to walk with me.'

They walked across the river, in silence, in step, the two stovepipe hats an even height. He walks here like a farmer, thought Only, not the quick short steps of shipboard. In what passed for a bar parlour of the Pickerel, Talleyman called for a bottle of brandy, and water, and glasses.

'So you have been ashore since you got married?' Only asked. 'That is, let's see, four years, or a bit more.'

'True. And yourself?'

'I have been to sea twice, on two of the expeditions to look for Franklin, once as a lieutenant and the second as commander of a steamer.'

'I thought you scorned steamers.'

'We can all learn. That second time, we spent the winter up there. We came back in May, too late to get a berth in the Fleet when it went to the Baltic. I would have thought you would have gone.'

'I wrote and asked for a berth. Five times. I have not been given an appointment.'

'So I gathered at the Admiralty. Did you not think it strange? We have two or three thousand lieutenants on the books, and when we need six hundred to man the Fleet for war, we cannot find them. We have promoted practically every Mate, and still there are not enough lieutenants, and most of our midshipmen have been made mates and cannot do the work. Yet, no berth for you? Have you not wondered why?'

'I have my suspicions. My father has a seat in the House, His allegiance is uncertain. A word from him . . .'

'And a name can be misfiled, an application put into the wrong drawer.'

8

'He has a gentleman. I am received where he is not. Nor my brother. He has said he does not want the only gentleman in the family to be killed.'

'So he does not want you to go to sea in this war. But what is your wife's opinion? I suppose she is quite familiar with the way in which your father controls the money.'

'You are right. She does not want me to go away from home.'

'She is well, I trust?'

'She is like the two boys: she grows in stature daily.'

Only sipped his brandy. Then he said,

'I have been given a ship, you know. Only for a short voyage, under specific orders. I am trying to find a crew, or at least officers, and that is why I have come to Cambridge. I spent this morning persuading a clergyman to come as Chaplain and schoolmaster. A Fellow of a college, and what I believe is called a muscular Christian, and I suppose we can stand the Christianity if only we have the muscles to heave on ropes and shift the coal, because I am sure I will have no one else who is competent.'

'Do you need an Engineer? I know someone who is qualified under the new regulations. He could be a a chief for a single commission. He wants to go. His name is Craddock.'

'I have asked Craddock, and he has agreed to come. We must get to sea by the middle of August, and we cannot stay after the end of October.'

'It sounds like a liner. Even the ones in commission. They sit in harbour from October to May.'

'Not a liner. A very strange ship, called *Flamingo*. I have explicit orders, and less than half the crew provided. For the officers, I must find them among the sick, the mad, the inexperienced and the unwilling. Would you not come, young Tal?'

'For a short voyage?'

'If there is to be a medal for this war you would be qualified. Could you not persuade your father? Where is he?'

'I do not know. He is somewhere between London and Brussels, always travelling to and fro. My great-grandfather sold pins and nails from door to door. My grandfather sold iron. My father sold iron works. My brother buys and sells money. They travel.'

'You might well be gone to sea and back again before they know.'

'As short as that?'

'If our plan is satisfactory, then probably no more than that.'

'Probably?'

'Almost certainly. This is going to be no more than a pleasure cruise. You say our liners will not go to sea in the winter? Do you think that the Russians will come into the storms and fogs of the North Sea? I may as well be honest, because you will see it in *The Times* in a week that *Flamingo* is fitting out to act as a guard ship off the north coast of Ireland in case the Russians make a raid from Archangel.'

'What do you want me to come as? Fourth again?'

'Second, and guns. I don't need you for engines, because Craddock seems a capable man –'

'*Flamingo*? He set up the engines.'

'Did he now? But he has found three or four young men who have finished apprenticeships and are qualified as assistants. So at least you will have someone to talk to.'

'I will think about it. As long as I'm not First Lieutenant. Dreadful job. All paperwork. And always with the Captain looking over one's shoulder. I could not stand that.'

'I know, I was, you remember, First Lieutenant to Pentstemon for one commission.'

'Pentstemon was a reasonable man.'

'Thank you very much. But make up your mind, young Tal, I have to go back to London tonight and I can get you appointed tomorrow. There are those of us who have influence and friends in middling places.

Talleyman drummed his fingers on the table. Only watched those enormous hands, made two sizes too big for the man. He's a ticklish man, Only thought, and I don't think there's a dozen captains could control him, and not more than a dozen captains he will tolerate, and I suspect I and Pentstemon are the only two who are in both lists. Pentstemon is in Bombay: he had enough sense to get himself honourably appointed to a sea berth where he would not be involved in any defeat. He observed, dreamily,

'Strange how popular this war is, and yet how few are willing to go to it.'

'People might go if they knew why we have a war.'

'It is like all wars,' said Only. 'The politicians and the ambassadors have not watched their backs, and they have slept when they ought to be awake, and they have gone to the ballet when they ought to have been reading their papers, and at last there is nothing left but a war, which comes, of course, as a surprise to them. It must do because they have let the Navy rot away and sent all the soldiers to foreign parts ready to fight the wars the last generation were afraid of, so we sailors and soldiers must go out and get killed to save the politicians' faces. But at least it gives us a chance to command, at sea or on land.'

'What is it the lawyers say? *Cui bonum?* 'Who profits?'

'Why, me, for one thing, young Tal. Don't tell anyone, but just as all number of incompetent Mates have been made Lieutenants, so I will be a Captain on Monday morning. I only have to live long enough me lad, and I shall die an Admiral. Think of that. All I need is sea time as a Captain, and I shall fly my yellow flag on a cab. And remember this: for many years to come no Lieutenant who did not go

11

to this war is likely to get a berth, let alone become a Captain.'

'True. And you could arrange that?'

'An Admiralty clerk who loses a letter when an MP writes to him will find it again when a Captain stands over him.'

'So – ' Talleyman mused a little. 'If I agreed to come. . . you mean I could be back to see my pump working? When do you want me aboard? I must see this casting cool. Then I must arrange for the bailiff to work the farm. Sixty acres of onions to lift.'

'Well, today is. . . yes. . .twelve days from now, young Tal, I want you aboard, in the afternoon.'

'For a short voyage? You have told me everything?'

'Since we must sail cheek by scowl through the next few months, young Tal, I can have no secrets from you. So, I will start with the truth – I have secrets from you.'

'I will join you. At Portsmouth, I assume?'

Paxton Only smiled like a seraph.

'Oh, no. At Dundee.'

'At Dundee? That sounds desperate.'

'I must find men, kerns and gallowglasses and kilted Highlanders with the heather growing between their toes.'

'How did you know where to find me today?'

'Someone at the Club said you were making machinery, and this was the most likely foundry.'

'At the club? The Agapanthus? Mr Bolton?'

'Who else? What other club would have me? Or you?'

'I will come.'

They rose, put on their hats and began to walk back across the river. Talleyman said,

'I will go home now and tell my wife, and if I survive I will pack my sea chest and bring a chess board. By the way, where are you staying in Cambridge?'

'The Coach and Horses.'

'Opposite the gate of St Tibb's? In Tibb's Lane? That's a fairly new name for the inn, you know. It used to be The Carrier because it was where the carriers' carts came in from Shelford. Then, oh, a hundred years ago, they started the stage coach, and he lost his trade, the innkeeper, and it didn't suit him. He used to stand at the door whenever the stage passed and shout at it, 'Whoreson Coach! Whoreson Coach!' 'So it got the present name. I'll see you in Dundee.'

Talleyman slipped in through the gate of the foundry. Only stood and stared after him. What have I done? he asked now. What have I done? A season of Talleyman's tales and his chess as well? I must be mad. I'm sure he is.

2

Talleyman had trouble with Harriet. He came home the next day, the twenty miles to the Dower House on Fen Dilney Manor. He liked the small house. He had been brought up there, as far as he was brought up anywhere, and his sister Arabella had taken full advantage of her four years precedence. Poor Arabella. When old Josiah had bought the whole estate, and moved himself and Arabella, and Richard, into the Manor House, he had given Tom the Dower House as a wedding present. He had given Tom the farm to run, too; not to own outright, of course, although it would come to him after Josiah was dead, and after that to his children. So Thomas Talleyman swallowed the anchor, simply by not applying for another ship after *Santorin*, not taking his half pay, and settled down as a farmer.

A farmer would not have been his first choice, he reflected as he trotted the trap along the turnpike. He had arranged for an overseer to come and look to the setting up of his steam when the castings were all done, and start the pumping out of the fen. It would not be as well done as if Talleyman were there himself, but even ill done it could begin by October and a year saved was a year gained. After that, Talleyman had an idea of a new way of ploughing by steam.

First choice would have been to go into the family business – not the business as it was now, but as it had been even as late as his boyhood. Once the Talleyman name had meant manufacture, the casting and finishing of parts for machinery. But the last of these factories that his father had directly owned was the boiler works, and that had been sold the year he went to sea in *Santorin*. Josiah had forbidden him, now, to have any part in what he called 'works' in general. The place of a gentleman was to live on his land, and not soil his hands with iron, or wheels, or coal or steam. But there were ways round this.

Talleyman liked travelling by road, in the trap. It gave him time to think and plan. In the back were his two gifts for the boys. For Albert, the elder, he had a wheeled railway engine, low enough to be pushed along by feet, wide based so that it would not turn over, a saddle mounted on the boiler outline by a system of springs. Angle irons and tube, thought Talleyman, you can make them small and yet strong, light but rigid. No need for massive structure.

Three miles from home he crossed the railway. Another three years, he thought, he would be in a strong enough positions to build a light railway from here across the Home Farm to the Dower House, to bring in the coal for the winter, to take out the potatoes and the barley and the onions he would be growing. Three years after that and he would have the stock pulled not by horses but by a small locomotive. Not yet, not till the soil was drained and settled. Drained by steam, not by a windmill like the one he had made for Edmund.

14

The boys, incidentally, seemed pleased with their presents. That hardly mattered. What was more important was that Harriet was pleased. He made sure she was in a good mood by bringing a pound of shop-made chocolates, and when she sat down to eat them in the middle of the afternoon he had a bottle or Marsala brought up.

Harriet liked sweet things. They did her good, Talleyman thought. When they were first married, she had been so thin it was touching. But now she had filled out into a fine figure of a woman. When she had finished the chocolates she oversaw the nurse putting the boys to bed. Talleyman took the big black horse and trotted him a little way into Dilney Fen, and planned ahead to where he would site the machinery for the steam plough and then where the light railway would run.

Dinner was simple. A soup, made from the garden peas. One of the Manor House gamekeepers had caught a pike the day before, and that appeared in a pie. A pair of young fowls, steamed. A home-cured ham, served hot. Raspberries and cream. Talleyman picked at it all, nervous, but Harriet finished what he did not eat. Finally over their dish of tea he told her:

'I had a visit from Only yesterday. He is Captain Only now.'

'And what was he doing, indeed, joyriding around the county?'

'He came to see me.'

'Why in Cambridge? Is our house not good enough for him, then? It would only be a step and we could easily have entertained him for a day or two – for a week; we could have given a dinner for him for there are a score of families still in the county even at this time of year. . .'

'He was pressed. He had other people to see in Cambridge. And he has not much time. He must be at sea in three weeks.'

'I would have thought he would have been at sea already. Does he not know that we are war with the Russians? I hope you told him.'

'He has just come back from a long voyage in the Arctic, and he has barely been ashore a month. Now they want him to go to sea again. He has been given a ship.'

'Obviously he has influence and favouritism. Of course he will not go into any danger. The Fleet is already at sea, and has been for months.'

'He has been given a special ship, for a special task. He offered me a post.'

'You pestered the Admiralty for a post for months, and never received an answer.'

'This may be the answer.'

'Your father will soon put a stop to this, and indeed he says he stopped the other applications. Just let him know, and there will be no pestering of you to go. There is no reason at all why you should go to sea.'

I have a reason, thought Talleyman. She would not understand it, even in one word. My honour sends me.

'The war is almost over,' Harriet went on. 'The Guards are on the Danube, and they are sure to destroy the Russians in one battle. And besides, you are a married man with children, and we all depend on you.'

'The Russians will not be defeated by one battle. And there are many men on the Danube, and outside St Petersburg, who are married with families.'

'They need not have gone. There are plenty of officers who have transferred or sold out rather than go to this war, and nobody thought the less of them.'

Talleyman saw the opening and seized on it.

'There is one person who will think less of me if I do not go to this war.'

'And who is that, now, tell me that, who will think the less of you?'

'Myself.'

16

She could not understand that. The argument went on for days. Harriet said,

'You gave Mr Only nothing in writing. It was all in words.'

'It was my word.'

'If you must be there on that day, you can be ill. You can have a cold. You may break your leg riding.'

'A cold? We will be cold enough at sea.'

'And how will I tell people where you are?'

He told her what Only had told him, not sure if she would believe it: he did not.

'It is possible, at least their Lordships think it possible. The Russians may send a fleet to attack Ireland. From north of Sweden. We must cruise there between Ireland and Iceland. To frighten them off.'

'Now, that is arrant nonsense, for who in their senses would want to capture Ireland, for it is a poor country is is not, and wet and hard to live in, and we only hold it out of charity for those poor peasants who depend on us English for their living. And the clothes on their backs and the food in their mouths, and what Russian would want to be paying our all that money?'

'It's true,' Talleyman allowed. 'Nobody wants Ireland for itself. But if the Russians take, say, only Ulster, they mask our ports from Glasgow through Liverpool to Holyhead. They could invade where they liked. Ireland has only a positional advantage.'

It was the most trivial thing that brought her round.

'If I do not, somehow, go to sea in this war, I cannot go to the Lord Lieutenant's receptions, or any where else where I am expected to wear uniform. Nor can you either.'

'Why not?'

'Without a medal? There will be a medal for this war. If I do not have it to wear, everyone will think I chose not to go. That I was afraid.' The medal for Navarino took twenty years to come but he did not think it necessary to tell her that.

17

'A medal? Really a medal?' Harriet had not thought of that. 'I can show the boys their father's medal?' She had seen a Navarino medal, and a Polar medal, small unimpressive discs of silver on shabby coloured ribbons, nothing to catch the eye. She was sure Thomas was worth more than a mere medal. Surely... what else was there? Once he got to sea, they would see what he was worth. She had heard of officers who were given the Companion of the Bath, and that might be very nice to have. She was realistic: she knew she could not hope for a knighthood for him as a mere Lieutenant and she would not be Lady Tallyman yet, but he would not stay a mere Lieutenant, not for long. She had heard of officers being promoted for brave actions and he must come back from this voyage a commander at least, perhaps a captain. Anything was better than to be a farmer's wife, even a small land-owner's wife, as if they were different things. But to be an Admiral's lady, to go in state, to be welcomed and recognized everywhere, oh, that would be something.

So Tom Talleyman's wife let him go off to the Russians war for the sake of a ribbon on his coat.

II

Harbour

1

It was the Chaplain who saw Talleyman come into *Flamingo*. The Reverend Arthur Dincombe was a fellow of St Tibb's College at Cambridge. He had been introduced to Only by French, the Senior Tutor. He asked for time to consider, and had written to his friend Mr Kingsley in Hamsphire. Mr Kingsley, well known as a muscular Christian, wrote back urging him to go and regretting that as he held a living in the church he could not take advantage himself of such a golden opportunity for violent activity. After making sure that a Fellowship did not count as a living, and that the College would give him leave of absence for a year, he had accepted.

About an hour before he saw Talleyman he had taken a four-wheeler for himself and his six trunks and rattled through the streets of Dundee to where *Flamingo* lay alongside a quay. Dincombe explained himself to a Marine sentry at the gangplank who, being a Cork man, understood very little of what was said to him, and then to Sergeant Madden, who sent for the Mate who was acting as Officer of the Watch. Mr Cricklade, being overworked, shouted, 'Silverwright! Take the Chaplain's bags to the wardroom: and the Chaplain.'

Silverwright was the wardroom steward, and therefore a petty officer and a man of some authority in his own little world. He left the mere handling of trunks to his subordinates, and led Dincombe to the companionway under the break of the poop, forward of the wheel and binnacle, past the Marine sentry and into the wardroom at the after end of the main deck. And left him there.

Dincombe looked around him. He was in a long room, with a table down the middle of it and a mast coming up through that. At the far end, which, he supposed from assiduous reading of Mr Marryatt, to be the stern of the ship, the room widened out and a row of small square windows gave some light. There was a skylight aft of the mast. Only had warned him that he would not have a comfortable place to live in, but surely this compared quite well with his sitting room in college. Down each side there seemed to be a row of cupboards. Dincombe walked to the stern, regarded Dundee harbour through the window, and opened the endmost cupboard door. It showed him a water closet. The one opposite seemed to be a shower bath. Very convenient. Dincombe wondered idly where his bedroom was. One of the other cupboards had some clothes in it, and a kind of swinging box hung from the ceiling with a few jumbled blankets. Presumably the property of the last occupant. He would speak to the steward about that, if he could find him.

Dincombe put on his top hat and went back on deck. The upper deck was a confusion of shouting, running men, and so the Chaplain climbed to the poop and looked at the scene. Men were unloading carts, and carrying things across the deck and down into the ship. They were bringing in sacks of what seemed to be coal by means of what Dincombe called a crane, but what he learned later was a derrick. From here he saw another four-wheeler pull up.

The man who got out was wearing a heavy pilot coat of brown tweed and a high top hat. He paid the cabby, left his two bags and a small trunk on the quay and went smartly to the gangplank. The Marine, recognizing authority in the step, came to attention and then, uncertainly and very badly, presented arms. The newcomer raised his hat to the Marine, came into the ship, turned to face aft and raised his hat again. Dincombe was pleased at this attention and raised his own hat in reply.

Talleyman looked round and saw the officer of the watch hurrying to him.

'Welcome aboard, sir.'

'Cricklade! You're a Mate. *You're* a Mate? You are barely ready to be a Mid.'

'Oh, I've passed, sir, and got my time in. I passed at the end of last year and I was hoping to go to the Baltic, but they said I had to go to *Excellent* and I've done the full course, six months, sir. I was afraid I wouldn't be finished in time for the war.'

'Oh, the war'll be over in a couple of weeks: the Guards have gone to the Danube, you know that. Captain aboard?'

'Ashore, sir. And the First Lieutenant. No other Lieutenants have come yet.'

'What are they up to?'

'Trying to make up the crew, sir. There's a couple of whalers in.'

'Chief Engineer?'

'Ashore, sir, at the Admiralty agent's. The Surgeon and the Pusser are either recruiting or with the agent. They're trying to buy the town out.'

'I'll change, then I'll report to the Captain.'

Dincombe followed Talleyman down into the ward-room, and was surprised to find that the newcomer did not entirely fill the narrow space. First impressions were deceptive. Talleyman was not in fact a tall man: he was under six feet, although Dincombe had thought him well over. He only moved, Dincombe realized, like a tall man, confident, thrusting, ducking his head under doorways that were quite high enough. His face looked at once both young and well used. Someone had broken his nose sometime. He threw his hat on the table, showing brown curly hair and brown eyes. Dincombe looked at the hat, coughed.

'I...er...I think you must be looking for somewhere else.'

'I beg your pardon. Who are you?'

'My name is Arthur Dincombe. I am the Chaplain and this is my sitting room.'

Talleyman raised his eyebrows.

'Been to sea before?'

'I've crossed the Channel.' Dincombe did not think it necessary to add, 'once'.

'This is not a vicarage. This is a wardroom. You'll be a member.'

'I don't live in a vicarage. I am a Fellow of a college and I live there.'

'In college you have. . . ?'

'A sitting room, a study, a bedroom, a guest bedroom, a pantry, a kitchen.'

'And a common room?'

'Yes, a combination room. And I dine in Hall.'

'This is a wardroom. Sitting room, study, dining hall, living room for nine or ten of us. You have a seat at table. You have a bed in one of these cabins.' He indicated the cupboard doors.

'Nine or ten?' Dincombe sounded horrified.

'Four Lieutenants, Master if we have one, Pusser, sawbones, engineer, soldier. And you.'

'Soldier?'

'Marine officer. Now, steward! Good God! Thought you were hanged. Remember you, Silverwright, gun-room steward in the old *Argyle*.'

'Yes, Mr Talleyman, sir. I remember you well, and Mr Pither and Mr Partridge.'

'Partridge is dead. Where are you putting me?'

'Where do you want to go, sir?'

'Am I in time to choose? First forward, port side. Nearest the hatch. Get out in a hurry if a shell comes in.'

'That's the First Lieutenant, sir.'

'First Lieutenant has his own cabin. Under the poop.'

'Ought to have, sir. But the Captain wants that kept clear, sir, for a passenger. And he wants the Master's cabin, opposite, kept clear for a chartroom, in case we does any surveying. Could put you in first to starboard, sir, share with the jolly.'

'What's his name?'

'Captain Fincham, sir.'

'Did he write that book? I'll go there. Sea chest, Silverwright, lay out undress, cocked hat.'

'Aye, aye, sir.'

'Where have you put the Chaplain?'

'Nowhere yet, sir.' Silverwright spoke through the open cabin door. 'I thought, both being day workers, I'd put him in port aft, with the Surgeon.'

'Very appropriate. You can pray if the shell comes in.'

'Appropriate?' queried Dincombe.

'Yes.' Talleyman was in his cabin now, talking through the door as he dressed. 'You have the same trade.'

'What's that!'

'Death.'

Dincombe blinked. Then it dawned on him.

'What? Do you mean I will have to share a bed-room?'

'This is a ship, Chaplain. We are too many men in too small a space. We leave many things behind. One of them is privacy. Only the Captain has a right to that. We must become friends. Very quickly. And stay friends. That means tolerance. It is not a common virtue. I know. My father-in-law is a parson.'

In what seemed to Dincombe an incredibly short time, Talleyman reappeared, his civilian clothes left in a heap for Silverwright to pick up. Now he was in a dark blue frock coat, white trousers, stiff white shirt and collar and black cravat. On his sleeve was the single gold stripe of a Lieutenant. He buckled his sword belt.

'No, no, Silverwright, cocked hat. Looks odd, chaplain. But it's regulation. Cocked hat ashore, always, even in undress. What's in all your trunks?'

'Captain Only told me to bring what I'd need for a term in college. I've brought my china, bed-linen, silver, books, clothes, everything. Is it enough?'

'Silverwright! Unpack the Chaplain's things. Keep what he'll need at sea. Repack the rest, get it ashore, let the agent have it.'

'But all my things – '

'You're going to war, Chaplain. Don't take anything you can't afford to lose. Come with me.'

They came out onto the quarterdeck. Talleyman called, 'Mr Cricklade!' Then to the Chaplain,

'Have you got warm clothes?'

'I find this costume quite warm enough, thank you. I have also brought an overcoat. Cambridge in winter is very cold, and I find – '

'I farm in the fens. You should be off watch soon, Mr Cricklade.'

'Yes, sir. I was hoping – '

'Defer your hope. Take Mr Dincombe ashore. Find a ships' chandler's. A good one. Where the whaling captains go. Rig him out for a winter voyage. Sea chest. Full outfit. Heaviest you can find. Three or four heavy jerseys. Seaboots. And waterproofs.'

'I am not afraid of a drop of rain,' said Dincombe defensively, trying to regain some control over the conversation.

'We are not talking about summer showers,' said Talleyman, coldly. Then, to Cricklade,

'Been in her long?'

'Just ten days. Joined her at Portsmouth, with the other two Mates. At once, the Captain said we were putting to sea, undermanned. Brought her through the Channel and up here under sail, with cold boilers. So we learned how to handle her, and the ten-year men got their first sea time in, most of them.'

'Captain sick?'

Cricklade laughed, and Talleyman joined in. The Mate told him,

26

'Sick as a drowned dog, first three days. But he just stood at the poop rail, all the time, with Silverwright holding a bucket for him, night and day. Retching away, and shouting in between, "Look at me, cowards! If I can do this, you can!" No proper sleep, just dozing leaning on the rail.'

The laughter, Dincombe had wit enough to realize, was not unkind, nor had the gossip been idle. Both officers had been watching the seamen. Talleyman observed,

'These are all regulars, Chaplain. Ten-year men. They've all got uniforms. Volunteers wear what they like. At first. We've got a couple of hard bargains here, Cricklade. That ginger man. Not pulling his weight.'

'That's White. The Bo'sun has hopes of getting him to desert tonight. There's a couple more like that. By the way, what have they given you in this ship? Third?'

'Second. And guns. I'll see a lot of you. I'd better report. Where are the recruiters?'

'Ivey Bush, just round the corner. You ought to be able to tell it by the crowd outside. We had a Marine sentry on at first, but the locals took so much pity on the poor sodgers going to the wars, in the practical way of slipping him drams and they just couldn't stand their ground. So we took the sentry off. The Russian war's very popular here, you know, among the townies. They won't come to fight in it, and they don't want to pay for it, but they're all for a war against the Ruskies. Perhaps it's just as well, when you look at them.'

2

Talleyman found the Ivey Bush, a respectable enough tavern, a place, he judged, where whaling mates would gather. Not quite high class enough for Captains. But good enough. There was a placard pasted to the big front window.

HER MAJESTY'S SHIP
FLAMINGO 18
IS FITTING OUT FOR
THE RUSSIAN WAR!!
SHE HAS BERTHS FOR
80
GOOD SEAMEN
WHO WANT
GLORY ADVENTURE
AND
PRIZES!

Talleyman found the door to the room behind the poster. He knocked and entered, announcing himself loudly and trusting that there was an officer inside it.

'Lieutenant Talleyman reporting, sir.'

Only was not there. Behind a table covered with papers were two officers. One was a paymaster, young, thin and pallid, dark shadows under his eyes. The other was a Lieutenant, a gross and bulky man, grey-haired. He looked up wearily and groaned:

'Welcome aboard. We could have done with you earlier. There is work, too much work, too much work. . . and too much haste.'

'Where is Captain Only?'

28

'Well may you ask,' said the Paymaster. 'We think he's gone to Stirling. At least he went there yesterday, and it sounded like that today. I'm Biddell. The Pusser,' he added, unnecessarily. 'Captain said he wanted to see us ready for sea when he got back. Captain always say that.'

'So much paper.' This man, thought Talleyman must be the First Lieutenant. What was his name? Sherman? Sherwin? He was complaining. 'So much paper. All this paper to be worked through. And all in a hurry. Nothing like my day. Can't make head or tail of it.'

Talleyman was regarding Sherwin in mounting horror. The man was fat, almost bursting out of what looked to be a brand new uniform. Might have been a big fellow when he was young, all muscle, but now just flabby. A red face which didn't look to have seen much fresh air lately. The hair was grizzled rather than grey, with no life in it. He repeated, 'All this paper, all new since my day.'

'When,' Talleyman asked brutally, 'did you last take a ship to sea? As First Lieutenant?'

'My last ship,' mused Sherwin, 'ah, she was a fine ship, that was the old *Kingfisher*, fine ship, seventy-four. Fourth Lieutenant, went out to Malta. It took us four months to make up a crew, all good stout lads, and here's Captain Only wants us to do the same job in a week. Can't be done, and I've told him so. It's all changed. All the forms have been changed, nobody understands them. I have to keep on asking the Captain.'

'Or me,' added Biddell with an aggrieved look.

'When did *Kingfisher* go to Malta?' Talleyman asked. 'Can't remember her.'

'No, went aground on Gozo, all broken up. That was in, oh, twenty-eight. Went into *Agamemnon*, then supernumerary, went on shore after Navarino. Never had another post offered till this war. But I knew they'd want me.'

'At Navarino?' Talleyman shuddered. This man had last been at sea when Talleyman was two years old. And senior then, much, to Only, who had been a cadet at Navarino. How old could he be? In his quarter-century on the beach, how much else had he forgotten besides how to fill in forms? And as fat as that, how would he get about the ship? Masthead would be well beyond him. And did he know anything at all about steam? Sherwin's next words answered some of the questions.

'I wrote my Member to get me a post. Must have written a dozen times. Missed the Baltic fleet, and they offered me this. Said there was nothing else suitable for my seniority.' And the whole Board, Talleyman thought, must have had fits when he accepted. Sherwin moaned on. 'New ship, no men, all to be done, and that lad Only wants everything done in a hurry. But a good lad, he's smelt powder, he's seen blood on the deck. But no men. The ship's no good if there's no men.'

Talleyman looked at Biddell.

'You were eighty short?'

'We had eighty-two to come up from Portsmouth, and the Marines had thirty-three and two drummers and at least they could haul on a rope. So we needed forty-eight. We asked for eighty, I'd have settle for forty, Only was ready to go with thirty, but we got sixty-two. Turning them away, we were.'

'But. . . how did you get them?'

'Oh it was Only who got them. He and the Bo'sun and the Carpenter, they've been drinking their way round the town nearly every night. There were three whalers paid off last week, and everybody out of them seemed to know who he was. Didn't he go on the Franklin relief expedition? Or one of them? Any rate, he got them to come. Twenty of them waving Navy discharge books as able seamen, another fifteen we've got were rated AB in merchant ships.'

30

'But how?' Talleyman repeated. 'The Baltic fleet, all those liners, couldn't get enough men.'

'Well, it seems it's who you are and who'll claim to know you. Who'll take your drinks when you buy them. I got a couple of farm lads on my own, but he got most of them.'

'Whalers' men? They'll be hard to handle.'

'But at least they're volunteers. Did you know Only before?'

'I sailed under him, in *Santorin*. He was First Lieutenant. Hard man. A driver.'

'He's driving me,' complained Sherwin. 'He's in a hurry, wants everything done at once, wants all the papers done in order. He drove us up from Portsmouth, it was a nightmare. I couldn't stand it, I was so sick I couldn't stand. And stores. She was fully supplied at Portsmouth, everything to scale. But up here, he's looking for more of everything, he's overloading her, and coal, coal, bags of coal stowed everywhere, didn't have anything like it in my days, not all this coal.'

'The Admiralty agent here's new,' said Biddell with relish, 'and not very knowledgeable at that. The Captain's been pulling the wool over his flaming teeth, let alone his eyes. We've got double of most things, especially small stores. Whenever the man objects, Only says, 'Normal for a steamer new commissioned', and finds new amendments in all the regulations that haven't reached Dundee yet. Nor ever will.'

'And all the papers, so confusing,' wailed Sherwin.

Talleyman could not let his smile be seen. If Sherwin could not understand the papers, surely nobody would ever understand the mess he would have made of them. The door opened without a knock and a surgeon came in. No, Talleyman thought, nobody I know, but maybe someone I would like to know.

'Talleyman, second and guns,' Sherwin introduced them.

'This is Dr Hacker.'

31

'Thacker, Thacker,' said the surgeon testily. 'The agent's gone back to the ship with the Chief.'

'The ship, the ship, the agent's at the ship?' Sherwin stammered. 'I must go to the ship, the agent will expect me, too much to do, too much to do, I must see him. Talleyman, you carry on, you carry on here, Biddell. I must deal with the agent, too much to do, all to do and only me to do it.'

He stuffed handfuls of forms into a green baize bag, higgledy-piggledy to Biddell's evident disgust. He seized his cocked hat and hurried from the room. The Purser shrugged.

'I hope he gets a sailor to carry the bag for him. Doesn't do to have officers walking about looking like solicitors, although perhaps they did in his day. What are we going to do with him?'

'No *Agamemnon* at Navarino,' Talleyman observed. 'Only really *was* in *Albion*.'

'Sherwin brought his valet with him and entered him as an AB for this commission. Now he's had his cook come out. Is the man fit?'

'He's fit for service,' Thacker told him. 'Fit but half dead and worn out. He got the telegram to come to Dundee, but the butler told him the ship was built at Newcastle and he ought to go there. So he got to some Newcastle in the middle of Wales and went looking for the ship in the salmon pools. He went home, and was sent up to the Tyne. He spent three days looking round the docks, and then found an officer who took him to the agent who sent him up here. So he's had five days in trains and is tired as a dog. I gave him a dose of opium and sent him for twenty-four hours' sleep in the sickbay. Silverwright will turn him out in the morning.'

'Ah, Silverwright, Silverwright,' mused Biddell. 'What would we do without Silverwright?'

'We'd live well,' Thacker retorted. 'How many more have you got for me?'

'Only two,' said Biddell, 'and then we're finished and back to the ship. And that last two you looked at this morning, that Sherwin keeps worrying over. You have a look at them, Talleyman, and take them, settle it.'

Talleyman took Sherwin's seat at the table.

'We'll have them in. I suppose we've got an olderly or two? Send him for something to eat, cold beef or something. I've had nothing to eat since very early.'

'And some brandy and water,' added Biddell. The Surgeon looked closely at him.

'Not beef, we'll have enough of that at sea, and you've stored us well with brandy. Make it cold chicken and beer. Are you feeling all right yourself?'

'Never felt better. Just send the food in as you go.'

'Last ship?' Talleyman asked.

'Oh, the old *Argyle*, still sitting on her beef bones, down on the sunny coast.'

'Blackwater fever?'

'Yes, or dengue or queasy fever or a violent ague or whatever the next surgeon likes to call it. I came home sick at Christmas, passed fit a mouth ago, and here I am.'

A petty officer, a ten-year man in a uniform, opened the door and ushered the last two recruits in. Talleyman looked hard at them, took a couple of sheets of paper from Biddell, skimmed through, then looked at the two men again.

'Moulton. . . and Calne. Which is which?'

Easy to remember once you knew. Moulton was smooth, rounded, with yellow hair sleeked down, Calne was scrawnier, dark-haired, stubble showing. Moulton seemed to be the spokesman.

'Let's see. Your last ship, the whaler *Hannah*. Captain Bathurst seems to think highly of you. Both rated AB. You're both Canadians?'

'Yes, suh, both Canadians, loyal subjects, suh. Want to fight for the old flag, suh.'

33

'Which part of Canada?'

'Prince Edward Island, suh.'

'And you, Calne?'

'Yes, sir. Prince Edward Island, born and bred, sir.'

'So. . . both of you?'

'Yes, sir. Grew together, came to sea together.'

'Why did you go to sea, Calne?'

'Better than potatoes, sir. Round the Horn, Canton, Foochow, Bergen.'

Talleyman listened, fiddled with a pencil, thought he understood.

'What's your religion?'

'Religion, suh?'

'Yes. We've a Chaplain just joined. Wouldn't like to be burried with the wrong prayers, would you?'

'No, suh. Episcopalian, suh.'

That told all. Talleyman smiled.

'Sign them on, Mr Biddell,' he ordered. 'No fuss, sailors don't take an oath. Not like Marines.' Then, 'One moment. That's a sextant, you're carrying, Calne.'

'Yes sir.'

'A whaling AB with a sextant?'

'Lucky at cards, sir.'

'And that's how you got your sextant, Moulton?'

'There's a game, suh, called poker. If you want to learn. . .'

'You might be surprised. These are valuable instruments. And we may have to fight. You must be careful. Lose them! Even in Her Majesty's ships the officers are capable of finding their position without aid. There is a pawnshop on the corner. The sextants will be safer there. And that gold watch, Moulton. They will be safe for the voyage.'

'Gold is easier to steal than sextants, suh. And coins gets rolled into unfindable corners. . . .'

'Bring your money to Mr Biddell. He will give you a receipt for it. We may put ashore. Then he will be your banker. Now carry on.'

'Aye, aye, sir.'

The seamen went out, the cold chicken and beer and hot fresh bread came in. Talleyman shuffled the papers he had been scribbling on. Biddell looked over his shoulder.

'Oh, I say, that's good. Make a woodcut out of it and send it round if Moulton deserts, and every police station in the country can pick him up.'

'You like it?'

'What I like. . . it's not just the face, but you can see the way he walks.'

'Clever to notice that. Get the way a man holds himself right. Not too worried about the features then. Here!' Talleyman worked away for a minute or a little more. 'Like that?'

'Oh, yes. Good Lord, yes. Can I keep it?'

'Of course. Send it home. To your wife.'

'I haven't got a wife.'

'To your mama, then. Someone. What do we do about dinner tonight?'

'Thank Sherwin. He had enough of Silverwright on the way here, that's why he sent for his own cook. But we've got an arrangement with one of the better eating houses here to send wardroom dinner aboard each night. I ought to get the order in on the way back. Anything you fancy?'

'We won't see lamb for a long time, at sea. Oh, hello, Thacker, will lamb suit you tonight?'

'I'll carve. I think that must be the lot.'

The door opened again, an apparition in scarlet and pipeclay crashed to attention, saluted. Then the Marine Captain relaxed.

'Talleyman, I take it? I'm Fincham.'

'I read your book.'

'I didn't write the book,' in a bored tone. Then, 'Are you ready to march your brood back? Sorry I didn't see you when you came, I was inventorying small-arms ammunition.'

'You haven't brought an armed escort?' asked Biddell. 'Won't do much for our popularity if we march these eager volunteers to the ship between two files of muskets.'

'Out of date, my boy. No muskets, we have rifles now. Much more terrifying. It's all right, I sent three sailors down and the Bo'sun's mate you've got here will see to it.'

'We'd have been done a bit sooner,' grumbled Biddell, 'if the Captain hadn't said he wouldn't have any Irish in the ship.'

'Lucky he didn't recruit the Marines. Most of my lot are Irish.'

'Strange prejudice,' mused Talleyman. 'He came to my wedding. Champagne was flat. Perhaps that's why. I married one.'

'You married a hairy illiterate ploughboy from Galway?' Fincham was interested.

'No. Thin daughter of a County Cork vicarage.'

'At least she speaks English.'

'So she tells me. Sometimes I have doubts.'

Talleyman fished in a pocket, brought out a drawing block, drew a few lines. 'Look here, this is a railway engine, d'ye see?'

'We've got one in the hold, haven't we?' Biddell pointed out. 'Or at least we've got an engine driver.'

'And this is the First Lieutenant.'

'That's good. You only saw him for five minutes.'

'And here is My Lord Sherwin as Puffing Billy.'

The officers laughed, conspirators against authority. Talleyman reflected that he had now established that he was capable of effective malice, tore the paper across again and again and scattered it on the floor.

'We're sailing tonight?' he asked.

'So the Captain said,' Biddell assured him. 'But ships sail when they're ready, not when they're supposed to. At least Sherwin says so, and it certainly agrees with my experience.'

'I've sailed under Only,' Talleyman reminded him. 'So has young Cricklade. If Only says we sail tonight, we sail tonight. Mind, we may come back tomorrow, but if he says we sail, then we sail.'

'We may have to come back,' sighed Biddell. 'We're still two officers short, and I've debited their mess subscriptions against them in the books. I've booked you for your share of this chicken, Fincham. And now we've finished it, I suppose we may as well get back.'

3

Biddell found it hard to believe. The last two officers had actually arrived. He inspected them with caution. As mess caterer, he was likely to get all the spleen produced by their indigestion or even by their bad taste.

'I'm Orton,' said one. 'I'm Fourth, or so they tell me. I hope this isn't going to be a long war, or a long voyage. I've got an appointment in December.'

Talleyman, changing from his long frock coat to his short brass-buttoned undress jacket for dinner, looked at him through the half-open cabin door. He was a slight man, with ginger curls. He looked younger and more innocent than he could possibly be. The other newcomer stood by the table, one hand against the mizzen mast, volunteering nothing till the combined gaze of the other officers prompted him to say,

'I'm Longville.'

The name meant nothing to Dincombe nor, plainly, to Sherwin; but the Chaplain sensed a sudden tension in the air, broken when a large pink figure, a towel around its waist, slid from the bath closet and into a cabin. Talleyman remarked,

'You've been out east, then.'

'I was not offered an appointment, so I have been broadening my professional experience,' Longville replied with an air of nervous bravado, 'sailing in merchant ships. I am,' he added defiantly, 'the holder of a Master's qualification.'

'You are qualified in steam?' Talleyman asked.

'Just. One must, nowadays. But I don't intend to make use of it.'

The last officer, a short man with small hands, long-fingered, came out of his cabin. Talleyman introduced him to the newcomers.

'This is the Chief, Charles Craddock. Take note of him, Mr Longville, he knows enough about the engines to do for the lot of us: he set them up.'

'Haven't seen you since we were at Maudsley's,' Craddock greeted Talleyman. To the First Lieutenant, waiting now by his seat at the head of the table, he apologized: 'Sorry to be nearly late, but I've been getting the condensers refitted together.'

'Will she steam?' asked Talleyman.

'Yes, she will now. Some botcher had been at her since I saw her last.'

'When I came into the Navy,' said Longville, 'we had only gentlemen in the wardroom.'

'What a dull place it must have been,' Orton told him with an innocent air. Sherwin made an obvious effort to regain control.

'The soup will get cold. Perhaps you will say grace, Mr Dincombe.'

Dincombe said grace, to his own satisfaction. He thanked Almighty God for their creation, preservation and all the blessings of this and the next life, for strength to eat, the talents to work and earn their bread, and for many other divine gifts for which at that moment the wardroom were not at all grateful. Dincombe was rather proud of his extempore and spontaneous prayers, and spent much time, which others thought dissipated in dreaming, in composing them. The officers glowered at their cooling soup, the fat forming in stars on the service. At the proper moment Sherwin saw his cue to break in and say 'Amen'. He then glared at Dincombe and told him,

'There is a tradition in the Navy. For grace, we just say, "Thank God".'

The soup was consumed, for it was now hardly worth eating or drinking, in silence. Then the lamb came on the table, and a fresh salmon, poached, and new potatoes, fresh peas, sweet new carrots. Talleyman beamed at the Purser, and told him,

'Food's good in this ship. Nearly as good as at Ding Pong's.'

'Do you mean,' asked Orton brightly, 'Ping Dong's? Ping Dong's in Hai Chow?'

'No. Ding Pong's in Chai How.'

'Yes, I remember, they're easily confused. The only trouble with Ding Pong is the limited menu.'

'Yes. Only serve eggs. Nothing else. Hens' eggs, duck eggs, peacock eggs, turtle eggs, caviare, skate eggs in the shell, octopus eggs. Frog spawn very good. All soft boiled. Must eat them with chopsticks. Ding throws you out if you bring a knife. Or a spoon.'

'I've never heard of it,' objected Longville. 'I've been all up and down that coast for three years, and I've never heard of it, or those towns either.'

'Ah, but you've probably only talked to gentlemen like yourself, in the merchant service,' Orton told him crushingly. 'You should have talked to some of the real old China hands, merchants who live there. They all know it. Ever try the hundred-year-old eggs, Talleyman?'

'Not hundred. Couldn't afford it. Tried twenty-five-year old. Not bad. Ding had some of the 1828 put down. Keeping them for 1928. Good year, twenty-eight.'

'A very good year,' Sherwin came back into the conversation. 'A good year for a good many of us. Navarino year.'

'Have you got your medal?' Talleyman asked him. 'Only's got his.'

'Yes, fine man, Captain Only, stood to his gun there, knows the smell of powder-smoke and blood. Powder-smoke and blood.' He returned to the lamb. Longville looked to the forward half of the table, beyond the mizzen mast, covered with a heap of papers.

'Bit of a clutter there, eh, Biddell?'

'I'll have it cleared as soon as I have any room in my office. First Lieutenant and I have been hard at it for the last three hours, making out watch bills.'

'When I came into the Navy, the Pusser always slept in his shop. I wonder you don't take your hammock down there.'

'I don't think I will,' replied Biddell. 'I've got two writers and a leading storeman sleeping in there already and they might not appreciate my rude habits.'

Dincombe watched the way the heads moved, the faces changed as the conversation flowed. He had a vague sense of parties being formed, battle lines being drawn, jockeying for position according to rules he did not know. The Surgeon said to him,

'Here, have some more claret. Won't have much at sea, it won't keep. All gets shaken up with the way these tarpaulins can't keep the ship still.'

There was fruit on the table now, bowls of new-picked whinberries served with jugs of fresh cream, hot-house peaches, fresh cherries, the first plums. Last year's apples were shrivelled but the sweeter for that. This is all the food, Dincombe reminded himself, that we won't get at sea. Fresh bread too, hot. Silverwright seemed now a little clumsy in serving it. Sherwin's own servant, Keate, stood behind his master's chair. The First Lieutenant seemed a fair trencherman: the new tunic was straining already over his waist, if he had a

40

waist. Natural if you ate like that. Dincombe caught at his thoughts, privately rebuked himself for the sin of malice. Talleyman was talking to Orton.

'You were ashore for three and a half years. What were you up to?'

'Reading for the Bar.'

'Four-ale? Or jug and bottle?'

'Middle Temple. Their Lordships asked me to come in March, but I said I'd really prefer to wait till I was called to the Bar. So I was called, and then I was called. They were very decent waiting. Beside, I hadn't been well and my doctor said a tonic and a sea voyage would pick me up.'

'I can't imagine you in court,' said Biddell.

'Oh, not too much time in court. The chambers I was in did a lot of marine work, insurance, all that. Meetings, bargaining, writing opinions. But I was devilling for a very good fellow, a silk, and almost the first meeting over insurance on a wreck, I saw something and I scribbled him a note. Now when the learned silk on the other side says – ' And Orton half rose, curved himself forward like a crow, and said in an elderly, pernickety voice – '"Now, Captain, knowing the Channel there as we all do, why did you not turn to starboard when you bore due east from the inner light?" it doesn't half stir you up. I saw what I could do to get a quick reputation early and so I want a cruise in a steamer. Not too long. Want to be back for a case in December.'

At this point the port came round and they drank the Queen's health sitting as Dincombe had heard sailors did. Sherwin was well into a fresh loaf and cheese. Most of the others refused cheese and sat, sated.

Only Sherwin was talking now. The others all had work still to go to, but could not stir before the president rose. Sherwin motioned for the port to come round again, to circulate faster. He was telling them tales of the old Navy, when he first joined. Dincombe couldn't work out when that was. He didn't actually claim to have served under Nelson, but everyone else came in. All the stories came back to the same theme, that everything had changed, it was all rush, rush, hurry, hurry, no place for a gentleman. No time to sleep, no time to think, no time to sleep and a man needed sleep and a chance to digest his dinner, even though the food was so dreadful at sea unless you could bring a good cook. . .And he was going to be working again after dinner, with the purser, on all those forms, and all the forms and vouchers all changed and made unnecessarily complicated and all for no reason at all . . .

It was dusk outside, early for August in Dundee, but the cloud hung thick and heavy, threatening rain but never going beyond a faint and depressing drizzle. Dincombe reflected that if Sherwin stopped eating soon, he might finish the paperwork before midnight. And his own bladder was pressing him. Then he forgot his bladder at the sound of a stamping of feet and a faint, apologetic whistle on the deck. Everything stopped, everyone stood up at once and made for the companion and up to the deck. The Marine sentry was almost trampled down. Talleyman was on deck first to see the Captain coming on board, Sladen, the Mate who was officer of the watch, getting tangled up with the sideboys and the Bo'sun. There were two wagons on the quay, driven not by civilians or even by local militia, but by regular soldiers, engineers. And there was a sapper officer with them.

4

There was someone coming up the gangway behind the Captain. Only was wrapped in his boat cloak, his cocked hat at an angle. The other was a spare man, wearing a brown tweed pilot coat like Talleyman's, the collar turned up around his face, his hat pulled low. But Talleyman, looking close, thought, I know you, yes, I have seen you and I remember who you are.

Only gestured at Talleyman and the huddle of officers behind him, and said curtly, 'The wardroom.'

The passenger melted away, into the cabins under the poop. He had the air of someone who was used to ships, but not a sailor. On the quay soldiers were manhandling things, canvas-wrapped bundles or boxes or bags, under the direction of the Engineers officer. Only snapped at the Bo'sun,

'Mr Harris, get that gear stowed under cover, you'll be told where.' To his steward, 'Abel! Supper for two in my day cabin in half an hour.'

In the wardroom, Sherwin was sitting, still, at the head of the table, as if the arrival of his Captain had nothing at all to do with him. He looked at Only with a half-guilty air, like someone accused of some minor fault which he was sure was not a fault. Only has been hard on him, thought Talleyman, and I have seen him hard. He has half ground Sherwin into the deck already. He poured Only a glass of claret.

'I am sorry to disturb this last supper, gentlemen,' the Captain told them. 'It will be simpler if you all sit down and listen. I see you are all here. We sail tonight, and anyone who is not here will miss the war. We sail

43

a little after midnight, and I have a tug ordered so we catch the ebb.'

He paused to sip the wine, and to let his announcement sink in. Orton spoke up, brightly,

> '"There is a tide in the affairs of men,
> Which taken at the ebb leads out to fortune,
> Salt water, gunsmoke, prizes and promotion."'

'Ah, yes, observed Only. 'That little-acted play of Shakespeare's, *Horatio Duke of Thunder*. I am sorry to be so late, gentlemen, but it was difficult to control the speed of army horses and arrive at dusk. We will not need our engines, Mr Craddock.'

'But we can't go on the ebb,' Sherwin protested. 'We aren't ready, we haven't enough men to work the ship, we have not rated them all properly. The watch bills are not yet made out. We have done nothing to work up the crew. There are a vast number – '

'We will sail upon the ebb. Most of this town knows these deficiencies as well as you do, Mr Sherwin, and they will wake to wonder at our empty berth. I have set the Bo'sun to bringing aboard the cargo for which we have been waiting and it will be stowed properly in – '

'No! No!' Sherwin shouted. 'This is all stupidity. We can't go, we can't go, we're not ready, we're overloaded, we can't take cargo, we must leave some stores behind. We're not ready, we must have time, more sleep, more sleep, more – '

Sherwin had already half risen, was trying to get away from the table to his right, the opposite side of the ship from Only. Now he suddenly stopped talking, gagged in his throat, and fell flat on his face across the table. The Chaplain immediately saw good works to be done to justify his existence. He leant over Sherwin's right ear, the left being in the Stilton, to say earnestly,

44

'Repent, passing soul, repent! Only believe in the Lord Jesus Christ and thou shalt be saved.'

'Quiet,' shouted the Surgeon, trying to push his way up from the other end of the table. 'Let me through! Pull his tongue out, someone!'

Talleyman unceremoniously thrust the Chaplain aside, forced open Sherwin's mouth and with a grimace of disgust inserted his fingers between the lips and teeth. The fat man was breathing heavily, noisily. Dincombe asked, in awe,

'Is that not the death rattle?'

Thacker was tapping the chest, listening closely, opening the eyelids, peering.

'No trade for you, parson,' he said. 'He's had a stroke.'

'Nothing more than a stroke?' asked Only.

'Apoplectic seizure, if you want it in long words. With his size and the amount he's been eating and drinking it's no wonder. It may not be bad, but we'd better get him off the ship. I know we are in Scotland, but there may be an infirmary in the town. Silverwright! Pass the word for my dresser. Rig a stretcher and put Mr Sherwin's blankets on it. We have to keep him warm. Nothing to be done till he comes round, and that may be days.'

'How long?' the Captain asked. Thacker considered a moment.

'Oof, who knows? He won't be fit to sail tonight, or this week either. And when he can talk and stand, I wouldn't like to have him in the ship. He'll not be able to work, he'll take all my time looking after him, and the rest of you will have to look after yourselves.'

'So I assume that we will not sail tonight?' asked Dincombe. Talleyman reflected that the Chaplain had not mastered the art of talking to captains. Only's expression was difficult to read.

'We cannot sail with him, but we must sail upon the ebb. Get him off the ship and make ready for sea.'

45

The Engineer officer had come, uninvited, into the wardroom. Talleyman wondered if the Marine sentry had challenged him. Now he was here, he could be made use of.

'Can we have one of your empty wagons? We have a sick officer here to get to the infirmary.'

'So I hear, old boy. I've sent one of my men to the infirmary for an ambulance.'

'Already?'

'You have to be a bit slippy ashore, old boy. None of your doodling along at a walking pace like ships do. Can someone go with him? Or shall I look after it?'

Silverwright was fussing around Sherwin, and another steward was with him, a man almost as old as the casualty.

'Keate, go with your master,' Biddell ordered.

Talleyman remembered that this was the valet Sherwin had brought with him. Only remembered too, and interposed,

'Mr Biddell, write out a discharge certificate for this man as unfit for service, conduct exemplary, and I will sign it. Have you any ready money, Keate? Or has Mr Sherwin?'

'Mr Sherwin has about thirty pounds in gold, sir, in his chest, and I have a couple of sovereigns.'

'Good. Stay with your master. I will write a note to the Admiralty agent and he will be up to see to you. And I will have a telegram sent to Mrs Sherwin.'

'Does that mean I won't go to the war, sir?'

'You've come to the war, and that's more than most of our fellow countrymen were willing to do. I said, "exemplary conduct". Look after Mr Sherwin, Keate. He was a good man, and willing too.'

The Engineer officer was listening. He observed,

'Made a mess of the dinner table, didn't he? Looks as if you'd had a shell burst here.'

There was a moment of dead silence. Talleyman told him,

'Not in the house of the hanged. Would you like to see our pretty Shrapnel's shells?'

'Oh. Oh. I see.'

'But you're not coming with us to the war, then?' Talleyman asked.

'Sorry, old man, I did offer but they won't have me. I've done the final unforgivable sin and been to India.'

'You've been in India?' asked Dincombe. Orton explained,

'Quite true. My brother-in-law was in a marching regiment in India, and he'd just exchanged into one at home. When they were warned for the Danube he was told, very short, to exchange out or go on half pay because they didn't want any Indian officers with their low customs. Like fighting, I suppose. Said they might teach the men bad habits. Like ducking when they're shot at.'

'Quite true,' the Engineer agreed. 'Nobody's wanted who's ever been in India. The Home army wants all the credit. Silly, really, seeing the war's just to keep the Russians out of India.'

Dincombe was curious but decided it could wait. He announced,

'That sounds like the ambulance.'

'I'll go with it,' said the Engineer. 'I'll stay with your man, and see your own doctor gets back to you straight away. You can't trust civilian doctors and regimental agents. When you come back, somebody come and tell me what happened. Ask for me at Woolwich. Everyone knows me, Little's the name, Willie Little. Unless I'm in Bangalore again.'

'Captain's passed the word for you, sir,' Silverwright whispered in Talleyman's ear. Talleyman found Only on the poop, leaning on the rail and looking down at the wheel and the binnacle on the upper deck. Talleyman saluted.

'You're the First Lieutenant,' Only told him.

'Till another officer comes up to take over, sir?'

47

'Till we get back, young Tal, or till you get killed. We *must* sail tonight. We'll go out on the ebb, and I want Longville with me when I take her out.'

'But if I'm First Lieutenant – '

'You'll be too busy with the watch bills and finding out what Sherwin has been doing. Besides, I've seen you trying to get a ship out of harbour, and I haven't seen Longville. You can stand and watch him. You know his reputation.'

'I know his reputations. In two fields. I'd rather *he* had apoplexy.'

'Is the wardroom clear now?'

'I'll make sure it is, sir.'

'Three minutes, and I'll see all the officers there. Commission officers, the three Mates, Bo'sun, Carpenter, Gunner. We won't be more than three minutes when they do come, but I want no excuses later.'

Talleyman got the officers together. They all stood and stared at each other. The stewards pushed about between them, still trying to get the wardroom straight. Only testily waved them away.

'Don't sit down, gentlemen, this won't take long.' The vague idea of a band of brothers always lingered in the Captain's mind. Brothers would either stand together or sit together. There was no room for this crowd to sit. 'We take a tug at the ebb. I want to slip out quietly. Thanks to Mr Sherwin's well-repeated song of disbelief, the whole town believes that we cannot possibly put to sea for another three or four days. I hope, Mr Biddell, that you have left sufficient money for the Admiralty agent to settle our bill at the eating house. The London papers said today, and the Edinburgh papers will say tomorrow, that we leave next week to take station north of Ireland to warn off an expedition from Russia to take Ulster and blockade the Clyde. Do not believe anything you read in the papers.

'Therefore we will not take stations for leaving harbour. I want her worked out by the duty part of the

48

watch on deck, and if the watch bills are not worked out by then Mr Harris will see to it. No pipes, no Marines band, not even the drummer.

'Next. Mr Talleyman is now the First Lieutenant. Mr Longville, you will be Second, but you have not been through *Excellent*. Mr Cricklade is the most up-to-date, and regardless of seniority he will have the guns. The First Lieutenant is qualified in steam, and will therefore be responsible and Mr Craddock will report to me through him.' I could not manage that, thought Only, if Craddock and Talleyman did not know each other already. And I know about Longville already and I will not have him disturbed. 'I have given you no extraneous duties, Mr Longville, there will be enough for you to do later.

'Now, as to dress. What is that you are holding in your hands, Mr Longville? Stow it somewhere. I know quite well that the regulations say that the proper wear with undress is the low top hat, but they also allow the wearing of the flat peaked cap. In this ship that cap is not allowed, it is required. Do not object, Mr Longville. You may think it very fine to be a merchant skipper and lean on the taffrail with your hands in your pockets and your cigar in your mouth and your topper on the back of your head, but in a Queen's ship you must be ready to work yourself. Flat caps, therefore, and blue trousers not white at sea, whatever the date. It is up to the discretion of the president of your mess what you wear at dinner – '

He paused, thinking he must give Talleyman a chance to give his first order as First Lieutenant.

'We will wear short undress jackets, sir, and white trousers till the season changes. I think that the gun-room mess will do the same.'

'Very suitable. But no undress jackets on deck. All officers will wear frock coats on deck at all times. I will further vary the regulations. When we get into bad weather, officers are not compelled to wear stiff shirts

49

and collars and neckties if they prefer to wear woollen jerseys or other fishermen's clothes.' That, Only thought, will tell them we mean business. What more? Oh, yes. 'Captain Fincham, I do not care what you say in your book – '

'I didn't write that book, sir.'

'Your modesty does you credit, but you are among friends here who know that there are several marine officers who can write and even read, some of them. I see no reason why your soldiers should wear stocks: we are going to war and not to a fancy-dress parade. No stocks at sea, except at your discretion, perhaps at Sunday morning church, for instance.'

'Aye, aye, sir.'

'Oh, yes, swords. You will please not wear swords at sea unless you actually intend to hurt someone with them, in which case I would recommend you to borrow the issue cutlass which is more effective and cheaper to get mended if you bend it on someone's skull.

'Further, I hear that some of you have brought your own revolving pistols. I know that they fit neatly into the side pocket of a frock coat, but I do not want you to wear them on deck unless we are going into action. All our men are volunteers in one way or the other, and many of them have come out of whalers where ruder manners prevail. I do not want them to see my officers behaving like merchant mates. The Bo'sun, of course, will make his traditional use of a walking stick, and the Master-at-arms under his direction. Now, if we are to sail in the small hours I suggest that all those whose duties permit go to take a few hours' sleep. Mr Talleyman, come with me and look at the charts.'

Talleyman lingered a moment.

'Finchman. Your Marine sentry. He let an Army officer into the wardroom. With no challenge.'

'I know. A man named Garvey. I'll skin him now, while he remembers.'

'Do that. But slowly.'

Dincombe was looking round the narrow slot he was to share with the surgeon when Thacker came in.

'How is poor Mr Sherwin?'

'He is. . . well, not better, but shall we say improved? He is looking round him and saying ugly things.'

'Like "barmaid",' asked Biddell from his nest of papers, 'or "army"?'

'More like "ug" and "ag", which is quite good progress for a stroke. He may find difficulty in speaking for a while, and I think he may limp, but there is nothing serious there and little to be done other than to nurse him. I've told the Captain. Now, I think us idlers ought to get some sleep.'

Dincombe felt affronted already at the thought of someone else telling him when to go to bed. He made an effort to be tolerant, and instead asked with a touch of acidity,

'We are idlers?'

'Only us,' Biddell reassured him. 'We're not watch-keepers, we just work all the time. In the Navy you learn to sleep where and when you can. Have you used a hammock?'

'Once or twice,' Dincombe admitted. 'In gardens. I can learn.'

'Not tonight,' said Thacker. 'Can't waste my sleeping time picking you off the deck. Silverwright! Get a cot rigged for the Chaplain.'

Dincombe watched the stewards bring in a long coffin-shaped box and sling it from hooks in the deckbeams above his head. They put into it a straw mattress and a couple of blankets, and left.

'I suppose they'll get my sheets up tomorrow, where-ever Silverwright has put them. And he hasn't put my night shirt in this chest.'

'Sheets? Nightshirt?' The Surgeon laughed. 'For Portsmouth Harbour, perhaps, or cruising in the Med in summer, but you're going to war in the north. Wear your oldest trousers and a shirt, in case you have to turn out in a hurry. We may get a sea through the stern windows, or a whale, or a couple of roundshot. For all we know there's a Russian liner waiting for us out there in the mist. But if they put a shell in, don't worry – we'll all be too dead to swim.'

5

Some time later, Dincombe didn't know at what hour, somebody was shaking his shoulder.

'You are sound,' said the Surgeon. 'But I thought you ought to see this. Just put a greatcoat on, and look through this scuttle here. Not too close, you don't want half Dundee to see you.'

Half Dundee was not there to see him. When his eyes got used to the dark, Dincombe saw there was no one to see him, no one at all. Through the thin drizzle, he could just make out the line of the quay, now ten yards away. Ahead, somewhere, he could just hear the throb of an engine, very slow, and the splash and beat of paddles. Is this, he asked himself, how one goes to sea, silently, dismally, unseen, in the dark?

'No bands,' Biddell told him, over his shoulder. 'No parades, no weeping women. We had all those at Portsmouth and that was nearly three weeks ago, We are not just going to sea, Chaplain. We are going to war.'

6

It was, in Dincombe's eyes, daylight all of a sudden. Not dawn but much later, bustle all about him and a steward, not Silverwright but another man – what was his name? Oh yes, Locock – offering him a mug of coffee.

'I brought you some hot water to wash, sir, but I can shave you after breakfast. I thought you wouldn't want to miss it, sir.'

All the other mess members were around the table when Dincombe appeared, in his frock coat, black against the blue, stock, white tie.

'Why, 'tis the sleeping beauty that walks upon the deck,' said Orton. He was wearing a woollen jersey under his frock coat. '"No winds or seas will break his doze, nor any sad shipwreck."'

'We. . . we are out at sea?' Dincombe could feel the deck moving under his feet, a variation on a permanent lean to one side. 'I did not know.'

'Look out there.' The Surgeon pointed to the stern window.

'The last of England?'

'Not England,' Longville told him, 'unless Talleyman has got the course wrong, or Orton has been sailing us backwards the last four hours. That's Scotland, that grey streak, if you can make it out. Tell us, Talleyman, where *are* we going?'

'Captain hasn't told me. Gave me a course but no destination. When you come on watch, come into the chartroom and see. I've laid it out. You can make your own guesses. Sit down, Mr Dincombe, please, and have some bacon and eggs. While you can. There's eggs

53

enough to last a fortnight. Craddock has let Silver-wright rig a galley on the engine-room floor plates.'

'Is the Captain coming. . . down. . .to breakfast?'

'Oh, no,' Orton told him. 'The Captain doesn't eat with us unless we invite him. He's not a member of this mess, but he eats alone above in solitary splendour. I don't know if he's doing as well as we are. I say, Talleyman, weren't you in *Argyle* with Fat Jack Pither and Partridge?'

'Partridge,' said Talleyman, 'is dead.'

'Is it true about Fat Jack and the boot?'

'Not as the story is usually told. First, he didn't eat it all: he left the lace tags. Second, it wasn't stewed, it was curried. Third, it wasn't a boot: it was a shoe.'

'Walking shoe? Or dancing?'

'Horse.'

Suddenly, there was another man in the wardroom, a scrawny figure in a disordered livery.

'Please sirs, please gentlemen, can you tell me where to find Mr Silverwright?'

Everyone looked at him.

'Who?' asked Longville.

'Mr Silverwright, sir, the butler.'

'No. Who are you?'

'I'm Nussey, sir. Mr Sherwin's second cook. He sent for me.'

'My department, I think,' said Biddell. 'Nussey, we are at sea, on our way to fight the Russians. Mr Sherwin did not come with us. There is no way of getting you back, and you have engaged yourself for this commission. Silverwright! Did you know you were the butler? Take this man forward to my store and fit him out in slops for work. Then find out what he can do – if he can cook better than you, for example.'

'That's done,' said Talleyman. 'Mr Dincombe, will you see me at nine o'clock? The Captain wants all hands mustered aft at eleven o'clock to make a speech to them. You will be asked to pray for the success

54

of the voyage. Do just that, and make it short. Very short.'

'I thought,' Dincombe asked Biddell, 'you counted time at sea with bells.'

'The sailors do, because they haven't got any watches. But here in the wardroom we tell the time in a civilized manner. If you're really curious, you'll see Talleyman at two bells in the forenoon watch and the Captain will speak at six bells in the forenoon watch.'

'Did you find that Marine?' Talleyman asked down the table. Finchman answered,

'Oh,, yes, Garvey, you can't miss him. Not just an ordinary Marine. County Cork man, but his English is good. He's a failed priest, of a kind. A fair degree of education – '

'Read *and* write?'

'Oh, more than that. Arithmetic, some Latin, a morsel of Greek. What in another walk of life you might call an able man. But he can't keep out of mischief. He's been up to Corporal twice and down again. Can't think why he joined, except to eat, or why he stays in, except that we'd flog him for deserting. I wish he would desert: I wouldn't chase him.'

'So? Any use?'

'Not really. Put it all down in your watch bills.'

'A long time before I get to Marines. I'm going up to the paper works now.'

III

The Voyage

1

At a little before nine o'clock, Dincombe set out for his interview with with the First Lieutenant. He had occupied his time by saying Matins, standing at the after end of the wardroom. No one came to join him. Then, feeling it appropriate, he read a little of the Book of Job and wondered what on earth it had relevant to his present position. Stuffing his pocket Bible into a drawer, since it did not fit very easily into any pocket, he followed Silverwright's direction. He passed the Marine sentry and climbed to the upper deck.

He emerged on the starboard side facing the bulwarks, a vertical wall six feet high. As he hesitated on the deck, the roll of the ship caught him and took him forward at a run. His back now to the ship's side, he looked round at a scene of confusion. The deck was full of hurrying men, men carrying round shot, men carrying flannel bags or leather cylinders, men at each of the black guns, hauling in, running out, grunting or shouting.

In front of him, Dincombe saw two men at the wheel, and behind them the doorway under the poop. His hand was on a ladder, he must remember to call it a companionway, which led up to the poop. Above him, he saw Longville leaning on the rail at the break of the poop. Longville beckoned. It was still only ten to nine. Dincombe clung to the rope rigged as a stair rail and climbed to join Longville.

'Come to see the fun?' Longville asked. There was a lad with him, about fourteen or so, dressed as a kind of miniature officer. Longville did not introduce him or explain him.

'Not sure of the way? Then Fox can show you. He doesn't know the way either.'

'What's going on? It all looks very urgent. It seems stormy. Are we in danger?'

'Not stormy, just breezy, force four from the north-west. We're headed north-east, under all the sail the Bo'sun thinks we can carry. As to what we're doing, we're sailing the ship. At least the Bo'sun down there thinks he is, and I know I am.'

'But all these men – what are they all doing?'

'Well, a very few of them are helping to sail the ship. About two dozen all told.'

'You can sail this ship with only two dozen men working at a time?'

'If this were a merchant ship and we wanted to make a profit, we'd sail her with two dozen all told, both watches and the afterguard.'

'Then why. . . I thought we had nearly two hundred.'

'See those guns? We need nearly two hundred to work them, and that's what the ship is for, to carry the guns and fire them. Half our trouble is keeping all those men busy and out of mischief. So now, gun drill, trying to find out if any of them are born gunners.'

'And are there any?'

'Oh, yes, they stand out. Parks, the ten-year man down there, the two Canadians, several others. We can find enough gun captains and number twos. Here, it's just about time. Fox, take the Captain to the First Lieutenant. Under the poop, just below where I'm standing now.'

Talleyman sat in a cabin under the poop, first on the port side. He was bent over a table covered with papers.

'Good of you to come, Mr Dincombe. Thank you, er, Fox. Carry on.'

'What are you doing? This is office work, I can see. What are all these papers?'

'Lists, Mr Dincombe. Lists of men. Lists of every man in the ship. What work he is to do. Where he is to be at

60

any given time. Where he is to work in normal weather. Where he is to fight. Which gun he is to serve. Where he is to be when we enter harbour. Or if we run aground entering harbour. And every man has to know exactly where he is to be when the Bo'sun gives a particular call on his pipe, or when the little marine beats his drum or sounds his bugle. Lists of everyone, seamen, Marines, warrant officers, commission officers. Including you, Mr Dincombe.'

'Me?'

'You are a wardroom officer, Mr Dincombe. What work in the ship do you think you are qualified to do?'

'Why, as if I were in a parish: to read services, preach the gospel, bury the dead. . .' Dincombe tailed off. Now it was put firmly to him, he could not think of anything he could usefully do.

'You may hold services, Mr Dincombe. And preach. If it does not interfere with your work. Or anyone else's. You are Fellow of a college, the Captain tells me.'

'Yes. I am a fellow of St Tibb's College at Cambridge.

'That is, you teach.'

'I. . .yes. . . the college tutor is in charge of teaching. But I coach privately, for the classical tripos, and for the mathematical tripos.'

'You are borne on the ship's books as Instructor-and-Chaplain. You have a class. We have four cadets. You have met one of them, Fox. The others are Chessil, Dyke and Pritchard. In theory they know the rule of three. If we are lucky, they may be able to count to three. On their fingers. Before they can become Midshipmen, they must know decimals, fractions, the first six books of Euclid. . .and so on. The regulations are in the quarterly List, page 220.'

'Euclid? In Greek or in English?'

'In English. Do you know it in Greek? You have them for two hours a day for mathematics. Start at nine o'clock by your watch. You will have them again in the afternoon, from two o'clock to four. You are to teach them geography and French. Later, when the ship is settled, I will take an hour of that to teach them drawing.'

'Where am I to teach them? Is there a schoolroom?'

'Teach them where they eat and sleep. In the gun room. On the lower deck, just below the wardroom, aft of the Marines' mess.'

'And the rest of the time?'

'They serve as messengers. There is always one with me, unless the Captain comes on deck and steals him. One with the officer of the watch. One with the Pusser. One with the Engineer. They rotate. That is how they learn their business.'

'No, I mean, the rest of my time?'

'In action or in shipwreck, your post is in the infirmary. You assist the Surgeon. He will teach you your duties as a dresser. For the rest, think a little. In three days, bring me a plan. How we can make use of you? Count your talents. Find out first what everybody does in the ship. Start with the officer of the watch.'

'Aye, aye, sir.'

'That's right. Learn the language. Carry on.'

Talleyman turned back to his watch bills. Dincombe went back to the gun deck, and climbed to the poop.

'I'm told I must find out what everyone does.'

'Indeed? See what I do for a living. I spend my duty times leaning on the rail here, looking at the sky and the sails.'

'There must be more to do.'

'A little. Fox, pass the word for the Bo'sun.'

Fox ran off, glad, Dincombe thought, to have something to do other than watch sails. It might be a pretty sight but as an occupation it must pall. The Bo'sun came up to Longville.

'Mr Harris. Look at the jib.

'Fluttering a bit, sir.'

'I have a suspicion that if we come a point to starboard, she'll fly.'

'I was thinking that, sir, on the way up to Dundee. Her best point is a point abaft the beam.'

'And she's on a point for'ard now. Let's come two points to starboard.'

'Aye, aye, sir.'

'How does she handle on other winds?'

'Well, sir, considering that it's like driving an ox wagon full of lead through a bog of porridge...I think they started to build her as a steamer and changed their minds halfway through.'

'We shall never know.'

'Hands to braces, then?'

'Carry on, Mr Harris.'

Dincombe heard the Bo'sun's pipe, saw the earlier pandemonium around the guns dissolve, reform into a different confusion as men ran, settled into other groupings, centred not around guns but around ropes whose function he could not understand. The two men at the wheel below him made fine, hardly noticeable adjustments. He felt the bow of the ship come round a little to his right. Then the confusion swirled back to around the guns.

'That will give us an extra knot,' boasted Longville. 'This ship may be awkward to handle, but treat her right and we'll get a fair turn of speed out of her.'

Are there many ships like this in the Navy?'

'No. There are no ships in the Navy like this one. Ask that question in any of the Queen's ships, Reverend, and you will get the same answer. We have a Navy of samples, and whenever a man goes into a new ship he has to learn how to sail her, since she may not behave like any other ship he has ever been in. I tell you, I have never been in any warship as small as this one.'

Then Talleyman was on the poop with them.

'We seem to have changed course, Mr Longville.'

'Trimmed her into the wind, sir.'

'That is the third time this morning you have trimmed her to starboard.'

'I am finding out that she sails better with the wind just on the quarter.'

'Sails faster, you mean.'

'Same thing, sir.'

'Since you came on watch, you have trimmed three points to starboard. That is three points to starboard of the course you have been given.'

'We gain a knot or more, and she handles much easier. With the wind forward, or just before the beam – '

'Your business is to sail the course the Captain has given us, not the course the winds dictate.'

'But if we sail on this heading, or even a further point to starboard, for two or three hours we can then come to nor-nor-east and save time and trouble by nightfall, and be in the same place.'

'You're gaining trouble now. You saw the chart. The Captain hasn't given us a destination. He has given us a course.'

'In a merchant ship – '

'I know merchant navigation, Mr Longville. You look at a compass which has not been swung or corrected. You keep your knife in your belt. You sail in the general direction of the continent you want to reach. When your water gives out, or your patience, you take a sight. . . if the fog in the sky or in your mind permits. Then you sail to the nearest shore. And ask the way.'

'That is an exaggeration.'

'I was hailed once off Scarborough. They asked if Baltimore was north or south.'

Longville considered this. When he could trust himself to speak, he argued,

'The wind will veer. Then we could turn due north with it on the beam.'

'It's been steady all night. You should watch the glass. I think it will back.' He took the megaphone that hung around Longville's neck.

'Smale! Powderman, number four gun. Smale! Here!'

Dincombe watched a man run aft. Thin, in a woollen jersey, one of the men picked up at Dundee.

'What'll it do, Smale?' Talleyman asked him. 'Haul forward on us, or draw aft?'

Smale looked up at the sails, at the clouds. He went to the port rail and spat. He watched where the spittle came back past him and landed on the deck. He said,

'She's steady now, but before dark she'll be backing on us.'

'Right. Carry on, Smale.'

'Why him?' Longville asked.

'I've spent all night on watch bills. He's had one voyage, AB on a whaler, but before that ten years' fishing in the North Sea. Come back on to the proper course. . . No, not yet. The men will think we do not know what we are doing. Wait another ten minutes from now. Then come another one point to Starboard. And a quarter of an hour after that, come four points to port. The men will think it is only training, to call them from the guns.' Talleyman swung on his heel and glared at the six sailors on the poop.

'Captain of the afterguard!'

The petty officer came running.

'Get this deck cleaned. It's filthy, filthy.'

He turned back to Longville, who said as smoothly as he could, trying to teach himself patience,

'I bow to your superior ignorance.' Then, urgently, 'The Chaplain. Look where he's gone now.'

Dincombe had wandered away, was leaning over the low poop bulwark. Talleyman called him,

'Mr Dincombe, Mr Dincombe. Come here at once, please.'

Dincombe came. Longville told him,

'Never stand there again.'

'Where? By the side of the ship?'

Longville waited for Talleyman to speak, and then realized that he was expected to explain. After all, as Officer of the Watch, he should have noticed earlier.

'The Captain may come on deck and wish to take the air. With the exercises going on down there, on the quarterdeck, he will want to come to the poop. Some captains prefer to take their air on the starboard side, in fact, most do. But Captain Only prefers to walk on the weather side, that is where the wind is coming from. So you must walk on the lee side if you wish to take the air and have nothing to do.'

'If you wish to take the air,' Talleyman added, 'and have nothing to do, do not let the seamen see you idle. Always come and engage yourself with the Officer of the Watch. Look busy.'

2

Harriet had heard of people going purple with rage. She had never seen it happen till old Josiah Talleyman returned to the estate six days after Thomas had gone. He had summoned her to his presence at the Manor House as soon as he had arrived, and she had ridden over on the bay gelding. She meditated that the horse must be feeling old, he seemed to have difficulty in carrying her at the pace she liked, while a year ago when she first had him he would usually pass from the trot to the canter without urging. Nowadays he seemed sluggish.

She wanted to look sedate, competent, capable of managing an estate, running a farm, with only a modicum of professional aid: no more than a bailiff twenty hours a day, seven days a week.

Harriet had tried to dress for the part. She had

picked out her second-best riding outfit, one more suited to the drawing room than her latest and best outfit, which she had chosen with the hunting field in mind. Instead of the navy blue of the new one, which went, or would go, so well with Thomas's uniform if he ever wore it, this was a very light blue. Not for wearing on a wet or muddy day, but perfect for paying calls if there were anyone in the neighbourhood to pay calls on. Halfway to the Manor House, she began to worry whether perhaps the navy blue might not be more suitable, perhaps more patriotic. But old Josiah was in no mood to notice clothes, either in style or colour. Nor very patriotic, either.

'Well, missus,' he began, 'and what have ya to say about all this? Is it ya that have brought trouble upon us?'

Josiah was proud of his accent, of showing that he did not talk like the nobs who had nothing to be proud of but the land they had inherited. But where his accent came from, except that it was within an area bounded by Oxford, Norwich, Darlington and Newcastle, no one could say. At least he could play at being the plain man. And the plain man spoke plain to this Irish slut his son had brought home. True, a man must honour his promises when he made them, but why did Tom have to make this particular promise at all? If Tom had his way, he would be living with her in Newcastle or Glasgow, and coming home on foot from a shipyard every night black with cinders and coal dust. In that he underestimated Harriet because she would have seen that in this Tom would not have his way. The life she lived did not entirely suit her: the life Josiah imagined would not have suited her at all. She asked, tartly,

'What trouble?'

'Could ya not stop him? There was no call for him to go off to sea like that. Why did ya let him go?'

'I did not let him go, and I did not send him. The

navy called for Tom, and he went like an officer and a gentleman. He had no choice.

Josiah ignored the question of choice. In this family it was he who made the choices, and he had made this choice in the spring. Or thought he had.

'I put Tom into the Navy to be made a gentleman of. He went through the Navy school, old Inman's school, and then he went to sea. And after that they cheated me, and they took him off to Africa for three year, as a Mid, and no sooner were he home again than they had him out there again as a mate. And after that, he went to that school, *Excellent*, because they told me that if he didn't go there he'd be a Mate till the end of his days. And then it took me months to arrange for him to go to sea again and be a Lieutenant, and a gentleman. So now he is, and he's been presented at a levee, and you've been presented too, and been to dinner with the Lord Lieutenant, and if he stays safe at home he'll be Lord Lieutenant himself some day, and it's all to hold the boy out of the works, and keep his hands clean. He's done enough: there's no need for him to go to sea again.'

'It was his duty.'

'Duty my eye. He wants a medal.'

'He is not as vain as that.'

'Ya don't know Tom like his own flesh and blood, missus. It's all he ever wanted, a medal to wear on his chest and swagger. This is where we want him, to keep his nose out of the works that we've all sold now, and out of the markets where we put the money that we got. Let him stay here in his proper place, and take his proper seat among the gentry.'

Richard Talleyman entered. Old Josiah, when in the country, always dressed like a moderately well-to-do working farmer. When he was in the Commons, whatever time of day or night, he dressed carefully like a very rich working farmer. He spoke there, as he was speaking here, in a coarse working man's accent, the hectoring tones of a foreman. But when he was at the office in the City, or when he travelled into the north to see, assess, value, urge on or close down an iron works here, a shipyard there, he dressed to the nines. He would wear a dark blue morning coat, mid-blue waistcoat and trousers, or a similar symphony in dark and light greys.

Richard, in contrast, seemed to have only one set of clothes, whether he went in the City, or in the house in Bedford Square, or here in the country in the height of summer. He always looked a trifle shabby, perhaps a habit he had acquired in his early days, learning how to be a solicitor. He would appear always, as now, in a black morning coat, a black waistcoat, a high stock and white cravat, like a clergyman if he had only worn black inexpressibles. But his trousers were always a dull grey. A year or two ago they had been plain, but now he had taken to a pair in what was called barristers' plaid, a fine grey and black check. This confirmed Harriet's suspicion that he only ever had the one suit, till it wore out: perhaps he bought his new clothes second-hand from his clerks.

'I've been round the farm,' Richard announced. He came forward, tripping on his toes. Oh, Agag, Agag, thought Harriet, no friend of ours. If only I could hew you in pieces in the parish church at Morning Prayer.

'There's a lot to be done,' continued Richard. 'That man Bretton needs an eye kept on him, to make him work.'

'Thomas appointed him,' Harriet pointed out, 'and he has the utmost confidence in Mr Bretton.'

'And I have no confidence in Mr Bretton,' said Richard.

'It was Thomas who chose him.' said Harriet, 'and it was I that Thomas left to keep an eye on him, not you.'

Arabella came in, and after her a maid with a tray, a pot of tea and cakes.

'Mrs Green,' Arabella said, 'has cooked one of her currant cakes specially when I told her you were coming.' She settled herself and began to pour out. Harriet said,

'Oh, I am always partial as much as these men are to Mrs Green's cake.'

'You might have it every day,' said Richard, 'if only you would be sensible and move from the Dower House.'

'Up to here?'

'It is hardly suitable for you to live alone in the Dower House.'

'I am not alone. I have the boys and. . . let's see, the butler and his wife, three maids, the boys' nurse, two grooms and a footman who sleep in the stables. Or over the stables.'

'But you have no other lady living there to be a companion and a chaperone.'

'Do you think I need a chaperone, Arabella?'

'It would be more seemly.'

'Then why do *you* not come to the Dower House, and we could act as chaperones to each other? I am sure you need one as much as I do.' Arabella looked daggers at her, then burst into tears.

'Ya must not make fun of Arabella,' said Josiah angrily. 'The lass is as God made her, and we must be thankful for her being so strong and sensible. And we must have her here in the Manor House, because Richard or I may come back at any moment, and who knows who with us? We need a mistress here who will keep her confidence and not get in the way.' Arabella stood and left the room. Her father looked after her, taken aback. He returned to the attack.

'Do ya mean to say, really, that ya will not move?'

'I will not move. I will not leave my own house. Look here, Mr Talleyman, it is the only house where I have ever been mistress and I have painted and papered and hung curtains to suit my husband. When he comes

70

home from sea in a month or two, I must be there to welcome him with all the things he needs, and that includes his children. They must be in their own home to see their father come back from the wars. I will not move, and that is final.'

Harriet pulled herself together and swept out. She had spent some time studying this movement, and had been looking for an opportunity to put her studies into practice. She went to find Arabella. Josiah guessed this.

'They're weeping on each other's shoulders,' he told his younger son. 'I still don't like it. She's a sight too independent, that one.'

'She won't weep long,' said Richard. 'Cooper's bringing her hoss around.'

'She's not riding that black? That 'oss is mine, I'll not have her riding him.'

'She says it's Tom's, and she's got a right to ride it.'

'Well, Tom was with me when I bought it.'

'*You* bought it?'

'Well, it was Tom that paid for it, out of the farm account, but it was bought for me to hunt. Tom knew that.'

'But she says it was Tom bought it for her to hunt. She's getting too fat for anything else.'

'Don't want her hunting that. What would we do if she got herself killed?'

'Better her than the horse,' said Richard flatly. 'You won't have too much time for hunting this season. You'll be in Bruges. Do you think he'll agree this time?'

'I'll be home to hunt. I don't expect him till the New Year. It'll be biting then.' There was something that Tom had said, like so many of the things he said, surprising in its subtlety for such a stupid lad, fit only for the Navy: or for farming. 'There are laws of nature about war,' Tom had said, 'and this is one. In the first three months of the first campaign, you will need three times as much ammunition and three times as many

71

men, and three times as much of general stores as you imagined you would need for the whole war. And nine times as much money.' Funny for such an idiot. But true. Perhaps he was better at sea out of the way, from now to the autumn. Richard, the sedulous clerk, had enough to do. And he was doing it, all the tedious detail of turning one firm after another into limited companies under the new Bill, so that as soon as that came into law they could incorporate.

'I'll give her a hint,' said Richard. 'She's coming through the hall now.'

He was standing close enough to Harriet to smell her, smell the camphor from her clothes, and the lily of the valley of her toilet water, and underneath it all, that musty, sweaty woman's smell.

'You should not ride that horse of Tom's,' he told her. 'It is dangerous.'

'It is dangerous to go to sea,' she replied 'especially in the autumn.'

'By the end of the autumn,' he said, 'there will be nobody at sea. The northern seas will be frozen, the Russians will not come out, our ships will come home.' This one, he thought, will not come home. She need not know. It had been a stroke of luck, to hear about this ship at the meeting at the Company's offices.

'I do not believe it,' Harriet told him. 'I half believe that he will never come back.'

'In that case,' he said flatly, 'you will die a very wealthy woman. You will be well provided for, and you need not worry.' It had been a stroke of high politics to find who was to command, and then to get himself taken to dine at the Agapanthus Club and meet Only 'by chance'.

'You have deceived Tom, as you are about to deceive so many people. You are deep in this idea of limited liability, which will let you gamble with other people's money, and lose nothing if the bets you make do not come off.'

'No one is being deceived.' It had been a stroke of high eloquence to let Only know, without seeming to, how Tom was placed, why he was still on the beach. Just as long as Only never let Josiah know who had told him.

'I think you are deceiving yourself,' he went on. 'But deceitful or honest, you will come at last to work with me. Work with me now. Do not ride that horse. He is too valuable to be risked.'

It stung her. She could not reply. She could only sweep to the door.

3

'Men,' Only began, 'I am proud to command you.'

That ought to be true, thought Talleyman, looking down from the poop at the crew, or most of it, mustered below on the quarterdeck. Not more than half a dozen short. Apart from the ten-year men, they are all volunteers. Three-quarters of them at least have actually been to sea before. And hardly any foreigners. They're all here because they want to come. There's going to be a catch in it somewhere. He listened critically to the Captain: he had heard addresses like this before.

'We are all gathered here in this splendid ship for a desperate and dangerous voyage.'

That's the catch. They had all come hoping for an easy voyage, a quick run up the Baltic to Stockholm and home for Guy Fawkes' day. They've come for the good rations, the good clothes. Pay not so good as in a merchant ship, not half so good as in a whaler in a good season.

'We are on our way to face a fierce and relentless foe. I recognize that it is a pity we are at war with the wrong enemy. Would we not all feel happier if we were sailing with the Tsar's navy to fight the French? Would there not be better employment seeking the lurking frogs in the mists outside Cherbourg? But we must go where the Queen sends us, and fight her enemies for the time being, whoever they are. We are sailing up into the far north, where the British flag has never flown before.'

So it's the Murmansk blockade. But aren't we a bit late? *Eurydice* went up there in June, and there are French ships there too. Back by November, then. We have ten weeks at the most if we aren't to be frozen in.

'We do not know what we will meet there. There are rumours that the Tsar has built ships in the waters north of Siberia. Frigates, perhaps, or even a seventy-four. Built, like most Ruskies, out of fir and pine, not meant to last, not fit to take the punishment of a good teak ship. One shell into them and they will shake to pieces before they burn.'

And everyone is thinking, what if there is a shell into us? But now we know why Moulton is here, and Calne. We want to know, yes, but the Americans want to know what the Russians have there, poised to threaten them from the harbours of Alaska. Surely the coast cannot be open at this time to let us down into the Pacific?

'There we will show the world that one British seaman is worth ten foreigners, that any British ship, however small, can take any Russian ship, however large, and come home to enjoy the prize money.

'So far I have only spoken to cheer you.' What will he say when we take a shell through the stern transom? 'Now, I will tell you things you may not have understood. First, there is the question of ratings. The First Lieutenant tells me that there are men here who are of age and have been rated as able seamen in merchant ships, but cannot understand why I will rate them only as ordinary seamen. True, you may be able to hand, reef and steer, and I will soon know if you can or not. But this is a Queen's ship, and we are going to war. I will have no man rated as able seaman and paid the extra till he can serve his gun, and load and fire a Minié rifle, and till he can use his cutlass.'

Well, that ought to tell them. The marines look happy enough. They'll do the teaching.

'Next, I do not like to look down on occasions like this on a rainbow of shirts. The paymaster has available a large stock of standard issue blue jean, and by the time I do my rounds a week on Sunday, I want to see every man dressed properly in blouses of the regulation cut. If you do not know what that looks like, turn to the ten-year men for help.' Hardly, thought Talleyman, a peacemaker's tactful instruction. 'And we are going into cool waters. By the time I make my rounds three weeks on Sunday, I want to see every man, ten-year man and volunteer in a suit of regulation cut made of thick blue wool. The paymaster has sufficient stocks, and will issue at the same price as the jean.

'Now, let me warn you that I run a tight ship.' I never heard a Captain say anything different. 'I will have discipline without brutality and without favouritism. My justice and that of my officers will be even-handed. Under their Lordships of the Admiralty, I am the law in this ship, and my law will be obeyed. It is a matter of choice. If any man chooses to disobey me and my officers, then he may do so and be flogged. I am empowered to flog, and it may be the last resort, but if in the end I must flog then I will flog.' Every captain says he is reluctant to flog: in the end, he does. The most fervent sermon I ever heard from a captain on his dislike for flogging we had a man triced up for twenty lashes within the hour.

'Those are my orders for the time being, and my warnings. We are setting out to seek action, and there will be time for talking when the action is over. We will splice the mainbrace today but, before that, God save the Queen.'

Talleyman remembered his manners as First Lieutenant. He ordered,

'Hats off! Three cheers for the Queen.'

The men cheered, in the proper manner. The Captain said,

'Carry on, Mr Talleyman.'

4

Dincombe followed the other officers into the wardroom. Cricklade took over as officer of the watch. Biddell went aft, to see the issue of the meal. The men's dinner, as always, was stewed beef and dried peas. The officers' luncheon, as always, was set out on their table: cold beef and ships' biscuit. Orton looked haggard and was shivering.

'Are you well?' the Chaplain asked him.

'Cold. Always get colds in a ship the first week at sea. Stupid keeping us out there all the time, just standing. Your long-winded prayers didn't help, either.'

The Chaplain, who thought he had been far too brief, blinked at him. Orton turned to Craddock.

'Isn't it time you started that deuced big fire of yours?'

Craddock nodded, went on eating. Orton demanded,

'Don't you ever talk?'

'No,' said Craddock. He took another bite of his biscuit, chewed, swallowed, then said, in a matter of fact way,

'I hit people, though.'

'Now, now,' said Thacker. 'Sail and steamer must agree, like little birdies in a tree.'

'Oh, it's time for my tonic,' said Orton. He went into the cabin he shared with Longville. Silverwright came round, filling coffee mugs. Biddell entered.

'All quiet on the frontier?' Talleyman asked him.

'Reasonably. Nobody's killed the cook yet, but I think he'll do for some of them before we're ashore again. Check your coal, Craddock, I think the man believes you put coke into the soup, not under it.'

'No fit work for a gentleman, watching sailors dipping meat out of a cauldron,' remarked Longville. Orton had reappeared, and took his seat again, his eyes shining. He asked, loudly,

'Tell me, Talleyman, how did you break your nose?'

'Ah'll tell that,' said Talleyman. He wasn't sure if his accent for these occasions was Geordie or Brummie. 'Ah wor a little lad, and we wor aworking on setting up Paddyguts Patent Crane on the docks at West Hartlepool.'

'Who hung t'monkey?' asked Craddock.

'It wor me and me da and me Uncle Ebenezer and me Aunty Hepzibah, and I were bottom-boy. Little snip I wor then. Not four year old. And me brother, he wor two year old, and he wor holding the rivets in the fire. We all started work early, us Talleymans. I were throwing up t'red-hot rivets to me Uncle Ebenezer, and me Aunty Hepzibah come along with some of her red-hot Carnish pasties for our snap. So I threw one up to me Da, he wor thirty feet up, he wor, and not too good at catching. And he missed it, and it fell back on me face.'

'Broke tha nose?'

'Aye.'

'What dist tha do then?' asked Craddock.

'Oh, Ah borrowed a 'acksaw and cut the pasty open, and ate it. Most of it. Me baby brother had the crust. That's why he's got good teeth.'

'But who cured tha nose?' asked Orton. 'It's a fancy shape the now.'

'Oh, Ah went to the farrier, and he put a slab of horse dung on it. Couldn't afford a doctor then.'

77

'Stupid!' Longville stood up and took down his cap. 'I don't trust the jib halliards.'

He left. Thacker observed,

'I wonder if he'd feel any more comfortable if I were a physician. Probably thinks a surgeon's the same as a barber.'

'I'll kill him, some day, I swear I will,' Craddock told them all, very convincingly. Talleyman shook a finger at him.

'Patience, patience. It's me he's after, not you. Wait till we get into some weather. I've not seen him go above the maintop yet.'

5

'Come with me, and with Mr Hook,' Orton told the Chaplain, 'and see how we earn our rations. But first of all, change your clothes. Put your worst trousers on, and a jersey over that starched shirt. Or better, change it. Wear your nice new seaboots, and follow your leader. The Carpenter will be behind you.

'Down here we go, and then down again, out of the light and the world of men. I don't suppose you thought there was anywhere further down than the orlop, did you? Up there it's all nice smooth walls and polished planking, but down here it's all rough and useful.'

Dincombe went gingerly down one ladder, and then another. Orton carried a candle in a lantern. So did Mr Hook and each of the two seamen with him.

'Here's George Fielder, petty officer caulker,' Hook explained, rather than introduced, 'and behind him's John Pulley, petty officer John Pulley. That's their ratings in the service. Good men, I was lucky to get them to come. Anywhere they'd be shipwrights, steady work in any yard.'

'I was foreman shipwright in a yard at Brindlington,' Pulley boasted. 'Only Mr Hook he came and ast me.'

'They'll see you don't hit your head, Reverend. No more ladders till we go up for'ard.'

'What is this under my feet?' asked Dincombe. 'It feels like metal.'

'It is metal,' Orton told him. 'Pig iron bars, the ballast.'

'Mr Longville's talking about moving some of it forward to trim her,' said Hook.

'We'll wait till we've steamed her,' Orton said. 'Trim for sailing may not be the trim for steaming. Want to keep her stern down for steaming, keep the screw in the water. We'll have Mr Craddock to ask, then.'

'And that's not right,' Hook grumbled. 'When I first came into the service, the Engineer, if you had to have one, he was one of the Carpenter's crew, and did what the Carpenter told him. And now they're commission officers, lording it in the wardroom over us all. There's no justice in the world, Reverend.'

'And the smell?' Dincombe asked. The others were not retching, so he would not: must not.

'Oh, she's pretty sweet,' said Hook. 'Old days we used to have gravel ballast and it got so foul sometimes the whole ship stank.'

'We're down at the bottom of the ship,' Orton explained more patiently. 'Everything you spill topsides trickles down here in the end. Seeps amidships into the well, and we pump it out. How's the well, now, Mr Hook?'

'Dry, sir, still, and sweet as a nut. She been put together proper.'

'Is this the bilges then?' asked Dincombe. He wanted only to show that there were some words he did know.

'Yes. When were they cleaned out last, Mr Hook?'

'In the summer, sir, when we got her out of ordinary.

79

Had everything out of here and scrubbed out. Now, George.' The caulker came out of the darkness astern. 'Is she dry?'

'Not a drop, yet,' the caulker replied. Then to Dincombe he explained, 'I got to go back there and look at the seal where the shaft go out of the ship. If that do leak, Mr Craddock he got to know at once. And he got to tell the Captain that minute.'

'Wait till we've been at sea six months, Chaplain,' said Orton. 'Come down here and smell her then. This is what we've come down to see. Look around.'

To their right rose the side of the ship. Now Dincombe realized that what on the upper decks he had thought to be the very walls that kept out the water were no more than an inner skin, ornamental almost. The ribs of the vessel rose, not vertically as he had expected, but inclined at an angle to the keel, sloping fore and aft and crossing each other, jointed together. Orton slapped his palm on a junction of great beams.

'That's the difference between a man of war and a merchant ship, Chaplain. This is diagonal framing. Mr Seppings invented that about the end of the French wars. You see, all kinds of cross support.'

'That be strong as nobody's business,' Pulley explained. 'It do mean a terrible lot of work, and more than owners would pay for, except the Admiralty.'

'And the scantlings,' said Fielder, 'that's terrible heavy for the size of the ship. Eight-inch beams and more, some of them.'

'I seen stouter,' Hook told them. 'I been in a Yankee frigate once, laid up in ordinary she were, in Philadelphia.' Dincombe wondered for a moment what a ship would be doing so near to Damascus, and then recalled the modern world. 'Fifty guns she were rated, but she were the length of a seventy-four and scantlings on her more like a ninety-two. But not diagonal. They put engines in her, and I wouldn't like to be in her in a bad sea. Break her back, soon enough.'

'But these side timbers,' said Pulley. Dincombe realized that these were things they had all been thinking about, worrying about, that they were glad of an audience to bring them out. 'Wouldn't ever see side planking like this in a merchant ship. Double diagonal planked, and eight inches thick each plank. I think they must have meant her to stand up to shell. Inner skin up there's eight inches, too.'

'Mr Craddock seen the propellor gland today?' asked Orton.

'Down here first thing,' Hook replied. 'Once we start steaming, we'll get some of that coal moved. No place for coal down here, not in the bunkers.'

'Right, let's go forward. Here, Chaplain, through this wing passage. The bunker wall is on your left. Bit of damp here, Mr Hook. Mind your head, schoolie, it's low here, and smellier. It's. . . oh, a bit of oil here. Smell it?'

'I think that's boiler spillage, sir, nothing to worry about. There's no knowing yet what we can expect here under the engines.'

'Are we under the engines?' asked Dincombe.

'Not exactly. We have to crawl here, under the bunkers. Those are the boiler base plates inboard of you.'

'What are we looking for?'

'Nothing, yet. But if we find out exactly how things are under sail, we know what we're seeing when the engines start and the vibrations begin. If she's going to shake to pieces I want to have first warning. Lot of coal dust. If anybody ever asks me what I did in the Russian war, I shall tell them I went walking through a coal mine during an earthquake. Only not so pleasant. Is your back breaking?'

'Nearly.'

'So is mine. Feeling it a bit hot?'

Dincombe was sweating, he could smell himself even in the stink of the bilges. The sweat was running down his body, around his groin. The close and stuffy air

81

was stifling him. They were out now into a passageway where they could stand upright again. He could tell that the side of the ship was curving round. But it was also sloping outward a little. Further aft, the side had been vertical. He said,

'Is this the shape of the ship under water?'

'Aye,' said the Carpenter. 'Now in a proper man of war, she's built like a box, see, and the bows are just rounded off in a semicircle, and the bottom rounded off into a vertical side for twenty feet up or so and then lean in a bit. Tumble home, we calls it. But this ship, she's more like what we'd call a clipper ship. She comes in sharp to the bows here, and the sides are sharper, a narrow bottom. It gives more speed, they say, if you have a sailer that's built light for it. But this one, now, she's shaped light but built heavy, you might say, and she's a bit heavy to steer too. But perhaps it's the best way to build a steamer. Nobody knows.'

'Look at this framing up here,' said the caulker. 'Scantlings like a hundred and twenty-one's, and the bow post, massive, that's all I can say. Massive.'

'Whaler to start with, you think?' asked Orton.

'That'd be sensible,' Hook agreed. 'A bit o' speed to chase 'un, but look for 'un under sail. But the ways of their Lordships be beyond the understanding of mortal man and we shall never know.'

'Well, time to take you up, schoolie. You look as though you've had the best of the day. Scrape along here and up, out of the bilges. Not much room in here for three. What are you up to, Biddell?'

'Counting peas, one by one. Enjoy Gehenna, Chaplain?'

'Something I've been wondering,' said Dincombe. 'Something you always hear about in ships.'

'What's that?'

'Rats. We haven't seen any rats.'

'That,' Biddell told him, 'is young Master Cricklade's doing. Sporting gent, is our Cricklade. He's brought

82

his pet shotguns, three of 'em, and he's afraid to ask the Captain for permission to use them. He and I were the first commission officers in the ship, and she wasn't too bad for rats. But she was clean empty, and we wondered how to take advantage. Cricklade brought along a couple of pairs of his ratters, terriers, nasty brutes, not much bigger than rats themselves and take your arm off as soon as look at you. They had high jinks up and down the ship for about three days, and at the end they were wailing after us on the deck to find them more. Haven't seen any rats since, touch wood. If you find any, Chaplain, let me know.'

Dincombe followed Orton, wriggling between casks and sacks, and up one vertical ladder into the orlop, and up another to the main deck. At last they came out on to the upper deck, and made their way aft, between the gun crews at their daily exercise. The Chaplain drank deep of the salt air, looked with affection at the grey sea. The narrow wardroom seemed as spacious as a cathedral.

'Now,' said Orton, 'wash and change. Silverwright will have coffee for us in ten minutes. Duty perks.'

6

Over the coffee, Dincombe asked,

'Have you done it before?'

'I do it every day. No, I tell a lie. I do it every even day.'

'And the odd days?'

'I start for'ard, go along the port side. I chop and change, saves me from getting used to things.'

'Only you?'

'It's on my bill, not anybody else's. If this were an old

83

ship, or if we knew what she'd behave like in a sea or under steam, I'd go perhaps every week. But I go every day, me and the Carpenter's crew.'

'Nobody else?'

'Oh, I see. Every officer has been along. Most days we take a cadet. Then we use it as a mild punishment for delinquent seamen, you know, make them come along and hold the lantern. A lot of them don't like it.'

'The Captain?'

'Once, before we left Portsmouth, I gather. The First Lieutenant comes once a week. Doctor comes once a week to test the smell. Paymaster will start coming when we've eaten enough to disturb the trim. You heard, the Engineer comes fairly often, to look at the leaks where the propellor shaft goes out of the ship.'

'You go through that awful passage just as a routine?'

'Just as a routine. But watch when the Captain goes again. We won't see him till we take a shell.'

7

Talleyman sat at the chart table, balancing watch bills and numbers. They seldom came out right. His door was open. The man in the First Lieutenant's proper cabin opposite, he must come out some time. He'd have to go to the heads. Or suffocate.

Midway through the afternoon, he did come out. The steps went along to the Captain's cabin, and in a little while came back. Talleyman stood in the way.

'I think we have met before. In Ireland.'

'Why, so we have, so we have. I think I sold you a horse. Good goer, wasn't she? Have you still got her?'

'Someone stole her. I think it was William Smith Bronterre O'Brien.'

'Did you have a nice time, shut up in the farm with all those peelers? It was good fun watching you.'

Talleyman stared. It all came back, rather it never went away, shut up in the farmhouse with the mob outside, firing once or twice in the quarter hour. He could remember, he could swear, every face outside, but he was sure that this man, a man he had dined with the night before, in a John Company officer's uniform, was not among them.

'Did you not see me?' Smith of Brighton, as he had called himself then, was smiling at Talleyman's bewilderment. 'I was in the Punch and Judy.'

'In there?'

'It was my turn. No show without Punch, they say, so we made sure that there was a Mister Punch at every show the would-be rebels put on. I was lucky to be there the day the excitement happened.'

'And now Mr Punch is in this ship.'

'I've just come for the ride, one might say.'

'Have you?' Talleyman thought a moment. 'This is not vulgar curiosity. What have you in that cabin?'

'Oh cargo, just a little general cargo, souvenirs of Ireland and such like. I'll take it all with me when I get off.'

'I am responsible for the safety of this ship. Under the Captain. I must know. Have you any powder? If a shell comes aboard, I must know.'

'Powder? Well . . . no, not what you would call a deal of powder. I have a Minié carbine and thirty rounds made up for it, and a revolver, with fifty rounds made up.'

'A revolver?'

'A Colt, and I bought it at the Exhibition, in Hyde Park. It seemed to be the best on offer.'

'I disagree. I saw the Colt. Navy pattern. I didn't like it. Single action is too slow. The calibre was too small. No stopping power. The half-inch bore will stop anybody. I bought Deane and Adams.'

'According to taste. Do we have to talk standing here?'

'Come into the chartroom. What are you doing here?'

'Hasn't the Captain told you?'

'He has given me a course to steer.'

'There is no need why you should not know now we have put to sea and nobody can tell the Russians. Have you heard of Shamyl?'

'It is a rude word. In Jewish. My father's financial colleagues often use it. About him.'

'No, no, Shamyl. He is leader of the tribes of the Caucasus. The Russians claim the land there, but so does Shamyl, and he would like to claim all the prairies of Asia.'

'But what has that to do with us? Or you?'

'Think of what this war is about, and where the Russians are. The most modern Russian army is before Petersburg, to protect the Tsar in case Napier lands. Their biggest army is in the Ukraine, mobilized against the Austrians, who have their main force on the Russian frontier. They have another army on the Danube, in the Principalities, Moldavia and Wallachia, and that is where our army has gone to fight them with the Turks. They have a small army in the Crimea to protect Odessa. But while those armies are ready for war, have been ready for many years, they have an army *at* war, at war for many years. The Russians are trying to settle the prairies of Asia, like the Americans moving into the west, and the tribes there, like the Red Indians, are trying to prevent them. The Russians are also trying to gain control of the Caucasus mountains and the land of Kirgizstan beyond the Caspian. This is important in two ways. In the first place, any soldiers who are tied up in Asia cannot come to fight us or the Turks. And in the second place, you know I am not a Queen's officer, I am a Company officer. If the Russians can take the Caucasus and hold it, or Kirghizstan, they can make their next step down into Persia, and from there they threaten India. Don't forget, the emperors of India at Delhi came from Persia.'

'Well?'

'What weapons do our soldiers carry?'

'Minié rifles, those who have not yet got Enfield rifles.'

'The Russian troops before St Petersburg have percussion muskets, about half of them, smooth bores. The rest of the Russian armies, everywhere, have the same flintlocks they used against Napoleon. With a Minié I can kill the man I want to kill at six hundred yards; with their flintlocks, the Russians can hit a man, not always the man they want to kill, if the whole company aim at him at two hundred yards. The tribes and the Caucasians can get powder and flintlocks from the Russians, if they fight for them, but if they had Minié rifles . . .'

'You are taking rifles to the Caucasus? To hold India? But you can't have got enough aboard to make any difference.'

'The Caucasians are very good smiths. First, I am taking them about two hundred Minié rifle barrels. They can make their own stocks to mount them, and their own locks, whether they prefer percussion or flintlocks. I have some percussion locks and caps, but they won't be able to steal enough caps to keep them going. And making caps will be beyond them. But I am also taking a dozen Minié barrels sectioned. The secret of the Minié is the rifling and the shape of the bullet. If the smiths know what they are supposed to make, they will make them by hand from very good steel. But the shape of the bullet, the long, pointed bullet with the skirt that swells from the explosion and fills the bore – that is beyond them at the moment. I am not taking bullets. They're too heavy, and the people there can steal lead from the Russians to cast them. So what I am taking, dozens of them, are Minié bullet moulds.'

'And that's all you have?'

'All I have.'

'I am not so sure.'

'Why not?'

'I watched the seamen who brought your cargo aboard. There were several parcels which the men thought were lead. I am inclined to believe them, from the weight.'

'Come and see.'

The Indian officer's cabin was filled with bundles. There was scarcely room to move, or even to sling his hammock.

'I've had it all very well packed. Each of these parcels is a load for a pack mule.'

'But the lead?'

'See here.'

He heaved up a much smaller sack, the size of a knee boot. Talleyman felt canvas outside, but under that leather.

'Yes, it is a riding boot. But full, feel it.'

'What?'

'Gold.'

'Gold? Gold bars? Or sovereigns?'

'Oh nothing so dangerous. Just think if you were a malevolent Siberian, and the Russians caught you and wanted to know what you were doing with all those Victoria Regina sovereigns, dated 1854. No, this lot is a fine old mixture, sovereigns and guineas back to George III, Napoleons, moidores, Spanish, Austrian, Persian, everything, and all well worn, rubbed smooth. And the rest, gold rings, all sizes, all eighteen carat, no hallmarks, all the kind of things you find all over the wild country. Men buy and sell with them, women wear them as ornaments, they go into chains for dowries, get melted down and hammered into pins and bracelets. But it's all gold, good gold, it's all money and for enough money Shamyl will go on killing Russians and drawing them out into the wilds, far away from the Danube and the Turks.'

'Much?'

88

'About a hundred thousand pounds worth.'

'So your cabin cargo is nearly worth the ship.' Talleyman pondered. Then he looked out into the passageway, called to the Marine who was standing a few paces astern outside the Captain's day cabin door.

'Now, you – Garvey, isn't it? From now on, your post is here, not down there. Challenge anyone except me and this officer. Don't let anyone but this officer into this cabin.'

'But Captain Fincham told me to stand here, sorr.'

'I give Mr Fincham his orders.'

Talleyman turned back to the stranger.

'Now, Smith of Brighton . . . .'

'That is not my name, in fact.'

'I never thought it was. Who are you, really?'

'My name is Esteron.'

'Well, Mr Esteron, a word of advice.'

'You probably have a great deal of that to give me.'

'Not really. Have you a uniform?'

'Naturally.'

'Then wear it. The men know there is a stranger on board. If the passenger is a civilian and he stays hidden, they will gossip. And guess. Wear a uniform. Take the air in it daily where you can be seen. If the men know we have an officer as passenger, they will take you for granted. They will know you have business and no business of theirs. And one more thing.'

'What?'

'Come to dinner in the wardroom. Tomorrow night.'

8

'Ah, Mr Wasely,' said Talleyman, who had passed the
word for the Gunner to come to the chartroom. 'I am
sorry to disturb you. Can you show the Chaplain what
to do, please?'

'What I do, Mr Talleyman?'

'What is the work of a Gunner, Mr Wasely.'

'Yes, the Captain says I ought to find out,' explained
Dincombe. 'How you fire the guns, I suppose, and so
on. I tried to see you this morning when the men were
at gun drill, but I couldn't make out where you were.'

'So you want to see me at my work, then, parson?
Well, my work is not in firing guns, nor in wreaking
destruction on the face of the waters. My work is in
keeping up my stewardship, and caring for the talents
that the good Lord almighty has been pleased to bestow
upon me.'

'Mr Wasely,' said Talleyman, 'is a man of God.'
Dincombe sought for the trace of a smile in the
first Lieutenant's face, but found none. Talleyman
continued: 'Mr Wasely is the senior warrant officer in
this ship. So he would be in any ship. He was in the ship
before we commission officers came into her. He will
be in her when we go out of her. He, the Gunner, owns
the ship when she is not in commission. He answers to
no one here but the Captain. He will, however, own my
authority.'

'Aye,' said Wasely. 'The business of the Gunner is too
sacred a thing to be left to underlings.' He was short,
red-faced and white-haired, although whether this was
due to age or to the weathered bleaching of a blond
man Dincombe could not make out. Indeed, the man

seemed ageless, immutable, eternal. 'Now, if truly you would come down and see the work I do upon the great waters and my stores and hear the power they have, you must turn out your pockets.'

'Turn out my pockets? But – '

'Yes, turn out your pockets, parson, here on the chart table. Mr Talleyman will not steal your property.'

'Do it,' said Talleyman. 'So do we all. I have given you into the Gunner's hands. You must obey him.'

'Now, let us see.' Wasely bent over the things that Dincombe had put on the table. 'Aye, that is what I thought to see, and proper things, all of them, for a gentleman to have about him, but though blameless in themselves, yet a sin to take where we are about to go. For here are the means of making fire, even though you do not intend it. Here are a knife, and a pipelighter of flint and steel held together by a tinder cord, that we commonly use to make fire. A pocket case of cigars, that are a temptation to make fire and then carry it about in your very mouth. Your watch you must leave here, for although the case is of beaten gold, yet the workings are wrought from steel. Now ... that is not all, for I see something glinting. You are in the habit, parson, of picking up stray pins and stowing them for safety in your lapels, and though that is an act praiseworthy in itself and loved by the Lord who enjoins us to thrift and even to parsimony, yet it may be a bringer of death on His servants. Put those pins here, and mark, you may have more of them than you thought. Put all those pins here.'

'Is that all?'

'Not yet, parson. Lift up your left foot behind you so that I may see the soles. You will have to take off your boots, and leave them at the wardroom door where there is a Marine sentry to see they do not run away of themselves, for they are well studded with iron. Yes, parson, put them there, and this child Fox, who has

91

learnt already all that you will learn, will bring you a pair of felt slippers.'

'Slippers? They are more like great boots of felt.'

'Aye, and no iron in them at all. Now have faith in me and follow me down into the very heart of the ship. Now we go down from the main deck where you live at the after end, and down to the lower deck where the seamen sling their hammocks, and where I live in my gun room and preside over the mess of the warrant officers and the Mates and, in this ship, because they have nowhere else to go, over the cadets. Now, let us go down here. I am sure, parson, that you did not know there was anyone lower in the ship than the lower deck. . . .'

'No, I do know that. I have been with Lieutenant Orton and the Carpenter through the wing passages and the holds.'

'Aye, but carrying their tools and their lanterns they would know better than to come near me. Remember that the whole ship is built for nothing but to carry me and my stores, and well they know it and respect me. True I have an armourer and his mates, and they work forward on the iron floor of the engine room, where they can pump their bellows and beat iron on the anvil, so that if ever we take a ploughshare from the Russians we may beat out a sword for ye, in token that it was a sword that our Redeemer came to bring among us. But the sword is a weapon of olden time, so the armourers there beat out rings and bolts and chains and all other gearing for the great guns when they need repair. Now it is here that I do most of my work, and here is my Gunner's Mate, Bathurst, a petty officer of the first class, who I think you have met before. He rules for me over the powder men.'

They were, Dincombe calculated, directly below the wardroom. On either side were racks of cannon balls. There was a stout teak bulkhead, which seemed to reach from side to side of the ship. Bathurst sat on a high stool at a desk fixed as a ledge to the bulkhead.

Four seaman sat on the floor. Three were scraping rust off cannon balls, and the fourth was painting them when clear and stacking them in a rack to dry. Dincombe indicated them.

'Why?' he asked.

'Oh, the men are defaulters who have sinned against heaven and the Captain and who because they have been seen dirty must clean our weapons. And this is not makework, as they will tell you, but they do it because a ball that is rusty and dirty and rough of surface will not fly true, and with a brush and a coat or two of paint we can do more to help our shooting than a week of practice at aiming the guns. Now come in here to the passage, parson.'

They went through a low door in the bulkhead into a kind of lobby, five feet deep. There was another door at the far end, with a sliding shutter in it, and a further door in the starboard side.

'Now, come in here and shut the outer door, parson, that the imps of hell that dwell in the stokehold do not enter. Now here to one side is another room, and you may see that a light shines into the passage from a scuttle in it, and when I open it, there is a compartment where three lanterns hang with candles. And see here, also, that there are scuttles which look through into the powder room and give us a little light to work there. Now, back into the passageway and through into the powder room.'

Mr Wasely opened the inner door and motioned Dincombe through. The sour, harsh smell that always hung as a faint scent about the Gunner's clothes and had been noticeable in the after end of the orlop, now became an overpowering stench, and the totality of the air that Dincombe tried to breathe. Wasely saw the Chaplain's wrinkled nose and smiled, saying, not unkindly,

'It takes a man time to get used to the smell of powder. Some tell me it is the smell of the devil's sulphur,

93

but I teach them that we must fight Satan with his own weapons and with none inferior. So the powder room here is the very being and essence of our holy task.'

The door was shut firmly behind them. Dincombe looked back at it, looked around him, and remarked in wonder,

'But the door. . .and the walls. . .and the floor. . .and the deckhead over us. . .they are all sheeted in metal.'

'Copper,' said Wasely briefly. 'Sheet copper will not strike a spark, but it will keep out the water and even the dampness of the air. The bulk of the powder is here, on either side of us, in casks of a hundred pounds, each lined with copper and well sealed down with pitch. For powder is not a dead thing, parson, it is alive and it breathes and makes its sustenance out of the air and the water in it. Or, to use the proper language, it is deliquescent. Let your powder get damp and you will soon lose half the strength, or sometimes more. So we do not open a cask till we must.'

'Don't you have a lot of small boys to run about with the powder in open tubs? I haven't seen any.'

'You've been reading too many romances about Napoleon, or looking at too many pictures of the death of Nelson painted by artists who never went to sea. We did once, and that's what I did at Navarino. Did you know I'm the oldest man in the ship, parson? Older even that the Captain by a few months, and we were both there in the same ship. Look here, we have the cartridges ready filled, canvas bags full of powder, in these copper-lined chests. Ten rounds, that is, full charge, and five rounds half charge. We pass them from here through that hatch, and then they go up through a hatch into the lower deck and then up again to the main deck, and so again to the gun deck. In action we would be filling cartridges here to replace the rounds fired.'

'And the shot is around the guns?'

'Yes, the solid shot, ten rounds per gun, in the garlands on the gun deck, and the rest in the orlop. But there is very little chance, parson, that we will have to engage enemy on both broadsides at once, so we have twenty rounds per gun for the engaged side. Let me tell you, twenty broadsides is a long battle, and one way or another it's one round will do the business.'

'What do you mean?'

'Look here, at these leather cases. There's ten rounds ready loaded for the eight-inch. Shell, man, shell. Feel the weight of that. As much as you can give one man to handle. There's ten pounds of the case, and inside it fifty pounds odd of iron shot, hollow, and inside that powder, and a fuse. So we have the shell here for the after eight-inch, and another shell room forward for the other.'

'After eight-inch? I thought there was only one, on the gun deck for'ard.'

'Oh, and there's another to match it, aft, on the gun deck. But – haven't you seen it? No? Then you haven't been into the Captain's day cabin, because that's where it is. He hasn't got as much room as you may think. I know it was there first thing this morning because I go in every morning to see to the breechings. Wouldn't do to have that take charge in such a small space. We wouldn't be able to lash it down again. But in a war like now, not like when the Captain and I were lads, an action wouldn't last more than one good shot. Take a shell, and you won't want to go on.'

'Why not?'

'You've had enough of the smell of the powder, parson, with the motion of the ship and all that, and I don't want my good men wasting their time cleaning up the deck after you. If you want to learn about shell, go and ask young Cricklade. He's an educated man. He's been to *Excellent* and don't let any of us forget it. Come on, parson, let's get you out of this.'

9

'Tell me,' said Dincombe. It was lunch time in the wardroom and officers were, as usual, doing frightful things to cold canned beef and coffee. Forward, the men were eating a hot meal, boiled canned beef and peas and canned potatoes. 'Tell me, what is shell?'

He was asking Longville, who seemed on this point the most approachable. There was a long silence. Everybody had stopped talking.

'Have I said something wrong?' Dincombe asked.

It was Orton who answered.

'You have seen the devil's evil hole? Didn't he show you shell?'

'Yes. But he did not say what they were, not in plain words.'

'Did he show you the enemy's shell, too?' Talleyman asked.

'Of course not, how could he?'

'You saw the size of the shells?' said Longville.

'Yes. Half a hundredweight, too much for a man to run with. Are they full of powder?'

'Not. . . full. Between three and four pounds of powder, to bring them all up to the same weight.'

'As little as that?' It did not seem a great matter.

'Enough,' said Talleyman. 'It has made war at sea impossible.'

'If we have to fight against shell,' put in Thacker, 'we are all dead men, and no need for burial. You can go ashore, then, Dincombe, you and I will not be needed.'

'They didn't have shell in Nelson's day,' Longville told the Chaplain. 'The army used them in mortars for high lobs. Then about twenty years ago, the French tried firing mortar shells out of a gun, long barrel, flat trajectory, that would hit a ship's side. Now if you are in a ship and a shot hits the side and doesn't penetrate you're fairly safe, but if it does penetrate, then the damage is done.'

'The shot bounces around inside the ship?' Dincombe guessed.

'Not the shot. What it does to the wood,' said Talleyman. 'Splinters.'

'The deck will be full of lumps of wood flying about,' Thacker explained. A jagged lump of wood a foot square will take off your head, or mash up an arm or leg so that all I can do is take it off, quick, before you die Wood does everything a lead shot will do, and worse.'

'But the shell?'

'Well,' Longville said, 'if a shell comes through a ship's side and the fuse works and it explodes, the three or four pounds of powder throws the fifty pounds of iron in small pieces, all through the 'tween decks. Just as bad as wood splinters, but sharper. And something else, too. What, Chaplain, is the nightmare in this ship? Why must you walk on deck to enjoy your cigar after dinner?' Longville irritated Dincombe with his schoolmasterly airs: the Chaplain felt that he was the only person entitled to draw information out of pupils, make them answer their own questions. Yet he answered,

'Fire?'

'Yes, fire. One bursting charge of powder inside the ship, and in a few moments all that powder old Wasely showed you will go up and we will all be dead men. If we meet an enemy at the old range, half pistol shot, it will happen.'

'That is what we think will happen,' said Talleyman comfortingly.

'What we know will happen,' Longville repeated in dismal triumph.

'You mean the Russians have shell? Are they as clever as that?'

'For a generation,' Longville told him, coldly, 'every fleet in the world has had shell. Nobody had used it against an enemy until last November. You may have noticed it in the newspapers: the Russians attacked the Turkish Black Sea fleet at Sinope.'

'Yes, I remember there was a battle. It began the war.'

'The Russians fired, oh, perhaps half a dozen broadsides, all shell. Five minutes, and seven Turkish frigates, three corvettes and two other steamers. . .they were all either sunk or burning or just blown into the clouds. That five minutes, Chaplain, made war at sea impossible. No training of gunners, nor skill at manouevre, no bravery can help.'

'Nothing?'

'Not it they see us first,' objected Orton brightly. 'The problem with shell is range. To be sure of penetrating with the fuse still burning, we have to fire at no more than five or six hundred yards. But with solid shot on a clear day we can engage him at a mile and a half and knock him to pieces before he gets to shell range. On a bad day we shall have to dodge in and out of mists and try to out-think him so that we come out a quarter of a mile from him loaded with shell.'

'Russian ships,' said Talleyman, 'are built of fir. Cheap. Not well seasoned. Shot will break them up. This ship is built to take shot. Scantlings like a liner. Teak sides. Two feet thick. Keep them at long range.'

'If we can,' said Longville.

'That is your task,' said Talleyman. 'Would you rather be here? Or in the Baltic? Going in against forts firing shell?'

10

Fat Jack Pither was not comfortable. That day he was on the quarterdeck of HMS *President*. He had been in Bombay Harbour, in *Forth*, under Pentstemon, wishing he had not taken the post when it was offered, wishing he were somewhere where there would be action, in the Baltic squadron, when Captain Pentstemon sent for him. He resented Pentstemon, who had persuaded him to come out here, but Pentstemon seemed quite affable, grinning all over his round face, rubbing his hands.

'Now, Jack, you saw *Virago* steam into harbour, did you not? And surely you realized why she is here?'

'No, sir.'

'Go along the paths of thought. *Virago* is part of Admiral Prices's squadron, and they are going to fight the Russians on Khamchatka. You saw in the papers that they have joined with the French in Hawaii. *Virago* has come from Hong Kong with an urgent message. Price wants more officers, he wants to borrow lieutenants and mates, a lot of them. So I am going to offer you to him, among others, and you will shift your gear into *Virago* this afternoon.'

'You mean I am to go supernumerary into *Virago*?'

'I rather think you are to go supernumerary into *President*. I can see you are delighted at the prospect of this. Can't you guess why?'

'Has someone died, sir?'

'Not yet. Now, try thinking. What do you know about Admiral Price?'

'I know he's seventy, sir. I know he was last at sea in, oh, twenty-seven. He was Flag Officer South America then.'

'Yes. And in the great war, he was a desperate and brave officer, he fought here and there till anyone else would have had a belly full. Frigates, mostly. There was one time he took a gig with a load of sailors inshore in a gale, and came out with a French ten-gun brig and three merchant men. And he learnt something then you may like to dwell on.'

'What's that, sir?'

'In big actions, it's the officers who get shot. He thinks he will be short of watch-keepers after he meets the Russians. So he wants spares. How if you are going to get into *Virago* before she sails, hadn't you better hurry? I did tell you I would make sure you saw action.'

It was now the end of August. In the castle of Petropavlovsk, Rear Admiral Zavioko, Governor of Kamchatka, was looking at *President* through his telescope. True, at that distance *President* was nothing but a blob of white sail on the horizon. But she was there to be counted, and her size guessed at, and for it to be seen that were were at least six, perhaps seven, sail with her, as well as a steamer.

In late July, St Petersburg had told the Governor that war was imminent. The dispatch had been sent in April, overland, through country wild with dissident tribes. Since then, he had had no confirmation.

He had worked night and day to get his three ships, *Aurora*, *Pallas* and *Dvina* ready for war. *Pallas* was now somewhere at sea. The other two were in harbour: their captains, having taken short cruise among the whalers, not daring to capture any in case there was not a war after all, had brought their fir-built vessels back, with some disinclination to try them at sea again without a good deal of reconstruction. Zavioko had barely begun to get the shore defences into order. He had batteries to mount twenty guns. Three were in position, the rest were still being hauled out of the cellars of the fortress.

'Eight of them?' said Zavioko's senior Captain. 'That's at least a hundred and fifty guns on the broadside, and big ones. The English use nothing smaller than thirty-two pounders.'

'You've grounded *Aurora* and *Dvina*. You can't take them to sea against this fleet, and at least we will have thirty guns.'

'Light ones,' said the Captain. 'Nothing more than eighteen-pounders. If we could get the rest of the fortress guns up, your excellency, we could give them a hard time. I wouldn't like to come in against a score of ten- and twelve-inch, land mounted, and a furnace going for heated shot. A pity we have no shell.'

'Colonel Lessoffsky tells me we will not have them in position till tomorrow late afternoon, and not ready to fire for another day after that. What then? What till then? We will have to make your crews fight to the last man, but until then . . . ?'

'Logs,' said the Captain, with simple logic. 'Stick logs out of the empty embrasures.'

Through the morning, *President* stood in, three more British frigates and four French behind her. Price paced his quarterdeck, looked at the fortress through his telescope, saw little. He called his Flag Captain, who had been scrupulously standing on the opposite side of the quarter deck.

'We should be in range about – oh – in another two hours.'

'We have been closed up to the guns for three hours,' observed Captain Burridge.

'Yes, so we have. Let the men have their dinners about their guns.'

'Aye, aye, sir. Bo'sun, pipe cooks to the galley.'

Pither watched the men eat, while he himself munched biscuit and salt beef. He felt useless. He had no task assigned him, except that if one of the lieutenants commanding the divisions of guns was hit, Pither should take over. He wondered how likely that was.

The Admiral wondered too. He had heard from a stray whaler captured a week earlier that the Russians had as usual dismounted the guns from their battery. They would take at least three weeks to mount them. He could make out now a couple of ships in the harbour. If he could tempt the Russians out to fight there would be no difficulty but ships moored inside a quay were more trouble to deal with, especially if they were on the mud, stable as guns in a fortress. At any rate, the ships would have no support from the fortifications. Nevertheless they would have to be dealt with: he would have to approach to within half a mile of the shore before he dared launch his boats. He would go first himself, in his own barge and show the French an example. He'd done it to them in the past and now they could see how it was done.

The seamen had finished eating. There was silence as far as there ever was silence in a ship. Pither looked glumly around the quarterdeck. The Flag Captain, the Flag Lieutenant, the First Lieutenant of *President*, the Master, the Captain of Marines, all stood looking at the Admiral. Captain Burridge revelled in his lack of responsibility. He did not regard himself as a staff officer, he saw his role as purely domestic: seeing that the Admiral had a clean ship, a willing, well-fed crew, a good table – although that was more the Flag Lieutenant's responsibility. Certainly there was no necessity for him to say anything. War was the Admiral's business, not his.

Price stood looking at the fort. It was still hard to make out the details, but ... but ... surely ...He called to the Flag Lieutenant.

'Look at the fort. What can you see?'

'See, sir?'

'Yes, see. Look at the fort, at the embrasures. What can you see?'

'Why ... guns, sir.'

'Guns? Are you sure?'

'Yes, sir. Big guns, twelve-inch or bigger. I can count, oh, nineteen or twenty of them.'

Price looked round. He called the Flag Captain.

'Burridge!! How many guns do you count there in the castle?'

'About a score, sir.'

Price stood silent on the deck. Guns, big guns. No one would install guns like that to fire solid shot. They were waiting for him, all ready, all run out. He would have to come well within range. They might reach him with solid shot a mile out, but there would not be much damage and at that range he could reply and smother the opposing guns. But to get in within that, to where he would launch his boats, he would have to get within the range of shell. They could engage him at half a mile. It would not be a question of solid shot annoying his boats, but it would be shell from shore-mounted guns. There would be no movement to disturb the gunners, they would have every approach through the shoals covered, they would be able to find the range. He imagined shell coming into *President*, the flame of the explosions setting fire to the decks, to the sails, the great splinters of flying iron, red-hot, smashing the rigging, the gun mountings, one hit leaving *President* dead in the water, unable to move, exposed even to the light guns of the ships, incapable of doing more than launching her boats to save her men's skins. He saw himself coming ashore to hand over his sword tamely to the Russian commander. And not only himself. The next ship astern was the French *La Forte*, under Admiral Fevrier des Pointes. He would go down in history as the man who lost two fleets, by wilful ignorance. They could not do it, could not face an undamaged stone fort firing shell at them. Shot, perhaps, but not shell.

But he had never avoided action in the last war. He had made his name as an attacking sailor, as a man who looked for war. He had been given this command, this last chance of smelling powder, simply because he had a name for being a man who could not be resisted. If he turned back now, he would be shamed even if he brought his ships out unharmed.

He looked again at the shore. There was a movement of a gun in one of the embrasures. What were they doing? Adjusting the fuse time? He could not sail this fleet into disaster. He had no choice. He slammed his telescope shut and looked round at the officers on the quarterdeck.

'Excuse me, I am just going to the heads.'

Price went down the companionway to his own day cabin. There was a long silence. Only the ship's noises, the cracking of timbers and of ropes. The other officers looked incuriously at the shore. Nobody had told them to look at the forts through their telescopes, so nobody did, least of all Fat Jack Pither, discarded and carried only in case somebody got killed.

Then, clear through all the ship noises, came the unmistakable sound of a pistol. Just one shot. The direction was clear. The officers on the quarterdeck looked at each other. For a few moments nobody spoke. Then Burridge took a decision. He wished there were someone else to take it, but there wasn't. He said to the Flag Lieutenant,

'What has happened? Go and ask the Admiral.'

The Flag Lieutenant wished there were someone else. After all, the Admiral had not ordered him to leave the quarterdeck, and he was doubtful about Burridge's authority. But Pither was there, Pither was a very junior Lieutenant, Pither was not a member of the Admiral's staff, was not a real member of the ship's company. He could be sent. The Flag Lieutenant therefore sent him.

Fat Jack Pither went down to the main deck, and aft to the Admiral's day cabin. Outside the door the Admiral's personal steward was leaning against the door frame, retching. Pither pushed past him, into the cabin, an act he regretted the rest of his life. When he reached the upper deck again, he was retching too. He controlled himself to explain. Burridge was sharp.

'He can't have shot himself. He can't be dead. He was here only a few minutes ago, talking quite rationally, you heard him yourself.'

'But he has done it, sir. The pistol is in his hand and the barrel in his . . . what's left of his mouth.'

'But surely he isn't dead. A little shocked, perhaps, if the pistol went off by accident, if he were cleaning it, or loading it, ready to go ashore.'

'There's his brains,' Pither told him grimly, 'all over the floor.'

There was a little procession down to the cabin. Pither excused himself: he had seen it already and wished he hadn't. When he had been sick, he felt a lot better. A sailor came and mopped up the mess, and then wondered uneasily if he would be flogged for acting without orders.

Captain Burridge returned to the quarterdeck. He also wanted to retch, and sent the Flag Lieutenant for a bucket. Then he wondered what to do. He asked the Flag Lieutenant's advice.

'We ought to haul his flag down, sir.'

'I couldn't do that. Not without authority.' Pither reflected that perhaps a dead body ought to be authority enough. But Burridge wore a captain's three stripes and had a mass of gold lace, so his indecision must be the result of some deep policy. 'I ought to have word from . . .from . . .'

'Admiral Fevrier, sir?'

'No, not from a damned frog. He mustn't know about it. Nobody must know about it.' Pither reflected that all the ship must know about it by now. Then Burridge said,

'Keep his flag flying till Sir Frederick knows about it.' Sir Frederick Nicholson was the next senior captain to the Admiral. He was in *Pique*, three vessels astern.

Burridge worried a little longer. Then he seemed to come to a decision.

'They'll court martial me for this, I'll stand trial but you'll all defend me, you'll all tell the truth. I have no choice, I must do this. Find the signals officer.'

The Lieutenant who had signals on his slop chit was below, on the main deck, commanding a division of guns. He came on deck rather bewildered, for the sailors had already passed from mouth to mouth information they thought their officers either already had or ought not to know. Burridge told him,

'I want a hoist made, but quietly, no need to tell everybody. To all ships –' The signals Lieutenant was a little puzzled as to how such a signal could be made quietly, but he knew better than to query his Captain – 'Break off the action. Course due south. Follow me.'

11

Esteron came into the wardroom for dinner, in uniform. Talleyman introduced him.

'An acquaintance from Ireland. A John Company officer.'

'Ireland, eh?' said Fincham. 'Talleyman has a sketch over his bunk of an Irish Marine.'

'Be quiet,' said Talleyman. 'Or I'll not buy your book.'

'Not my book. But that's a gorgeous rig. Sky blue with melon facings.'

'Fourth Ghats Irregular Horse,' said Orton. Everybody looked at him. He explained.

'My father was a Company officer, and he made a pattern book, sketches of all the uniforms. He made me learn them all off when I was a boy. He said that there was no use going to India not knowing who I was supposed to shoot.'

'What's your name?' Esteron asked him. 'Orton? Oh, was your grandfather in India as well?'

'Oh yes, he was collector of Madripore. He retired and came home, and when he died four years ago my father came out and came home too, and I left the Navy.'

'Your grandfather cut up pretty warm, did he?'

'Not quite the word for it, old boy. Say he cut up steaming red hot. You know Madripore?'

'A little. I was there two years ago for the old Rajah's funeral. When they came to crown the new one, they got out all the regalia the old boy had kept under his bed – that's the tradition, you know. The tale was that the aigrette for the turban and the belt and the scab-bard and all the rest were encrusted with diamonds, but when we looked they were nothing but paste. The big ruby was real, though. Very funny that. Your grandfather knew the old Rajah well?'

'Oh, yes, very well. We were brought up on the tales. But as you say, funny that, about the diamonds.'

'You been in India?'

'No, not yet.'

'You ought to come. You can meet a splendid fellow, Hodson. Great character, none of his friends like him, good company. They tell me you're a sea lawyer.'

'I will be when I get back.'

'Well, why come at all? Did you have to?'

'Not absolutely. I haven't been drawing my half pay, so I suppose I could have just ignored them. But I thought it would look a bit odd if I didn't. After all I have a commission, and I supposed people would think it rather odd if I stayed. A bit like poor Sherwin.'

'But why this war?' Esteron was probing, pushing. 'You may get killed. What are you risking that for? What do you think the war is about?'

'Well, stopping Russia, of course.'

'Stopping Russia doing what?'

'Invading Europe. They've taken the Principalities, and next they will cross the Danube and come down to the Adriatic and the Aegean. Once they've done that and destroyed Turkey, they can turn on Austria and go into Germany. So we and the French must act with Turkey to stop them before they reach the French frontier and the Low Countries.'

'The Russians? Or the Tsar?'

'Does it matter?'

'It does matter,' said Thacker. 'The Tsar is the absolute ruler, what he says must go. So masses of poor Russian peasants must go to war because the Tsar says so. If we do not fight then we will have that evil system spread all over the world. What do you think, then, that the war is about?'

Talleyman sat at the head of the table and watched the talk flow. Esteron answered Thacker.

'The war is about India. The Russians are not at all interested in Europe, or in making a great war. They only want to go to the east, and to the south-east. They are intent on invading India, and we must stop that or we will all starve. We have got the French and the Austrians to act with us, and we now have to break the Russian power by defeating them in Europe. We are as interested as the Russians in destroying Turkey, but in our own time and for our interests. If we divide the Turkish Empire with the French, we want to be able to do that without any interference from the Tsar. I agree, though, it makes no difference whether we say Russia or the Tsar. If there were a revolution in Russia tomorrow and they elected a parliament on the purest chartist principles of democracy, we would still have to fight them within the next ten years to keep our hold on India. And it is from India that we get our wealth, as you well know, Mr Orton.'

'I had thought,' Dincombe contributed, 'that we went to war with Russia to preserve the holy places. If the

108

Russians take the Turkish Empire, they will close the sacred sites of Jerusalem and Bethlehem to all travellers as they have closed their own borders.'

'So we fight the Christian Russians,' said Thacker, 'to keep the Christian shrines in the hands of the Turks.'

But to Talleyman's surprise, it was Longville who joined in, bitterly, destructively, as always.

'It doesn't matter what the quarrel is about, a set of clever statesmen could settle it by talking. Even a Tsar can be bargained with. But we have the usual situation. The politicians and the ambassadors have been careless, been lazy, they have let things drift, till affairs are so complicated that no one can understand them. So they fight a war to simplify things and it's poor soldiers and us sailors who get killed.'

'So you come to war,' asked Esteron, 'to save a politician's reputation and to encourage them not to work in future?'

'It is not my place to ask why there is a war,' said Longville. 'But I was a naval lieutenant on half pay and claiming the money. So when there was a war declared, it was my duty to come back and report to the Admiralty and ask for a ship. And this – ' He spat the words out with hate – 'is the ship I got.'

'We must face it,' interposed Orton. 'We are hardly the cream of the Navy, except possibly the Pusser. We have all come late and unwillingly, dragging our feet over the rough pavements of our consciences. Talleyman from his potato patch and me from my green bags, and you, Longville, if you had been as anxious as that to fight, you could have gone from Hong Kong not to London but to Bombay and been received in a Queen's ship there, or even a Company's ship.'

'I hoped for a liner,' said Longville. 'I have never been in so small a Queen's ship as this.'

'In any case,' Orton asked Esteron directly. 'Why are you here?'

'I am a Company man,' Esteron told him. 'I may be civil or I may be an officer as the Company orders, or I may travel on the Company's business. I go where I am sent.'

'What business,' asked Talleyman speaking for the first time, 'had the Company in Ireland?'

'Oh, that was a case of someone doing a kindness to Dublin Castle, and providing men whose faces were not known in Ireland. And since I was in England on leave, and since I had done the same kind of work before, I was sent. It was cooler than Bengal, and not quite as wet.'

'Did you have Irish in Bengal to watch from the Punch and Judy tent?' Talleyman asked him.

'Not quite. We have Irish. The European regiments in the Company's pay are recruited mostly in Ireland.'

'Like the Marines,' volunteered Fincham.

'Exactly. But they are no problem. But there are plots and counterplots on the western frontier, dealings between Rajput and Mahratta chiefs, the emotions of kings and mobs, and a king, even the Tsar, does behave like a mob. So I watched kings there, and I watched mobs, and Indian mobs are very like Irish mobs, and Mr O'Brien was very like a rajah. And Irish famines are very like Indian famines, and if there had been a dozen men out of the Company's civil side sent to Ireland to do what we have to do in India, well – I do not say there would have been no famine, but the famine would not have killed half the population. But let us talk of other things. Why are you here, reverend sir?'

'Well, I was given the chance. The captain came to the senior tutor of Tibb's, and asked for help, and Dr French brought him to see me. I had then hopes of making a way in the learned world, and I had made study of the ancient Russian Church, so I agreed to come because I thought we were going to Russia and I could see the Church at work.'

'Do you speak Russian?' Biddell asked.

110

'No, not really. I have learnt . . . taught myself from a grammar, to read Old Church Slavonic, which is the language their service books are written in. But I do not know how near that is to modern Russian. Indeed, I have been told that it is impossible to learn to speak Russian without living there many years, and I have never met a person who speaks Russian.'

'You have now,' said Esteron. They all looked at him. 'It is a knack I have. I was a cadet at Addiscombe where as you know the Company's officials are trained, and there I learned Sanskrit – it was obligatory. So when I went to India at sixteen, I found to my surprise and everybody else's that I was able to pick up first Hindi and then Urdu with good accents in a few months. Then two or three other Indian languages, like Tamil, and then Persian which is the court language at Delhi. It is merely a trick I found I had, and when I went into Ireland I learned the Gaelic in a few weeks, and when I came to England again on Company business and was told that I would not go back till I had done what I am here to do, I learnt Russian. I found a teacher in London, very reasonable. I will give you the address. But you could have seen the Eastern Church in Greece.'

'But that is where I thought we were going,' said Dincombe in exasperation. 'It is very expensive to get there and I half understood from Captain Only . . . well, that is one reason.'

'And the other?' Talleyman asked him.

'I have a friend, a Mr Kingsley – '

'The muscular Christian,' said Craddock unexpectedly. 'Doesn't like machinery, wants us all to play cricket instead.'

'He was very envious, but of course since he had a benefice he could not come as a chaplain. But he advised me that the fresh air and the hard work and the company of the honest sailors would be a corrective. I have spent all my life in schools and colleges, you see.'

'As for the muscular sailors,' asked Biddell, 'what were you doing with a seaman, Smales I think, in the forepeak yesterday?'

'I . . . I was teaching him – '

'A purely Christian act,' Talleyman interposed, to save the Chaplain. 'But, Mr Dincombe, you are in a ship. You must never, never, ever have two men together in a compartment. One man working alone. Or three. But never two.'

'Why not?' asked the Chaplain. 'Why not?'

'Think back,' Biddell told him, 'to the story of Lot and where he came from. You were in a boarding school you told me, Winchester I think. What did you see there?'

Realization came to Dincombe.

'Not . . .? Not . . .? Little boys, I have seen, I can understand, but not grown men. Surely, not grown men?'

'Yes,' Talleyman told him. 'Grown men.'

'Such immorality, in the pure air of the sea?'

'Immorality does not matter,' Longville said. 'The sea has no moral law, but destroys as it will if we let it. What we must guard against, Chaplain, is love.'

'Love? Love, not lust?'

'Oh, both. If a man loves another, the day may come when he has to choose between saving his love and saving his ship. And there must be no doubt that he will save the ship. And if a man lusts for another who is below him in rank, then he may make demands which cannot be refused. It is . . . was, very easy in the Navy, in the old Navy, for a petty officer to get a man flogged for something he did not do. There is no morality at sea, Chaplain, and no honour, no loyalty or love. There is only the ship.' Longville stood up. 'Mr President, sir, I know that our guest is still with us, but I am due on watch in a few minutes. May I be excused?'

Esteron also stood.

112

'I am afraid I have kept you all talking,' he said. 'I feel that I must go back to my quarters, and let you return to your normal round. I am most grateful for your hospitality and conversation.'

'I will see you back,' offered Talleyman. 'Would you like to walk a little on the deck and enjoy a cigar?'

They walked on the quarterdeck. There was a fresh wind, and occasional brief flurries of rain. Once or twice they saw the moon.

'You have, I suppose, all sailed together before, for a long time?' Esteron asked.

'We have only been in this ship as long as you have.'

'But the way you all talked, as if you were old friends sharing the same memories, the same slang, the same friends.'

'It is the Navy. In the Army a man joins a regiment for life. You can take your time to get to know him. In the Navy, you join a ship for a commission. Two years, or perhaps three. You must live with the other officers in a small space. You learn to make friends quickly.'

'Do you know no one in this ship?'

'Oh, yes, the Captain was in *Santorin*, my last ship in Ireland. So was one of the Mates. Craddock, ten years ago. He was an apprentice to Nasmyth. I was a Midshipman hoping to get a berth as a Mate. The chief steward was in my first ship, *Argyle*, in Africa. But we know each other, some of us, by reputation.'

'Some of you?'

'The Gunner. A noted preacher. Orton, reckless, can lose anything from an anchor to a ship. They were glad when he went ashore. And Longville. Think of your Mr Hodson. None of his friends likes him. If he joined your club you would check the books and leave it. Came home a slow way. Thought there might be an early battle.'

'Hoping for a death vacancy?'

'Something like that. But . . .'

'But?'

'He is well known. He has another reputation. As a ship handler. And . . . what shall I say? As a seer. Or rather as a smeller. They say he can smell his away along an unknown coast, in darkness or fog. Or guess the depth of water under the keel. Faster than the lead. And as accurate.

'When we got to where I am going, we will need him. Good night.' He left Talleyman, wondering.

12

Next morning, the Captain came on deck. He looks green, thought Talleyman, and worn out. Probably been seasick the whole week.

'First Lieutenant!' Only called.

Talleyman came to him on the weather side, saluted.

'Mr Talleyman, ship the figurehead!' Only went back towards his own cabin. Talleyman called the Bo'sun.

'Captain wants the figurehead shipped.'

It was not much of a figurehead, just the Navy standard issue for small, cheap ships. Only an oval slab of wood, convex, with the royal arms carved deep into it; fixed to the stempost with dowels. It was not easy to get at. Mr Harris told Talleyman,

'It's all right where it is. Not much wear on it, paint's hardly touched.'

'The Captain says ship it, so we've got to. Much of a job?'

'Not most days. But it's a bit of a blow, and she's pitching.'

'You want one of the Carpenter's crew?'

'No, there's a couple of the lads who can do it. That Smales, he knows what he's about, and Middleton, he's a ten-year AB.'

'Put them on a bowline.'

'You don't have to tell me.'

Harris went for'ard. Talleyman considered, and then called the petty officer who was captain of the after-guard.

'Get the quarter boat hoisted out. And a crew in it.'

He could see a discussion on the fo'csle. He went for'ard.

'What's up, Mr Harris?'

'Smales says he don't want a bowline, sir.'

'In this sea? No bowline, Smales, then no lifebuoy when you float past. I'll tell the Marine sentry my-self.'

He had Smales down on one of his lists to try as a helmsman. And Middleton, and Calne, and Moulton. Strange how the good men were good all-rounders. Smales accepted the lifeline, and with Middleton went out on to the beak head. The pitching was now very bad, occasional seas coming in over the forecastle. To get at the figurehead, two men had to get down, putting their feet on the martingale stay. Talleyman and the Bo'sun leant over the side for'ard of the catheads and watched. Suddenly,

'He's gone,' Talleyman said. 'Haul him in, there!' The bowline had been rove through the tackle on the cat-head. Smales (it would be Smales, thought Talleyman) was soaking wet and out of breath. He told those around,

'There's a ring bolt on the top back side of it, and we ran a line through that. But the dowels are stuck tight, they'll need a hell of a thump.'

'Going again?' asked the Bo'sun. Middleton was back on the deck now. He had not fallen in but he too was soaked. Talleyman shook his head.

'You two, get below. Get dried. Put dry clothes on. Quick! You don't want to freeze! Now, who's next?'

The whole crew of the forward eight-inch came to him at the run. Talleyman laughed.

'No, I'm not issuing extra rum. Now, let's see, I'll take the biggest. That's you, Parks. And Moulton.'

'No. It's "and me",' said a voice. Only had come forard almost unnoticed. 'What's the trouble?' Talleyman explained.

'I'll go. Pass the bowline around me.'

'No, sir,' said Talleyman. He hoped he sounded polite and not worried. 'I think it's me next, I was here first.' He was nettled now, he ought to have gone himself in the first place. He could see Esteron watching, in a great coat open over a scarlet shell jacket.

'My ship, my fighting dogs,' Only said firmly. He stuck the mallet and reamer into his belt, and asked, 'Who's with me? Yes, it had better be you, what's your name? Parks? Right.'

Over they went, Only to starboard, Parks to port. Talleyman leant over, watched the Captain, right-handed, tapping away with the mallet, Parks on the other side pulling the dowel pins through as they came loose. Talleyman felt the ship pitch again, and shouted a warning. Both the captain and the seaman vanished under a boiling cloud of green water and spray. The Bo'sun had one end of the captain's bowline fast round a belaying pin, and watched the taut line from the cathead. As the ship's bow came up, Talleyman saw them both still clinging on. Only gave a last tap with the mallet, and then shouted,

'Haul away!'

He guided the panel with the royal arms round his body, and saw it hauled clear end up to the cathead. Then he clambered back on to the bowsprit and then to the beak and was pulled in over the bulwarks. Parks followed. Only clapped him on the shoulder.

'Good lad. I'll remember this.'

'You'll catch your death of cold to remember this by,' Talleyman told him. 'Come aft, sir, and get some dry clothes on.'

116

'Walk back,' said the Captain, 'and you, too, Bo'sun.' Three of them climbed to the poop and aft to the taff-rail. Only leaned over. He pointed down to the name, *Flamingo*, painted on the stern nameboard.

'Bo'sun, can we rig a cradle for ten minutes or so and paint the name out?'

'Ten minutes, sir? Not much of a job, that.'

'I don't want dockyard standards, Mr Harris. I just want enough of a daub that people can't read it.'

'Aye, aye, sir.' But Harris caught Talleyman's eye, and frowned. Only shook himself like a dog. His face looked blue with cold and he was shivering, but he smiled and said,

'You can't catch a cold from salt water. And there's colder to come.'

Talleyman watched the Captain go below. Inwardly he was furious. He felt that he had been taught a lesson, that Only had chosen this way to remind him that an officer ought not to ask for volunteers for a job he could do himself. He looked up to the mastheads. It was blowing hard now, and worsening. Longville, officer of the watch, had taken in the royals, double-reefed to'gallants.

'Mr Harris!' Talleyman called.

'Sir?'

'Didn't you say you had thoughts about the main to'gallant parrals?'

'Needs a bit of work, sir.'

'I'll go up and see.' Talleyman looked round, still full of resentment, then saw the Chaplain come on deck, blinking and eager for fresh air after two hours of mathematics by candlelight in the gun room. He called,

'Come and see what I do, Mr Dincombe, and the Bo'sun.' Dincombe came dubiously.

'What are you going to do?'

'Climb.'

'Up that rope ladder?'

117

'Tis not a ladder. Except for convenience. The upright ropes are shrouds. They hold the mast upright, side to side. These lines across them –'

'Rungs?'

'No, we call them ratlines. You can climb on them. We're going up there. First stage. To the maintop.' Talleyman had done this so often now with cadets on their first day at sea.

'But we're leaning over.'

'Safer. Remember, keep one hand for the ship, and one for yourself. If there is doubt, hold on with both. We're going up the lee side. If you fall, you'll go into the water. Not the hard deck. Try to push yourself if you go. There's a boat still manned and hoisted out. They'll have you out in no time. The Marine at the stern, he's watching. He'll throw you a lifebuoy on a line. Hold it. Now, if the Bo'sun goes first, and I follow, you'll be all right.'

Dincombe felt he had no choice. He had to climb. He had always said he had no head for heights, but in fact he had never tried himself. He clung on, took each step gingerly, kept his eyes fixed on the Bo'sun's backside. At the top, he saw the Bo'sun swing out, but Talleyman's voice from behind told him,

'You don't need to do that, not yet. Push up through the lubber hole.'

Dincombe found himself on a square platform, about twelve feet each way. The main mast came up through the centre, and the topmast rose in front of it, the two well fastened together for the first ten feet to the masthead. Another set of shrouds came down to the sides of the top. There were three men already in the top besides the Bo'sun, and they laughed to see the Chaplain come through.

'Stand here, Reverend,' they welcomed him. 'Stand up here and hold on to this. Don't mind the swaying, you'll get used to it.'

Talleyman, having pushed the Chaplain up through

the lubber hole, swung himself out on to the futtock shrouds like the Bo'sun and came into the top over the edge.

'We'll be having you do that before we finish. Now, you wait here. Mr Harris and I have another stage to do.' Dincombe watched the two officers go up the topmast shrouds to where the to'gallant and royal yards were down to the topmast cap. They hung there, talking, pulling, taking their time. At last they came back.

'Captain of the maintop!' Talleyman ordered. 'To'gallant yard parral is wearing. That's the piece, Mr Dincombe, which holds the yard to the mast. It has a lot of friction; it's a rope lashing. We will watch it, see how fast it wears. Later we may have to replace it. Petty Officer Longden here will keep an eye on it and let me know each time he renews the lashing. Didn't Lieutenant Longville notice it?'

'He don't never come up here,' said Longden. 'Let alone up to the cap. He says he learns enough looking through his telescope.'

'Different men, different methods,' said Talleyman. 'Now, Chaplain, if I go in front of you, and the Bo'sun comes after, we'll have you back on deck.'

They are all, Dincombe thought, once he was back on the deck, trying to establish themselves in others' eyes. Orton, ready to go down to the dirtiest job in the ship, and much more often than necessary. Longville takes the pose of the distant expert, who seems to know no man by name, never speaks direct to a seaman, only goes through the Bo'sun or a Bo'sun's mate. Talleyman is hard at work being the opposite, knows everybody, goes anywhere, shows that he knows how the ship works. Even the Captain, who is hardly seen, makes sure that everyone knows he can do a seaman's work, and doesn't mind being dipped.

119

13

Harriet called for the trap. Barnet the groom brought it round to the Manor House, where she had moved in as soon as she could. Arabella was not the best of company, but at least the two children liked her, and she could take most of the load off Harriet's back. In fact, she was so much with the boys that Harriet wondered if she could, perhaps, dispose of either their nurse or the nursery maid: preferably the nurse as she was the more expensive and Harriet needed the money for clothes. She would need them for the winter in London, her best evening gown was now too tight.

The riding horses she wanted to see were in the far paddock. They stayed out for a great deal of the summer, and there was a set of stalls and a tack room. Another groom, Cooper, was there, doing something – she didn't know what but probably quite unnecessary – with a saddle. She ignored the two men for a little while, and strolled under the horse chestnut trees. The conkers were falling, some ripe and opened, others still unburst. The prickly cases were everywhere.

'I'll ride Emperor,' Harriet told Cooper.

'He's in the paddock, mum.'

'I can see him.'

'The master said that nobody else was to ride him but himself. He had a proper do yesterday, couldn't hardly keep his seat.'

'You've seen me ride him.'

'Aye, mum. But you'll have to catch him yoursen, and put a saddle on him.'

Harriet laughed at him, a short sneering chuckle that hurt Cooper, but made Barnet grin. She walked out into the sunlight, over the grass. The big black horse was grazing apart from the three or four others. She took no notice of them, didn't even bother to see which they were. She snapped her fingers. The black horse stopped grazing, raised his head and pricked his ears. She snapped her fingers two or three times more and he trotted over to her. She dug into the loose pockets she had had made in her riding coat, fashion or not, and brought out a few pieces of apple, lumps of sugar chipped off the cone. Barnet laughed.

'Arr, she can do that, and there's not many as will dare to try.'

'I won't, I know that,' Cooper snarled at him. 'I'll have no more to do with that beast than I have to.'

Harriet twined her fingers into the horse's mane, and led him peaceably over the grass to the fence. Cooper brought the bridle out, and while Harriet put it on, he went back for the sidesaddle.

'Hold his head,' Harriet snapped at him. He gingerly took the extreme end of the reins. Harriet picked up the saddle, carelessly threw it over the horse's back and busied herself with the buckles. She jerked her head, and walked over to the mounting block. Cooper cautiously led the horse over to the block and brought him to face the right way. Harriet climbed the steps of the block, swung herself daintily into her seat, crooking her thigh around the post. A quick jiggle of the reins, and she walked the horse out into the paddock.

She brought Emperor calmly to the boundary fence, and rode him all the way round the paddock, first at the walk, the second circuit at the trot. Now the canter. And the men, the *men*, all of them saying they couldn't manage him, even when they took a whip to him. Now round once or twice at the canter, and then a little out from the fence. There was a course laid out, she had seen it done two days ago, three poles laid across the tops of buckets, a brushwood hurdle. Nothing too high to start with, just let her teach him to jump, quietly,

121

easily. Just take him around at the trot, talk to him all the time, soothingly. Nothing you couldn't get out of a man if you soothed him and wheedled him and talked to him as if he were the cleverest, the wisest, the richest, the most powerful creature in the world. And what was this young horse but a four-legged youth? Hup, yet again, perhaps tomorrow the hurdles higher, the brushwood in them a bit stouter.

Tom and his father had bought this horse in the spring, going off together. Still a four-year-old then, a mere colt, hardly been ridden, never been hunted. But they were both nervous of his size, worried in case they had bought more than they could manage. Perhaps he was more than they could control, but she could do it, make him do whatever she wanted. She could handle him all right, he had learnt that, had learnt enough to make the grooms, the men, afraid to touch him. She had been out almost everyday to groom him, her voice always gentle, her pockets always full of apples and sugar and carrots and raisins even. He liked them.

Oh, there was no pleasure in life like this. Her thigh hooked round the post, her legs working, her body working with the movement of the horse. No, there was nothing any man could give her that was like this. On the horse's back she could forget men and their demands. All those wasted years of her girlhood when she could ride but had no horse, only the loan of a nag from the stables of the great house when she could wheedle Jane to talk honey to her father. And there she'd only hunted the once, and it was sheer heaven, riding at the fences, nothing to think about but the way to go and when to lift the horse and the streaming of the wind in her face.

Perhaps she would be able to hunt this horse this season, or next. This wasn't hunting country, but Tom knew people who lived a few miles away on the chalk or the stonecrop, out of these dismal marshes, who would give her a day or so out. A couple of nights

122

away, Barnet to hack the beast over for a day's rest before the run. There was no way of getting to know gentlemen like a day's hunting. And then – there was a voice calling, a well-known voice, a voice she disliked.

'Missus! Hey there, missus!'

Harriet turned her head, and saw her father-in-law at the tack room door. She finished the round, and brought Emperor over, reining him in by the mounting block. Josiah said bluntly,

'Ya can't do that, missus. Ya can't ride a horse like that. That's a man's horse, and ya can't ride him.'

'I can ride him,' she replied, 'and I do. You can see me.'

'That horse is too big for a woman. Ya'll get killed, gel, ya'll get killed.'

'I won't get killed.'

'Ya'll get killed. The horse is too big for ya.'

'What other horse is there in the stables which I can ride? This is the only one that'll bear me.'

''Tis ya own fault. I bought that horse to bear me.'

'How is it my fault if the horse will bear you?'

''Tis ya own fault. Ya stuffs. Ya stuffs every scrap ya can cram in, ya eats it all, potatoes, suet pudding, cakes and cream, all as if ya were going to starve, as if there were no more coming.'

Does he watch every mouthful? thought Harriet. Or does Arabella present him my accounts to be approved every time I go into the Manor House? And the grooms there, hearing every word, even though they've got their backs turned. Oh, this odious man, if it weren't for those grooms I would fetch him a good one across the face with my crop. Now, now, Emperor, there's no need to get restive, sure they're as good as humans these horses, they understand every word you say. She patted him.

'Now, come down off that hoss, my girl,' Josiah went on. 'Come down off it. Beggars on hossback, that's all ya Irish are, putting on airs as a passon's daughter and poor as church rats ya all are.'

'I am not Irish. We were English, we only lived there. I'm not Irish, I'm no Catholic potato-scraper.'

'Ya're Irish, and it shows every time ya opens ya mouth. Come down off that hoss, missus.'

His voice gets thicker, she thought, as he gets angrier. Let him get angry enough and there's Irish she'd give him. He went on,

'And Tom to marry the likes of ya, and persuade me to let him. Misery guts that ya are, no wonder he went off back to sea rather than stay here with you.'

'He went back to sea because it was his duty, a word you don't know the meaning of.'

'I know my duty towards my flesh and blood, and I've always done it. Now, 'tis ya duty to get down off that hoss, and do ya duty by ya elders and betters as it says in the Prayer Book, if ya ever heard of the Common Prayer. Come down now peaceable, or I'll pull ya off by strength, with them yokels looking on and half the county to know about it within the week.'

That she could not stomach. Be pulled off, that would be too much. She disengaged her leg and slid down on to the mounting block. She let go of Emperor's rein, let him edge nervously away from her. Josiah shouted,

'Hey, Cooper, change that ... that thing for a proper saddle.'

Cooper looked at Emperor.

'I'll not change a saddle on that hoss, mester, nor the bridle. I been bit once and kicked three times. He'll let me stroke him and brush, but he won't let me put no tack on him.'

'Don't be impertinent, get that saddle changed. D'ya want to see me ride him bareback?' Chance would be a fine thing, thought Harriet. One day ... 'The day's passing, and the year's passing, and there's schooling to be done and I want to hunt this beast in November.'

'He's too savage, mester, I won't – '

'Ya take this saddle off, and ya'll change it. And if the Boss is too savage, we'll have to beat it out of him.'

'I will change the saddle,' said Harriet. She was determined now, she knew what she would have to do, but this man should not beat her Emperor, should not ride him to hounds. She walked over slowly to the horse, snapped her fingers, dipped into her pocket where the food was, and all the other jumble. He bent his head to follow, took the apple quietly, and then a piece of carrot. Harriet waved to Cooper who brought the man's saddle over. She worked precisely at the buckles, singing an old meaningless chant in the Gaelic she had learnt when she was a child. It soothed and steadied the horse, it always did. She slid the sidesaddle off, and carried it a little distance where Cooper could pick it up. She held out her hands for the man's saddle, and threw it over the horse's back. She dipped her hand into her pocket again and again for apples and carrots and raisins and this and that. She adjusted the saddle, remembering where the pressure would come now, how it would change when there was a rider on it. Luckily, she had the horse's body between herself and the men. She stroked the horse on the hindquarters, then looped the reins around the post by the mounting block.

'There, ya's cowards, both o' ya, afraid to put a saddle on a hoss, when a woman can do it. Ya've seen it, ya knows how to do it.'

Harriet ignored her father-in-law, she simply beckoned to Barnet and walked to the trap. The horse was still in the shafts, and she made a note to tell the groom off when she found opportunity. She settled herself, and ordered,

'Back to the Dower House!'

They had gone about eighty yards, Barnet could swear to that by the tree they had reached along the drive, when they heard the screams. Whether it was the

125

horse or a man who screamed first, Barnet could never be quite sure. They had gone another twenty yards at a round trot, before Harriet told him,

'Draw up! Listen! What was that?'

Barnet took them back at something nearer a gallop than a trot. At the tack room, Harriet waited for the sprag to be set on before she was down. Barnet could understand her hesitation. The black horse ramped and raged high over a dusty bundle of rags. Cooper was crouching in the lee of the mounting block, his arms oddly set as if he wanted to protect his face and could not.

Emperor foamed at the mouth. Harriet saw the hooves come down, the cutting edges of the shoes gleaming where they were not clotted with bloody mud. Barnet told the story as he saw it to the coroner, and before that it went through every servants' hall in the county, and into every drawing room. 'She just went up to 'im, that great savage beast that was killing people left right and centre and all roaring and kicking it was and she just snapped her fingers and he followed her like any little lamb and she took him by the forelock and led him away.' And whenever she heard it, Harriet found it easier to say nothing, just to look as if it were true and she were being modest. But it had not been like that at all.

Never be in a hurry, Tom had told her, never rush, always take time to think. The pump was outside the paddock, near the outer wall of the tack room. There were buckets there. She turned to Barnet who was making little runs up and down and wittering.

'Draw a bucket of water.'

'Aye, mum, and over which one?'

'Which one?'

'Over Charley or over the master, mum?'

'You won't go in there. Take it along this fence, and put it down inside the paddock, there, by the horse chestnuts.'

126

Now was the bad part. In, very slowly and gently through the paddock gate, and stand a moment here, twenty yards from the broken men. She whistled, as she always did, twice, and thought she saw the horse hesitate.

'Emperor!' she called softly. 'Emperor! Come to me, there's a good Emperor. Come.'

Now his ears were twitching her way, and he stopped his bounding and prancing.

'Come, Emperor, come to your love, come.' He hesitated between his target and the sound of her voice. 'Come!'

It took longer than you would think from what Barnet said. A while of coaxing and soft talking, and after a little, a snapping of the fingers, and a pantomimed searching in the pockets. And after a while, it seemed ages to her, he began to come, to edge stiffly towards her, his eyes alert for the least threatening movement, for the renewal of pain. Can anybody ever have been so frightened? Harriet asked herself. At least it was not one of her headache days, he seemed to know those, to behave badly then. But now it was all right, he could smell her scent. Tom had told her, so often, animals know if you are frightened, they can smell it, a change in your mind, so she always used plenty of the scent he had given her, lily of the valley. She stood upwind of Emperor, what little breeze there was, and let him smell the lilies, and the carrots she held out, the carrots and the apple, and the raisins. She had never known a horse which liked raisins, or was it simply that she had never fed raisins to a horse before? She took a step backward, and then another, and at last to her relief he followed her, keeping close to the smells he knew and wanted. She went in front of him, stepping backwards, hoping that there was nothing in the way, a bucket or a log, for her to fall over. If she went down she knew quite well she was a dead woman. This, she hoped, was what Tom would do, and therefore she did it. Her steps were shorter, and the horse came closer to her, At last he was close enough to take a piece of carrot from her outstretched palm, and then another, and a piece of apple. She was alongside the bucket now, and she tapped it with the toe of her shoe, making the surface shimmer and the smell of the water, if water had a smell, to come to the horse and remind him that he was foam flecked. A handful of raisins, and she was talking to him all the time, and at last he bent his head to drink, shivering with his own emotions. She reached softly for the bridle, and in another moment she had him tethered to the post of the fence. A little more sweet talk, humming and singing and soothing, and she could get round him to loosen the girths, to slip the saddle off his back. And the three conkers fell to the ground, the spines bent and broken.

Harriet backed away, carrying the saddle till she could drop it over the fence where Emperor could neither see it nor smell it.

Now she was safe, it was time to deal with the men. Barnet was inside the paddock now, darting from one body to the other, sobbing,

'Are ya all right, mester? Are ya all right, Charley? Art hurt, Charlie? Can ya stand up, mester?'

'Stand still,' Harriet snapped at him, 'and be quiet!'

Old Josiah was lying more or less on his face, crumpled up in a way no well man could lie. One eye was visible, shut. He was breathing loud, in snorts. His left leg was bent back at the knee. There was a lot of blood on flesh and cloth. She turned to Cooper: at least he was conscious.

'Help him up,' she told Barnet. Barnet enthusiastically took hold of Cooper's arm and tried to haul him to his feet. Cooper screamed. Harriet had heard a horse scream like that once when it was impaled on a stake in a hedge. Cooper vomited, and, from the smell, had voided his bowels inside his breeches.

'Get water,' ordered Harriet. She knew what she was

128

doing, she was trying to behave like Tom, or like Jane, people who did what was needed. They managed to swab Cooper's face with the end of a towel, and to let him have some water to drink. He opened his eyes. Harriet said again,

'Help him up.'

'Nay, mum, he do stink horrible.'

Harriet shrugged. It was only men with their inexperience of real life who were put off by the smell of vomit and faeces, let alone with blood, and shrank from all the bother of mopping up and wiping off. She said patiently, as she had been used to doing to Irish peasants before she had ever met Fen Tigers,

'Get behind him. Put your arms round him, under the armpits, and walk forward as you lift him. I'll get the trap.'

Between them they got Cooper into the trap, sitting up and leaning back against the seat rail. Harriet said,

'Listen. Take Cooper back to the Manor. Tell Miss Arabella what has happened. Get someone to go for the doctor. Find Mr Fadden. Tell him to bring a wagon down here and some men.'

'The Manor, mum? Please, mum, which door do I go to for Miss Arabella? The front door or the back?'

Harriet tried not to scream: this was worse than in County Cork. She was patient.

'The back door. Get cook out of the kitchen, and the maids to help.' Kettle the butler would be of no use, he must be all of sixty. 'And don't go too fast on the way back, the jolting will hurt Cooper.'

'And the Master, mum? Can we get him in the trap, too?'

Harriet shook her head.

'He had better lie here till we can lift him flat out. But Cooper has both collarbones broken and one upper arm. Go carefully.'

14

Harriet stood and looked down at old Josiah. Old? He could be no more than his fifties. He lay on his face, or, more accurately, on his stomach, his cheek to the earth. She had not meant to be as drastic as this. She had bargained on no more than a throw, what you would expect on the hunting field, perhaps a twisted knee. Something to convince him that he would not be able to hunt Emperor. But he must have had a better seat than she had expected, he must have stayed on long enough to use his whip.

He'd used his whip on Emperor, and he deserved what he'd got. But something must be done. Harriet knelt by him. The hoof marks were clear, by his shoulder blades to around the waist; there had been a kick on the back of the neck. Josiah was unconscious, breathing like a set of bellows.

He'll be in bed a long time, Harriet thought. The Dower House is nearer, but I'll not have him there, not with all that work to do. Take him to his own room in the Manor House, let Arabella look after him. It would be easier if he were dead, much less fuss. She wished Tom were there, he'd have known what to do, he'd do what he liked, not wait for the old man to approve everything, count out the money coin by coin. He'd have his own way about the funeral.

Sure, and then Tom would have his own way about everything. If the old brute were dead, he'd be his own master, Oh, then they'd not have to stay here in this swamp that had to be drained before it could grow so much as a potato, they could go to London for the Season, more, they could even go to Paris, oh there was the gay city, with balls and dinners everywhere, so she'd heard.

She did not know what to do with Josiah. He burbled and gruntled in his throat, he jerked and gagged. Perhaps he would be better on his back, but if she moved him over and he died, she'd be blamed. Oh, more than freedom, if the old man died. Would not Tom have the estate, the money? Sure, he was the elder son, it'd be to him that Richard would have to come for permission to do anything, just as he now came to the old man. Not that he needed to come, he was with his father everywhere, knew all the secrets. The wonder was he was not here now. Yes, if the old man were dead, there was the wealth and the power Tom would have, would come into the moment he was back from sea, back from Belfast or Londonderry as soon as he put in and heard.

She had already put a horse blanket over Emperor. She went into the tack room and found two more. One went over Josiah, sure he needed that, he was shivering and sweating at the same time. She wetted her handkerchief, and cleaned his face a little. He was bleeding at the mouth and nose, and even at the ear. She folded the other blanket. It could do no harm to lift his head up on a pillow. She had heard ... she shrank from it, pulling his tongue out to make sure he did not swallow it. If he hadn't done it already he wouldn't do it now.

She got the folded rug under his cheek, raised his face out of the dirt. When she had done that, he gagged and choked a little, more blood came from his mouth and ear. The fit passed, and he lay there, gulping in the air through his mouth, noisily and with effort. Ah, and a long time it would be before he was well again, if ever. He might be lying there for months, perhaps for years, with no more life in him than he had now, and all that trouble running back and forth and all that cost for people to look after him. She had seen that once with her mother's second cousin, Auntie Liza, after she had the

131

apoplexy and lay there for eighteen months not able to move or to speak and nothing to be done for her except to keep her clean and fed, and all that time and the way the relations argued over the will and her sister Auntie Fanny had given that jet necklace of hers to Harriet, and when she died in the end and the will was read the necklace was bequeathed to another cousin and Harriet had had to give it back and she had missed that necklace more than she could tell.

Oh, sure, Harriet had seen it all and it was worse than children in the house and more expense. People like that were better off dead and no burden to their relations. And so much easier when people were certain what was to happen to the property and sure wouldn't it be all due to Tom, and him not able to touch it till . . .

There was no noise of wheels yet and she wondered what they were doing with that cart and whether they had been able to find Fadden and whether they were waiting for the doctor and whether Barnet had got the message right. There was nobody to be seen, or to see her where she knelt in the dust of the paddock close against the tack room. And nothing to be heard, no voices, no footsteps or hooves, only the noise of Josiah gasping as the blood pulsed from his ear. Oh, sure, and 'twould be a mercy. Harriet reached up to the nape of her neck and drew out the hatpin.

15

'Join the Navy, I tell the lads,' said Biddell, 'and be a shopkeeper. It's a dreary life. I sit below the waterline and I keep my books, and once or twice a day I come up for air. And I serve the customers. It's not merely that every day is like every day – every hour is like every other hour.'

'As bad as that?'

'Well, perhaps I exaggerate. But that's how it feels. Look, Chaplain, every mouthful we eat or drink in this ship goes through my books. If there's any wasted, I have to find a way to make it up. If we starve you may want to put it down to navigation or the weather or the enemy, but every seaman will blame it on the Pusser.'

'You do all this by yourself?'

'I have two chief petty officers. There is the chief cook, who looks after all the issues of food and sees the fires are kept going to boil the beef and that the cooks of the messes are quiet and orderly. And I've got a captain of the hold and five seamen to fetch and carry and lift and shift and move things about so that we keep our trim. And a cooper and his mate. And if anybody makes a mistake, I have to explain it. If you can write a clear hand, Chaplain, any time you have a spare hour I can do with you to copy.'

16

'What do I do all day?' Craddock repeated. 'Now, with drawn fires and running under sail? If you've got three or four days to spare, I'll tell you.'

'I thought you didn't talk,' said Dincombe.

'Not up there,' Craddock replied. 'No one intelligent to talk to. Only Tal.'

'But down here?'

'Well, look at it. My engine – I say it's mine because I built it. Well, there were about sixty of us on it, but I'm the only one of them on board. But I know it all. And the boilers. Eight hundred horsepower, more or less. Made to cruise for days and days at about six knots, but she'll work up to twelve in an hour or two, and there's not many will pass us. No liners, at any rate. We're made to carry three hundred tons of coal in the bunkers, but Biddell and I did a bit of lying to the agent, and we've got another hundred and twenty in sacks in the lower deck and down here. Massive overloading, and that's why Longville hates us. The ship's a bit cranky and hard to handle.'

'I thought Longville hated everyone.'

'Oh, he'll feel better once we've done some steaming and got the trim worked out. Once we do get steam up and come under power, it'll be the Carpenter who'll hate us more.'

'Why?'

'Well, once we start to use the engines – there's those pistons to thump up and down, and the shaft to spin round, and the screw to fight with the waves, the whole ship will begin to shake. These planks will begin to move, trennels sliding out, caulking free . . . it'll find out anywhere the carpenter's skimped his work.'

'And yourself?'

'Oh, it'll find where I've skimped my work, six years ago,' said Craddock. 'If the ship's vibrating, what do you think the engine's doing? There'll be me down here, most of the time, and my four assistants, all done apprenticeships, two artificers, two petty officer stokers, and the black gang, anyone we can find. We've got a hundred or more bearings here, and we've got to look at each of them every twenty minutes or so, and make sure they're still well oiled, otherwise they'll run hot and jam and that's an end to steaming till we can free them. There's a couple of hundred places where the engine is held together and to the ship by bolts and nuts: every watch, sometimes more often, we have to look at each of them and tighten up where necessary. We've got miles, literally, of copper piping for steam, or water, or even oil in some places, and we have to search along them all continuously for leaks. And there's the vibration and

134

the noise, and it's as hot as hell, Chaplain, literally. Our air comes in through that skylight and down to us below the waterline, and out again through the funnel. Come down and stand a watch with us sometime, when we're steaming.'

This man who does not talk, thought Dincombe, will lame a herd of donkeys if you ask about his work.

'So you could steam for three weeks with the coal you have aboard?' he asked.

'As the ship is now, yes.'

'Could you do better? And how?'

'We could use superheated steam.'

'What is that?'

'We boil water for cylinders. We make the steam condense to move the pistons. That steam, when it comes into the cylinders, is already below boiling point – it is moist. But half the power we get from burning coal goes up the chimney. So we could take the pipes from boiler to engine through a box around the base of the funnel, and get it well above boiling point – that is dry steam. It can put the power up, and therefore the range up, by anything from a quarter to a half. I could fit a steam heater here in three days.'

'Then why not?'

'The Admiralty says no private experimenting. They are carrying out trials.'

'Is this your own invention?'

'No, Chaplain. This is an elderly engine, it's six years old. There are a lot of merchant ships around using superheated steam. But once you increase the power, you get more vibration and every part of the engine must be made stronger and the hull also. So unless you mean to steam through a sea of riotous carpenters, you have to design the ship to take the engine designed to use superheated steam. God,' said Craddock unexpectedly, 'does not give you power, He sells it you at a fair price.'

17

They were five days out. Dincombe sent Fox, who was the Captain's messenger for the day, to ask if he might have an interview with Only. After a time Fox returned and ushered Dincombe past the Marine sentry and through the bulkhead door into the Captain's quarters.

The Captain's day cabin, once the Chaplain had passed between the sleeping cabin on the port side and a pantry on the starboard, as well as a private bath and lavatory, struck him as comparable in size to the wardroom. But then he remembered that the mizzen mast came down through the middle of the wardroom, while here it had been set against the first bulkhead, so that the door was on the side. The day cabin was lit by the stern windows. There was a carpet on the deck, but it was not a very good one, and covered only a part of the space. The Captain had an elegant dining table with chairs to the starboard side, and a mahogany desk covered with papers on the port. There were two bookcases against the forward bulkhead, filled with a couple of hundred volumes, all colours, all bindings. But the thing which took his eye was the great gun.

He knew there was a gun here, mate to the gun on the open fo'csle. The one for'ard looked big: the gun here, in this enclosed space, looked enormous, threatening, terrible. There was no shot stored here. Half the deck space was taken up by the system of ropes and eyebolts which held the beast still. Only followed the Chaplain's eyes.

'Not the kind of thing you would like to have in your rooms in college, eh? But it would never do if the beast carried away when I was holding a party. Now, is this so formal a visit that you feel you must remain standing, or can you relax enough to sit in that basket chair?'

Dincombe sat. It was, he thought, rather like visiting French, the tutor of St Tibb's, to talk over an undergraduate Dincombe was coaching. But you did not look over French's shoulder and see hanging on a hook in the bulkhead a leather belt with a pistol in the holster and in a sheath the regulation issue cutlass. And on the next hook a cap and a greatcoat, and below them a pair of knee-high seaboots. All ready for action in the night. Had French ever known action in the night? Or passion either?

'Are we alone, sir? We always have a steward hanging around in the wardroom. Nothing we say there can be kept secret for an hour.'

'Are we to talk of secrets? I have ordered Abel to make us some coffee, and when he comes in I will send him on some errand. But he is for'ard at the moment, and we will have warning of his coming. So, unless Silverwright is standing on the wardroom table with his ear to a knot-hole, we are perfectly private. Private Garvey, in fact, is on call in case the tables and chairs rise in mutiny. Captain Fincham tells me Garvey is so incompetent the only place where he can do no harm is in watching over my door. But I digress. What is your problem?'

'It is your problem, Captain. It concerns two members of your crew.'

'Well, that sort of thing used to be common in the Navy once, after a long voyage. But I agree we have not been at sea so very long.'

'I do not believe we are thinking of the same thing.'

'Oh? Strange. In my young days we rarely thought of anything else. Except just before dinner time.'

'No, sir. It is a matter of . . .we are in grave danger.'

'Of divine retribution? I recommend prayer, Mr Dincombe, prayer and fasting.'

'No. In danger from men, in danger of treachery. I have been listening to what the men say, to what they tell me, and I am sure that there are two in this ship who are not to be trusted, who must be watched day and night. It would be safer if you could keep them in confinement.'

'Indeed? Who are these great sinners who will contaminate us all?'

'It is those two men who ... masquerade as Canadians. Calne and Moulton. They are not Canadians at all.'

'So? What are they, then? Whitewashed Hottentots?'

Dincombe leaned forward and whispered,

'They are Americans.'

'Well?'

'I tell you, they are not British. The Canadians are British, but these are Americans, and not the Queen's subjects.'

'There is no rule, Mr Dincombe, that forbids us to sign on foreigners. Indeed, there is an instruction from the Admiralty that we should not take into the same ship both Norwegians and Swedes, they fight with each other.'

'But they have concealed the fact that they are foreigners, and if they have lied then I must assume that they have come aboard with some evil purpose.'

'Mr Dincombe, you must be the last man in the ship to find out we have two American cuckoos in the nest. Did you not note how they walk?'

'How they walk?'

'They have been drilled, and taught how to march. Calne and Moulton, my friend, are passed Midshipmen in the United States Navy. The Americans have even fewer posts at sea for junior officers than we have. These are both gentlemen of property. Calne comes from the north of what I believe they call the Pearson-Dixon line, and Moulton from the south. Could you not tell the differences in their accents? Neither talks

138

like a Canadian. They are doing what Longville was doing, they have been improving their professional knowledge by shipping in merchantmen. They wish to know the coasts of the Americas well, so they have taken one engagement in a sealer, and one in a whaler. And now they want to go to war.'

'Why?'

'To see how it is done. There is a Prussian writer called Clausewitz – have you read him? He writes on the art of war, and he was in fact a general in the Russian service. He says that an army ought to keep itself in constant practice, and if a country cannot manage a war more than once in a generation, then they ought to send officers abroad to serve in other people's wars. So we have Moulton and Calne. We have them written down as Canadians for their protection. If we accept them as Americans, and especially if we write down HMS *Flamingo* on their discharge certificates, they will be in danger of prosecution when they go home. But they cannot give false names, because they need the discharge certificates. Everyone will know what they have been doing but for want of written evidence a charge will fail.'

'So you knew?'

'Of course I knew. They approached me in a tavern in Dundee, and I told them how the thing was to be managed. I was a better sea lawyer than they were. Those two men are as qualified to work a ship, to command a ship, as anyone in the wardroom. Remember, Chaplain, that apart from yourself, the Marines, the ten-year men who are ordinary seamen and a few of the idlers, we have nearly a hundred men in this ship who have been rated able seamen, able to hand and reef and steer. They know as soon as the officers when we are going to have to tack or to take in sail, and they make themselves ready and wait for the order. The officers, for these day-to-day matters, do not decide what is to be done because that is determined by the weather and the sea. But the officer gives the order, and it is from that order that everyone takes their time. What the seamen do not know in advance is the orders for the week, for the voyage.'

'But how did you find so many good seamen?'

'I asked them, and they came. Half of the volunteers have sailed with me before. I will tell you something, Chaplain, that no other officer knows. While I was on the beach, between 1840 and '45, I made three voyagers as mate of a whaler. It was legal and profitable.'

Abel brought in coffee. Only said, loudly, clearly, distinctly,

'Listen now, Chaplain, to my confidential orders. Up to now, we have been exercising how to work this ship. For the next three days, we will do our live firing and expend the ammunition allotted for the quarterly practice. Then I will make my decisions and rate men as AB if they can serve their guns. And after that, I will order: make steam, up funnel, down screw. Then, Chaplain, we will really go to war. Thank you, Abel, you may go about your business now.'

IV

The Northern Seas

1

On the ninth day of the voyage, *Flamingo* sighted another ship. It was not for half a generation that Dincombe, travelling to Norway, realized what a feat of seamanship that lonely voyage had been in such a crowded sea. His first warning came just after breakfast when the drum began to beat that old rhythm of 'Hearts of Oak'. Nussey and Silverwright were moved into instant action, clearing away the crockery, rushing into cabins, packing property huggermugger into sea chests. Orton, who had only just come off watch and turned in, came rushing out again, pulling on his frock coat and strapping on his revolver belt. He asked Dincombe,

'Have you got a telescope?'

'Yes.'

'Then bring it on deck.'

Dincombe, clutching his telescope, followed the Third Lieutenant up to the quarterdeck and then to the poop. There was an animated group on the weather side of the poop, pointing their telescopes at a white dot on the horizon. Even through his glass, it still looked a white dot to the Chaplain, although after some concentration he made out three masts.

'Is it?' Only said to Talleyman.

'I'll see.'

Talleyman went down to the quarterdeck, made his way between the seamen rushing to run out their guns, climbed into the mainshrouds and went up to the maintop. He stood there resting his telescope on a sailor's shoulder. Then he called down,

'Deck! *Eurydice*!'

Cricklade came to the quarterdeck, and said,

'All guns ready. If it is *Eurydice* shall I stand them down, sir?'

'No,' said the Captain. 'Remain closed up. Hoist the ensign and a recognition signal. It will take about half an hour. Make ready a boat.'

Dincombe listened to the chatter among the officers.

'*Eurydice*. What's she? Twenty-four?' asked Orton.

'Twenty-six,' Biddell told him.

'Would you like to fight her?' asked Longville.

'Mmm, yes,' answered Talleyman. 'After we've had another three weeks of this crew. She's just come back from the North American station. Well worked up.'

'In this?' asked Orton.

'Yes.'

'Giving away eight guns?'

'I've seen her handled before. Under steam we will run rings around her. We'd be across her stern in a wink.'

'But as we are?'

Flamingo was under sail, but funnel hoisted, the fires lit, the propellor still at the top of the gallows.

'Yes. In three weeks more. Or in an hour, when we'd got the screw rigged. Ideal fighting ship.'

'Armament suit you, sir?' asked Cricklade.

'Well, perhaps swop a pair of thirty-twos for a pair of eight-inch.'

'Swop three pairs,' said Cricklade. 'At least.'

Dincombe followed the exchange. The other officers were showing deference to Talleyman as First Lieutenant, but not as a seaman or as a fighting man. Longville said,

'With that armament and the engines taken out, I'd fight her. Good enough, but not ideal.'

'What is your ideal?' Orton asked. 'A liner?'

'Oh, no. Much smaller, smaller than this. I'd go for a brig, no steam, and a few pairs of eight-inch shell guns.'

'You'd lose some speed,' Orton objected. 'How would you get within range?'

'Yes, how?' asked Dincombe, anxious to show that he had learnt something about the sea. 'A brig has only two masts. Isn't it a much smaller ship? And slower?' He had some confused idea about the ratio of possible speed to waterline length.

'Not necessarily,' Longville told him. 'A brig with a good spread of sail can crack on a fair pace. But if it isn't as fast as a ship of the same tonnage, it is much more manoeuvrable. Look at all the collier brigs bringing coal down into London River from Newcastle, and dodging each other and the shoals in a crowd. Two masts, you see, each giving about equal amounts of power to speed the ship along But if you remember any mechanics from your mathematical studies, it should be obvious: with a smart crew to back sails on either mast when ordered, you can spin the brig on her centre point, dead amidships, while a ship with her three masts must come about clumsily. So the brig can come in dancing, dodging the broadsides till she gets across the liner's stern. But we can be nippy even in this tea kettle. Watch!'

Dincombe already knew that Longville was officer of the watch. He had heard him order the Bo'sun to furl royals and and to'gallants. Now, he called,

'Mr Harris. We'll have the courses clewed up, if you please.' Longville explained: 'With those two large sails loosely bundled up, we lose a great deal of speed.'

Esteron came on deck, wearing a heavy dark cloak over his garish uniform. Talleyman stepped across to him with sheets of paper, rolled into a tube.

'You'll need these.'

'Makes me feel rather a criminal, old boy, scattering my likeness among half a dozen ships to be recognized.'

'It may save your life. One each for *Miranda* and *Brisk*. Spares for the French. Don't want them to throw you back, do you?'

'Now we're under topsails only,' said Longville. 'Barely slipping along. Now, when we're in close to *Eurydice*,

145

we want to stop, heave to in proper language, dead in the water, but with our bows coming round to meet theirs. Mr Harris! Stand by to back fore tops'l!' He stood, an eye on the Captain, his hand raised to drop when Only moved. Dincombe had a vague sense of being in the way, and drifted across the deck to Cricklade. The Captain went down the poop ladder, Esteron after him. Sladen shouted an order, Longville another. *Flamingo* turned into the wind, slid forward, came to a stop in the water parallel to *Eurydice*, barely twenty yards away. The boat went down, touched the water as *Flamingo* stopped, the sideboys piped Only and Esteron down the ship's side. The boat was rowed across to *Eurydice*, Fox at the tiller with a seaman's eye on him.

Dincombe understood all this, understood why the boat's crew paid little attention to Fox's squeaks, took their own way in coming up dead to *Eurydice*'s entry port, oars vertical. This was all a piece of swagger. *Flamingo*'s men, hurriedly rushed together into a crew, were telling *Eurydice*'s Atlantic veterans how good they were. Dincombe said so to Cricklade, and added,

'I suppose if she were a Russian we would be broadside to broadside.'

'Not,' said Cricklade, 'if either captain had any sense.'

'Why not?' asked Dincombe.

'Shell,' replied Cricklade. 'Excuse me, I have something to do.' He went forward. Dincombe joined the group of officers standing at the rail, looking at *Eurydice* and the boat bobbing beneath her entry port. Talleyman stood back and looked round. He tapped Longville on the shoulder and pointed up. Longville raised his megaphone and shouted,

'Maintop!'

'Deck!' came the answer.

'Don't spend all your time looking at the frigate. Keep a lookout to starboard as well.' Longville turned to Dincombe and grumbled, 'Sailors are like children.

146

Once something happens, they all want to look at it.'

After half an hour, they saw Only and Esteron get back into the boat, come briskly back to *Flamingo*'s entry port. Only returned to the poop as the afterguard hauled up the boat to the davits. The Captain called,

'Signals officer!'

Longville came at the run. The Captain spoke to him briefly. Longville called the Yeoman. Meanwhile Only spoke loudly,

'Mr Talleyman!'

'Sir!'

'Pass the word. All hands to cease shaving.'

'Aye, aye, sir.

Fincham felt moved enough to address the Captain.

'The Marines, too, sir?'

'Yes, Captain Fincham, your Marines too. And the cadets, to the best of their ability. Now, make sail.'

Dincombe heard the Bo'sun order,

'Fill!' The backed main topsail came round, courses and to'gallants were shaken out. *Flamingo* came round to her original course. Talleyman touched the Chaplain's shoulder, and pointed to the signal flags now fluttering from *Flamingo*'s spanker gaff.

'What does it mean?'

'It says,' Talleyman told him, '"Go in, go in, and God go with you". And *Eurydice* makes, "Psalm 20. Verse 1".'

'"The Lord hear thee in the day of trouble,"' the Chaplain recited, '"The name of the God of Jacob defend thee." What does that mean?'

'I do not know,' said Talleyman. 'But it does not cheer me. It does not cheer me at all.'

'Something the Captain said,' observed Longville, 'comforted me even less. He orderd "Strike the Ensign, from now on fly St Andrew's Cross".'

'St Andrew's?' asked Dincombe.

'Russian ensign reversed,' Talleyman told him. 'It may pass.'

2

Only came quietly into the chartroom. Talleyman got to his feet. He had the table covered with papers.

'You are enjoying your exalted rank and your authority?' the Captain asked.

'If I had any sense I would not be doing it.'

'Why, young Tal, are you bored with the sea?'

'I might as well be on the farm. I ought not to have agreed to come. I knew it half an hour after I promised you. I certainly ought not to have come when Sherwin collapsed.'

'What? You are what, twenty-eight? And First Lieutenant of a ship going to war. I had to wait till I was nearly forty before I was First Lieutenant, and then it was a rusty iron paddle steamer giving away maize to the Irish. You remember that. And I would not be a Captain, either, if there had not been a war. You have had advancement beyond my wildest dreams.'

'These are not my wildest dreams.'

'Why not?'

'My wildest dreams were what I was offered, Second and guns. Going to war, that is. And not this war, either, or this ship.'

'In a liner, eh, and in the Channel mists outside Cherbourg? Wouldn't we all. But we have this war, and this ship and these orders.'

'And half the time, I am a housemaid. And half the time a clerk. All these vouchers. You cheated the agent every way. Even Biddell can't make sense of them.'

'What are you at, at this moment?'

'Learning. How do I audit the wardroom's mess accounts?'

'Why not let Biddell do that?'

'You know why. I have to guarantee to their Lordships that Biddell's accounts are correct. He's been trained as a bookkeeper. He can't make sense of what he's signed for. How should I?'

'I see, young Tal, you need some instruction. You have all the regulations, on victualling, on public and non-public funds. Draw me up a seat, and I will teach you.'

3

'I would like to come with you,' said Talleyman. 'Better than staying in this ship.'

'You think you are good enough?' asked Esteron.

'If I am good enough to manage this ship – '

'It is not management,' Esteron told him. 'First we have to ride. I know you can ride a big horse. And you hunt? Oh, you do. But that is not what we are going to do. Can you sit on a sheepskin thrown across an untidy half-broken pony, fourteen hands at the most, ambling along, and that for fourteen hours a day, and every day for three weeks. You'd be lost most of the time, you'd depend on native guides whose loyalty you may doubt. Can you ride three weeks each way like that? And perhaps not be able to ride back but face another six weeks going on south over the mountains.'

'Oh. I – '

'Can you eat like the natives? They may eat anything at all, I don't know what, worms for all I know. Not as a final ration in hard times, but every day as a staple food. And drink foul water or whatever else they may think a delicacy, or even a staple. The sour milk of mares will be a delicacy. You may think you can do that, but, really

149

can you? I've been trained to it for nearly twenty years, but passengers can't get used to it, any more than your passengers can get used to the motion of the ship.

'And fighting. You're willing to fight, I don't question that. But can you ride a pony at full tilt, till he drops, and while at full gallop, shoot down a man with your pistol at thirty yards, first shot? Or have you the heart to ride a man down, and then turn to finish him off with a spear while he lies still? I can do it, because I've spent half my life learning how. But you could no more do it than I could handle this ship. I could learn, and you could learn, but we have no time to teach you.

'And the language? Are you quick at learning languages? How many do you speak?'

'French,' offered Talleyman, feeling a little deflated.

'Only Russians speak French here. Some of them speak English. I could make you look like a Georgian or a Pathan, with your brown hair and brown eyes. But can you learn a new language in three weeks well enough to be taken for a native? By ear, without book, a language which is unlike anything you've ever imagined, where ideas like verb or noun have no place?'

'I've never tried.'

'No, and there's no time to find out if you can. And you don't walk like a man who began to ride before he could crawl, or like a man who has never gone out without a musket slung on his shoulder. Anywhere we go, you'll see every man carrying his musket, not because he expects to use it but because it is the most valuable thing he owns and he will not trust its safety out of his hands. You walk like a sailor, young Tal, there's no hiding it.'

'I thought,' said Talleyman with what dignity he could still manage, 'I walked like a farmer.'

'Never. You can be recognized at a hundred yards.'

Esteron decided he had been too hard. 'I'd like to take you, Tom Talleyman. I've seen you fight, and

I'd like no one better at my back. But I'd have to be guarding your back, and I can't afford it.'

He looked at Talleyman's face. He ought to be a little kinder. 'Look, can't you understand I want you here to guard my back? I don't care how far I go, as long as I know that when I get back here, you'll be here, with the ship.'

4

Talleyman came out to the quarterdeck and then up to the poop, where Longville leaned on the rail, looking forward. Longville asked him,

'To what am I indebted for this visit? Am I half a degree off course?'

'If we hadn't sailed the exact headings we were given we wouldn't have kept the appointment with *Eurydice*. But you heard what the Captain said. Just keep as near to due north as you can, till you see the edge of the ice. Then come east.'

'This is the best I can do, as near north as I can do in this wind. I've just had the royals taken in.'

'No ice?'

'Not yet.'

Talleyman looked up to the to'gallant crosstrees.

'How often do you change the lookout?'

'Can't have a man there more than half an hour.'

'It must be killing cold. He's in the wind. Four changes an hour.'

'Are you going up yourself?'

Talleyman sensed the challenge. He went up on the lee side, looking down at the water as the ship heeled. He wondered how long he would live if he fell into the sea. It was as cold as he had ever known. It was Smales at the to'gallant crosstrees.

'See the ice yet?'

'Not yet, sir, not out there.'

'Not out there? Where then?'

Smales pointed to the shrouds.

'Starting there, sir.'

'Will it build up? You know these seas, I don't.'

'Aye, it'll build up fast once it starts.'

'Enough to affect the trim?'

'I don't want to be below decks when she goes over.'

Talleyman looked at him. Smales' hands were blue and he was shivering. 'You've been up here too long. Follow me down.'

5

Flamingo dropped in gently between the island and the shore.

'Who made this chart?' asked Longville testily. 'Edmund Chancellor?'

'You mean Richard,' said Talleyman. 'But his nibs up there is sure that this is where he wants to go. By latitude and longitude. And a written description.'

'Time for the Chaplain and the cadets to do their trigonometry again.'

'Wait till I finish my sketch,' said Talleyman. 'Time for exact surveying after that.' Longville and Fox leant over the elephant sheet, watching the coarse lines of charcoal developing. It was all there, the mainland shore low and undulating slightly, with here and there a mound rising a couple of hundred feet. The Chaplain looked at them, remembered a book he had read which had made the Master's eyebrows rise, and murmured.

152

'Glacial moraines.'

Two of the mounds came down close to the sea. The land between them sloped gently up, to a ridge perhaps half a mile from the water, and, all assumed, sloped downwards again out of sight. On the opposite side of the channel, two miles away, on a similar shore, rose a cluster of buildings. Half a dozen of them were huts, sheds, shacks – what you will – put together out of unplaned wood, driftwood probably, Longville thought. There was another building, he saw through through his telescope, larger, higher than the others, made of trimmed planks, with a window in the side. Orientated east and west, Longville noted, and a cross on the rooftree. And last, a long low building, also of rough planks, probably some kind of warehouse. There were two or three pillars of smoke, one behind a long mound, and some men moving around.

Only climbed on to the poop. He looked down at the seamen closed up to their guns, with the ports closed. St Andrew's flag hung from the jack staff. Esteron came with him. Only inspected the town through his own telescope. Esteron took Longville's with only a muttered request, and swept the mainland shore. Only ordered,

'Get my gig into the water. Make the crew all whalers' men, tell them to wear their own clothes. Mr Longville, lend me your top hat.'

'Regulation round hat, sir?' Longville corrected him.

'You know what I mean. And bring some waste paper – I think your head is bigger than mine. Mr Talleyman, is that your oldest hat?'

'I think so, sir.'

'Take the badge off, and send for that tweed pilot coat.'

The Captain smiled down at the cadet. 'You see, Mr Fox, the exigencies of the situation demand that we go ashore as civilians, and perhaps as Russians. We

153

need the Chaplain. He knows some Russian. Wear that high-necked jersey, Mr Dincombe.'

'Wouldn't it be better for Mr Longville to go, sir?' asked Talleyman. 'In case of accidents.'

'If anyone gets hurt,' said Only, 'it won't be any of us and it will be no accident. Besides, Longville can't draw, can you, Mr Longville? Oh, thank you, Silverwright, but I don't think you have put enough stuffing in the brim. Now, in Mr Longville's fine hat, I hope I look the image of the merchant skipper. Now, last of all, Mr Wasely! When my gig pushes off, will you be so good as to fire three rounds from the signal gun? And after that, you are to let off three signal rockets, one after the other. Colour? Oh, red, if you please.'

'No Marines, sir?' asked Fincham.

'Think of the effect of the red coats,' Only told him. 'Stand your lobsters by, and do what Major Esteron tells you. Mr Longville, neither my commission nor my conscience will allow me to tell you to obey a Company officer's orders, but I will advise you most earnestly to conform with the major's actions and intentions.'

Talleyman went down the port accommodation ladder into the boat. Only followed, the senior man, last in, first out. The oars went into the water, and Mr Wasely dropped his upraised hand. The white smoke hid the boat for a few moments. Fox asked Longville,

'Please, sir, why give them warning? Why not take them by surprise?'

'It'll have been surprise enough,' said Longville, 'for them to wake up and find us sliding in through the morning mist and the dawn. They probably haven't had breakfast and we have. Now, young Fox, work for your living. Go to the Bô'sun and tell him we have to get the longboat into the water on the starboard side, now, and you are to supervise the operation. Think you know the orders to give?'

'Yes, sir. Oh, thank you, sir.'

'After that Pritchard is to have the launch out on the port side. Dyke and Chessil can get them in afterwards.'

An hour passed. Longville watched the shore through his telescope. Fox tried to do the same, but he found his glass heavy and hard to aim.

'Practice, lad, practice,' Cricklade told him. 'And size. That thing is too big for you. Or balance it on the mizzen ratlines.'

Fox did his best, and after another half hour was able to call, 'Flag signal from shore, sir. Making semaphore letters A–C, sir, repeated.'

'Very good, lad,' Longville told him: it rankled that Only had been forced to point out to him, in confidence as if it were a thing he had never heard of, that part of his duty lay in training young officers, not bullying them. 'Mr Sladen, take the launch ashore with your working party. You can have the services of Mr Dyke.'

Dyke grew an inch visibly as he passed Fox. As the launch, well down in the water with men, began its pull to the shore, he was able to report:

'Gig coming off, sir.'

The gig arrived in the charge of the Master-at-arms. It was rowed by four men, and was making heavy work of it. Biddell had already had the Boatswain rig a derrick, and out of the gig they lifted six bales, almost cubic and wrapped in sacking. These Biddell had moved down to the main deck. Chessil replaced the Master-at-arms, and the gig went back. When the launch returned, it brought not bales but sacks of coal.

'Best Welsh,' Craddock exulted. 'We burnt a hundred and five tons getting here. Fill the bunkers first, and then restack in the orlop.'

The two boats continued to go back and forth between ship and shore, the natty gig with the mysterious bales, the launch taking empty sacks ashore, and returning with full ones. The ship filled with a mist of coal dust, insidious, penetrating everywhere, into locked sea chests, into folded hammocks, into the sick

155

bay and into the wardroom. Only the magazine, sealed against damp, remained clear. The bales slowly filled the forward end of the main deck. At noon, and again about halfway through the afternoon, Esteron had Wasely send up three rockets.

A little after that, Orton went ashore with Craddock. Talleyman and the Chaplain came back in the gig. Esteron saw a group of men leave the village, if you could call it that. He remembered seeing better villages than that in India, and worse too that the collector would have on his map and had tax tallies for. He watched them come along the opposite shore, and then across the sandbank at the far end of the bay. It took them two hours, and then they struck off inland. Esteron told Wasely,

'No more rockets today, nor tomorrow, but the day after,' then he went back into his cabin, with his own cargo, and kept the door shut against everyone except Nussey.

Wardroom dinner was late, an hour late. Everyone was back from shore, not because the light was failing, which it was a little, but because the men were dead tired. Talleyman ordered an emergency watch, two hours on and the rest of the night off, of two complete gun crews and six marines, as well as one officer. The tale of the day came out over the dinner table.

'A reasonable day,' said Thacker. 'Four ruptures, one an old one restarted, six crushed feet, various contusions. Are you finished?'

'Not yet,' said Craddock. 'The bunkers are topped up, but we'll need all the empty sacks refilled before I'm satisfied. I'd never have expected coal here.'

'Esteron expected it,' said Talleyman. 'This was where he wanted to come. And the people of the place were expecting us.'

He remembered them, would always remember them, the big figures in bulky padded smocks, belted, patched and mended.

'Beards,' he told the table, 'as bad as ours. Nobody spoke English, and the Chaplain's Russian wasn't any use.'

'I've never heard it spoken before,' Dincombe excused himself, 'although I can understand it a little when I see it in print. Print doesn't teach you the tone of the language, the stresses, the way a sentence sings. But we did agree on a few words at last – coal, for instance, and water.'

'They weren't very useful,' Talleyman went on, 'till one of them turned out to speak French – after a fashion. He said he was the schoolmaster. I asked where was the school and who went to it. He told us that the women and children had gone south for the winter. He said nobody could live here in winter. They were keen to get off themselves, and go south before the snow started. They may start coming back, the men that is, when the snow is deep and well frozen, by about February. But they were waiting for a ship. They insisted we were the ship.'

'Comes every year,' the schoolmaster had told them. 'You are company ship, is it not? Every year, brings coal, takes off cargo. Never ship with steam before.'

'Plenty of coal?' asked Biddell.

'About a thousand tons,' Craddock answered.

'Which company?' asked Orton.

'How should I know?' Talleyman said. 'He brought me a mass of papers to be signed. Couldn't make out anything. Lots of royal arms on them. Theirs, that is. I signed them everywhere.'

'What name?' asked Orton.

'Franklin Pierce,' Talleyman replied. He remembered what the schoolmaster had said: 'Here I am schoolmaster, I am postmaster, I count dead and born, I am only man here who can read, perhaps in ten years when children grow up are more, but if they can read, they go off to city. Life here too hard.'

'You signed for the coal, then?' asked Craddock.

'And for the cargo in that godown.'

'What is the cargo?' asked Biddell. 'It's all wrapped up in leather, every bale.'

'"Contain your soul in patience and be still,"' Talleyman quoted unexpectedly. Then he explained, 'The Captain will address all hands. On that subject. Tomorrow after the seamen's breakfast.'

'But this means,' mused Longville, 'that we were expected, that someone had spent years stocking up coal for us. And the cargo, whatever it is.'

'But the headman told us, through the schoolmaster, that the cargo was all they had collected this year. So it is only the coal that was laid down. He said the cargo was for the company. What company do you think he meant?' Dincombe asked. There was a silence. Then Orton told them,

'Esteron did not go ashore. He stood and watched the shore all day, waiting. And Esteron is a Company officer.'

6

The ship was quiet, now, anchored in the dark. Some were asleep, some not, depending on the mood and the duties.

The Chaplain lay in his cot, still now after the weeks of swinging and lurching. The frame of the ship was no longer vibrating with the spin of the engines. He has as much alone now as ever he had been since the voyage had started. No, he remembered, this morning he had been alone. He has been into the little church. The schoolmaster had asked him if he were a priest, and then showed him where the keys were kept. Three sets: one set was left under the eaves, on a hook, a second set went off with the schoolmaster, the third set was given to Dincombe. To keep?

'Only against animals,' said the schoolmaster. 'Men not so wicked.'

In the gloom of the church, Dincombe sought for God. It was a bare hall, furnished with a few benches. There were no decorations, except carved on the door-post the date, 1794. It looked like a Baptist chapel, fit for Mr Wasely. One end was closed off by a curtain, the east end. Behind the curtain was an altar, oak wood, bare except for a crucifix five feet high, flanked by half a dozen brass candlesticks. But on the walls, three or four pictures, crudely painted to Dincombe's eyes. The subjects were plain enough: The Virgin and Child, a Crucifixion, and two Martyrdoms, easily recognized, St Andrew and St Peter. The colours were soot-covered, but gold leaf shone everywhere.

Against the wall stood one or two cupboards, their doors wedged shut with pieces of wood. In one he found familiar things, chalice and paten in silver. Other things were less familiar, but he had read enough to know their use. A ciborium in silver, and a sanctuary lamp: in brass, thurible and incense boat, candle snuffer, a bell. Other things were there, in brass or silver, whose use he could only guess at: the silver spoons, for all he knew, were for holy oil or for holy water or even for the communion. All very popish.

In another cupboard there were bundles wrapped in tanned leather. He opened one: the white altar frontal, for the Great Feasts, encrusted with gold wire embroidery. Where, Dincombe ask himself, could he find his God? Out there in the bare austerity of the nave, or here before the splendour of the sanctuary? It was before the altar he had knelt, it was that altar he saw in his sleep.

Esteron did not sleep. He lay awake and looked into the dark, a dark in space and in time. It had not begun today. It might not begin tomorrow, but within a few days it would begin. The long journey, the terrors and the tasks he had offered to Talleyman. Talleyman had refused them: why should he have imagined that they did not frighten Esteron also? He lay in the dark and tried not to dream, tried not to whimper.

Orton tossed and turned. How long before the morning, and his dose of tonic? How long before he would, for a few hours, cease to shiver?

Cricklade also dreamed. He had a good dream, he had seen the dodo, a giant dodo, tall as the foremast, coming to him through the snow, striding from iceberg to iceberg. And he had shot it, and had it ready for stuffing. If only the seamen did not want it for their dinner.

Longville leaned on the rail of the poop. He looked down into the waist, and counted seamen, the part on deck of the watch below, huddled against the bulwark. He looked out into the bay, to the land on either beam, showing under the moon. He tried to count Chinamen – he had done that often enough out there, in *Waterwitch*, in waters as cramped as these. It was a mild night, the land broke the force of the wind, and even the wind had been little more than a breeze. He wished it was time for Talleyman to relieve him and watch the dawn come on.

Talleyman was almost asleep. He was as near real sleep as he had been since leaving Scotland. He mused that that was why he did not want to be a First Lieutenant, the man who knew everything about the ship, knew about everybody. But they had come to this place – and hard it had been to find it exactly – for a purpose, and tomorrow, or in a day or two, the task would be done. Then they could go home. He would go back to his marsh draining and to his potatoes, and to Harriet. He ached for Harriet, for her voice, for her smell, for the sight of her coming down a corridor, sitting across the table, on the edge of his bed, undressing before the fire. And yet – why was it? – when he tried to conjure her up before his eyes, what he saw was not her living face, but one of his own pictures. He had her pictures in his portfolio and he looked at them sometimes in the day when he had a few minutes away from the lists, the charts, the tables of stores consumed. Perhaps when he got back, in another six weeks or less, he would find someone to teach him how to work in colour. Not oils – you could not handle them in a ship – nor watercolours either, but perhaps pastels. But why not oils? He would never go to sea again.

Only sat at his table, with a lamp, and sank himself into Mr Dickens' latest novel, *Bleak House*. His mind was at peace: he knew exactly what he would say to his gallant men in the morning. That big warehouse of furs and skins had been a godsend. They would have to be issued tomorrow, and the work started. There were a sailmaker and his crew, and every man now could use scissors and a palm. In a week from now, he would tell them, he wanted to see every man in a fur coat, knee-length, long sleeves, and a hood. It would be pleasant to have them all the one colour, or perhaps coloured by watches, or between watch-keepers and idlers, but they'd have to come as they were, take their chance. He had his speech ready, off by heart, to give them heart, too. But he was nodding over the book.

Outside the Captain's door, Marine Garvey stood sentry for his protection against the evil seamen. He had his rifle in his hands, with the bayonet fixed and four rounds in his pouch as well as one down the barrel. No cap fitted. The ship was still, the shore was a hundred yards distant, the duty was ceremonial. Marine Garvey dreamed on his feet, as he always did, about ways to harm the English.

7

Abel got Esteron's fur coat made first. He wanted to make it out of white fur, bearskin and ermine, but Esteron wouldn't have it. He said he wanted something to hide in, not something to be shot in. Talleyman offered to take the white coat, half made, off the steward's hands, for a consideration, but they must make Esteron's first, out of beaver. They were standing on the poop, trying the beaver on, on the third day when they heard the call from the main to'gallant top,

'Deck!'

'What d'ye see?' Talleyman called.

'Smoke to the south. Three fires. About two miles.'

'Three fires?' asked Esteron. 'Let me have my three rockets again, please, Mr Wasely.'

The rockets went up. The seamen were still bringing coal from the north side of the bay. It was about an hour before the lookout reported people coming towards the ridge from the south. One man came forward, to where, Talleyman guessed, he could see the top, not quite realizing that the man in the top, close in among the to'gallant shrouds and a furled stay sail, was watching him. Just below the ridge, he fired three shots, well apart because it took him time to load. Esteron signalled Mr Wasely for another three rockets. Talleyman hoped that they could be charged to the Company's account.

The cutter was, as on the previous two days, in the water, and half a dozen Marines in her. The boatswain had a handful of seamen handing down the cargo, all dozen bags of it, while Biddell and one of his clerks

162

checked it off against Esteron's list. Talleyman came down into the boat and the two officers sat in the sternsheets.

The boat grounded. The Marines jumped out and scattered, each going to the post Fincham had pointed out from the ship. The sailors stayed by the boat, cutlasses handy. Behind them they were conscious of the guns being run out and loaded with grape. The strange horsemen came nearer and separated out into a dozen mounted men and as many pack horses.

At a quarter of a mile, Talleyman held up his hand, palm out. They recognized the signal, obviously, because they halted. At least most of them halted. One alone came riding on. He came close enough for Talleyman to see his face, round, yellow, smooth. Esteron shouted,

'Bahadur, oh Bahadur!'

Whether this was a name, or a title, or only a word of greeting, Talleyman did not know. Or maybe a password. Esteron said,

'Yes, I know this one. It is safe.'

In spite of this, he felt sick at the pit of his stomach. He hoped it did not show. Talleyman watched him reach up and embrace the horseman. He caught the smell of a nomad not washed since the Caspian, and did not envy Esteron his journey; for he thought, Esteron will smell the same when he comes back. He asked, as if it were something forgotten,

'Should we not give them some rations for the journey? And yourself, too?'

'I eat what they eat,' Esteron told him, 'or they will not trust me. Beside, if you gave them five days rations each now, they would sit down here and eat it all by tomorrow night and not move till they had slept it off. But you can feed us all when we come back.'

'When you come back? I thought you were hoping to go into India.'

163

'There is a limit to the height I can climb. I will see you again here.'

'Here? But . . . how long?'

'Oh, not long. Only will be back for me in about eight or nine weeks.'

'You mean we have to wait here for another eight weeks before we can go?' Talleyman also felt sick. An extra eight weeks before he would see Harriet, an extra eight weeks before he would see what that idiot of a bailiff had done with his onions and his drainage. 'Wait here?'

'If you are not here when I get back, I am a dead man. You will wait for me, Talleyman? You will know when I am coming for I will be smoking my pipe, puff-puff-puff. You know the way.'

The yellow man had been bottling something up. Now he burst out in an odd-toned garble, a strange rhythm of sounds. Esteron listened and answered in what sounded like a beginner's version of the same tongue, slowly stumbling here and there, trying, it seemed, to establish the meaning of new words. He looked back to Talleyman.

'He says there has been a battle.'

'On the Danube?' Talleyman guessed.

'No, at Archangel. He knows the difference. The English attacked a town, tried to put an army ashore. He would count a hundred Marines an army. All the Russian soldiers in north Siberia have gone there to fight. So now, young Tal, you know what our blockading ships were there to do, and how they did it. We have come this far to the east without being seen. Tell Only. Ah yes, here is more. He says the English were defeated and went back to their ships when ten times their number of Russians appeared.'

'Very sensible of them,' said Talleyman.

'He also says that they found Russians near here yesterday.'

'Did he know?'

164

'He says they were coming from the village here, by a path south-west across the bog. They are now dead, all four of them.'

Four of them, thought Talleyman, only four of them. Will he bring a real army down on us? There will be no catching him. But who would want to be a single man, lonely, lost in this desert?

The seamen had brought Esteron's baggage ashore, the canvas-wrapped bundles of rifle barrels, of lead, of bullet moulds, some good powder, some caps. Mixed with the bundles of lead was the gold. Talleyman wondered how Esteron would tell them apart. He could see no markings. The small yellow men began to load them into saddle bags of untanned hides, slung ready on the packhorses.

One of the strangers brought Esteron a pony, rather larger than others. It still looked too small for Esteron. The Indian officer was wearing the gaudy uniform of his unnamed regiment, sky blue with melon facings and gold lace. He had on a hussar's cap.

'Put on a bit of show,' he observed, 'for Mr Punch.'

'Hold that a moment,' Talleyman told him. A few strokes of the pencil and he had it, the tall man on the drooping horse, the fur cap, the pistol in his belt, the Minié rifle across his back, and the sabre at his side. 'That's before.'

'See, see?' said Esteron plaintively.

'When you come back I can do the after,' Talleyman said. Unbidden, Sergeant Madden had fallen his Marines in line.

'Field officer on parade, present . . . ARMS!'

He's got more sense than I have, thought Talleyman. One sodger to another. He turned to the seamen by the boat.

'Come on, lads, give him three cheers!'

Esteron saluted, and turned his back on friends, safety, food, warmth, a dry bed. What hero, he asked himself – for like every man he was a hero in his own

eyes, and his eyes were colder and clearer than most –
what hero ever started a great expedition by being sick?
But that was how he felt.

8

'I told you you would work with me, in the end,' said
Richard. 'I told you that the ship would not be back until
the spring. And I have work that only you can do. You
are the only one I can trust.'

'You would trust me?' Harriet asked. 'No one can
trust you, how can you imagine that there is anybody
that you can trust?'

'Oh, I know I can trust you.' They were in the drawing room of the Dower House. There had been frost on
the lawn that morning. The leaves were going. She was
still in black, as she had been since the funeral, and she
felt it so boring. Richard lived dressed for a perpetual
funeral. Only in that, she felt, could she trust him. He
went on: 'Would you like to come abroad?'

'Abroad?'

'To Bruges. It is in Belgium. For a few weeks, over
Christmas.'

The short staccato phrases caught at her memory. It
sounded so like Tom. 'How? And why?'

'I am engaged on financial negotiations. My father
started them last spring, and you will remember he
was abroad several times. His part in the negotiations
has fallen to me. I have a small number of English
colleagues, men of substance and standing, but nobody
who understands the finances as I do. The chief nego-
tiator on the other side – he is a baron from Livonia,

166

and there are certain incidents in his past which make him unwilling to come to England. On our side, there are a number of people who must rely on me to make them in harmony. We have two or three French noblemen, gentlemen of title in any case, titles bestowed on them by the Emperor, in whose confidence they stand high.' He watched her interest. 'Whether they are two or three depends on my skill. We have a citizen of Brazil, who has interests in the diamond mines there, but the driving force comes from – ' She expected him to say 'from myself', but instead he said, 'from this kingdom. Our foremost names come from either side of the House. We have Lord Dunscore, and Lord Denain.' Philip Suttle, she thought, her Philip, stolen from her, and Richard watched her face. 'The noblemen do not matter, except to talk occasionally in the Lords, but these foreigners, you know, if they are a count or a baron, with never two ... sous ...' He had almost said 'kopecks', but had caught himself in time ... 'to rub together, they will not talk to anyone who has not his own title.'

'But what can I do, if you are meeting such great men?'

'We began these negotiations last spring. Bruges was suitable, because it is convenient to both London and to Paris, and has communications across the Prussian frontier which enable our ... adversary ... to consult with his colleagues. Those negotiations came to nothing, or almost to nothing. Now, however, conditions have changed in the international monkey market.'

'Because of the war?' she asked. He must be careful, she was cleverer than he thought.

'Yes, because of the war. Last year my father found it convenient to take a lease on a house in Bruges. A furnished house, with servants. He and the English principals lived there, or at least stayed there, and on occasion other of our more important employees. In this kind of negotiation, you know, it is necessary

167

to make a show, to entertain. If we have a house, we must have a hostess. We need a lady to keep our house for us, to be the hostess at our dinners, to receive at . . .em. . . yes, at our receptions, perhaps even to preside at a ball.'

'So you wish me to be a housekeeper for you.' She was flat, disappointed.

'Not a housekeeper. We have servants, we have a housekeeper in our sense of word. A lady of your standing is not required to cook, or even to hire a cook. Your place is to approve the menus. If that.'

'There are other ladies,' said Harriet, probing, 'who would be better placed than I am. Lady Dunscore, for instance?'

'Lord Dunscore is now seventy-five,' Richard told her, seeming to make a joke of it. 'He married for money, a lady ten years older than himself, and she is still alive. In any case, his tastes do not run to women.' Harriet wondered idly what he meant, brushed her puzzlement aside. 'The money he married for he will now treble in a year through this business.'

'Or Lady Denain . . .Jane?'

'I will not deceive you. You expect me to be dishonest, but I am honest now, and you may ask her. We had intended that Lady Suttle should be our hostess, and she was proposing to ask you to join her if Tom had not returned. She was waiting till winter set in and you were still alone. But now she will not be able to go, not to spend Christmas and the early spring out of the country.'

'Why not?' She was frank in her demand.

'Has she not told you? They expect again an heir to the Barony, and after the long history of mishaps, she proposes to spend a period at absolute rest.'

Harriet did not know at what she should be the more offended, that Jane had not told her about the Bruges expedition, or that she had not mentioned her new pregnancy. If she could not go to Bruges, and Philip

168

would be there, her Philip, alone with her at last. . . She came back to the present, and objected,

'How could I go, not chaperoned?'

'Your husband's brother is there to protect you. What better chaperon is there than myself? Remember, this is a matter of great delicacy. We need a lady who will so manage the establishment that there will be perfect secrecy. We cannot trust anyone who is not of our own families, not of our own blood.' He knew this sounded absurd and melodramatic, but he knew too that it was the melodramatic which would take her attention, that there was no absurdity for her.

'Then why not – ' And she grasped at her own notion of absurdity, asking to be reassured – 'why not your sister?'

'Arabella?' He continued to look surprised. 'You know that Arabella does not go into society, and you know why. She has no experience of these functions, she has never seen the great world. And what is more important, we could not have a young unmarried lady as our hostess. It would resemble too much a market, a kind of auction. You are so eminently respectable, a married lady whose husband is at the wars.'

'I might come,' Harriet said after some thought. 'The boys would benefit greatly.'

'Oh, I am afraid there would be no place for children. You could not spare the time. Understand, my dear Harriet, that this is a business occasion, not a social one.'

'Leave the boys behind?'

'Why not? Arabella will be glad to look after them. She dotes on them, you know. And they love her.' True, thought Harriet, they seem sometimes to love her more than they love me. Certainly she loves them more than I do, these squalling brats, uncontrollable boys, who had each deprived her of a whole season's riding. Tom wanted the boys, Josiah had been delighted to see them come into the world, everybody welcomed them but

169

herself, everybody loved them, and the more they welcomed, the more they loved the boys, the less, she felt, they had time to love her, the more she could be made to feel the foreigner, the Irishwoman, the stranger who had done what she was imported to do and could now be discarded. All right, if Arabella wants them, let her have them, for the winter at least, let her see them any hour of day or night. Let Arabella argue with nurse, nursery maid, cook.

'But what about clothes?' Harriet asked. She might as well get what she needed out of this. Almost all the credit Tom had left her at her dressmakers in Cambridge had been exhausted on her mourning clothes. 'I cannot go to Bruges for such an errand always dressed in black.'

Richard noted that no direct answer had been given, the proposition had merely been accepted with no further discussion. He still had some talking to do with Arabella, but here the principle had been conceded.

'Certainly not. We will have to get you some proper clothes. Not mourning.'

'But would that *be* proper?'

'We will be outside England. Mourning,' he improvised desperately, 'is never worn outside England, except for great personages in Court mourning, and then only an official business. Mind you, black silk or purple, with gold or silver lace does look very rich and dignified, but if we are there for a month or two. . . monotonous.'

'I might. . . could I go to London for clothes?'

Bind her now, make sure, and after all we will have to equip somebody to play the hostess's part, let Harriet benefit, rather than a stranger.

'No, not London. We may stop there to buy you a suitable travelling costume, and perhaps tea and evening gowns, one or two, to tide you ever. But for the most part we will have you some clothes made in Paris.'

170

'We will have to go to Paris?'

'It is our most expedient way. There are bankers there, business acquaintances. I will have to see them. You can see the dressmakers, the milliners, during the day. I suspect we will be entertained at dinner.' He hoped so, these men owed his father, the family, that hospitality. 'We will go to the theatre. Or perhaps you do not like Paris?'

'Oh, I loved Paris. I have only been there the once, you know that, after Tom and I were married, a good place, he said, for a honeymoon. And it was so wonderful, all the streets and the great houses and the wonderful shops and we went to the Opera one night and we saw the Emperor only he wasn't the Emperor then only the President and he wasn't married and do you think I might be able to see the Empress?'

'I think something may be arranged.' I could probably get her presented at court there, not certainly so I don't dare promise it, but it will certainly help, to be escorting a lady in that good odour, wife of a brave Navy officer who is now at sea fighting for France. Can I trust her not to say too much? Well, the less she knows. . . She is almost decided.

'Bruges is colder than England. I think you ought to have a fur muff or two, at least. And perhaps you might like a fur coat?'

Her eyes were round, bright.

'Fur? A fur coat? I have never had a fur coat. I have always wanted one, I have asked Tom, but he always says when the farm is really prosperous, I suppose when the potatoes are selling. Oh how I detest potatoes, I seem to have been governed by potatoes all my life.' Then, anxiously, 'Are you sure that Tom would approve? What if he comes back while I am abroad?'

'I know he would approve. And as for his return, my friends at the Admiralty tell me he cannot now be home before the spring. And if he does come home, he can

171

be here or you in London in two days, whichever you prefer. Arabella will cable to us.'

'When,' she asked, 'should we go to Paris?'

'Oh, there is no hurry. We must be in Bruges before Christmas, and you will need two weeks in Paris to get your clothes.'

'I must take a maid.'

'Not necessary. Maids talk, and we are going to Bruges to be secret, all of us. You will have a maid there, entirely to yourself, one who speaks some English. And no tales told around the city. Tell no one else, do not talk even to Arabella unless you are both alone together in the open air. All that I have to do abroad must be done in secret. If we keep it secret, then Tom and I will be rich: if it leaks out, then you and he will have only the Dower House and the potato fields to depend on.'

V

The Ice

1

Flamingo came back, slowly, under fore and main topsails, jib and spanker, her engines turning slowly, into the bay. Dincombe leaned on the poop rail watching the shore. The whole crew were at action stations, also watching the land. He himself had nothing to do, and he did not want to go to the sickbay yet.

The sky was grey. It was a little after first light. How Longville had brought them in through the middle of the channel in the half-light, the Chaplain could not understand. There were only about four hours of daylight now, but the rest of the time, when the sun was not visible, was hardly night. There was the moon, visible a great deal of the time, and the aurora, bright and sparkling, turning the ordinary humps and hillocks of the shore into living creatures haunting the ship as it came close to land. But just as there were silent shapes there were also wolves that howled when nothing could be seen. The evidence of eyes could not be trusted.

There had been little incident. Within the ship one of the whalers' men, Bloxham, was caught in what Orton called *flagrante buggeratio*, with a marine drummer. Craddock caught them in one of his inspections of the propellor gland. Only awarded Bloxham twelve strokes of the cat, 'six for the sin and six for stupidity in committing it in a place and time where and when an officer was well known to poke his nose.' The drummer was given twelve strokes, allotted in the same manner, of a rope's end on his bare backside, held down like a child across the Bo'sun's knee. Thacker, making sure no permanent harm had been done, gave his medical opinion that it was not the first time, nor the dozenth neither.

Later, among the islands, an ordinary seaman named Hallen fell from the main topsail yard into the water, fell straight in and did not come up. *Flamingo* hung about there for another day, cast the lead and found the depth a hundred fathoms, tried nevertheless dragging with a hook, found nothing. Hallen was a ten-year man, not six months in the Navy, and never in any other ship. Only blamed himself that the boy had not been well enough trained to go aloft, and Talleyman and the Bo'sun also blamed themselves, but not each other. The next day was a banyan day, so declared by Biddell on account of a great amount of fish just caught; but the men would not eat the fish, mostly cod, either then or later in the voyage.

Cricklade brought out his shotgun, permission granted, and granted a great number of birds. At first indiscriminately, but when the novelty wore off he only shot birds singly when they were a species he had not shot before. But once or twice, given an opportunity, he provided enough geese or duck for a different kind of banyan day. On one occasion he was allowed to go ashore with a rifle and bayonet to have a try for a bear spotted on the beach. But when he got near to the beast and saw how big it really was, he backed off. When it turned and stood above him on its hind legs, Cricklade turned too and ran back to the boat. The sailors cheered on both contestants in the race, and since they saw how big the bear was they did not blame the Mate for running.

Flamingo came east, to 100 degrees, where the chain of islands ran north. The sea was dotted here with ice, big floes. They turned a little north, and then back. Clearly, no ship could come through here, between the Tajmyr peninsula and the islands. There was no need now to hide, instead the task was to coax any Russian men of war out to fight. The Cross of St Andrew was stowed again in the locker. In a calm bay, Walter Hook

176

and his carpenter's crew put the figurehead in place again. The Bo'sun asked Only,

'Shall I have the name repainted, sir?'

'No, no, indeed, there's no need to overdo it. Let them worry about who we are.'

Flamingo, nameless, sent men ashore at a couple of score of settlements, villages, sometimes even one hut alone where a trapper spent his season. Several times they found their fame had gone before them, but no Russian came out of the mists. There was the damp smell of winter, but never powder smoke. Dincombe saw things he had only heard of, high cliffs of cruel rock, crueller floating mountains of ice, pancake floes with the water already porridge thick between them. He saw wild reindeer in sheltered spots, and herds of seals, swimming or on shelving shores. And he ate both seal and reindeer, ostentatiously so that the men would see him and perhaps follow suit.

'We're well stocked,' Biddell told him, 'but there's ne need to waste what the Lord has sent us. Plenty of food here, for eating and for thought. You'll have a fair number of sermons out of this.'

When there was little light left in the day, and the water was beginning to feel mushy, *Flamingo* came back from trailing her coat, into the bay of the Glory of the North, Vladi-Sevier. As they came up the water, everyone saw the smoke.

'I thought,' said Only, 'they said they were all pulling out for the winter, but that's a lot of smoke for a dozen huts. Why are we going so slowly, Mr Longville?'

'Mr Craddock is still eager to conserve coal,' Longville answered. 'Fox, my compliments to the Chief, and we would like to have more speed.'

Talleyman came up on to the poop, and took one look at the smoke.

'That's not peat burning, or wood. That's good Welsh.'

'Welsh?' Only was disbelieving.

'If you'd spent all your life with steam, sir, you'd read smoke for the fuel too. Coal burning, in the open, without a draft to stir it.'

Even Longville could guess what that meant, only Longville found it needful to put it into words.

'They've set fire to the coal dump.'

'But not long,' Talleyman told him. 'That's a lot of smoke for a village, but not very much for a couple of hundred ton of coal. Shall we prepare to land, sir?'

'Obviously,' snapped Only. Then, 'Man even number guns, Marines to go ashore first, crews of odd number guns to follow with spades, shovels, picks, any tools we have that look suitable, and buckets and tubs. Mr Craddock to go with them.'

Talleyman went into the maintop and watched the burning coal dump as *Flamingo* came up opposite the village, where she had anchored on her first visit. At least, he thought, Longville could bring a ship to where she was supposed to be. He saw Fincham take his Marines ashore and, after ten minutes, wave a signal that the rest were to follow.

'Not a great deal to it,' Craddock reported at dinner that evening. He had come back with the coal grimed into his skin, the tarry smell on his clothes. 'Not a big fire. Might have been burning an hour, so probably he lit it at first light, at the earliest, probably as soon as he spotted us coming in.'

'They were watching for us, not expecting us, not with any certainty,' said the Chaplain.

'A deduction?' asked Taberon.

'If you lived up here,' Craddock challenged him, 'and winter coming, would you burn four hundred tons of coal on spec?'

'Well the sooner you coal and we can get out of here, the better,' Longville told him. 'If we sit here close in to the shore much longer, someone's going to get shot.'

2

It was, after all, Orton who got shot. At least he was the first. It was another bad day, the iron grey clouds low, the wind bringing little flurries of snow. Orton was officer of the watch. He had gone forward to look at the sailors clearing ice from the martingale stay, and was standing on the jib boom, clinging to the forestay with one hand and bending down to see what was being done. He had his fur hood thrown back, so that he could hear properly. His peaked cap was pushed to the back of his head. As he straightened up, he felt, he said later, a Clydesdale kick him above the knee, in the back of the leg. He swayed, his leg was crumpled beneath him, but he heard a dozen long-gone voices remind him,

'One hand for yourself!'

Orton was certain later that he had heard the shot, just after the kick. Other men heard it too, and as the Lieutenant sagged slowly to his knees, the Bo'sun was alongside him, and another two seamen, sliding on the ice-covered part, supporting his weight, easing his fingers from the rope. His hat fell on to the ice below.

Talleyman came out of his cabin on to the deck. The Bo'sun shouted,

'We're being shot at, sir. Mr Orton's hit.'

Talleyman looked around. The shore was to port. He bellowed.

'Everybody shelter under the port bulwarks. Bring Mr Orton back on this side. Get those men back aboard!' He looked up to the man in the maintop.

'Sterling! Did you see anything?'

'Not sure, sir.'

Thacker called down to the gun room for the Chaplain to join him in the sickbay. Only came on deck, took in the situation and joined the seamen crouching among the port guns. Longville put his head up through the after hatch and asked,

'Shall I call to quarters, sir?'

'No,' snapped the Captain. 'Get everybody below who hasn't got to stay on deck. Don't let anybody more up here.' Then, to Talleyman, 'Where is he? The man with the musket?'

'Don't know. I'm going to see.'

Talleyman went up the ratlines on the starboard side. He felt, oddly, that the mass of mast and shrouds would at least hide him, spoil the shot. He reached the top.

'Any idea where?'

'I think I caught a wisp of smoke, sir. There, on that hillock. Among the rocks.'

Talleyman opened out his telescope. Sterling, unasked, offered a shoulder to rest it on and pointed. Talleyman looked along the seaman's arm. This time he saw the flash, the smoke. Sterling sagged back against him, bleeding. Talleyman decided this was no place to stay and dress a wound, and called for a rope to be thrown up to him.

'Nobody come up,' he shouted. 'Keep your heads down.'

'That's no way to talk,' said Smales. He went up the starboard shrouds, took the weight of the body as Talleyman manoeuvred it through the lubber hole. He backed slowly down as Talleyman paid out the line. There was, he sensed, someone coming up to help him, Longden by the grunting. Talleyman watched the wounded man touch the deck, reached out for the mainstay, and slid down to reach the deck before Sterling had gone down the hatch to the sickbay. He rejoined the Captain. Only called,

'Sergeant Madden!'

180

The Marine came to the officers on his belly. Only asked,

'Who's the best shot we've got?'

Talleyman knew that, knew he had it in his lists, down in his pile of papers. He kept quiet, while Madden answered,

'Four or five good ones, sir. There's Moulton, the . . . Canadian, Parks, Mr Cricklade, Private Garvey . . .'

'Yourself?'

'Not as good as them sir.'

'Captain Fincham?'

'Aims at the plughole and misses the barrel, sir.'

'Call Moulton. With a rifle. Now, Mr Talleyman, did you see where?'

The drawing pad was out.

'That hillock, sir, about halfway up. . .'

Moulton was with them, rifle in hand. Talleyman passed him the sketch.

'He looked to be about here. Keep your head down!'

Snowflakes whirled about them, then ceased. Moulton said,

'Forward gunport, this side.'

The Bo'sun and three seamen slithered forward. Moulton followed them, and the two officers. Mr Harris and the other three had laid on to the gunport hauls. Moulton lay on his face, close to the port, his back to the great gun trained fore and aft amidships. He had already loaded his Minié, and now he carefully pulled back the hammer and placed the percussion cap. He took another look at Talleyman's sketch, and asked,

'Range?'

'About four hundred,' Talleyman told him. 'Perhaps a trifle more.'

'Lahk shooting fish in a barrel, suh. Haul away.'

The seamen laid hold of their ropes, began to hoist up the gunport lid. It was not easy. The snow and ice were crusted heavy on it. The first pulls did little more than shake it. Talleyman and Only took hold of the ropes too, heaved on the Bo'sun's word, and felt the ice crack. Slowly the port lid came up, the weight of ice not letting them do anything but bring it up in jerks. If he sees this, thought Talleyman, he must fire, he'll be easy to spot. The lid was now well clear, showing a slit at the bottom a foot or more wide. The Bo'sun asked,

'Is that enough, Moulton? Have you got a view?'

'Just about,' said Moulton. I think I've – '

They all heard the shot, let go the ropes, let the lid slam shut. Moulton had sagged forward on to his unfired rifle, his head streaming blood. The snow swept in, great swirls that hid hill and shoreline and maintop and even the poop rail. Without orders needed, two of the seamen picked up Moulton and carried him aft at the run.

'Everyone off the deck,' said Only. 'Under the poop. We'll get a view from my cabin windows.'

'Put a man in my cabin,' Talleyman told the Bo'sun. Then to Madden, 'Have a squad ready, bayonets fixed, loaded, some under each hatchway. I'll call for boarders if I see them.'

3

Thacker looked at Orton as the seamen brought him in.

'This cot. No, on his face. Bayford, cut away his clothes, let's have a look. Ah, Chaplain, stand back there and do what you can to help. Don't touch anything. Drink this, Orton, it'll dull the pain. Here, Chaplain, have you seen a gunshot wound before?'

'It looks very bad,' said Dincombe. 'It's swollen and black.'

'So would your leg be if someone hit you with a hammer there, even if it didn't go through the skin.

I must know something before the swelling really gets bad. The first thing is to see whether the bullet went through. Help me turn him over here, to see the front.'

'It's an honourable wound,' said Orton loudly. 'I don't care which side, I didn't turn my back on him. He went round to the back of me. Most unfair.'

'I thought I gave you enough opium to make you sleep,' snapped the Surgeon. 'If you can talk, you may as well help. Tell me when it hurts.'

'It all damn well hurts.'

'I should think so. Now does it hurt more here? Or here?. . . or when I do this? Oh shush now, Orton, you needn't be so explicit about where it hurts and when. Remember that the Chaplain is a man of education and probably doesn't know these words. Ah, that's good.'

'Nothing's good here.'

'And here? No? Well, we know the bullet is still in there, but it hasn't broken the thigh bone. Now, if we twiddle our thumbs for a few minutes, we can try to get the bullet out. No, we can't twiddle our thumbs. Put *him* down here. Funny ship this, we don't have starboard and larboard any more, we have Orton and Moulton. You men, get out, we haven't got enough room here as it is. Barford, find some water and wash his head. Cut the hair away.'

Dincombe leaned over Moulton. He said,

'Only believe in the Lord Jesus Christ, and you will be saved. Call on His holy name – '

Moulton opened his eyes and said, very clearly and with a tone of malice,

'I'm an Episcopalian.'

'Right, Moulton,' said the Surgeon. 'Can you see my hand? How many fingers have I got up? Two fingers and the thumb? Nothing wrong with you. Just a crease across the top of the skull. Wonder where the bullet went? You haven't got it inside, anyway. Now, Bayford, call a couple of seamen. He won't be able to get into a hammock, so have them rig a cot somewhere near here.

183

Moulton, I'm going to give you something to ease the pain, and you're off duty for at least twenty-four hours. Come and see me in the morning.'

'Will he be all right?' asked Dincombe.

'Of course, he's no worse than if someone dropped a block on him from the top. Now, let's have a look at Master Orton and – no, here's another one.'

'My turn first,' Orton complained.

'It's Sterling,' Dincombe said, in what he intended to be reverential tones. '*He*'s dead. Receive, O Lord, into the bosom – '

'You'll frighten him to death,' snapped Thacker. 'Here, Chaplain, if you can stand the sight of blood, hold a lantern close. Now Bayford, make sure he doesn't swallow his tongue. Someone else – is that you, Nussey? – get a lot of water, it's oozing here, not pumping, wash the blood away . . . make a pad and hold it here, press hard. Now, turn him over, let's see his back. . . h'm, I can feel it here. Chloroform, Bayford.'

Only stood at the door.

'Ah, you're busy.'

'How many more?' Dincombe asked him. He felt he didn't want to know about what the Surgeon was doing with his knife.

'Oh, no more, not for the moment. Everyone's under cover, and the snow is giving us protection. How is Lieutenant Orton? Now, now my boy, there is no need to be so explicit. I don't like these places either.' Only went out into the companionway. Dincombe heard him call for Abel, and then begin to retch into the bucket his steward brought. The Chaplain congratulated himself on his strong stomach. He went back into the sickbay, saw what the surgeon was doing, and realized he had been premature in his conceit.

'Welcome back,' Thacker observed genially. 'I've nearly finished off Sterling.'

'Not the right words for a doctor,' complained Orton. 'I was here first.'

'What is that smell?' asked Dincombe.

'Something new,' Thacker told him. 'I have a young friend called Lister. I promised him I'd try his idea, and wash wounds in a solution of something called carbolic acid. He says it stops gangrene after operations, and he wants to know how it does with war wounds. Now, if these two don't get gangrene, they ought to be all right.'

'But why did I have to wait?' Orton still complained.

'Because he was unconscious when they brought him in, and you were most objectionably conscious. I had to give him chloroform, but I had to keep you awake long enough to find out if you had a broken thigh.'

'Will he be all right?' Dincombe asked.

'Who? Oh, Sterling? I think so. Bullet entered below the right collarbone in front, broke a rib, was deflected, travelled round inside against the rib cage, finished at the back, short of the spine, nearly at the surface. Now, if we can keep him still for twenty-four hours and if he doesn't get gangrene ... that should be enough. Now, hold the lantern, Chaplain, and don't run away again. I'm getting this bullet out.'

'Save my bullet,' said Orton. 'I want it on my watch chain. Don't get it mixed – Aah! What in hell are you doing?'

'What Lister told me. Carbolic acid on the knife, carbolic acid on the wound inside. Be carbolic acid on my hands next, I suppose.'

'Hell, I hope so. You've no idea how much that hurt.'

'Do not go to meet your maker and endanger your immortal soul with such language on your lips,' Dincombe reproved him. The Surgeon snorted.

'Immortal soul? I tell you, I've dissected the human carcase a dozen times, and there's nothing there. Nothing there.'

Dincombe decided that this was not the time to convert the heathen. Thacker bent over his forceps. Orton grasped the Chaplain's free hand and squeezed. He was concentrating his strength on keeping his lips together. But he groaned a little. The Surgeon said, suddenly,

'There you are. No worse than having a tooth out, was it? You can have a look at it when I've finished.'

'Haven't you finished? You're not going to do anything more to me?'

'Oh, yes. There's a few bits of your trousers still in there I can see. We ought to have those out, on principle. Fine tweezers, Bayford. I'll swab with carbolic down to the bottom. . .right. Needle and gut, all gone through the carbolic, and we'll sew up.'

Talleyman came in.

'Sorry to be so long. How's Sterling?'

'He'll work again, barring accidents.'

'He was in front of me. Silverwright's cleaning my fur coat. Got Sterling's blood all over it. How are you, Orton?'

'Here's my bullet. Isn't it a good one? I'll be holding this up in court next year and saying, "I who have have suffered wounds for my country . . ."'

'In the backside,' said Talleyman cruelly.

'No, not in the backside, not exactly. It feels a bit low down to be called the backside.'

'Look here,' Thacker told him, 'you've got to stop chattering and go to sleep. You've had enough opium to kill a normal man, and you'd better lie there still.'

'I'm not staying here,' said Orton firmly. 'You'll boil me in carbolic acid. I'll be fit to stand my watch as soon as I've had my tonic. I haven't had my tonic today. And I want to show the Captain my bullet. Look, Tal, isn't it a good bullet?'

Talleyman took the bullet with the amused air of someone pacifying a child. Then,

'Good God! Good God! Did you get one out of Sterling?'

'Here it is.'

'Don't mix them up, don't mix them up,' Orton warned. 'I want my own.'

'All right, here's yours. Show it to the Captain. He's in the wardroom. I think you ought to sleep there. Here,' Talleyman bellowed out of the sickbay door. 'Half a dozen men! *Now!* Nussey, rig a cot in Mr Orton's cabin. You men. We have to get Mr Orton into the wardroom. Go very easy on his leg. If you bump it, it'll jar like hell.'

4

The wardroom was crowded. The Captain was there, all the other commission officers, Mr Wasely, Cricklade, Sladen. The other Mate, Neve, was on deck. On the long table was Talleyman's new map of the coast, backed by his sketch of the shore as seen from the anchorage. Somehow the sailors got Orton inside, and into a cot slung from the deckhead alongside the table.

'Now,' said Talleyman. 'Orton will show you his bullet. Orton will show you all his bullet.'

Orton held it up, gave it to the Captain to pass round. Biddell said,

'A funny bullet. What's it made of? It's not lead, is it, and it's been knocked about a bit, not a ball any more. I didn't know your backside was so destructive, Orton.'

'It's pusser beans that did it,' Orton replied. He was sweating. Only said,

'Nussey, get the patient a large brandy. Or his tonic if he prefers. Now, gentlemen, Mr Talleyman seems to think this bullet is important.'

'It is,' said Talleyman. 'How many know what it is?'

'I do,' said Fincham. Cricklade and Wasely also nodded. Fincham explained,

'This is not a lead bullet. It's not even iron. It's cast steel, drawn out into a wire, a very odd thickness, and then machined into a hexagon. Very expensive. I suppose Talleyman could make one here, but it would keep him busy.'

'Yes, very expensive,' agreed Only. 'I saw it at the Great Exhibition, but I couldn't afford one. Besides, I couldn't think where I would use it.'

'Too expensive?' asked Dincombe. 'One bullet?'

'Oh, no,' Cricklade told him. 'Not the bullet, although Lord knows that would cost enough, but the rifle. Look, most rifles have a groove inside the barrel, a spiral going round and round all the way. Spins the bullet. The bullet is lead, so the problem is pressing the lead into the grooves to give the turn. But the Whitworth has a six-sided barrel – inside. And the six sides make a spiral. It turns gently at the lock end, and then the spiral gets tighter and tighter. The bullet stays its proper shape, smooth, and carries well. Whitworth says it is accurate at a mile – you'll hit the man you aim at at a mile, and hit him hard enough to kill at three-quarters.'

'Theory,' said Fincham. 'That assumes that you're lying down and he's standing up. That you are calm, that you haven't been running, that you aren't frightened, that you can see the man plainly against the background: most of all, that there's no wind.'

'I've fired it,' said Talleyman. 'It *is* as accurate as they say. Whitworth claims a round a minute. His engineers can do that. In theory. Start with a new rifle, all the ammunition, ramrod, laid out ready. In shelter. Say "go!". Shot comes in one minute, perhaps a second under.'

'What's wrong with that?' asked Dincombe.

'I've seen it too,' Cricklade told him. 'Those engineers built the gun, they've been practising for a year. But you and me, even on the range, we've got to start the bullet in the spiral, coax it down, get it right home.

188

And getting the cap on the nipple is a niggly job. So for a trained man, a good soldier, it's still more like two minutes between rounds.'

'A round a minute?' mused Talleyman. 'But not ten rounds in ten minutes.'

Again the Chaplain it was who asked, 'Why not?'

'Fouling,' Cricklade explained. 'Even with the best powder, fouling, ash, clinker, call it what you like, accumulates in the barrel. It spoils the fit of the bullet, and with the Minié you'd do better to clear it out after ten rounds or so. But with the Whitworth – well, they claim ten rounds without serious fouling, but I had trouble after six.'

Only sat silent, listened to the talk. It was Orton who spoke now from his cot, drinking something, perhaps his tonic, whatever that was.

'I was listening to the doctor. You say this rifle will kill at nearly a mile?'

'It will,' Talleyman said.

'Well, there's been three of us hit. What's the range to the place he shot from?'

Talleyman looked at his chart.

'I've measured it. Four hundred and twenty yards.'

'But he hasn't killed anybody. Hit us all right. Mine stuck in my thigh.'

'Your backside.'

'My thigh. Knocked Moulton out, but didn't break the bone. Sterling – broke the collarbone, just went round under the skin, didn't have the force to come out again. Nussey, get me some more tonic.'

'Powder,' said Mr Wasely. 'If he don't keep his powder proper the way the Lord willed us, he won't get the range. Either it were bad powder to start with, or it's damper than we'd want. Either way, he loses the range. And there'll be more fouling.'

So look at it this way,' said Only. 'We have here one Russian officer – '

'Why an officer?' Talleyman asked.

'Because it's his own rifle. No government would buy that rifle to issue. It's the kind of thing that a rich man would buy to go shooting elk. He knows it well enough to adjust the elevation as his powder weakens. If he has that money and that understanding of ballistics, then we must assume that he is an officer. And alone, or nearly alone, if that is all he can do. Mr Talleyman, how long were you in the top, getting Sterling down?'

'About three minutes,' Longville put in. 'I noted the times for each shot in the log.'

'That is a realistic reloading time. If he could have shot at you again, he would have. So we need posit no more than the one weapon.'

'Here, Talleyman,' asked Biddell, 'what were you wearing up the top? On your head?'

'My peaked cap.'

'And you, Orton?'

'The same. Oh, I see. You mean he's shooting at officers' caps?'

'So we have the one man,' went on Only, 'and we must posit a telescope. He is shooting at officers only. He knows them by their caps. He picked Mr Orton out of the working party on the jib boom. He does not bother to shoot at seamen. Therefore I would suggest that he is short of even his bad powder, or of percussion caps, or of Whitworth bullets. Or of all three. So this one poor lonely man, ill-supplied, can terrify two hundred of us, warm in a well-found steamer. What can we do about it?'

'Break out and rig the sun awnings,' said Biddell, 'before dawn. I can start it now.'

'Hardly a remedy. And how long will the awnings last in a blizzard? Will you go out and clear them, Mr Biddell? No, let us think what he is afraid of. He shot at Moulton without waiting to see his cap. He does not want the great guns to open on him. Only the for'ard eight-inch will bear. Mr Talleyman, can you give us range and bearing from your charts?'

'I can, sir.'

'Then I want the gun crew closed up, and the gun trained out of the port where Moulton was hit, five minutes before dawn. Don't start proceedings too early, Mr Cricklade. No men on deck other than the gun crew. Any officers who must go on deck to wear coats with hoods, no caps, and seamens' trousers. If you can't get jean trousers made in time, Silverwright will steal them for you. The Gunnery Lieutenant, the First Lieutenant and I, in order of usefulness, will see to the gun. Mr Sladen, I would like you to stay on the poop, well hidden, and see the fall of shot.'

'Shot, sir?' asked Cricklade.

'We shall wait till dawn, and when I blow my whistle, Mr Cricklade, I want three explosive shells on the target as fast as can be.'

'Aye, aye, sir,' said Cricklade. He had been looking at Talleyman's sketch of the shore, at the chart. He would make his own arrangements.

5

Dawn was about eleven o'clock in the morning. Dincombe felt he could not bear another day in the sickbay locked below while the great guns fired. He stood, huddled in furs, under the break of the poop. The snow flurries came and went. Six bells sounded and, as always, a working party came up the after companion way, all hooded, in denim trousers, with brooms and shovels. They worked along the deck, clearing the night's snow. They were not slow about it. Once they were well forward, hidden now under the bulwark from the watcher on the hill, they broke up. Only and the other two officers stood aside. The fourteen men of the gun crew moved fast, sliding the gun carriage on its runners to point toward the port, still lidded.

The Chaplain heard the words of command. He knew them now by heart. 'Search!' and the Number Four probed into the muzzle with his spiral worm, making sure that the gun had not, by some accident, been left loaded.

'Load!' The small forward hatch opened, a cylindrical case was passed up. Number Five, took it, Number Three slid the flannel bag of powder into the muzzle, Numbers Four and Six rammed it home. Five drew the shell from its case, passed it to Two. Two held the shell up for the gun captain to see, as he set the fuse. Then he slid the shell into the muzzle, fuse out. Four put the shaped end of the rammer over the shell so as not to hurt the fuse, and with Six drove it home. Then on that they rammed in the wad of old rope.

Now it should have been 'run out!' but the crew had their orders: Number One went straight to 'Prime' and Two slid the powder-filled quill into the touch hole, while one pulled back the hammer against the ratchet.

'Point!' and the gun captain, Number One, looked along the barrel till the hand-spike men, following his hand movements, had the gun aimed at the white mark Talleyman had already made on the inside of the port lid.

'Elevate!' and the hand-spike men lifted the breech to free the wedge. Cricklade bent over as Number Two slid the wedge backward to give an elevation of four degrees. When he called 'Down!' they lowered the breech and stood back.

'Ready!' and Two cocked the lock. And now, out of order, One called 'Run out!' The handling numbers hauled on their ropes, and the port lid came up with a run, the gun pushed out.

'Fire!' shouted Cricklade. Number One pulled the lanyard, the hammer fell on the cap, the powder caught. The noise of the gun deafened every one in the ship. But as the smoke rolled round him, Dincombe heard the orders, 'Stop your vents!' as Number One put his calloused thumb over the touch hole, so that the next order, 'Sponge!', when carried out should not bring a spurt of flame from the touch hole to set off the new cartridge or the fuse. Then it was 'Load!' again.

But before the gun fired again, there came the longer, rumbling roar of the shell bursting on the hillside. There were three rounds fired, and after the third the orders were, 'Sponge!' 'Secure the gun!' 'Search!' Before the explosion of the third shell had died away, the Mate, Charles Sladen, stood up, looked through his telescope, and shouted,

'Good shooting, sir. Three on. No – '

The Whitworth bolt hit him in the back of the neck. He pitched forward down the ladder. Dincombe jumped forward, caught him and lowered him gently to the deck. Sladen was still breathing, trying to say something. Longville came forward, and Silverwright, to help bring him down to the main deck, to the sickbay.

Cricklade shouted to his guncrew,

'Secure! Then get below!'

Only said to Talleyman,

'If there is only one rifle, we have a moment's grace.' But Cricklade was running along the deck, and a group of seamen came up the rear companionway and went before him under the poop. In the Captain's cabin, he found them already with the eight-inch cast loose, coming round with a will to the port. Abel pointed out of the Captain's stern window at the patch of scrub by the shore. The small hatch in the deck opened, and the cartridge was handed up. Cricklade bellowed down. 'Shrapnel's! Six rounds!' Then to Number Two, 'Elevation fourteen degrees!'

Dincombe, on the poop, saw the shot leave the gun. He had heard this was possible, but had not believed it. He followed its flight, saw the flash, and could

193

imagine the forty-pound weight of balls scattered over the scrubland. Only came into his smoke-filled cabin. Parks, Two, pulled the Captain with him to the right of the gun and safety as the second round was fired and the ten-ton gun on its carriage came thumping back.

Only coughed and flapped his hat to clear the smoke from, at least, a foot in front of him. He circled the auxiliaries as they sorted out the ropes for running out again and got to one of the big-framed windows. Abel had opened them, and there was no glass smashed. He tried to see the shore.

Talleyman had decided that there was little profit in going into the cabin. He climbed to the poop and stood a little distance from the Chaplain. He saw the shrapnel burst over the patch of bushes, and through clouds of smoke thought he could see something move. But he was not sure. He counted the rounds, and the times between them. After the sixth, the interval seemed longer. Cricklade had ceased firing. The smoke was drifting away.

Had this expenditure of costly ammunition been worth it? Only one way to find out. Talleyman heaved himself up on to the taffrail, stood holding the jackstaff. No shot. Perhaps not enough provocation. Nothing else for it. He snapped open his telescope and scanned the shore. It was hard to hold it steady, and even in the cold, sweat was trickling into his eyes. Only spoke from the deck,

'What are you doing there? Come down, you're a target.'

Talleyman dropped to the deck.

'It seems he isn't engaging targets, sir. We've either killed him or driven him away.'

'Have we? asked Only. 'We haven't, not you or me. Cricklade did it.'

Talleyman waved his arm in the air. The other officers, all of them, came on to the poop, and gathered round the Captain. Only turned to Cricklade.

'Who told you you could make a mess of my day cabin?'

'We're in action, sir. They're my guns, you gave them to me. I engaged a target with the only gun that would bear. I commend Abel, sir, for spotting the shot.'

'You must have arranged this. You know what's the trouble in this ship? It's Pentstemonitis. I had enough of it, no direct orders, let people use their initiative. It may be all right for small boats on the coast, but not in a big ship. If you have strokes of genius, Mr Cricklade, or if you want to do unusual and effective things, tell other people first. Tell me. Or nobody knows what they are to do next. Tell *me*!'

'I have a working party clearing snow, Sir,' said the Bo'sun. 'And breaking ice in the rigging.'

'Think you're bullet-proof? There's only one way to be sure he's dead. Find him. Captain Fincham!'

'Sir!'

'Let me have a corporal's guard of Marines to take ashore and beat those covers.'

'I'll be ashore in ten minutes, sir.'

'No! Not you. *I* must go.'

'It's getting late, sir.' Talleyman objected. 'It's nearly noon. You've only an hour of light left, if you can call it light.'

'It must be done today. In the dark he can change his position, recover from the shrapnel, clean his fouled piece. He can engage us again tomorrow. We have the initiative, and we must keep it. It must be to-day.'

'You cannot go. It is too dangerous. I – '

'Mr Talleyman. You are the First Lieutenant. Your task is to run this ship, sail her, keep her clean and orderly. My task is to fight her. I must fight our enemy. This Russian has held us at his mercy. He has almost made our anchorage untenable. He has killed an offic-er, wounded another, brought down two seamen. The people of this ship are afraid of him. Can I ask any of

195

them to go and do something which I appear afraid to do? I *must* go.'

'I would do just as well,' said Talleyman. 'I have a reputation too.'

'Then let me acquire one. Now look, young Tal, that man wants to force us out of this anchorage, into the open sea. He may know this or he may not, but we have to stay here whatever he does, because we must wait for Esteron. Somewhere down there in the south is Esteron, trying to get back to us. For all we know he is sick or wounded or starving, and do you want him to get here and find that the ship is gone and nothing to welcome him but a Russian with a rifle?'

'No, but I – '

'No, not you. I am the Captain and I am responsible. I must make this shore safe for Esteron. So it is my task to go and make certain we killed that Russian dead.'

Only went down the companionway rigged for him into the longboat. Corporal Egan and six Marines followed, arranging themselves with difficulty, without packs but their long fur coats hampering them, the pockets in their tunics stuffed with biscuits and cans of salt beef. Only had left his sword behind. He had a couple of pistols stuck through his belt, and a regulation cutlass. Talleyman wondered if he had signed for it. Before they pushed off, Only called up and another Marine passed down to him his musket with bayonet fixed and a couple of packets of cartridges.

Longville spoke earnestly to Talleyman.

'Why did you let them go? Couldn't you keep them back?'

'The Captain goes where he wants to,' Talleyman answered.

'Not only the Captain. He's taking seven men with him. And in this weather.'

'It's not snowing much,' Talleyman consoled him. 'Only these short showers.'

'Sniff,' said Longville. 'Can't you smell it? 'Look to the north-east. It's all coming in on us, we've only had a few showers for starters.'

'This isn't the China coast,' Talleyman told him coldly. 'Not the monsoon season.'

'Wasely has the right idea,' said Longville. The Gunner and a couple of his men were readying the little three-pounder saluting gun on the poop. Forward he had an armourer rigging a batch of rockets.

The boat was halfway to the shore. Suddenly, Cricklade in the Captain's day cabin shouted his orders. One, two, three rounds of shrapnel burst over the scrub, spattering the snow with dark holes, throwing up branches of the dwarf willow. The last shell scattered its balls into the water, close to the boat. It grounded and Only leapt out.

'Fool,' grunted Longville. 'He's got his feet wet, and in this.' The sky was suddenly darker. Only waved his little party to spread out in line, himself on the inland flank, Corporal Egan near the water's edge. Bayonets thrust forward, keeping their dressing as best they could, the Marines began to move into the patch of bushes. The longboat was almost back to the ship. And now the snow began to fall in earnest, blotting out the shore.

Talleyman stood at the rail, peering into the murk. Below him were the duty part of the watch on deck, half of them huddled in the chartroom; every half-hour they changed with the other detail at the bottom of the boiler room companionway. The snow built up, an inch deep, two inches in under half an hour.

At six o'clock, Mr Wasely's men came on to the poop and fired a saluting charge, half a pound of powder, but loud enough. They continued to do this every half hour.

6

Cricklade came up about seven o'clock. It was pitch dark. He brought Talleyman a mug of steaming coffee.

'What's in it?' Talleyman asked. 'Either the spoon will stand up or melt.'

'About one third its bulk in rum,' the Mate replied, 'and nearly a quarter of a pound of sugar.'

'Whose rum ration?'

'Let us say, medicinal.'

'You've had yours?'

'There was more rum in it.' The two officers paced up and down the poop, to keep the blood moving.

'My feet are blocks of ice already,' said Cricklade. 'I'll have a working party up to keep the deck clear.'

There was a shot. Talleyman counted thirty. There was another. Thirty again, and a third. The exact timing told him a great deal. He realized that the ship was silent, the buzz of living noises, movements and talk, was noticeable only when it stopped. He cupped his hands, and shouted,

'Who's that?'

Cricklade repeated the question, using his speaking trumpet. Talleyman murmured, 'Don't put your mouth too close to that or you'll need new lips.' There was an answer from the shore.

'Egan. Corporal Egan, sir! Take us off. Please take us off.'

The Gunner's men forward let off a rocket. It burst and for a moment or two spread a flickering light over the shore. Talleyman counted seven men. Cricklade shouted,

'Boat away!' Then he left the poop at a run, but his

gun crew were in the Captain's day cabin before him, the eight-inch run out and ready to cover the Marines. But they were not needed.

Talleyman was at the side to see the frozen men come ashore. Six Marines.

'Get down to the boiler room and dry yourselves,' he told them. It was plain they had all been in snow up to their waists, one over his head. The last in was Egan, carrying two rifles. Only did not come. Talleyman called to the corporal to come with him to the chartroom. Other officers crowded in.

'The Captain, sir. . .we lost him.'

'What do you mean by that?'

'He was with us, sir, going into the bushes. He wasn't so good, he'd had his boots full of water. He couldn't keep up – '

'That's absurd. It was your duty to keep back with him, not his to keep up with you.'

'No, sir. Yes, sir. But he kept on shouting, "Hurry up, go on, after him, catch him!" So we had to run on. The Captain said his feet were freezing. He were the other end of the line, I couldn't get across to see. Then Garvey next to me on my left, he called out he'd found something, and we all went to see. That's when the snow started properly.'

'What had he found?'

'This sir.' Egan laid the extra rifle on the chart table.

'Well, well,' said Biddell. 'A genuine Whitworth. I've not seen one before.'

'I have,' said Cricklade, 'and that's no part of their trademark.'

It was engraved on the lock plate. An octagon, deeply incised, and a line, a ray, extending from each corner. The two upper rays were each forked at the end. And under the octagon, the letter 'P'.

'So,' said Craddock. 'It was a gentleman, an officer, a nobleman, something like that, and he's put his crest on it.'

'It's thoroughly fouled,' Cricklade pointed out. 'Perhaps he didn't have his valet or his gamekeeper handy to boil it through. Or just no fire or no water.'

'Even simpler,' said Talleyman. He looked at Egan, who laid something else on the table. It was a cardboard box, subdivided inside into a dozen compartments. The name was printed on the outside.

'Whitworth cartridges,' said Cricklade. 'He dropped the rifle because he was out of ammunition. So that's him accounted for.'

'What about the Captain?' asked Longville. 'Did you just leave the Captain there to die, you cowards?'

'Indeed no, sir,' protested Egan, looking at his own officer for support and getting none. 'It was the snow, sir, it was when we found the rifle that it started. It was so heavy we couldn't see each other's faces as we looked down together. When I realized that Captain Only was missing, sir, then I started to look for him. It was hard enough finding my own boys. It was coming down like a galloping horse. I got the lads in a line, like Mr Fincham told us, and arm in arm. Then we walked back the opposite way as far as we could guess, across our line, sir, till we thought we'd passed the place where we saw the Captain last. But we couldn't find him.'

'His footprints?' asked Longville, throwing the question like an insult.

'No, sir, couldn't see any sir, it was coming down that fast and thick we couldn't see our own marks when we looked round. So we shouted, and we went fifty paces in each direction, north and east and so on, but after a bit we didn't know which way we were going. Then we heard the gun, and we argued over which way it was, and we agreed, and when the gun went again we were going away from it. And it was a long time between signals. And then we were on the beach, and we all saw the flash of the gun. So we fired off the signal like Captain Fincham told us, and shouted, and then we saw the rocket and we heard you. And sure, sirs, we

200

were near death all of us, and we couldn't have walked further in the snow except as ghosts.'

Talleyman looked at Fincham.

'Any point in another party?'

'Not with the snow like this. I think we were lucky to get these men back. We might try in the daylight. The working party can hardly keep the ways clean on deck.'

Talleyman looked at Cricklade.

'Two men from each gun crew out there, keeping the guns and tackle clear and ready to fire. Changing every five minutes. Mr Fox is being the time-keeper.

'Corporal! The guns too long between?'

'Yes sir, a lot too long between. Couldn't get a bearing.'

'Mr Dyke! Run to the Gunner. My compliments and could he let off one round every ten minutes. Now, Corporal, get below somewhere, boiler room I suppose, and get dry. Mr Biddell?'

'My storemen, sir, issuing hot grog, hot soup, dry gear out of store. Full record being kept.'

The Pusser, Talleyman noticed, a theoretical lieutenant, had called him 'Sir'. Did that mean anything? If anything, it meant pessimism. There was no need to keep all these men here. As First Lieutenant, Talleyman spoke.

'Get below. Start wardroom dinner. Send me something up here. Mr Neve, get something to eat. I'll stand this watch. But Mr Chessil, go and find the Bo'sun for me.'

Nussey came with a mug of pea soup, almost boiling. He heard Talleyman say,

'Mr Harris. Are we icing up?'

'A fair bit, sir. Hard to keep it off the rigging in the dark.'

'Have a party ready. As soon as it's safe enough to go up, have the men send down the to'gallant and tops'l yards. And the topmasts. Everything above the tops.'

'We'll not be able to sail, sir.'

'No. Let Mr Craddock know that. And his mates. We'll have to have funnel up, screw down, permanently.'

Nussey came with curried beef, boiled rice. He had the small chop with him, onion, coconut, chutney. Talleyman asked,

'D'ye cook like this for Mr Sherwin?'

'No, sir. He do like plain food only, and he'd call this too fancy. I've been cooking things for you I'd never have had the nerve to try with him. Things I've never cooked before, only heard of. I've got a couple of cook books, sir. If you'd like to have a look and order anything, I'd do the best I can with the ingrediments we've got.'

'What does Silverwright say? And Abel?'

'They was a bit disapprovalizing at first, sir, but now they don't say nothing, only watch. I think they're a bit jealous.'

'It'll be a comedown to go back to Mr Sherwin.'

'Oh, I'm not going back, sir. I've had other offers. Trying to find the ship, I had an offer.' He paused a little, offered the dish of curry for Talleyman to help himself again, then said, 'Do you think we'll find Mr Only tomorrow?'

'Ask Mr Dincombe to pray,' said Talleyman. Pray for Only out there in the snow, probably frozen to death, at least with his feet frostbitten. No hot supper for him even if he were alive, but only ships' biscuit and bully beef.

Do not mourn the dead, fill up their places at table and rejoice in life. Do not mourn the dead, just push the bodies over the side and serve the guns. Do not mourn the dead, keep your own hand hidden, give the other to the ship.

Do not mourn the dead. But Talleyman waited till what ought to have been dawn, till the ship again was full of noises.

Only was not dead. He was wrapped in furs, his stomach full of stewed pork and his head full of vodka. Strapped to a sledge, he was of as little use to Talleyman, or Esteron or *Flamingo*, as if he had been dead.

7

At about two in the morning, Talleyman checked his watch bills. He knew, he was sure he knew, but it was better to be sure. He called a seaman: the cadets were day workers and would be asleep now down somewhere inside the ship, closed in, stifling. He told him,

'I want Calne. Part on deck of the duty watch. He ought to be clearing snow, for'ard.'

Calne came, glad to be under shelter.

'You're from North America.' Tact, there. 'So you're used to snow.'

'Yes, sir.'

'Can you walk on snowshoes?'

'I have done, sir. Not since I was a child, and we played in the snow. I was brought up in a big town.'

'Go to the Carpenter. Tell him I want some made.'

'Wake him, sir? He's a day worker.'

'Tell *me* when you see some daylight. By then I want three or four pairs of snowshoes. A party to go ashore. You're one of them.'

'I think it's cooper's work, sir.'

'Tell Mr Hook.'

'Aye, aye, sir.'

The night crawled by, the snow came drifting down. Talleyman sat at the chart table, occasionally getting up to take a turn on deck or peer through a scuttle at the shore. At first he relied on the signal gun to keep him awake. Later he dozed. He was lulled by a muffled hammering from for'ard, where Walter Hook and his crew were making a coffin for poor Sladen. At each change, the new officer of the watch came in to him with fresh hot coffee. At a little before eight, Silverwright brought coffee and said,

'Breakfast nearly ready, sir. Nussey's made some kedgeree with eggs out of the waterglass cask.'

Talleyman came out on to the upper deck, looked up at the iced masts and yards. Had he left it too late to send the spars down?

'We'll do it,' said the Bo'sun. 'If we don't we'll go over when a wind gets up. There's some men here I can trust to start it in the dark. We've all had our breakfast, so you go and have yours, sir. At least we'll have the royal yards down before you finish it.'

The wardroom was chill, the food at least hot. Talleyman asked Biddell,

'What's it like on the mess decks?'

'Warmer than here. They're getting heat from the forward boiler and the stokehold. Most men are slinging their hammocks somewhere warm. Forepeak's empty.'

Talleyman turned to the engineer.

'Craddock, can your people make us a coal stove and fit it in here? Set it on a big iron tray, and ask the Carpenter about where to put it and how to fit the chimney.'

'It's all worked out,' said Craddock. 'Midday do you?'

'Last us till we get home,' said Longville. 'Home for Christmas.'

'Not likely,' said Talleyman. 'Find the Captain first.'

'You won't find him,' said Longville. 'And he won't find us. It's coming down outside thicker than Silverwright's porridge.'

'We'll find him,' Talleyman said firmly. 'Mr Biddell, I'd like to see your ration count at ten o'clock. Mr Craddock, I'll have the coal state at half past.'

'We'll have to go in a couple of days,' Longville pressed. 'I've been over the side, and the water's beginning to glaze over.'

'Interesting,' said Talleyman.

'It'll be getting very icy outside,' went on Longville. 'We must go, or we'll be iced in.'

Talleyman did not answer. He finished his kedgeree and went back on deck. It was time for his usual rounds, but first he called the Mate, Neve.

'Mr Orton can't get into the orlop. You'll have to do his job. Go round with the Carpenter today. Extra careful. We fired yesterday, remember. Now, Fox! Go to the Chaplain. Say we're in action, no time for classes. Then come around the mess decks with me.'

The Bo'sun said,

'Royal yards down, sir, fore to'gallant yard down. Topmasts'll be a job, but we'll manage. We'll have to.'

'How are you stowing the spars?'

'Amidships, along the engine room skylights and hatches.'

'Will they get in the way of the gun crews?'

'Don't think so, sir.'

'Anyone hurt?'

'One or two slips and sprains, sir. Nothing serious.'

Thacker was mixing plaster of Paris for a twisted ankle.

'Now, get in your hammock and stay there till this time tomorrow.'

'No, sir, I'm all right, I'll get around.'

'Get on your back,' Talleyman told him. 'Listen to the Surgeon. Keep your weight off it. Your mates will feed you. Heads? Shit in your trousers, but stay on your back.'

'Never had all this fuss in a whaler, sir.'

'In a whaler, you don't have to fight. Bayford, find two seamen to carry him back and sling his hammock for him. This your log, Mr Thacker? How was it you treated Moulton before you looked at Sterling?'

'His fault, or his mess mates. He told them he'd only had a bit of a knock, and he'd be back on deck after a bit of a sit down. So they brought him past here and back to the mess deck, and it wasn't till he fainted that they thought of asking me to have a look.'

'Better the devil he knew. . . Right, Fox, let's go round the mess decks, and then to see the Pusser.'

When they reached the Gunner's kingdom, they found Cricklade there too.

'Early orders for the market,' the Mate told him. 'If you are sending men ashore, I want to be able to cover them.'

'If. With one eight-inch?'

'I have been working on it. If we let out a little aft and take in half a turn on the bower, then with a bit of hard work by the hand-spike men, we can cover as far as the scrub with the whole starboard battery. And not move enough to be noticed, and still cover the village with the port broadside. So I'm having a few rounds of canister sent up to mix with ball. And half charges, that ought to do it.'

'I would have liked to be consulted if you want to move the ship.'

'You remember how Captain Pentstemon said we were to see what was to be done, and do it. So in the absence of a Captain. . .'

'In the absence of a Captain. . . Captain Only is a different person. Mr Cricklade, Mr Wasely. . . Make it so. Be ready to see the boat into the water as soon as the sun shows. . . no, the sun may not show. Have your preparations ready by eleven o'clock, and wait for the whistle to run out.'

Thank god the gunnery officer will speak with the Gunner, thought Talleyman. Sitting there thick, with Davidson's book on gunnery on the table between them.

The snowshoes were not an entire success. There were three pairs, one with soles of twisted rope, one with leather straps, and one with soles of interlaced strips of wood. Calne, as inventor, took the wood. Fincham claimed the rope. That left the leather straps for Corporal Egan. Talleyman left the sodgers to equip themselves, but called Calne.

'Use a revolver?'

'Yes, sir.'

'This is a Deane and Adams. Single action. Hope you've got a strong forefinger.'

'I've used a Colt.'

'Too flimsy, and feels a bit silly in my hand. Don't lose this. Or steal it. Got my name on the barrel. Here's twelve extra rounds. And caps. Want 'em back.'

It was not, at that moment, snowing. The boat went down into the water, and as soon as it did so the broadside guns ran out, the barrels hard against the right-hand sides of the ports. Everyone waited for a shot, rifle or gun, even, but nothing happened. Longville had had a mixture of hammocks, spare sails, oddments of gear crammed into the hammock racks on the bulwark aft, so that one could look between them and not be seen from the shore. The boat slid through the water, crackling the ice, reached the shore. The three men went across the snow, bending low, and floundering even in the makeshift snowshoes.

They went, Talleyman decided, as far as they could, as far as anyone could, creditably far over the wide sheet of snow. They reached the skyline, and Fincham turned and waved his arms, Then they came back, and were taken off. Talleyman reclaimed his pistol and twelve rounds, and followed the Marine officer into the wardroom. The stove was installed and alight. Silverwright was waiting with rough towels and dry clothes. Fincham talked through his open cabin door.

'No hope of finding anything. It's hard enough to keep upright on those shoes, and we couldn't have managed it in boots. But the snow stretches as far as we can see, deep as anything, certainly over a man's head. And it's smooth, smooth, untouched. As far as the eye can see, just smooth shining white, shining with the sun, bright enough to hurt your eyes. You can tell where the scrub was, because it's a bit bumpy on top, but there's no saying where anything has been.'

'It's freezing,' said Talleyman, looking at the chart-room thermometer. 'Hard enough to walk on?'

'Not yet. Ice thick enough to bear you for about a yard from the shore.'

'Well, that's it, then.' Longville was drinking Nussey's thick mulligatawny soup. 'We can't stay here and get frozen up, we'll just have to leave him and go. It's easier for him to find us than for us to find him. If we can't get ashore and look for him, then he can't look for us. I don't think there's anything to do but to leave him. You talked about the sun, Fincham, but it won't last the next hour. It's coming on again from the west.'

Talleyman considered an answer. He was saved by Thacker coming out of Orton's cabin, prompting him to ask,

'Is he well?'

'Well, there's no gangrene started yet, but it's early days. He seems very bright this morning, and I gave him a dose of opium to calm him down, but it didn't do much good.'

'When will he be fit to stand a watch?'

'Without gangrene? Oh, not for a month, and even then he won't enjoy putting his weight on that leg.'

'That is a blow. And Sterling?'

'Still very poorly. Well, you saw him, and, given no gangrene, we'll still have to carry him ashore. Moulton, though, let him have three or four days' light duties, and he'll be all right.'

Biddell came in from overseeing the men's dinner and the rum issue.

'Any complaints?'

'No, they're still in the mood where they'll eat any-thing. When rations get short, that's when they begin to object to the tastier dishes, like rat.'

'Serve the rat now,' said Talleyman. He went back on deck. The Bo'sun told him.

'I mustered all hands this morning, sir, and we've got all the spars down and stowed. We could just make way under fore and mainsails, and I thought it wasn't safe to depend entirely on the steam.'

'Quite right, Mr Harris. I'm sure that Captain Only will approve.'

'Any news, sir? Have you looked at his orders? It may be he planned something with the Marines and it's their fault they're not with him.'

'Nothing helpful there, Mr Harris. But I know what he came here do do, and when. We must wait a week.'

8

'Nice to greet us with snow,' said Mr Strand, looking out over the market square in Bruges. 'Give my hot Brazilian blood a treat.'

'I claim you are Brazilian,' said Richard. 'I hope you can speak some Portuguese. Wouldn't Mexican have been simpler?'

'No, no choice. I haven't been far in Mexico, not as far as Mexico City. But I have been a banker in Rio.'

'You say, "have been". Is that all over? Can you go back?'

'Oh, certainly. I still keep an office there, and a few clerks. I shall move my commission there, and pray for the safety of the republic. I mustn't keep it where Uncle Sam can lay hands on it.'

'If you earn your commission.'

'I've earned it, all right.'

'If you don't find the money, we will have to make up the difference here, Dunscore and myself.'

'Denain?'

'Only a figurehead, to have one on either side of the house.'

'Hm.' Strand was drinking gin and water, Richard only lemonade. 'When this began I thought it was Dunscore was the main mover, being a lord.'

'Lords aren't important. Not nowadays. My father and I started this, a long time ago.'

'What, as soon as the war started?'

'Oh, no, no, no.' If this was the wily Yankee trader, Richard thought, there would be no trouble. 'A long time before that. I met Rakoff just when we started to plan it, in '50. We thought it better that we should not be seen together from then on. The rest is details. We spent enough on this war not to want to waste it now.'

'Spent enough. You mean bribes?'

'Say, lubrication.'

'What? You bought politicians? Or the Tsar?'

'No.'

'Rakoff then?'

'He thinks he's been buying us. He is planning to get his profit out of the loan.'

'Who then?'

'Oh, small fry, embassy clerks, translators, couriers. Not at all difficult to get double meanings turned into single ones, diplomatic prevarication into straight-forward demands, get replies delayed till it looks like rudeness. You can always inflame politicians, if you go through the channels.'

'Then what is the trouble now?'

'Rakoff. He wants too much.'

'His commission?'

'Oh, no, that's all arranged. Even the distribution, so much to the war minister there, so much to the minister for the Imperial Court. And for the Tsar – Rakoff tells me, "the first priority in every financial dealing is the welfare of the Imperial Household". Fancy a British politician saying something like that about little Mrs Coburg. Or about the Pierces, if it were an American.'

'If not his own cut, then what?'

'He has property. Mineral rights. He is doing nothing with them, does not intend to. But I want them. It will cost him nothing. It may later be to his profit, but it is certain to be to mine. Unless he agrees to this, he will find it hard to get the loan arranged. He knows there is no one else who will arrange it, nobody who has the patience. He backed out over it last year. But now the war is becoming serious, and the Tsar has expressed his displeasure. Yet, he is still dragging his feet.'

'So, what?'

'Next week, my sister-in-law arrives. And Rakoff likes large women.'

9

Talleyman came up to the poop, following Fox. Cricklade, who was officer of the watch, was looking over at the knoll where the rifleman had been ten days ago.

'What can you see?'

'Nothing,' said the Mate. 'But I think I can hear something. As far as you can hear anything with that noise from the main deck.'

'Battle of Agincourt on the main deck,' said Talleyman. 'Orton directing. Christmas carols on the lower deck. Chaplain conducting the orchestra.'

'Out there, sir,' said Cricklade, 'I think it's sleigh bells. Fox here heard them first.'

'Sleigh bells, sir, and a rattling of chains, like Marley's ghost. And I thought. . . I thought. . . but it couldn't be.'

'What?'

'I thought, sir, I heard a horse snort. Once, sir, not neigh, but a snuffle the way they do.'

'Your ears are better than ours,' Talleyman told him. 'Mr Cricklade and I have spent too long listening to machinery. Makes you deaf. Early.'

'Going up the top, sir? May be better to see and hear.'

'No Sterling. Once bitten... you're welcome, Mr Cricklade at your own discretion.'

'No, thank you.' The three stood silent, listening. Then Fox said, 'A voice, sir.'

'Yes, there was a voice,' said Talleyman. 'Sounded like the way you coax a horse. And...'

But then the voice again, coming across the ice. Not one voice, but two, shouting in a measured chant, versicle and response. Talleyman threw himself down on the deck, pulling the cadet with him. Cricklade started to duck later, was on the deck before them.

'I don't know Russian,' said Talleyman, 'but I know what that sounded like.'

'Yes,' Cricklade agreed. 'Land or sea. Search! Cast loose! Load! Run out! Prime! Point! Elevate! It's a song with the same tune in any language.' He stood up and offered a hand to Talleyman, who said,

'Now, Mr Fox, be a messenger.'

'Beat to quarters, sir?' asked the cadet, bubbling with excitement.

'No hurry. If he were going to fire, he'd have done it. He's waiting. Can you hear anything?'

'More bells, sir. Further off.'

'Coming this way?'

'Yes, sir.'

'Then there's at least one more gun. If they let off a round, there's no need to sound a bugle. Go down and quietly, very quietly, send up here the crew of the for'ard eight-inch. Just tell Parks, he'll find them. And Captain Fincham, and Mr Wasely. Oh, yes, and we'd better have Mr Longville, or he'll sulk. Then find the Surgeon and the Chaplain and tell them

212

they may have trade. And back with a sharp pocket knife.'

They came up quietly, one by one. Moulton was among the powder men.

'Is he fit enough, sir?' Cricklade asked.

'Would you want to be below in action?' Talleyman asked. 'Here, Parks, listen to the gunnery officer.'

'Shrapnel, Parks. The target is the hollow of the knoll, where the rifleman was that first day. Can you make it out well enough?'

'Needed two degrees elevation,' said Parks. 'So with shrapnel, another two and a half degrees, sir?'

'Make it a five-pound charge, and cut the fuse. . . I suppose as close as this, we need, let's see. About two inches.'

'They'll come up set to four inch, twenty seconds, and Number Two will cut them. Load with the port down, sir?'

'Yes. By the sounds, he'll have a gun or two over there on the knoll, and we want to open on him before he unmasks. When you hear my whistle, run out and fire. We have another weapon up our sleeve.'

'You heard all that, Mr Wasely?' asked Talleyman.

'Aye, 'tis the wrath of the Lord we must bring on them, and break their souls with a light beyond the day. If the gun will fire on your second whistle, the first one will let my man send up the rocket.'

Talleyman peered into the flickering light of the Aurora. There were moving shadows. . . mere flickering or moving men? The Marine officer came to the poop. Longville came, somewhat grudgingly, and got up into the main shrouds. The Chaplain came on to the poop, too. He doesn't like being below when we're firing, Talleyman thought, but his place *is* below with the Surgeon, I must say something to him about that. Now, forward to that eight-inch, keep an eye on Cricklade, see that everything goes off well. A little voice reminded him that there he would be well hidden by the bulwark, but he stifled that. Fox and Fincham came with him. Only Dincombe remained on the poop.

'We'd do better,' said Cricklade, 'with a bit of light. Handling shell and cutting fuses in the dark isn't what I enjoy.'

'Calm yourself,' said Talleyman. 'I've just sent Fox to Craddock. As soon as the first round goes off, he's going to throw back the boiler room hatch covers. That'll give us some light.'

'Make us a better target,' said Fincham.

'How are you going to hide a ship?' Talleyman asked.

'If we're all ready, then, sir?' Cricklade was asking for permission to fire. From the hillside they could hear the shouting of orders, the jingling of the harness bells, the casting off of the trace chains.

'All right,' said Talleyman. 'Catch them while they're still taking aim. Up ports, then.' He held up his hand. Cricklade blew his whistle once. The port cover came up as the auxiliaries hauled on the lines, and then changed to the gun tackle to run out the gun. Parks was kneeling at the rear of the gun, his weight on his left foot, leaning over as he pulled the lanyard. The hammer of the lock fell on the copper cap at the head of the primer. The powder fired, Parks leapt aside as the gun came back on its carriage.

'Stop your vents!' Cricklade shouted.

Parks replied,

'Well! Sponge!' And then there was another shout from aft.

Dincombe had come on to the poop, as far as he could get from the Surgeon's place of bloody business. He came astern to the very taffrail, and shrank back against the stepping of the jack staff. He looked forward, where the Aurora flickered on the hummocked ice, and the sailors stood around the rocket mount and the gun. He saw Talleyman's hand raised and brought down, heard Cricklade's whistle. The rocket burst over the hillock, and there was a second whistle. He saw

Parks pull the lanyard and leap back to one side, returning as the gun slid to a stop to clap his thumb over the touchhole of the lock. Moulton was ready with another shell while the first was in the air, tearing the sealing strip from the fuse. Dincombe felt, no, no, he could not watch men killed again, he could not see bloodshed. Why had he ever come? He turned his head away to starboard. And he saw the shapes in the mizen shrouds.

A whole stream of images swept through his mind. He saw the blood and confusion that must come, he shrank from the clash of steel, and these men had steel, they came with swords in their hands, he heard the click of pistols being cocked. Half his mind told him that a man of God had no place in a pitched fight, hand to hand. But the men forward were his friends. And his hands were empty. There was no solution in trying to jump over the side, in swinging himself up on the bulwark. But a strange memory came to him, a tale of bishops going to war but carrying a mace so that they should not shed blood.

There was a row of belaying pins in their rack at the foot of the jack staff. Longville's voice rang in his ear, 'They're not for hitting people with: let Mr Harris see you damaging one of those pins and you'll be in trouble.'

The first man into the ship stood with his back to Dincombe, counting the rest over. The first men up were already going down the accommodation ladder to the starboard side of the upper deck. Dincombe fumbled for a belaying pin. He shouted. Shouted anything: 'Help! Fire! Russians!'

Dincombe ran at the nearest of the invaders. The man turned, raised his arm. Dincombe saw the pistol coming up. He swung the belaying pin with all his might. He heard the arm crack. The pistol went skittering across the deck. He did not wait to pick it up. He had heard the other man cry out. In pain? In

215

surprise? It did not matter. Dincombe was on the port accommodation ladder. He went down with his arms taking his weight. He had seen the sailors doing this, had not tried it before, was surprised how sensible the method seemed. The after eight-inch fired again.

Dincombe reached the upper deck at the same time as the Russian. It must be a Russian. Longville was coming up the after companionway. He went for the Russian bare-handed, was pushed aside. He recovered, stood to block the way into the chartroom, pulled a pistol from his peajacket pocket, and fired once at the Russian. The smoke from the gun rolled back over them.

'Don't shoot into the brown,' Longville shouted. Men were coming up the after companionway, with pistols, cutlasses, axes, even stokers' shovels. Longville got some kind of control.

'Master-at-arms, take ten men on to the poop! Never mind about stations, just take them and hold it. After eight-inch crew – get in to your gun. Hold the stern windows. Corporal Egan, take ten more men on to the poop. Shoot anybody who goes over the side. Let the sailors hold the taffrail. Sergeant Madden: make two sections, one down either side of the ship. Bayonets. Don't load.'

For'ard, Talleyman heard the Chaplain's shout as the boiler room hatch was thrown back. He looked astern, and in the glow of the fires, he saw men, too many men, men in furs, coming down off the poop. Then the smoke swirled about him, reflecting the glow of the furnaces, making a fog in which he could not see the width of the ship. He fumbled for his pistol. The enemy were already about him, pushing aside the men of his own crew already coming up the fore hatch. Moulton was on his knees, fumbling with the third shell.

Talleyman saw Moulton tear the strip from the fuse as someone kicked him in the back. The powder man fell forward, and one of the strangers clutched at the shell. Talleyman pushed forward. There was the flash

216

of a pistol, close to the shell, and the bullet went past Talleyman's ear.

A shell, thought Talleyman, with the fuse lit. The pistol fired to light the fuse from the pan. The boiler room hatch open, not ten feet away. Even a shrapnel's shell down there, and we won't steam her again. On deck, it'll sweep us all away. Shoot and it'll be kicked around till it goes off. Fuse not cut – maximum timing. Twenty seconds.

He dropped his revolver, leapt forward. He snatched at the shell, with its smoking fuse. The other man held on to it. Parks slammed the long handle of the rammer under Talleyman's arm, into the stranger's stomach. Awkwardly, not hard enough to do real harm, but the grip on the shell relaxed a moment. Talleyman had it. Half a hundredweight of death. Twenty seconds, and half gone. Talleyman sensed, did not see or hear, Parks behind him. The way was for a moment clear to the side of the ship. He had never thought half a hundredweight was so heavy. He held the shell in both hands, bent his elbow to bring his right hand close to the shoulder. Then he did not throw, he pushed the shell forward and up as he let go with his left hand. He'd put the shell like a shot. Well, it was a shot, wasn't it?

For a moment Talleyman thought he could not clear the top of the six-foot bulwark. But it did, curving up in an arc which would take it on to the ice, clear, if not far clear, of the ship's side.

'Down!' Talleyman shouted, ducking himself, even while he thought it stupid, that he would be well enough protected by the stout timbers. He waited for the explosion, waited, it seemed for hours, for at least as long as he had carried the live shell, breathed the smoke of the fuse into his nostrils. Then from over the side there came not a bang but a crackle. The heavy shot had gone through the ice.

Others had seen what he had done, had heard the ice break even over the noise of the fight. A voice shouted

217

something in Russian. The invaders clustered together, retreated in a group into the port forechains. Over the side they went, leaping down on to the ice, moving among the hummocks and dodging in the shadows that still flickered in the Aurora. The Minié rifles on the poop began to open up, but the targets were elusive.

'Stop wasting powder,' Talleyman ordered. He leaned against the eight-inch gun, his shoulder aching. Now for the mopping up.

'Eight-inch crew, stand fast! All seamen clear the deck! Marines. . .' He looked enquiringly at Fincham.

'Sergeant Madden! Hold the poop. Other Marines, to me.' Fincham stood on the gun carriage, the Marines closed up on him. Talleyman told them,

'Sweep the deck. We don't want anyone hiding in the ship.' He had himself slammed shut the forehatch when he had seen the Russians. 'At least Longville knows what to do. He's at the after companion looking in every face.' The Marines formed up in a double line of steel points, from one side of the ship to the other. There were a couple of bundles of furs lying on the deck. The nearest of them, Talleyman saw, was Moulton. Bending over him, unexpectedly, was Nussey. As the redcoats moved very steadily, step by cadenced step, Talleyman followed to stand over Moulton.

'Is he bad?'

Moulton groaned,

'My back, my back. Has he killed me?'

Nussey held a small pewter pot, a quarter pint, to Moulton's lips.

'Drink this, it's best wardroom brandy, that'll put life into you.'

'Don't dare give that man brandy till the Surgeon's seen him,' Talleyman snapped. Moulton answered, snatching at the mug,

'You cannot deny a dying man his last request.'

Talleyman straightened, his voice full of fury.

'I ought to give you vinegar. I ought to kick you in the kidneys till the blood runs. I ought to break every rib you have. I ought to have the hide flogged off your back. I ought to. . . I probably will. You nearly killed us all.'

'That Ruskie's nearly killed me.'

'Have you no sense? Have we taught you so ill? What do you mean by that? Stripping a fuse seal behind the gun? Sitting there with a shell to be let off by anyone with a match? I'll have you for this! I'll make you remember the ice for ever! I'll – '

Moulton leaned forward, vomited on the deck and fainted. Nussey looked up at the officer and said,

''e won't be no good till the morning, sir.'

There was a shout from forward. Then a shot. Talleyman ran past where Bayford and Silverwright were bent over another man, to where Fincham stood with his pistol smoking in his hand. There was a man dead on the deck.

'Lying doggo?' Talleyman asked. 'You should not have killed him. He might have told us something.'

'Like that?' asked Fincham. He turned the Russian over on to his back. The man's stomach was ripped up. The regulation issue cutlass, thought Talleyman, cheap and effective. 'An act of mercy,' Fincham added. 'Carry on the sweep.'

Talleyman went into the sick bay. He asked Thacker,

'How many?'

'Not bad,' the Surgeon answered. 'Mundell and Toller, sword cuts. Tebbs, broken upper arm. And Moulton. Perhaps he ought to sling his hammock here permanently.'

'Is he bad?'

'Not really. He's been rammed with a blunt instrument – '

'Kicked. I saw it.'

'Yes, that may be it. But in the side, two or three times, two broken ribs. If he'd been kicked in the

219

back he'd have a pair of bad kidneys. Perhaps even the spleen ruptured, and that you can't sew up. Too spongy.'

'Is he conscious?'

'Just about.'

'Then keep him fit to be flogged.' Talleyman hoped he sounded fierce and frightening. Thacker changed the subject. 'And the Chaplain looks sick as a dog.'

'At the sight of blood?'

'Not really. Just emotion. He'd never hit anybody really hard before, and that to save his life. He looked at Tebbs and realized what he may have done to a Russian.'

'He'll learn,' said Talleyman. 'He'll learn. What's the time? Look, I want all officers, the warrants as well, in the wardroom in half an hour.'

10

Talleyman looked round the officers in the wardroom.

'So we're all here, except Mr Neve. Good. Now – '

'Before you start,' said Fincham, 'I think this is yours. Deane and Adams.'

'Thank you.'

'Found it on the poop, sweeping up. How did it get there?'

'It was brought on board,' said Talleyman. 'It's been well kept. But it's not mine.'

'You've got the only Deane and Adams on board,' said Fincham.

'Still not mine. I dropped mine forward. It has my name on it. Engraved on the frame, just over the cylinder. Look at this.'

'So he's still here,' said Cricklade. They all craned to

see the octagonal star, with the forked ends to the two upper rays. Under it a Capital 'P'.

'If he is the same man,' said Talleyman, 'then he's dunned us twice.'

'I think,' said Dincombe, 'that it was the pistol the first man had. I knocked it down with a belaying pin.'

'I'll forgive you,' said the Bo'sun. He smiled and broke the tension. Dincombe caught at courage, and went on,

'He was the first man up. Then he stood back, looking for'ard, and motioned the others up, one by one. He was counting them, waving his hand. I went forward myself and hit him. He was surprised, and shouted. He dropped his pistol and ran after the others. He was holding his right forearm with his left hand.'

'There was a man killed,' said Talleyman. 'Did you search him?'

'He was in furs,' said Fincham. 'Under them he had a green tunic, riding breeches, high boots. All very ragged and worn. And he was lousy. No papers or anything else in his pockets. And nobody had hit him on the arm. There wasn't a mark.'

'What uniform?' Talleyman asked. 'Know it, Orton?'

'Not in my father's notes, but I know it. He was, or had been sometime, in a Guards cavalry regiment. I don't know which one. And not an officer, I think a sergeant.'

'How was he killed?'

'Private Foley put a bayonet into him when he was trying to spike number four port thirty-two-pounder.'

'And now?'

'We brought Orton out to look at him, and then we dropped him into the hole in the ice, the one where your eight-inch went in.'

'This pistol threw me. I knew before we came in what I wanted to ask. Mr Harris, was there much damage?'

'A good deal, sir. They came down that deck at a run, just hacking about them. There's three shrouds to be spliced, and a few halliards and other ropes. Someone had a go at the mainstay. Big hole in the bottom of the gig.'

'Three guns spiked, or they tried to,' said Cricklade.

'So they came,' said Talleyman, 'knowing what they had to do.'

'The shell,' Cricklade suggested, 'was a bonus?'

'Not entirely. They were ready for it. But the guns. . . Mr Wasely?'

'The power of the Lord fought against them, and the work of the devil is botched as it always is. We have cleared two guns, and my armourers are at work on the third.'

Talleyman shook himself mentally. This was untidy, all the information coming in piecemeal, he had lost control. Fincham got his oar in again,

'We can now muster eight pairs of snowshoes. Sergeant Madden has taken seven marines off to where the noise of the horses came from. We may have hit some of them.'

'There'll be nothing there,' said Talleyman. 'Face it, gentlemen, he's conned us again.'

'The same man?' asked Orton.

'Our mysterious Mr P. I think it must be. He drew us all to look one way, and then attacked us from another. He out-thinks us. He'd have had us, half a dozen of them against two hundred of us, if it hadn't been for the Chaplain. Now, what's he trying to do?'

'Wear us out,' offered Orton. 'He wants to keep us stood to all night and day, keep a lot of men out in the cold, frighten us. So what he wants us to do, we don't do.'

'We'll do some of it,' said Talleyman. He wanted to shout, to storm, to demand why there had been no one looking out over the ice. Someone ought to have been looking out all round, someone ought to have

222

been posted where he could have seen these Russians coming up on the disengaged side. But what he could not forget was that he had been there himself, that he ought to have kept an eye, or someone's eye, on the rest of the world. He had concentrated all his attention on the target, he had never looked the other way.

He looked round the officers. Cricklade was all right, he had had a couple of years of Pentstemon, the man who had never been known to give a definite order. He would think ahead. He worked well with Wasely, they had never lacked for ammunition, and always the right ammunition before it was called for. Fincham would behave as if he were on a field day, with his eye open always for anyone who forgot his part: but Fincham could not split his attention, not with his raw Marines. Neve was stuck in the Longville mode. Each of them had already been spoiled by some Captain who had taught them to be more afraid of him than of an enemy, taught them never to act without a direct order. All right, then, give them direct orders. If only Orton were fit enough to stand a watch. He confessed to the assembly,

'We have all been at fault. There is a man out there who is dangerous. He thinks he can deceive us when he likes. He has traded on our inattention. If he does it again, he must suffer. Mr Longville, you are doing the duties of a First Lieutenant. Your main duty is to see that what the Captain forgets is done. Do that in regards to lookout. Show me what you have done at my morning rounds tomorrow. Next – '

There was a timid knock at the wardroom door, and Fox came in.

'Please Mr Talleyman sir, the Marine. . . Sergeant Madden is back and says he has something to say. He doesn't know if it's you or Captain Fincham he ought to speak to.'

'Bring him in,' snapped Talleyman. 'He can tell us all.'

Madden came in with a clank and a tinkle. He held up for all to see a length of trace leather with bells hanging from it, a yard or so of chain.

'That's all we found, sir.'

'Very good, Sergeant. Nussey, find the sergeant a double tot of brandy.'

'Thank you, sir. We got to the shore and we went up a bit, to the top of the rise where the shells busted. No cannon there, sir, no dead men, not even any horse droppings. Nothing. Only these.' He downed the brandy. He had not been in here before. There were always tales about the luxury officers live in in big ships, but this bare cabin, he wouldn't have put a pig in it at home. He had done much better in the box where he and the Master-at-arms slung their hammocks.

'No tracks?' asked Fincham.

'Some, sir. It looked like there'd been one man up to the ridge, did a bit of trotting around up there, and then went down again. Don't think he was hit, sir, tracks going away looked as good as those coming.'

'That's a very valuable observation, Sergeant. You weren't shot at?'

'No, sir.'

'Saw no one?'

'Quiet as the grave, sir.'

'Good. Then get yourself and your party into dry clothes and warmed up in the boiler room.'

'Yes, sir.'

'What's the condition on deck, Mr Cricklade?'

'All gun crews closed up and ready, sir. Shall I stand them down?'

'They won't come back while they think we're awake. Keep four guns manned, stand down the rest. Mr Longville! Make arrangements. Besides the lookouts, I want the duty part of the watch on deck always ready to go on deck. I want every man to have a cutlass and pistol ready. I want that part of watch always to provide crews for one section of thirty-two-pounders. Gun working

224

numbers and auxiliaries. Always two pairs of guns loaded, locks and sights in place.'

'The powder won't keep,' objected Wasely.

'The First Lieutenant will see that the guns are fired at random, singly, so that the powder is changed in each one every... twenty-four hours, you think, Gunner? Good.'

'Tomorrow, sir,' said Biddell, 'is the twenty-fifth of December.'

'I am aware of that. First Lieutenant will see that all duty men for morning watch tomorrow are Roman Catholics. Clear main deck by five bells in the morning watch. Seamen's breakfast will be half an hour late. Mr Dincombe will administer the Sacrament at five bells.'

11

On the Thursday after Epiphany, Talleyman dined in the wardroom. He had done this every Thursday since Only had gone and he had moved himself up into the Captain's sleeping cabin in the poop. He visits us as an act of grace and a show of his own good favour, thought Dincombe. How does advancement change a man. Would I behave like this were I to became a bishop or an archdeacon, a dean even? Yet it is not a deference Talleyman assumes from us, it is a deference we all give him, as Captain. In our minds already he is Captain, Only is forgotten. But if he were to come out of the snow again, would Talleyman be diminished in our minds?

He has been still and strange these last weeks, hardly speaking to anyone, even when he comes to dinner in the wardroom. Most of the time he hovers in the chartroom, looming over Longville as if he does not trust Longville to look after a still ship, wedged into the ice. This is the first time I have heard him even begin to talk as he used to, he's even starting to tell one of his outrageous stories of the way the world works. The port had gone round, the Chaplain had, as vice-president for the evening, proposed the toast of the Queen, had heard echoing in his own mind the bidding words, *over all causes and over all persons within her dominions supreme.* In this little kingdom the Captain was supreme, a true Sir Oracle, superimposed himself on the little noises.

The timbers creaked, easing themselves into each other. The ice scraped audibly against the sides, just below the rubbing strake. Burbling, rattling sounds, rattle of rakes and shovels, from where both boilers were kept, at best, warm enough not to freeze. A hum of talk from the two mess decks as the hands took their supper, hot cocoa from a kettle in the galley and the unused part of each mess's biscuit and cheese and beef for the day.

But the sound here, that was more like it, cheering at last after these gloomy weeks locked in the ice. A monotony of outlook, a monotony of routine, a long chain of hard work, by Dincombe and Biddell and Orton, trying to make each day different. There were the theatricals. *Macbeth* they had staged, easy, from Orton's pocket edition. *Julius Caesar* next, another one with few women's parts, and no romance.

Now Talleyman had a familiar look in his eyes, something they had not seen since Only had. . . gone. He was on the brink of one of his dreadful fabrications. It had started when Orton had said,

'Cricklade has shot just about everything that flies, now. Can't we persuade him to go after seal?'

'Or walrus,' Biddell had added.

'He might,' said Talleyman, 'shoot the famous red-tusked walrus, if it exists. It would be an important product of these regions.'

226

'There's no red-tusked walrus,' said Biddell. 'At least not in the inventory.'

'There was a red-tusked elephant,' said Talleyman. 'Orton's family put paid to that.'

'My family? How?'

'Your grandfather – I thought this would have been part of your family history. Now you must know that if you go into any mess or club or hotel in India, you will find a billiard room. None of these existed fifty years ago. It was Grandfather Orton who took the game out there He was a famous player in London, There were at the time only half a dozen tables. One was in Lord Denain's house. Old Mr Orton, when young, was often received there. I had the tale from old Lord Denain, who knew him well. When he went out to India, and went to that city, what's it's name? – '

'Bunkumpore,' Orton contributed.

'What? Oh, yes, there. He hired a number of Indians. One he taught to make billiard tables. Another he taught to cut and carve the slate beds. One learnt how to weave green baize. One was a fisherman and made nets for the pockets. One made cues. But his difficulty was with his balls. White balls, of course, were made from the tusks of the common white-tusked elephant. Mr Collector Orton it was who located a few specimens of the red-tusked elephant, even then rare. He shot one to make him the single red ball to go with his white balls. However, to give employment to the Indians he had trained, he encouraged them to go about selling their tables to messes and clubs. But they found it impossible to find balls fit for the Sahibs. In every mess there were men who went out to shoot elephants to make the billiard balls. If someone invents a new game, there would he hard times for the even rarer yellow, green, blue, brown, pink and black-tusked elephants.'

Amid the laughter, Dincombe was aware that the human noises from forward had changed their pitch, their rhythm. Orton was saying,

'I suspect that it's true of my grandfather, but I'm sure there are no green or black-tusked elephants.'

'Oh, but there are. The black-tusked elephants are very bad-tempered. They have constant toothache. I was hunting the black-tusked elephant in Timbuktoo once; it's how I broke my nose. I – '

Silverwright was in the wardroom, saying to Fincham,

'It's Sergeant Madden, sir, Sergeant Madden, he wants a word with you, sir, or the Captain. It's all very distressing.'

Fincham got up. Talleyman called from the after end of the table,

'No, Silverwright, bring the Sergeant in. And pour him a glass of brandy. Put it on my book.'

Madden seemed somewhat taken aback by this reception. He messed with the Master-at-arms and the other chiefs, and he had told them before, I never believed it before, and it wasn't like that in any other ship I been in, but they live in there like naked Indians wrapped in their blankets. But their brandy was good stuff, and he drank the Queen when old Tal told him to. They live hard, but they drink well. And eat. He told them,

'It's Marine Garvey, sir.' Madden was paying respect to Talleyman, but it was Fincham he was talking to. 'He's gone.'

'Gone? You mean he's deserted?'

'No, sir. He's gone mad. It's the ice, sir, and the quiet, and the nothing to do, sir. The whalers' men, they say it's not unusual up here if a ship gets caught in the ice.'

'Where is he?' asked Fincham.

'Well, sir, he was due for his turn to go sentry at the lifebelt, sir, and he threw his tunic in my face, and he took his rifle and his pouch and said he was going to go for the man who did for O'Brien.'

'For who?'

'For Mr William Smith Bronterre O'Brien, sir, and that was a name to conjure with not seven years ago.'

'Was he drunk?'

'And where would he get the stuff to be drunk, sir? The spirit locker is in order, for I checked that myself, and the whalers' men they say that it's better he would be if he were drunk for he would sleep it off and be none the worse. But he didn't smell of drink, and he walked straight and his speech wasn't slurred – '

'That man's not drunk,' said Orton aside to the Chaplain, 'I saw his hand move.'

'That's as may be, sir,' said Madden angrily, 'but he's moving himself entirely, and as if there's only one of everything he can see, and he has his rifle and four rounds in his pouch and one down the hole – '

'That means in practice,' said Talleyman, 'he's got one round. Where is he now?'

'He went to the forehatch, sir, but the Master-at-arms was there first, on the deck, and dropped the hatch cover shut on him, and if he'd waited half a second he'd have hit Garvey on the head with it, and then he looked at us all there and shouted, "I've no quarrel with them that didn't do for O'Brien," and other things in the Gaelic that I do not think it would be helping much to repeat. And then he saw one of Mr Craddock's Mates with a shovel in his hand, and so he went into the forepeak where the drummers sleep, sir, and he turned them out and there he is.'

'What have you done? Have you told the officer of the watch?'

'Yes, sir, I told Mr Cricklade, and he said to clear the main deck and I told him that I'd done that, and he told me to come and tell you, sir, and sir.'

'Very well done, Sergeant,' Fincham told him. 'Where have you got the rest of the Marines?'

'I told Corporal Leary to get them fell in, sir, on the poop.'

'I suppose the best thing to do,' said Fincham, 'could be to tempt him to fire off his five rounds and then go in after him.'

229

'And where do the bullets go?' Talleyman asked him. 'There's a lot of piping coming up into the main deck. There's more if a shot ricochets down to the lower deck. Can't have all the machinery go up. Put that in your book, Fincham. Somebody'll have to go after him. As he is.'

'I was afraid of that,' said Fincham. 'Don't suppose I'd better take my pistol, either. Sword, I suppose, the regular issue cutlass that Only was so fond of? Or something more brutal, a boathook or a long iron rake from the boiler room?'

'It's a bit cramped up there in the forepeak,' said Longville, 'and you're a bit big for the job. I've hooked men out of that kind of space before, Chinese mostly. I'll go.'

'It's my responsibility,' said Madden surprisingly. 'I gave him the order he disobeyed, sir, and it's my place to make him obey it. It's what I always was taught, sir, since I first joined the corps.'

'Well,' said Talleyman, 'you can back me up, Sergeant. Stay well down and behind.'

'You can't go,' said Longville. 'We've had enough already of this "I am the Captain and it's my part to take the risks." We lost Only that way, and we can't afford to lose you, too.'

'I am gratified,' said Talleyman, sounding like enough to Only's voice and style to make the others smile: it was what he intended. 'To find that I am in such demand as a chess player. No. I must go.'

'It is my responsibility,' said Fincham, 'as the only Marine officer on board.'

'No, no,' said Talleyman wearily. 'It is nothing to do with responsibility. Nothing to do with being Captain. Nothing to do with courage. I do not think any of you gentlemen will prove acceptable.'

'Why not?' asked Thacker. 'I'll have to do the patching up in the end, and I'd like to know why.'

Talleyman took off his coat, handed it to Silver-wright.

'This is a personal thing. It is myself he has asked for.' He put a little of a brogue into his voice as best he could. 'Then it is myself he must be getting. For 'twas myself that did for O'Brien. At least I fired at him. I missed, as usual. It was my reputation I had to keep up. So 'tis myself alone he is wanting. This is not an affair of officers and soldiers, eh, Sergeant? Nor an affair of sodgers and sailors. Just a personal affair of me and the Irish.'

'So it is, sir,' said Madden. 'Will you be taking a cutlass, sir? Or a rifle and a bayonet?'

The wardroom door was open now. The Marine sentry was standing at attention and the voices were carrying up the companionway to the seamen on the quarterdeck. Talleyman, in his shirt, the sleeves rolled up, the collar and bow left on the wardroom table, began to move forward.

12

Fox went forward too, close behind Talleyman and the sergeant. Nobody had told him to come, but nobody had told him not to go. It was his turn as Captain's messenger, and he had long learnt that where the Captain went there he must go, an invisible presence no more noticed than the Captain's watch or his glove. So he alone saw all that happened from beginning to end.

They went forward from the wardroom door, along the port wing, between the tangle of small compartments where men worked all day making shoes or pills or grommets, and the coaming of the engine room hatch. When the hatch in the upper deck was open, you

231

could see right down to where the machinery lurked, below the waterline. The draft came down here in a rush of air, forward into the boiler room, sweeping up the funnel by way of the furnaces.

And forward of that, stretching away into the bows, was the great empty space of the upper deck, the mess deck. It was cumbered with mess tables, hammocks, all the disarray of the transition from working day to night. The row of working lamps down each side gave enough light to get by: at lights-out only two or three safety lanterns would be left alight. At the far end, right up in the bows, a frail partition closed off the compartment where the boys slept. There was a door into it from the mess deck. The door was open. Fox looked hard at it, was able in a while to make out something moving in there, could at last recognize that it was a rough grey shirt, warm flannel, and below that the sheen of the bayonet.

They went close, perhaps to twenty feet, before Sergeant Madden noticed Fox. Without a word he reached out and pushed the cadet, not roughly but firmly enough, into a space of dark behind a mess table. He followed Talleyman forward for a couple of paces more. Talleyman stopped, and said loudly,

'Where's the man who wants to speak of O'Brien, the King of the Cabbage Patch?'

A soon as he had spoken, Talleyman knew he had made a mistake, not only a mistake in speaking, but a mistake in coming here forward on the mess deck, in coming into the ice, in ever coming in this dreadful ship at all. A step further and he would be finished with mistakes, would have made the last mistake, would not see the land again, would not see Harriet And there was no point to anything unless it meant he would get back again and see Harriet. But now it was done, he would have to go on.

'And is that yourself, then, Talleyman, that thought himself King of the Widow McCarthy's midden?'

'Oh, that was a long time ago, Garvey, and all dead and forgotten.'

Fox heard it, and he also heard from long ago and far away the first thing Talleyman had told him: 'Remember, remember everything I say and do while you are with me, burn it into your little mind deep enough to last at least an hour so that you can make a report.' Fox was trying to understand talk of things long ago.

'So it's all dead and gone, is it then? And in one way true enough, with the greatest man in Ireland dead and gone with it.'

'Now, don't be exaggerating, Garvey. You know well enough that Mr O'Brien is living in Bermuda, in the Governor's household. In the lap of luxury.'

'But he's gone from us, that was the greatest man is all Ireland, and if he is not dead it is not for the want of yourself trying. Oh, that was a great day for you, and that day I saw him plain, as near as you are now, and I heard Doheny talk, too.'

'I had Mr O'Brien plain, in my sights,' said Talleyman, 'and I could have killed him then. But I did not kill him. Nor the man in the white coat either. And if you spoke to Doheny that day, then it was nowhere near the cabbage patch you were.' One side of his mind said, don't be sidetracked, don't let him get you into an argument: the other side said, talk to him gently, talk, talk, talk him down. The first side of his mind was winning, made him say, 'But you've sworn an oath to the Queen, Garvey, you're not like the seamen, so now keep that oath.'

'What care I for the Queen of England.' answered Garvey. His voice sounded far way, almost unearthly. 'She is a Protestant and oaths to her are void as we all know. But if you like, Talleyman, come you forward and fight for her and for your oath.'

And there was a curious mechanical noise, grating of metal. They all heard it, Talleyman and Madden and Fox, and it took Fox a moment or two to recognize, and then it came to him: Garvey had cocked his musket, had pulled back the hammer to fall on the cap.

It came like a hammer blow itself to Talleyman. He wasn't cocked, he wasn't cocked, we could have jumped at him any time in the last five minutes, it would have taken him a moment to bring up the hammer, one of them could have knocked him off balance, pushed that muzzle out of line. Madden heard it too, and understood it, and cursed himself for being slow. He moved past Talleyman, and murmured,

'Leave him to me, now, sir, I can handle him.'

He stood forward before he could be stopped, came across Talleyman's field of view, and said soothingly,

'Come along now, Martin Garvey, come along now, you know you wouldn't shoot me.'

Garvey shot him.

Fox saw it all, in a vast confusion of sound and movement. There was the flash of the rifle, and the cloud of salty white smoke swirling about them all. The noise of the shot boomed off the bulwarks, or perhaps it was the ricochetting bullet, he couldn't tell. Fox found his face and his jacket wet, splashed with blood, Madden's blood. Through the smoke he saw Talleyman launch himself forward, but not quickly enough, for the bayonet came thrusting forward to meet him. He heard Garvey grunt with the effort of the thrust, as Madden had taught him. There was another noise he never thought to hear, Talleyman squealing in despair and pain. Not to wonder, for in a moment Fox saw the gleam of the bayonet point come through the cloth, somewhere near the armpit. Talleyman was still squealing, no, more like roaring, his two hands up around the fore end, and pulling the musket into himself, against all Garvey's efforts to bring it back through the door. Then it seemed to Fox that intelligence came to Garvey, overcoming rage, terror, whatever emotion it was, and he pushed instead of pulling.

234

Talleyman had been pulling. He was thinking, lucky I'd been moving when he made the thrust, I took it well, not much more than a scratch, I heard the steel grate on the bone, but the point went round the outside of the ribs. Well through. But if I had been a moment quicker, it would have been through my arm, and if slower, there'd have been no going back to Harriet, I'd not have seen the boys grow up. Lucky he put such effort into it as I came forward. It's gone well through, and a good thing too. As long as I can keep my arm hooked over the tangle of gear at the fore end of the muzzle, the foresight, the locking ring, the piling swivel. . . pull on the stock, pull. . . don't think of the pain, think of Harriet, think of this year's barley, think of the two boys. . . God, now he's lunging again.

Talleyman thought he grunted. Fox thought he squealed like a stuck pig. He saw Talleyman's knees bend, saw him come flat on his back on the deck, twisted over by the rigid steel. The twist, obviously, threw Garvey to his right, against the mess table still rigged. Then there was a new flurry of limbs, with the rifle on the deck. Fox dared to leap out of his cover and pull it clear. There was blood on it, blood on Talleyman's shirt, the Sergeant's blood on the deck: Fox was sick at heart.

But Talleyman felt the lunge begin, and thought, I know a trick worth a dozen of that. This man hasn't been on the coast, hasn't wrestled with the Kroomen, hasn't learnt to fight dirty. Talleyman rolled back with the thrust, and felt the breath go out of him with agony as the bayonet point hit the deck. He was twisting to his left with his hands on the forestock, and the rifle came sharply over. He saw that Garvey had lost hold with the hand that was on the small of the butt. There was a tempting target now looming over him. Talleyman thanked God that he never wore pumps with his number ones afloat, that he still had on his seaboots, over his ankle, heavy and nailed. He kicked up into Garvey's crotch. Not a good contact, a Krooman would have laughed it off, boots and all, It unsettled Garvey, no more. He didn't like it, though. He went with it, sideways, against the mess table. That was enough to force the other hand off the stock. Talleyman rolled away.

Now to get rid of this spike. Christ, it's taking an hour to get it out, no, an hour and a half, hurts like hell. There it goes. Drop it. Blood over the deck. Garvey's scattered things, tin mugs, a couple of clasp knives, someone's hussiff. Don't let him get the bayonet again. He's in practice, an hour's drill with it every day. He'll have me skewered proper. But he can't wrestle, neither clean nor dirty.

But Garvey tried dirty. His groin ached, but he came back while Talleyman was still on his knees.

'Aye, kneel to me, ye English bastard, kneel and kiss the toe of my boot.'

The kick was aimed at Talleyman's teeth, but Garvey found his foot caught, twisted till his ankle grated, and even from his knees Talleyman's strength and weight told, pushed him away again against the mess table.

Fox saw Talleyman come again to his feet, blood all over his shirt, some of it his, some of it Sergeant Madden's, he couldn't tell which. He saw the white shirt move in toward the grey. Garvey looked around, desperate, for the rifle. It gave Talleyman a moment to close, to grapple him. One arm was around Garvey's body, pinning Garvey's arm. The other slammed one, two short cruel punches into the Irishman's kidneys. Garvey had one arm free, no room to swing a blow where Talleyman was forcing him back against the bulkhead. He got his free arm up, bent in front of him, and hammered with his forearm against Talleyman's face.

That's my nose again, thought Talleyman. Harriet will have to get used to another face. Think about anything but what you're doing, anything but the pain,

236

anything but the damage you're doing to another human being. The forearm came in again, Talleyman felt the bone grating and the blood running down into his mouth. He spat the blood into Garvey's eyes. He remembered the Krooman, a stoker in the old *Winchester*, who had told him that trick. Garvey ducked away, making vomiting sounds in disgust, and Talleyman's hurt arm couldn't hold him.

Garvey looked around in the dim light for the bayonet, for any kind of weapon. Talleyman was coming at him again, his face bloody and distorted. No time to look for anything, only time to run for the forward companion ladder, time to get his eyes over the level of the coaming, to see the seamen standing round, the hard faces of the Master-at-arms, the Bo'sun, the Captain of Marines. Talleyman's hands caught at his calf, pulled it backwards so that all he could do was slide down the ladder again, and lash out backwards with his heel. He felt contact with something soft, a face or a stomach he did not know. Fox saw it was a stomach, saw Talleyman stagger backward making retching noises. Garvey had time to look for a weapon, but he was too frightened, now, to seize the chance. He went for the ladder, anything up there was better than this nightmare in the candlelight.

The upper deck was lit by the Aurora, fitfully. The hard faces around flickered at him. No one moved. No one spoke.

Garvey wavered towards the foremast fife rail. He thought there he could find something, a belaying pin at least, to defend himself with. But the Bo'sun was before him, his back to the fife rail.

Garvey turned. Talleyman had come to the upper deck. His shirt and his face were smeared with blood. He was coming forward, his eyes vacant, as if he were in a dream. Only three steps, and he was close enough to the Marine to reach out with his good arm and haul the grey shirt close against the white. The other arm

237

was the bad one. He held the upper arm close against his body. He swung his fore arm, pivoting on his elbow, held the first sideways as if it were a hammer, struck blow after blow against the Marine's kidneys as if he were a steam hammer.

Talleyman only knew now he was hammering hard against an enemy. This was someone who would have kept him back from Harriet, someone who would have Ireland up in arms, threatening Harriet. He struck again for Harriet. He hardly felt Garvey's fists on his back, Garvey's knee into his groin. He was even past seeing Garvey's flushed face, the fierce blue eyes, the ginger hair, he could only see that someone was threatening Harriet.

Then the strength went from his arms, and Garvey stopped struggling, stopped hitting, simply tore by his weight from Talleyman's grasp and crumbled to the floor. Talleyman felt the world come back around him, the darkness, the cold, the pain within him, the men around him. Silverwright was there with a fur coat to wrap around him, and then said,

'Your hat, sir, you'll need your hat.'

Talleyman put on his hat. Slowly, he felt himself changing back into an officer, not a man with a ferocity born of fear for himself and for his family. Ferocity born of fear, born of love, he thought. Fincham put an arm round him, and said,

'Better get you back to the Surgeon.' Then, to the Master-at-arms, 'Get that criminal below. Chain locker.'

Biddell looked fresh at Talleyman. He had heard Talleyman boast of having killed his first man when he was in his teens. He had heard tales on the coast of Talleyman and of Pither, too, and Partridge. Partridge was dead. He had found it hard to link those tales with the soft-eyed bustling man, always tied up with the business of the ship as much as Biddell was, always counting in his head men and rations and coal and water.

Talleyman, sweating and expecting the sweat to freeze on him, unable to walk faster because of the shattering pain in his groin and arm, moved aft along the port side of the ship. The seamen who had been cleared out of the mess deck stood on the starboard side, separated from him by the boats on their cradles, the spare spars outside them, then the engine-room hatch gratings and the main mast fife rails. There was a murmur of voices, and then out of the crowd, someone called out,

'Good old Tal!' and someone else shouted,

'Come on, give him a cheer!'

And there was a confused, disordered shouting, loud but more like a crowd at the hustings cheering a candidate. Talleyman waved a dismissive hand. He wanted to tell them to stop, but his mouth was bruised and he could not make the words come. He looked up at the break of the poop. What in God's name had Fincham been thinking of? The rest of the Marines were there, fallen in, rifles at the order. Through his mind went all the tales he had ever heard of mutinies, where the Marines had defended the officers. Was he going to see a new phenomenon, where the seamen defended their officers against the Marines?

Then he heard Corporal Egan's voice,

'Three cheers for the Captain!' And the Marines cheered, in a proper way, the way they had been trained. And Talleyman knew that his ship was safe. He moved to the companionway which went down to the sick bay. And his knees crumpled and he did not remember being helped down the steps.

13

When Talleyman came to, he was in his cot in the Captain's sleeping cabin. He tried for a moment to understand what had happened, and then it all came through his mind in an instant: the bruises did it, he thought. Fox, who had been watching, asked him,

'Shall I get the Surgeon, sir? I said I'd call him.'

Talleyman tried to think of something to break the spell he had, somehow, cast over the cadet that he could see in the lad's eyes.

'I hope you learnt a lesson from that, lad.' He was glad he could make any sound at all, and only knew it was an intelligible noise when Fox answered,

'You mean, sir, never say, "You know you won't shoot me"?'

'No. Don't wear your best shirt for a fight. Call the First Lieutenant. When he can be spared.'

Abel came first, with a mug of hot soup, a jug of water, a bowl for Talleyman to spit into when he rinsed his mouth.

'What time is it?' Talleyman asked.

'Ten o'clock, post meridian,' said Thacker, entering.

'Feels like post mortem,' said Talleyman. 'Which day?'

'I gave you a dose of opium last night, quite a good one, and another when you tried to wake up this morning. You've broken your nose.'

'Again,' said Talleyman.

'Second time?' asked Thacker. He was looking, through the slit in a nightshirt, at the wound in Talleyman's left side.

'Fourth.'

240

'You shouldn't lead with your face.'

'Way I was brought up. When you set it, please. . . set it twisted the other way. Give my wife a change.'

'I've set it straight.'

'Nobody will know me. Garvey. . . ?'

'Not bad. Bruised worse than you, but no real damage, not even to his kidneys. He's tougher than you are, Talleyman, but not as hard. You're a hard man.'

Talleyman wondered where he had heard that expression before. He asked,

'Can I get up?'

'You could. But you'll be better a lot quicker if I give you another dose of opium, and you lie still for twelve hours more. Let things knit.'

Longville was in the cabin, now, looking over Thacker's shoulder.

'I'll keep the ship's routine running, sir,' he said. Talleyman noted that he was wearing his hard round hat again. And he had called Talleyman 'sir'. He had done that before, but always as a conventional response, in a manoeuvre. 'Sir' then would mean an order heard and completed. But now he had called Talleyman 'sir' in conversation. He was, Talleyman realized, the last member of the wardroom to do it. Why? Because he had behaved like the mate of a merchant ship, going in with his fists when he had a Bo'sun and a Master-at-arms to do the job for him? Longville went on,

'What shall we do about Garvey, now?'

'I had a hat like that, once. Last one was in Ireland. Lost it overboard. In a dead calm. In a churchyard.'

'I beg your pardon, sir?'

'Nothing. Quiet. I'm thinking.' A pause, then, 'What would you do?'

'Me? A quick court-martial, and have him to the yard arm by sundown, not that there is much of a sun up or sun down here.'

'No.'

'No, sir?'

241

'I've been thinking it over.' Listen now, will he still call me "sir"? Will he jettison me as indecisive? Will he understand? I am acting as Captain of this ship. I am not *a* Captain by rank. I have no permanence in this position. *The* Captain may return at any moment. He is a Captain by rank.'

'Only's dead.'

'We do not know that. I am merely minding the ship for him. In this position. . . I am not sure of my position. As a Lieutenant, am I legally justified in calling a court-martial? And am I legally entitled to pass a sentence of death? I suspect I am disqualified. After all, I fought with the man. It may be argued I am prejudiced against him. It might be that I too would be court-martialled. Let a Member of Parliament get hold of it, and start asking questions in the House. . . . Fox! Ask Mr Orton to do me the favour of calling on me. Within the next three minutes, if it be convenient.'

Orton came, heard Talleyman's brief. He tried to hide his astonishment. There were enough tales in the Navy about Talleyman, and he had heard them all. Was this the Talleyman who had been on the coast, in Ireland, who always did the first thing, went straight ahead, acted with force and violence, the Talleyman who would drive at once to the heart of the matter? He had done that last night, throwing off hat and coat and taking on the armed madman with his bare hands. And yet. . . Orton was thinking harder about Talleyman than about Garvey. What was the Talleyman fable? After all, it was the man who went straight forward into the dark, into the swamp, and never tripped, never fell. And here he was, still making sure that he would not trip. Orton read it clear. Talleyman wanted to do nothing, wanted support, even advice, to do nothing. And, in addition, the facts determined the advice any sane lawyer would give.

'Do nothing,' Orton advised. 'Hanging is most convenient, stone dead hath no fellow. But not safe. Not if you want a calm and trouble-free life. Hang him, and you will be court-martialled yourself for allowing him to go mad. And for letting Madden get killed. Everything will come out, they will find against you, and every Irishman with a grievance will feel free to kill you. Or any other officer. Take him home and let him be court-martialled. You might prefer to see he is shot attempting to escape. The crew would be pleased enough, and the jaunty would arrange it. I had somebody in my chambers who used to laugh at court-martials. He would say, "If God almighty cannot fix a court, God Almighty is not fit to be a Captain." Don't tell the Chaplain, sir, please.'

'Right. Keep him in the chain locker. Put him up for court-martial when we get back.'

'Shall I tell him that?' asked Longville.

'Certainly not. Tell him nothing. Let him stew. Now, go and look after the ship.'

Orton lingered after Longville had gone.

'May I have a private word, sir?'

'Speak.'

'I have a complaint against the Surgeon.'

'A complaint? Has he been putting rhubarb in your coffee?'

'No, sir. This is serious. He has stolen some of my property.'

'I cannot believe that.'

'I have witnesses. He instructed Silverwright to conceal it from me.'

'What property?'

'My tonic. My stock of Dr Wormset's tonic. Efficacious in all cases of exhaustion and debility. It is true, I rely on it. Without it I cannot work, I cannot. . .I cannot. . . you have seen me, you know I always take my daily dose about mid-morning, I get edgy and bad-tempered if it is late, I'm not fit to live with. And now the sawbones has stolen it, he's hidden it somewhere, he thought I wouldn't know, I've had none today. . . .'

'All right. I'll talk to the Surgeon. It's not your watch. Go back to the wardroom. Get your head down. Fox! Ask the Surgeon to come here again. Tell him I'm dying.'

Who'd be a Captain? Talleyman asked himself. I've nearly been killed. My side's hurting like hell. I have a broken nose. I have a headache like the inside of a boiler. I have to decide whether a man is to be hanged. And now I have to look at a squabble between gentlemen. A storm in a Madeira glass.

'I had to do something,' said Thacker. 'I've had the story out of him, bit by bit. It was all quite harmless at the beginning. He'd been working very hard, and was finding it hard to sleep. Wormset is better known for his social connections, which give him his practice, than for his medical skill, but the tonic is well known. It is supposed to be composed according to a secret formula, handed down in the Wormset family since the days of King James, but I have tasted the version of which Orton brought six months' supply, and I have no doubt of the main ingredient of that. It is a tincture of opium in brandy – probably about half and half by weight.'

'Strong?'

'Almighty. And he was on a very small dose when he came abroad, but, of course, he's been taking bigger and bigger helpings. And the bigger the daily helpings, the more you feel you need it, and the more difficult it gets to take smaller helpings, or to miss a day.'

'An addict?'

'He's approaching the stage where he can't live without a sizable dose every day.'

'You gave me opium last night.'

'A quarter grain – twice. And that is half what he started on. You're only getting opium from me, and I'll see you don't get enough to have an addiction.'

'Shall we tell him?'

244

'I think we'd better, or there'll be bad blood between him and me – between him and all doctors – for a hundred years.'

'Mr Fox! Fox? Oh, Dyke, have you taken over? Please take my compliments to Mr Orton and ask him to come here.' Talleyman smiled and winced because that hurt his face. 'He'll probably say, "Sir, Old Tal wants you." So long as I don't hear it. . .Ah, Mr Orton, How good of you to come back. Please sit down. . .there. And stay seated till I tell you to go. And the same to you, Mr Thacker. Let the Surgeon speak first.'

'That's better,' said Orton brightly, although Talleyman could see that he was biting his lip half the time, and that his hands were shaking. 'Have it like a court, with proper long statements, and you to be the judge. Biddell will be my second, if it comes to a gentleman's affair.'

'Quiet. Listen to your – our – medical adviser.'

I could have done without this, thought Talleyman. My head aches, I suppose that's the opium. It hurts to talk, and I have to breathe through my mouth. I have a foul taste there, blood and mucus trickling down my throat. My left arm strapped to my side as far down as the elbow, and my rib cage aching, part bruise, part carbolic acid. Did he bath me in it? My crotch aching, my privates black and blue and swollen. . .and with all that I have to command the ship, hold figures in my head, soothe hurt feelings, deal with opium fiends. . .Thacker has finished. Orton is sitting still, looking at him. Will he ever speak?

'So Dr Wormset has turned me into a drug addict? For the whole of my life? What ought I to do?'

'Well, that's up to you. Many well-known figures in society are similarly dependent. Have been for many years, and you can get laudanum easily enough at any druggists. And you mustn't blame Dr Wormset. This is a standard treatment for the condition you described, over-fatigue and worry and uncertainty. Of course, you know that the immediate effect of a dose is calming, a general feeling of well-being, and that this wears off with time, so that before your habitual time for a dose you seem – what shall I say? – crabby. You may find it more convenient to take smaller doses several times a day, to reduce these oscillations in mood.'

'You mean that my moods, my thoughts, will always depend on my taking the tonic?'

'On taking opium, yes. You'll probably have noticed other symptoms, too. You haven't much of an appetite. At luncheon, you are usually content with some coffee. Silverwright knows better than to serve you large helpings of anything. You are constipated – how often do you go to the heads? You have indigestion, often, do you not?'

'And that all my life?'

'As long as you keep on taking opium.'

'I can't live like that. I can't walk out of court, or out of a meeting, in the middle of proceedings, because I must take my opium.'

'Oh, it's no worse than having consumption, and going out for a coughing fit. Many people have led useful lives for some years with consumption. You probably have a rather better expectation of life than if you had consumption.'

'Consumption?' Orton was silent for a while. Then, 'I will take no more of the tonic.'

'That's difficult.'

'Life is difficult.'

'It might be easier to taper it off, gradually reduce the daily dose.'

'If I were a seaman, what would you advise?'

'I'm not here to advise seamen, I'm here to cure them. I'd have you in the chain locker for three weeks.'

'I will abstain.'

'If you chose that course on shore, I would advise that you commit yourself to an institution where you could spend the period under close medical supervision.'

'So that I could not get any more by cheating? Do you think I will find it easy to get more opium in this wardroom, at sea, and surrounded by friends and servants who will try to prevent me? There is no secrecy in a matchboard mansion like ours.'

He went. Thacker turned to Talleyman.

'Well, I'm taking him off the opium, but I'm putting you on it. Take this. I want you still again now for at least another twelve hours, without you trying to move your left arm and opening that stab again, and without you talking and trying to blow that nose, not now I've set it straight again. I wonder who it was botched you up last time? You need your rest, because we'll be having a hard time in the wardroom for the next six weeks. He'll be pitying himself first, and crying for himself, and after that he'll be crying for laudanum, and looking for it, and begging you and me for it, and bullying the stewards, and bribing my dressers, and trying his skill at burglary and lock-picking.'

But Talleyman was past hearing. Talleyman was far away. He was in his new-drained forty acres, in the drying peat. He was moving steadily down the row, turning over the potatoes and watching the busy hands picking them up. Harriet's hands.

14

Talleyman was sitting in the Captain's day cabin, trying to read by a candle in a lantern. Abel had made him up a fire in a stove, but he was still cold, cold through to his bones. They would be warmer in the wardroom, all together. He wished that this man Elliot was a little less stiff. Strange, he only read in moments of enforced inaction. He had read at least five novels at Eyories, when he was getting better from the typhoid. Pritchard, the duty cadet, came to call him. He felt annoyed. He wished it were Abel with his lunch, hot soup and a couple of biscuits.

Mr Longville's compliments, and would you please come on deck, sir.'

Talleyman moved stiffly. The bruises were nearly all gone, but his arm still ached when the cold got at it. He still did not dare put a strain on it, in case the cut came open. He huddled himself into his fur coat, and pulled his hood up over his peaked cap. He felt in his pocket for his – no, it was someone else's Deane and Adams.

'On the poop, sir,' said Pritchard. Longville leaned on the taffrail, his hood turned up over his top hat. Talleyman asked him,

'Can you hear something?'

'No.'

'Or see anything? The lookouts? You have a man up in the maintop?'

'He hasn't *seen* anything yet.'

'Then why?'

'Wait for a breath of air. The windy's very light, but gusting a little. Here we come.'

Talleyman felt the wind on his cheek. He pushed back his hood from his ears, to listen, but he heard nothing but the soughing of the wind across the ice.

'No,' said Longville. 'Don't listen. Sniff!'

'Sniff?' But Talleyman did. He sensed something, tasted something, but it was incredible. No one could smell that here. There were all the smells he expected, men and food and oil and damp steam. But there was something else. He looked again at Longville.

'I was sniffing for a wind, or a thaw, or something. And there it was.'

'Horses. At least, horse manure.'

'For us to smell it at any distance, there must be a lot of horses.'

248

'Anyone can shout orders and rattle chains, but you can't have that smell without horses.'

He was right, thought Talleyman. Even an ignorant opinionated man could be right sometimes.

'How long before we have real light? Ten minutes? Plenty of time. Mr Pritchard. Go and find Mr Cricklade. And Mr Wasely. Send up the duty gun crews. Very quietly.'

Cricklade came up, sniffed as he was told.

'It can't be.'

'The French did it at the Texel, in ninety-two I think. Captured the whole Dutch navy.'

'It's still stupid,' said Longville. 'It's another trick.'

'It's not stupid,' said Fincham. 'The snow's frozen deep, now. We don't need snowshoes any more. I think that the horses will manage it. Now, look at it this way. They're about three-quarters of a mile away, over the ridge in the dead ground. There's no cover, and they have to get over the ground as quick as possible, not to surprise but to avoid our fire. Yes, if I had horses, I think I'd try a charge too. This isn't the calibre of the man we had before, and not a gunner. We need range markers. If we choose carefully we can get two broadsides in before they get near us. Do you agree, Cricklade?'

'Markers at, say, three hundred yards and five hundred?'

Beat to quarters,' Talleyman ordered. 'Don't load, Cricklade, till you have made your mind up.'

'Made it up,' said Cricklade. He called to the gun captains as they came on deck. 'Six-pound charge, double shot with grape and shot. Number one gun, elevation one half-degree; number two, elevation one degree. All others elevation one degree. When I blow my whistle, numbers one and two only to fire, reload and elevate to one degree. When I blow two blasts, fire a broadside and relay at one half a degree. When I blow again, fire broadside.'

The deck was full of armed men. Half the Marines were serving a pair of guns, one on each broadside. The rest were on the poop. Talleyman went to the engine room hatch, shouted down,

'Craddock! Bring your people on deck, with cutlasses. We're going to batten down.' That would mean no way below for any boarders: no way to the deck for those caught below. The Chaplain was on deck. Can't stand being locked up, Talleyman reflected. And he's got a cutlass. He said he'd done some fencing. Sabre, I hope. No point in my staying here. He pushed down between the guns, and swung up into the main shrouds on the disengaged side. There was a good view here, and he was fairly well hidden. Should he stay or should he go further? Up into the top, thought Talleyman, let the men see me.

In the maintop, he looked down at the deck. For'ard, thirty sweating, cursing men were bringing the eight-inch to the starboard broadside. With the usual four-teen men it would take five minutes: this crowd looked to be doing it in three. He checked the officers com-manding the sections of guns, each with two guns a broadside. Fully manned, this would be a midshipman's job: now there were Biddell, Neve, Orton sitting on a chair, and... oh, yes, Fox with Cricklade's hand on his shoulder. Pritchard was at the skylight over the Captain's day cabin, in nominal control of the after eight-inch, watching Talleyman's hand.

The youngest cadet, Dyke, was under the break of the poop with Longville and the Bo'sun. The fourth, Chessil, was battened down with the Gunner, and the Carpenter with his mates somewhere in the wing pas-sages of the orlop. There were the stokers, but Crad-dock must still be down there, with his artificers. A shot in the boilers, or even a burst pipe drenching everyone with scalding steam, perhaps they could do something.

The forward half of the Bo'sun's damage party, under the Master-at-arms, had left the handling tackles and hand-spikes of the eight-inch. The ship was still, now, and quiet. Talleyman remembered what he was there for, and looked round. There was nothing moving on the ice, or in the village. Nothing on the hillock. A gun there would be terrifying, but there was no movement. Smales was in the foretop, he was watching that side, did not move even when, far away, Talleyman heard a bugle.

Talleyman watched the ridge. Now, surely they were coming. It was light enough to see, little enough to gallop a horse and pick one's way between potholes at speed. In a moment – merciful Christ, how many, how many? They came out of the dead ground, seemed to fill the whole front from horizon to horizon. Ten thousand? Twenty? He made himself think, some witnesses swore there were forty thousand at the Cabbage Patch, some four. It had been more like four hundred, and even then not more than a dozen who mattered. He called down,

'Now, Mr Cricklade!'

Numbers one and two fired together. The billowing smoke would hide the attack from the men peering through the ports. The two shots fell into the snow, well short of the advancing line. They splashed, throwing up clouds of ice, marking the ranges. Perhaps the Russians thought it was a miss, and it had encouraged them. Talleyman set himself to counting. Horsemen, five feet apart. How wide the front? Estimate, count, multiply, divide, work it out. No, about four hundred. And how many were important? There was a group in front, the long line behind them. They were all coming down the slope at a deliberate trot. Why?

Talleyman looked around the horizon. Still all clear. Smales still watching. Now to snap open the telescope, to invite the rifle shot. But nothing came. Ah, that was why they were coming on so slowly. There were men on foot coming forward with the cavalry, either infantry or men who had lost their horses. Put the number up by about another half. Twice as many, three times, as we are.

The leaders were about ten yards short of the outer marker. Talleyman shouted,

'Now, Mr Cricklade!'

The whistle blew twice. The broadside went off, Talleyman noted with his professional mind, very well together. The cavalry coming up to the marker took it badly. There seemed a hole, almost, blown in the middle of the line. The flanks seemed almost untouched. Talleyman signalled to Cricklade to spread the volley and, he saw the Mate shouting at the hand-spike men of two guns to train a degree left, a degree right. The crews were working to reload, to run out again. Men were throwing off their fur coats.

Talleyman flung out his arm, pointing straight forward. He saw little Pritchard in the act of shouting down to his gun between decks. At five hundred yards the charge ran into a curtain of shrapnel. The slope was covered now with bodies, men and horses, many of them struggling to get up, to move out of this wall of fire, to crawl away, up the slope. But the line, what was left of it, came on.

Nearly three hundred yards. Talleyman called again to Cricklade, heard the broadside, now had the attack hidden even from him by the billowing white smoke. He looked forward and saw Smales still turning his head, sweeping the disengaged side. He looked down and could guess what Cricklade was shouting.

'All guns, point-blank range, quarter charge, double load grape, fire at will!'

The noise of the shots now was ragged. Men came out of the smoke, some running, some on horses, their backs to the ship, struggling up the slope. Talleyman motioned upward with his hand. Cricklade ran from one section commander to another. The firing stopped for a moment. Talleyman watched as the main body of the enemy came up towards the nearer ranging point.

252

Bearded men, men in long fur coats, they might have been his own Marines. They rode, those who still rode, small hairy ponies, not well kept, their coats matted and strained. The rear was brought up by four or five horsemen, whippers in, Talleyman thought, urging their men on, rounding up the stragglers. The main body was almost up to the inner marker. Talleyman called,

'Now, Mr Cricklade!'

The full salvo came again. Better now, thought Talleyman. Cricklade handles these guns very well, complete control, probably better than I could manage. The grape went humming over the slope like bees, hissing into the backs of the Russians. More men, more horses, were down on the snow. Talleyman shouted,

'Cease firing, Mr Cricklade. Come up and look. Mr Biddell serve something out – anything.'

Cricklade came up to the top.

'Good God! Did we do all that, sir?'

'I did not observe the Army helping. But it's always the same. When you fire, you think you've killed the lot. Men falling everywhere. When you stop and count, it's remarkable how few you have hit. Most will have got away. But it's bad enough. Blood all over the snow. And the horses.'

'It's horrible.' Cricklade fished in his pocket and brought out a flask. 'You want some brandy, sir? No? Well, you won't mind me.'

'Most of them are left. They'll come again. We'd better burst some shrapnel's over the ridge when we hear them.'

'Three-quarters of an inch of fuse, seven degrees elevation, full charge,' Cricklade calculated. 'I'll start it.'

Talleyman went down to the deck. The buckets were coming up. Talleyman took a dipper full. Hot coffee almost stiff with sugar. He caught at Fox.

'Had yours?'

'Yes, sir.'

'Then take a mug up to the man in the foretop. And have a look round.' Talleyman got himself on the step of a gun carriage. The seamen gathered around him. Someone started a cheer, but nobody took it up.

'That's right,' he told them. 'Don't cheer. Not over yet. We've done a great deal of damage. Not enough. They'll be back. We've had two months practising this. Nothing to marvel at. Back to your guns.'

There was a high-pitched call from the foretop.

'Deck! Something's happening!'

Talleyman went back up the main shrouds. How long since they had opened fire? Half an hour? He got into the top. Fox called,

'It was a bugle.'

'Back to your guns, lad. See anything, Smales?'

'Not to port, sir. But there's something going on on the bow.'

Talleyman looked. There were dark shapes flitting in the hummocky ice. Suddenly there was a flickering of flashes.

'Not to worry,' he called back to Smales. 'Out of range.' But how to drive them off? Outside a musket's lethal reach, but within a Minié's range. He shouted to Fincham, and pointed. Fincham went forward with a party of his redcoats, and opened in reply. Talleyman heard the bugle again. No knowing what that call meant, but no point in waiting. He called to Cricklade,

'Shrapnel's!'

The eight-inch fired. As the shells bursts over the ridge, the new attack came over, stumbled in the gust of balls. They took the next broadside, of grape at six hundred yards, and came on, fewer of them, into the next blast of shrapnel's. They were not in the same formation. The cavalry were in the centre of the line, the two clumps of infantry on the flanks. A shout from Cricklade had brought the eight-inch training round, to burst that last shrapnel's over the men on foot. The line wavered, turned into a crowd, a mob. It came to

254

a halt, then the Russians turned raggedly, not, it was clear, in response to an order, and began to go back up the torn and bloody slope.

'They're running,' said Dincombe, almost over Talleyman's shoulder. 'Let them go. Let them go, have you not killed enough? Spare them.'

'You came up here to say that?' asked Talleyman. 'We are a target for riflemen. Mr Cricklade, you can get one more round in when I tell you.'

'This is a massacre,' shouted Dincombe. 'I know there is no humanity in a ship, but in the name of humanity, let them go!'

'They ran once,' Talleyman told him. 'Then they rallied and they came again. How many more times will they come? They are coming to kill us. We will have no rest till we know they will not come again. You saw the damage one man could do. Watch now, there are still a few hundred left to kill us.'

'I heard Mr Kingsley preach. He talked about the glory of the clash of strong men, about praising God by the exercise of the body. But he had never smelt what I have smelt.'

'What?'

'Blood, and gun smoke, and fear, my own fear.'

'We have not finished. What time is it?'

'Noon, just about.'

'Then another hour and a half of some kind of light. In that time, be afraid. They may come again.'

Talleyman went down to the deck, leaving Dincombe to follow. At least he can move in the rigging, he thought. He couldn't do that when we first had him.

'Mr Harris!'

'Sir?'

'Relieve Smales. Send up someone as good as Smales, if we have anybody as good.'

'I'll find one, sir.'

Talleyman looked round the deck, the guns run out. Biddell asked,

'Hot coffee again, sir?'

'Yes. Mix some rum in it. About a quarter tot per man. Enough to taste and talk about; not enough to get them drunk. A tot to Smales, when he's thawed enough to drink it.'

Smales was down. The Chaplain was still in the maintop. Talleyman looked at the log. At least, Longville could do this, had all the times down, exact for each salvo. Fox brought Talleyman his coffee. Cricklade was pouring half the contents of his pocket flask into his mug. He was shivering. He asked Talleyman,

'Those men, all those men. Did I kill them? Or did you kill them? Or did they kill themselves?'

'We all killed each other. And ourselves. Most of all, the people who killed them are not here. Someone must profit from this war.'

They waited, in the cold, under a clear sky full of frost, looking at the low sun, and awaiting a new attack.

15

'Deck!' called the Chaplain. 'Someone coming down the slope. With a flag?'

The officers on the poop huddled under the boats on their davits and poked their telescopes between keels and the bulwarks.

'It's a white flag,' said Fincham, 'and two men to carry it.'

Everyone watched the slow trudge. Only Talleyman thought to hail the foretop, and tell the new man to keep watching on the disengaged side. Then he asked Biddell,

'Is there food ready? Pipe cooks to the galley.'

The two Russians came on within earshot of the ship. One of them shouted.

'Is that Russian easy enough for you?' Orton asked Dincombe, who replied,

'Listen. He's calling in French.'

The man was shouting, '*Je veux parler, je veux entrer.*'

Talleyman replied, '*Un, seul. Un.*'

He held up one finger. He looked out through the entry port when it was hauled up, and saw the water alongside the ship. The ice had been broken about a foot wide, and even that was glazing over now. He motioned the Bo'sun to lower a rope ladder. That would do.

'Bring him into the chartroom,' he ordered. 'Business as usual.'

Furred and bearded, the Russian would have passed for anyone in *Flamingo*. He got up the ladder, came in through the port. He saw the long row of gun breeches, the men who might have been his twins, furred, bearded, with cutlasses in their belts as he wore his sword. He looked around in a puzzled way, then with the air of a man who knew something must be done but who was not sure what, he faced forward and saluted. Nobody laughed, nobody spoke. The Russian asked in French,

'Where is the Captain?'

'This way,' Dincombe told him. Talleyman was with Longville in the chartroom. On the table was his sketch of the shore, the ranges of every mound and hummock marked. It was in full view: Longville moved to make sure the Russian could see it. Talleyman motioned the Chaplain to stay. The Russian came noisily to attention. Talleyman regretted that he had not called Fincham in.

'I am Captain Brassov of the Preobrazhensky Guards. Who is the Captain?'

'I command this ship. Talleyman, Lieutenant. You wish to talk?' This man's French, at least, is as good or as bad as mine. But there is no guarantee that he does not speak English.

'I have come to ask for a truce. To bury our dead, and to recover the wounded.'

'For how long? We have another hour and more of clear day, and then some twilight.'

'As long as it takes us. There is a moon tonight.'

'You represent the commander of your force?'

'I am, now, the commander of our force.'

Everybody senior to him is dead, thought Talleyman. He pondered. Brassov went on,

'If you could signal. . . One rocket for "no", two rockets for "yes".'

'Mr Fox! Pass the word for the Gunner and then the Bo'sun. Ah, Mr Wasely, the wonder-worker. We have not fired a fused round yet which failed to go off.'

'It's how I keep them,' said Wasely, as if ashamed to acknowledge praise.

'Have your demons fire two white rockets.' Talleyman translated that into French, holding up two fingers. 'Mr Harris, pipe "Run in and Secure." Then pipe starboard watch to dinner. Tell them they have twenty minutes to eat and then to relieve the port watch.'

They listened to the unmistakable sound of gun trucks on the deck, and then the slamming of the port lids. Fincham did come now, his furs hanging open to show his red coat, and flung a salute of great ceremony.

'Sah! No casualties. Forty-seven rounds small arms expended. I have ordered the Marine gun crews to stand down, and rifle section to stand to. Sah!'

'We have a truce.' Talleyman had returned to French. 'Let that poor devil on the ice have a hot drink and a bit of beef and biscuit and send him back. He is to say that we will not fire on unarmed parties, and will allow the use of pistols to despatch horses, but we will recommence firing at sight or sound of muskets.'

258

Longville caught Fincham's eye, and went out, saying, 'I'll see to that.'

Fincham addressed the Russian.

'I take it that you admit defeat, since by tradition if you ask for a truce to remove your wounded you yield the field to us.'

'There is little I can do,' replied Brassov. There was a noise outside, the after eight-inch crew going to eat. Talleyman explained,

'My men are complaining that their dinner is late. If they are not required to shoot, they want to eat. But I have difficulty – they could prefer to shoot.'

'You have the capability,' said Brassov, bitterly.

'Mr Fox, pass the word for Abel or Nussey to bring us something hot to drink and anything hot to eat they can make up. Mr Dincombe, you will join us? Our priest, you know.'

'It is obvious, from the beard,' said Brassov with a straight face; in this situation, Dincombe reflected, there is no other face he can put on things. Nussey brought in three more steaming mugs of hot coffee, well laced with rum.

Silverwright came in with a tray on which were three plates of curried beef with rice. Brassov said,

'I do not think that I should deprive you. . . .'

'I think you mean,' said Talleyman brutally, 'that you cannot eat if your men do not. Send for Mr Biddell, somebody. Ah, Pusser, that was quick. Break out enough biscuit and canned meat for, what shall we say, three hundred men, is it, for one meal?'

Biddell repeated the order back, in English, saluted and went.

'That will be enough, I think to allow you to pack up and start your journey back to your station?'

'Why,' asked Brassov blandly, 'should we leave?'

'Because,' Talleyman told him, as bluntly as he could manage, 'three hours after the moon has risen, I will resume hostilities. You must now be bivouacked

259

just beyond the ridge. I will drench the area with Shrapnel. You need send no message of farewell. Fox! Find Mr Thacker. Do you enjoy your curry, Captain Brassov?'

'Is this a peasant dish, for the English winter?'

'In a way. Indian peasants. For the summer. Ah, Dr Thacker, I am glad you could be spared. Were our casualties heavy?' Talleyman hoped the Surgeon was good enough at French. He was.

'Marine Hanlon burnt, touching his gun when it was heated. Mears, able seaman, stupid enough to have a gun run over his foot. Otherwise, Smales reports a bullet embedded in the fore crosstrees.'

'You can't treat that. Have you a doctor, Captain Brassov?'

'We had a doctor, when we arrived. And a priest.'

'Well, if he volunteers –'

'I volunteer,' interjected Thacker.

'I will allow him and a few other men, and the Chaplain if he wishes, to go ashore and do what they can in the way of mercy.'

'Brayford will come,' said Thacker, 'and one of the stewards, either Nussey or Silverwright, they can toss for it: they are used to the work. And a couple of seamen. Calne wants to go ashore, and if Calne goes, Parks will go.'

'I did not think they loved each other so much.'

'They hate each other so much,' said Thacker, 'that they will not let each other out of their sight.'

'Take them both, and up to three others. If you are going, Mr Dincombe, I suggest you leave your cutlass behind.'

'Your priests fight?' said Brassov.

'Usually each other,' Talleyman told him. Biddell reported,

'Biscuit and beef stacked, sir, ready to go ashore when you say. The men grudge it.'

'Let them grudge it. Your people in St Petersburg,

Captain Brassov, must be very much in need of a victory to boast if they send so many of you against a stranded ship.'

'St Petersburg? They never talk to me, I am not in favour there. But I think you have no news of the war, since you came on this coast?'

'None, I was not sure there still was a war.'

'Oh, yes, there still is a war. And I must return to it.'

16

'It is two and a half hours after moon rise, sir' said Neve.

'Where', Talleyman asked, 'is Mr Cricklade?'

'He is indisposed, sir. At least, not fit for duty.'

'Drunk?'

'I am afraid so, sir. He thinks he was responsible personally for every man killed.'

'Well, don't *you* think so. Look, is that our party coming down to the ice?'

'Looks like it, sir.'

'Have the eight-inch crews stand to. I've spoken to the gun captains.'

'They don't like it, sir.'

'Like it or not, they'll fire.'

The companion ladder went down, the men came on board from the ice. Parks, Calne, Nussey, the Surgeon. Last of all, Dincombe came up. One of the seamen – who was that? Oh yes, thought Talleyman, Orme, foretop man, sponger on number four port broadside, out of a whaler, done one commission in *Electra* ten years ago, yes that's the man – reached down to help him and said,

'Come on up, vicar, come into the warm.'

In the wardroom, Talleyman asked,

'They are moving? They really are moving?'

'They're marching,' said Dincombe. 'Marching and singing. Did nobody hear them singing? Those who could sing?'

'How many?' Talleyman asked.

'How do we know?' Dincombe asked. 'Who could count them?'

'I counted, as well as I could,' said Thacker. 'And Calne did, too. We agreed. There were nearly two hundred and fifty to march away, those who could walk and those could not. They had about twenty sledges, and loaded the worst cases on those. There were others who were fit to ride, and others again who walked alongside the horses, holding on. There were nearly a hundred and fifty horses.'

'And dead?' pressed Talleyman.

'Easier to count. About a hundred and eighty. They brought them and laid them like firewood, layer on layer, in a pile. And they covered them with snow. Very deep, to last, they said, till spring. They will bury them then. I told the Captain, Brasso or whatever he was, about Sladen and Sergeant Madden; he said they would be buried too.' He paused.

'Pass the word for Calne,' Talleyman ordered. Thacker went on,

'It was the cold, as much as the lead. They were all clean wounds, from the balls. No splinters, nobody burnt, like in a ship. They were bleeding and losing heat with the blood, they were dying as we were bringing them in.'

Calne came in. Talleyman asked him,

'What did you see? We know how many.'

'Very strange, sir. They were all in furs, but under that, oh, a dozen different uniforms. And a lot of elderly men, forty or more. A lot of them spoke French, or German.'

'You speak French? And German?'

'I thought that was why you sent me, sir.'

'I sent you to look after the Surgeon. And Parkes to look after the Chaplain.'

'More of them,' said Thacker, 'spoke English than they wanted us to know. Things like doing what I wanted before I translated into French.'

'Beg pardon, sir,' said Fox, 'but Mr Neve asks, permission to fire.'

'No need to fire again,' said Dincombe, 'they've all gone.'

'I must fire,' said Talleyman. 'I promised. And they must hear it is Shrapnel's. Two rounds, spaced, Mr Fox.'

'Aye, aye, sir.'

'Their priest was dead,' said Dincombe dully, as if talking to himself. The after eight-inch went off above their heads, shaking up the dust around them, the smoke wreathing down through the rough cracks between the beams in the deckhead. 'Someone gave me his service book. Brassov showed me the place. I could read it aloud. I didn't understand it but I could sing it. It had the music. The kontakion, the prayers for the dead. Those who were near me sang the responses.' The for'ard gun fired. 'There was one dead man, he seemed a very old man. Brassov said his name, he said "*C'est Polkovnik*", as near as I can pronounce it. Brassov opened his fur coat, and he had a picture pushed into his tunic. A holy picture. It wasn't hurt, just the frame chipped. Brassov kissed it and gave it to me. I kissed it and gave it back. I remembered to cross myself their way.'

'Their way?' asked Fincham. 'You mean not like my paddies?'

'No, the opposite way.' Dincombe demonstrated, and brought out the picture. 'Brassov wrapped it in some scrap paper, and gave it to me again. He said "Take it" and I said no, but he said "yes", and a lot of the others said Yes and *Oui* and *Ja* and *Da*. So here it is.'

He unwrapped the picture and laid it on the table. It was a Virgin and Child, very stiff and strange in style, the gold still shining but the paint darkened. They could hear Orton crying in his bunk, Talleyman asked,

'The food? Did they want it?'

'I took it up,' said Calne, 'at least I saw they did. Their quartermaster, I suppose, took care of it. He told me, "*Beaucoup pour deux jours*", enough for two days, or plenty for two days.'

'Two days on half rations,' Talleyman interpreted. 'Then two days on nothing. That's how far his base must be.'

'Half of them will be dead,' said Thacker. 'At least half.'

'There was something very strange about their weapons,' put in Calne. Talleyman noted that he was behaving as if the wardroom was his proper habitat, as indeed it was: or the gun room at least. 'They were all different kinds of guns. Not everybody had a musket. Some had sporting guns, some only had pairs of pistols. Different kinds of swords. And not everybody had a sword. There were a number with axes or even pikes.'

'Pikes?' asked Talleyman. 'Spears? Sounds Irish.'

'Look here,' said Craddock suddenly. He spoke so seldom, unaddressed, that everybody stopped talking, and looked at him. He was at the forward end of the table, holding a lantern close to the surface. He had a jumble of untidy scraps. 'Look here. You didn't look at the wrappings. Look at them. Look!'

Biddell was the nearest. He looked, and said,

'Good God! We didn't look. I suppose it was so familiar we didn't take any notice. It's in English.'

Everybody grabbed together, even Calne. Talleyman stopped them.

'One at a time. No, not even one at a time. Only one. Mr Biddell, lay these scraps out.'

The Purser did so. Fragments, one by one, some the size of a palm, others larger, the largest was nearly half a page. Everyone knew the paper, the type. Biddell fiddled, moved pieces about, turned them over, put together at last perhaps half a dozen larger scraps. They were all dirty, all worn smooth by fingers.

'Is there any more?' Biddell asked. The officers were promptly all down on hands and knees, looking under the table, all over the floor. They found three or four more scraps, the size of thumbnails; three fitted into other scraps, one was unidentifiable, even unreadable.

'Read them,' said Talleyman. 'Stand and look. When we've finished, turn them over. You too, Calne. Read them. Take the news to the seamen. Stop rumours.'

They read in silence, changing places. Talleyman waited, then said,

'Right. What have we got?'

'Two pages of the *Illustrated*,' said Biddell. Two different issues.'

'Turn them over!'

Biddell did it, very carefully. They read again, almost in silence, with little noises of drawn breath, of surprise. They were, Dincombe thought, like thirsty men waiting in turn for a drink at a slow tap. Talleyman said,

'Right. We've all read the lot. What have we got?'

There was a moment of silence, then Longville said,

'There's been a battle.'

'Mr Biddell,' Talleyman called, 'be secretary. Take it down.'

'Not a battle,' said Fincham, 'but two battles. One on the twenty-fifth of October, one on November the fifth.'

'Where?' asked Talleyman.

'Sebastopol,' said Neve. 'What on earth for?'

'No point in taking Sebastopol,' agreed Fincham. 'It's to protect the fleet. The fleet is to protect Odessa. If we're attacking Sebastopol, then they can land there, which means that the Russian fleet is out of action, which means again we must have had a naval battle and won, and we must have taken Odessa already.'

'Doubtful,' said Longville. 'We must have taken the army from Moldavia to the Crimea. If they've got ashore, then as you say the Russian fleet must be out of action. But if the fleet got into Sebastopol, then our brilliant admirals and generals will simply have followed it. We're fighting the Russians where they want us to fight.'

'Two days,' said Fincham, 'and two battles. A week apart. The first day, it looks like a pursuit, and an ambush. Almost all cavalry, and light cavalry at that, the eyes of an army. My cousin's husband is there dead. Thirteenth Light Dragoons. Most of the regiment, come to that.'

'Second day?' Biddell asked.

'Nearly all infantry,' said Fincham. 'The Guards took it hard, but a lot of other regiments too. First day, only a few, and nearly all in the Ninety-third. So it was probably only a vanguard affair. But the second day, marching regiments, Rifles, Highlanders, all sorts. Staff, even. A big affair.'

'No Navy, and no Marines,' Thacker pointed out.

'They'd be a separate list, if there were any engaged.' said the Purser. Everyone felt he ought to know. Then Craddock spoke again, and at this rare sound, everybody listened.

'Here's old Sherwin. Didn't you notice? All looking for deaths. Here's old Sherwin, a bit torn, but it's Henry Sherwin. He's standing for Parliament.'

'Must be a bye-election,' said Talleyman.

'Let me see,' and Biddell took it. 'Torn down the edge, but it says ". . . nry Sherwin, candidate for Wra. . . said last night that spea. . . who through the peace had spoken often ag. . . ministration and waste in the Naval. . . and returned broken in health from the wars. . ." That's all. It's a hoot, isn't it? Returned from the wars, indeed!'

'What seat begins with WRA?' Craddock asked. Talleyman knew. He moved to the wardroom door, then told them,

266

'We have won a victory. We should celebrate it. I will order an extra issue of rum for the people of the ship. If you will allow me to use this table. . . I will pay for dinner tonight. If you permit I will ask the Mates, also. Abel will break out some wine. I will settle with Captain Only's . . .estate. I am going on deck.'

17

Talleyman stood on the poop, looking out over the slope where the Russians had charged. The sky was full of small clouds, coming in from the west. The moonlight would not last long. He listened. There were strange noises he had not heard before. He sniffed the air: he had learnt that from Longville. Nothing.

A bye-election at Wrackham. His father had held the seat for ten years. If there were an election, then he must have left the seat vacant. It was not something he would ever resign. If he had taken office, he would have to be re-elected, but old Josiah had sworn he would never take office, not even as undersecretary of woods and forests. He would vote the way he wanted, usually with the Tories but that could not be relied on. And the seat was too valuable, and even, so far, too delicately balanced, to be risked. There was only one other reason for a bye-election.

Talleyman leaned on the taffrail, under the jack staff, and began to face the likely truth. Almost certainly, his father was dead. He would go back, to, in some degree, freedom. What the will would say, he did not know: but to some extent the chains would be loosened. He felt that on this night he ought to weep, but what was there to weep for? Tonight, he had ordered a celebration. The Irish would call it a wake. Then let there be a wake.

Cricklade came on to the poop. Talleyman asked,

'Your watch? Are you fit for it?'

'Much better now, sir. Had some black coffee.'

'What have you got there?'

'Came to ask permission to use it sir. Captain Only said I could keep it abroad for emergencies.'

'A rifle? Why?'

'I brought it in case I had a chance at. . . well, up here I suppose elk, but I was really thinking of mountain goat or something. I haven't seen anything to use it on till now.'

'Our friend with the Whitworth?'

'I was waiting till Moulton had finished.'

'What are you going to use it on, at last, if I give permission?'

'Listen, sir.'

They listened. The noise was closer, and unmistakable now. The moon was flickering behind the racing cloud, throwing shadows from the hummocks that were dead horses.

'What rifle?' Talleyman asked.

'American, a Sharps, breach-loading.' Cricklade was half proud of having such a weapon to show, half afraid that Talleyman might want to try it himself. But Talleyman only asked,

'What about all those birds? You've shot enough in the islands.'

'I've got them skinned, got the bones, when I'm back I'll stuff them. Moulton showed me how.'

'You get on with Moulton?'

'Yes. He's an officer in his own navy, we know what to say to each other. But Prince Edward Island, of all places! You know anywhere in Prince Edward Island called Flah'da?' He took out a flask. 'Care for a tot, sir?'

'Thank you. Here's your first customer.' They looked at the wolf, sliding from shadow to shadow. Cricklade shook his head.

268

'Too far to be certain. Sighted to eight hundred yards, but can't trust it over four hundred. Cheaper than the Whitworth and quicker to fire, but a devil to keep clean. I don't like the idea of only wounding an animal.'

'If you wound one to draw blood, it won't last long. Aim about a finger to the left, for the wind.'

'It throws a little high, and to the right. I reckon I should aim dead centre.'

'Do what you think justice calls for. Only remember, Cricklade. . .' Talleyman paused.

'What, sir?'

'Contrary to popular opinion, even a wolf has a father.'

VI

Spring

1

'Would you like,' asked Baron Krabbe, 'to drive out into the countryside?'

They were in the big house in the St Armand Straat, in the first floor salon which ran across the whole front of the house. Harriet liked to call it 'the salon', a much more elegant term than drawing room. At least it was warm in here, with the great stove in the centre of the back wall taking place of a fireplace, and taking it much better. Harriet wondered if there were any possibility of persuading Tom to install one in the Dower House when he came back. If he ever came back. If he did not come back, Richard said, she would be a very rich woman, and why should she not begin to enjoy riches now and get used to them. True, she supposed a stove called for a good deal of work in the morning, raking it and carrying out the ash, and again in the evening when the family were at dinner and the salon empty. But Harriet had long passed the stage of householding where she ever got up in time to see the grates cleared and fires lit, so she need not worry about ash.

This was the best of all, to be mistress of a house and yet have no responsibility for it. Madame Marnix appeared each morning to present the menus for the day, to receive warning of new arrivals, of guests for meals, acting as if Richard had not already given her a list. She spoke English, as did the French maid provided as Harriet's own personal attendant, with no other work to do than to keep Harriet's clothes in order and to help her to dress and bring her coffee and fresh rolls in bed in the morning, and perhaps two or three times if there were no reason for Harriet to get up.

273

'I have seen the town, a great deal,' said Harriet.

'Do you like the town?' This was going to be a dull few days, with Mr Talleyman conferring with his French colleagues, and the three English lords all back in England, two for the debates in Parliament, and the third because his wife was pregnant and in danger of a miscarriage. Although, Krabbe gathered, she was eternally in danger of a miscarriage.

'I like it well enough. With the houses along the canals, close to the water, it is rather like Wisbech, or perhaps even parts of Cork.'

Krabbe had never heard of Wisbech. He knew London well but had never been further into the interior of the island, and did not much care to.

'You have learnt to skate while you have been here? Six weeks is long enough, I think.'

'Oh, I could skate before I came here. We skate on the Fens, you know, when they freeze over. I have been skating here, on the canals, with Mr Strand.'

'Ah, Mr Strand. He skates well?'

'Very well, for a Brazilian. And he speaks English very well, too.'

'Did he learn to skate here?'

'No, he learnt to skate when he was a boy, in a town called, he says, Acushnet. In Brazil.'

Krabbe smiled, his smile hidden in his rich brown beard, his lush moustache. Oh, she was an innocent, this woman, a big, glorious innocent. At home, he enjoyed women like this, he enjoyed their company, their prattle, their ignorance of the world and of money and of politics, while their husbands thought themselves so clever, so sophisticated. Not the wives of peasants or of serfs, depending on which of his estates he found them, but the wives, the daughters of gentlefolk, of small farmers, who called themselves his neighbours to cover up the truth, that they were his tenants, or his debtors, or both, men who dared not offend him.

'So, he is Brazilian as you are English.' She did not

see the irony. Oh, he liked women like this, he liked their warm closeness, the perfume, cheap or expensive, mingled with the sweaty smell of their bodies. Innocents, thinking themselves so wise, so sophisticated. He might push further. 'Perhaps you would like a to go for a ride in the country? We could take a . . . a picnic. I shall furnish all the provisions.'

He waited. He considered. Young Talleyman was not here, but he could not afford to object even if he were here. He could not afford the risk that Krabbe might again withdraw, go back to St Petersburg to consult his superiors. In truth, Krabbe thought, I dare not go back, I must have this bargains struck before the end of the month, before the snow begins to melt in the south, before the new columns begin to make their long way south from the depots. These men had to have rifles, and powder to fire them with, and bullet moulds and boots. But there would be no trouble, no danger.

'But, would it be proper? Richard cannot accompany us. Only my maid.'

'Oh, but my fast carriage will not have room enough for your maid. It is a light affair with seats only for you and myself. And where is the harm? Everybody knows we are here on the same business, we are part of the same group of foreigners.'

'But my reputation!' But she could hear what Richard had told her. The others do not matter so much, they are on our side. But Krabbe – Count Rakoff – is the adversary, and we must keep him sweet and hold him here. So charm him, Harriet, charm him and hold him. Be agreeable at all costs, very agreeable.'

'Reputation? Here, where nobody knows you? The only people who care for your reputation are ourselves, our small group, and we know each other too well. We are, almost, a family in ourselves. You will come? Otherwise I have nothing to do all day but sit here with you behind closed doors, in this quiet room, and the servants not to come unless they are called, in case they hear our business. And what could do more harm than that to a reputation? At least if we drive out together where everyone can see us there will be no suspicions.'

He went to bring the carriage round, clattering in the slushy streets. Harriet went to her room and rang for Marie-Annette. She considered what she should wear, decided at least that warmth was the most essential thing. Warmth with elegance; she would wear her riding habit, the one she had had new to wear that once in the Bois before they came on here by rail. If she had had any sense, she would have worn it in the train, chamois riding trousers and all. But she would not need those for a ride in a carriage, just her high buttoned blouse of silk and the jacket and skirt of good solid English cloth, put together in Paris. And for warmth, the beaver coat Richard had helped her buy – she did not dare to think how much that had cost him – with the matching muff, a small one as was now the fashion.

She heard the wheels in the street, and went down to be by the door as Velde opened it. She couldn't remember all his real name, so she just called him by last part of it and he seemed pleased enough, and was a good butler. And she saw the carriage.

It was not a carriage, not properly so called. It was a two-wheeler, high light wheels, everything light. Two seats under a tall hood, almost, one might say, a trap with a hood, but that air of foreignness about the woodwork and the brass. But the horses were even more foreign; there were three of them, *three*, and Harriet was on the brink of coming out to see them, when Baron Krabbe said,

'You cannot go out in this weather if that is all you have to wear. You must have furs, real furs. You deserve real furs, and I have brought them. Stay inside a moment, keep the warmth.'

He was himself almost invisible in a fur coat cut like a coachman's and a round fur hat to match, his hair and beard almost blending, so that only the blue eyes and the full red lips showed. In a moment he had returned, saying,

'Put this on over the others, keep well warm.'

It was black, a vast black cloak of fur, almost drowning her in its soft bulk. Marie-Annette, her eyes round, helped to drape it about her shoulders, tied it at the neck, clasped it lower with a brass clip, so that only her hands showed. There was a matching muff, vast also, quite out of fashion, and the maid brought up the hood over the riding hat so that Harriet's face peered out, almost as hidden as the Baron's. She giggled.

'Our reputations are safe. Nobody will recognize us now.'

'My reputation is worth nothing,' the Baron corrected her. 'In any case, everybody in the town will know that it is myself. Nobody else drives three horses.'

Harriet did not know any more how long they had been driving. Or in what direction. She was muffled in the great black cloak, and before they had started Krabbe had brought another fur, a snowy white rug, out from the dim interior of the trap and spead it across their knees.

Some miles out of Bruges they had found a long straight stretch of good road, under only a thin skin of slush. There she had let the muff dangle about her neck, and took the reins. She had driven two horses before, once tandem, but three was a different matter. These horses were, at least looked, a spirited trio, and could get up a rattling pace, but in spite of that they were easy to handle, forgiving of errors.

'When I get back to England,' she said excitedly, 'I shall try three horses in a trap.'

'It is not so easy,' Krabbe told her. 'You have to train them to this from the first.'

'Where did you find them?' she asked.

'I bred them on my estate. They were trained to run like this from the year they were born. And see *how* they run. They are not going as fast as some, but they can run at this pace and run and run. They are bred for these long journeys, with only a light load, but they can keep on all day and all night. They go as they are handled. The only trouble is for us to keep warm. And keep awake.'

He reached under the seat, to a box filled with straw. He brought up for her two covered cups of a strange soup, warm and sweet-sour tasting.

'What is it made from?' Harriet asked.

'Beetroot. It is the soup of my country.'

'Who made this?'

'My cook.'

'What? In. . .Courland?'

'Oh, I brought him here, and a dozen other servants, as well as my horses and carriages. Only my wife would not come. She did not think I would ever come back.'

'Do you have any children?'

'I have a son, not much older than you are.'

Harriet had no clear idea of where Courland was: she thought perhaps a part of Prussia, or of Austria. She asked,

'Is he at the war?' For all she knew Courland was at war with Russia.

'He serves his sovereign. He is not at any war. Try this.'

It was another sealed cup, kept warm in the straw, coffee laced with something. She asked what. Krabbe answered,

'With this.' It was a fiery spirit, harsh and burning her throat.

'They make this out of potatoes at home,' she said.

'It is a peasant drink, a kind of eau de vie, they make this too out of potatoes, or out of rye. It is very useful. Without it life is not possible in the winter.'

'It makes me sleepy. It makes me feel I could nestle down for ever in this wonderful cloak. Is it truly sable? I have heard of sable. Now I can tell everybody that once I had a sable cloak.'

'It is yours, to keep. I thought you understood that. It is not polite to lend a garment to a lady, either you give freely and for ever, or you withhold absolutely.'

'But sables – it is worth a king's ransom.'

'Sables? They cost me nothing. They are vermin. On my estate, my gamekeepers catch them. It costs me only a little for the silk lining, I have my own tailor on my estate, he makes it up as part of his normal work. It is nothing to me, but it seems it is a great deal to you. It makes you happy. Keep it.'

She snuggled back into the cloak and drowsed, her head on Krabbe's shoulder. Suddenly she was awake, but kept still. She felt his hand warm on her thigh, under the cloak. He stroked slowly, smoothly, comfortingly. She snuggled down again, felt his exploring hand and dozed off.

2

She awoke. It was twilight. She did not know how long she had slept. They had stopped outside a long low building, timber framed, brick filled, the roof thatched. Ostlers were at the horses' heads. Krabbe held his arms out for her to get down. Now they had stopped, the cold wind stung her face, as it had not done on the journey.

'Where am I?'

'We are at Les Sapineurs. It is a hostelry tolerably well known. We will rest the horses while we have dinner. Then we can ride back through the night, under the stars.'

'Let us first see,' she told him, 'to the horses.'

He approved of that. They followed the ostlers, saw the beasts rubbed down, fed, watered and put into stalls with blankets over their backs. These horses, she thought, will never run the same distance back again, not tonight. They will need a much longer rest.

Dinner was set for them in a private room upstairs. There was a fire in a grate, piles of logs dry by it. The table was small, covered with a cloth edged with lace. The cutlery was silver-handled, the glass fine crystal. If this, she thought, were a well-known hostelry, then it was not a cheap one.

The people of the house came and went, smiling. They seemed to know Krabbe, addressed him as *m'sieu le baron*. The candles flickered in the draughts as the door opened and closed, as each dish, each bottle came in, showed pictures on the wall, the patchwork coverlet on the bed against the wall.

'The food is different here,' Harriet remarked.

'In what way?'

'In Bruges we have. . . well, they can cook dumplings and game and thick soups and oysters and mussels that come in barrels. But this here, it is lighter. I can taste other things. Are they olives, these? And have they used olive oil to fry in?'

'Probably.'

'That hot soufflé – so light, and made in the last ten minutes specially for us. And they seem to use so much wine, and I think it's brandy, but a heavy brandy, a bit sweeter. In Bruges I think they might get as far as showing a gin bottle to a dish, but not opening it.'

Krabbe laughed. The hostess came in, enquiring if all was satisfactory.

'Oh, *madame*. Baron, help me if my French is not good enough.'

'I have a little English, *madame*.'

'But the food has been wonderful.'

'Oh, is nothing, *madame*. Is only peasant dishes. Carp and an eel and a tench in a matelote, *poulet à la Saint Menehould,* an *estouffade de boeuf à la Provençale* as *monsieur le baron* ordered, yes – a *pâte de porc du Périgord.*'

'And the wines!'

'Oh, nothing, a Graves, and then a Bordeaux as *m'sieu* ordered, an Hermitage of forty-eight, chambré'ed and left to breathe an hour, and now with the apple *tarte* and the cheese, not a Sauterne but a Monbazillac.'

'Wonderful.'

'No, but the best our cellar can do. If you come to France, *madame*, you must expect French cooking.'

'France?'

'Thank you, *madame*, and if you would send up a bottle of Armagnac – that is the heavier brandy you detected.'

'But she said France!'

'Yes, we are in France, but only just. I brought the horses by a forest path, for it is so boring going through the customs. Besides, we are in France, and I would be hanged if they know who I was.'

'Hanged?'

'In England I would probably be sent to Dartmoor like the French sailors.'

'Why?'

'Surely you know, I am Russian. I am in Bruges on the Tsar's business.'

'And my brother-in-law?'

'He is here on his own business, and I believe on his own, too.'

'But why? Why have you come into France, if it is so dangerous?'

'Because it is dangerous. Think. It is the bravest thing I can do. It lets me laugh at the French. Laugh with me.'

Later he thought, yes, it is the bravest thing I can do, but it is brave and stupid things that add zest to life, more of a tang than sauces of wine and brandy and fennel and mustard. To go to bed in an enemy country with the wife of an enemy, and to do it smoothly, with courtesy, with such exquisite enjoyment.

Harriet lay across his chest, her fingers entwined in his beard. For the first time that day an image of Tom flickered across her consciousness. She was convinced by now that she would never see Tom again. This was better, after those stupid dull years in that stupid flat fen country, to eat well, and now to sleep well, to be treated in bed for the first time with tenderness, with courtesy. And to do it where she might be caught, be tried as a traitor. . . it was the danger that made it worth while.

3

'Deck!' Smales shouted from the maintop. 'Smoke. Fine on the starboard bow.'

'Fetch Mr Talleyman,' Longville snapped to Pritchard. But Talleyman was already on deck, and in the main shrouds.

'Where?'

'Over the knoll,' Smales told him. There was scarcely any wind. The smoke was standing up like a pillar. Ought to have Dincombe up here, Talleyman said to himself. His telescope would show him nothing. Then he did see something, a break in the column, then smoke again, and a break again. It was as if someone had held a blanket over the fire, Red Indian fashion, but nothing to bother Calne with. Or like someone puffing on an enormous pipe.

Talleyman slid down the mainstay. He hung over the engine room skylight, open in the slightly milder air, only cold enough now to freeze your face off.

'Mr Craddock! Have you steam enough in that boiler to blow the hooter?'

'In five minutes, sir.'

'When you are ready, three long blasts. Three. And make as much smoke as you can.' But it may not be,

Talleyman told himself. Be cautious. Beat to quarters? Not yet, give them five minutes, perhaps more like ten, don't get the men chilled before they have to come on deck. He must send first for Cricklade, and for Moulton. The smoke rose again in three puffs.

'Mr Cricklade, I will beat to quarters in a minute or two. When I do, delegate your gun deck duties. To Neve. Bring your elephant gun up here. Moulton, get yourself issued with a Minié. I want some sharp shooters. Poop is the best position. Captain Fincham! Who is your best shot now? Hurley? Send him up here, with his rifle.'

Five minutes were up. Craddock put his head up through the boiler-room skylight, and waved. For the first time for months, the hooter blasted out, whooo. . .whooo. . .whooo. Before the pipe sounded for action stations, the seamen were crowding and jostling each other on the companionways, around their guns. Moulton and Corporal Egan were standing on the poop, rifles in hand. Cricklade was watching his gunners on the upper deck, prompting Neve, vanishing with him under the poop to check the after eight-inch in the Captain's day cabin. Neve came back to the gun, quickly numbered off the gun captains. The ports came up, the guns were run out, as Smales called,

'Deck! Man coming out of dead ground.'

The three marksmen brought their rifles to the ready, but Talleyman waved them down. The ship was silent, except for Garvey, in the forepeak, shouting to be let out. It was his right, if they were going into action. To hell with his rights, thought Talleyman; he shot his sergeant. There was someone coming out of the dead ground, a man on a horse, pushing wearily through the snow up to its withers. It must be getting warmer, Talleyman thought irrelevantly, the beast is breaking through the ice crust. He called to Craddock and the hooter sounded again, three

283

times. The man on the horse raised his arm and came on down the snow slope. At length Talleyman said,

'Time to stop him. One round a yard either side of him. One in front. One at a time.'

The snow spurted up around the horseman. He reined in, watched by all the officers through their telescopes. They saw him fumble in his furs, raise his arm again and wave something, a piece of cloth, coloured. It might be the Union Jack, but it was hard to tell. Talleyman called,

'Bo'sun. Hoist the ensign. I'll go and meet him.'

'No, you must not,' said the Chaplain. 'Captain Only went ashore, and never came back. We cannot afford to lose you.'

'Only went,' said Talleyman. He was tucking his trouser legs into his sea boot tops. 'The men must know I am not a coward.'

Talleyman went up the slope. The horseman was a hundred yards from the edge of the frozen sea. Soon he could be seen clearly, a small yellow man, smooth-faced. The same small yellow man? Talleyman wondered. He was not sure. But he *was* holding the Union Flag, now stretched out between two hands. Talleyman opened the front of his fur coat to show his uniform. He was close to the yellow man, perhaps ten feet. The horseman spoke.

'Punch Judy man. Punch Judy man.'

Who else would remember the Widow McCarthy's farm? Talleyman ordered,

'Fetch him!'

The yellow man looked a question. Talleyman pointed over his shoulder at the ridge, made beckoning movements. The yellow man said,

'Poof-poof. Poof-poof.'

Talleyman turned to face the ship. He lifted his right hand and jerked it up and down, up and down, mimicking some one pulling the lanyard of a hooter. In a moment, he heard the hooter sound two blasts, a wait while one could count to twenty, then two blasts again. Talleyman asked,

'How many? How many?'

The horseman spread his hands, looked blank. Talleyman remembered one of the words that the Chaplain had tried to teach him. He asked,

'Kolik? Kolik?'

The yellow man understood at least that much Russian. He let go one corner of the flag, and with the free hand held up five fingers, then again and again, Talleyman said 'Come!' and turned to walk back down the slope. The horseman followed him. Talleyman waved to the ship, and saw the back up party come on to the ice, Fincham, half a dozen Marines, Parks. Reaching them, Talleyman told Parks,

'Back and let Mr Biddell know it's hot food and a rum issue for about twenty, more or less. And an extra biscuit ration. I suppose the horses will eat it.'

There was a gaggle of horses and people coming over the ridge, out of the dead ground. The artificers brought ashore a couple of iron plates from the boiler room flooring, and a brazier of burning coal. Biddell's crew carried ashore a kettle full of a stew of tinned beef and dried peas. They put the kettle on the brazier, and someone gave the horseman a tin bowl of stew and a couple of biscuits. He ate as though he had starved for a fortnight. It turned out later he had. The cavalcade was now only a hundred yards away. Talleyman went up to meet it and recognized Esteron sitting on a small horse, hunched into his furs.

'Good morning. I hope we have enough food ready. You look more like forty than fifteen.'

'You asked Kaiuk? He probably only counted the men. The older men have their families: they couldn't live up here otherwise.'

'Will they eat stewed canned beef?'

'They're devil worshippers, they'll eat anything.'

They had reached where the sailors were handing out the platters. There was a clatter of women unloading horses, putting up tents on the snow. Parks was holding Esteron's horse. 'Please can you help me down? I broke my leg in November and it isn't well yet.'

'Don't ye worry, sir,' said Parks. 'We'll carry you to the ship.'

'I'll say my goodbyes first. They want to get back to their main camp and their horse herds. That's about three weeks. Would you give them some biscuit and dried peas? They understand those. And, say, half a hundredweight of good powder, and the same of lead? They'll remelt and make balls for their own pieces – every one in a different bore. Now, carry me to Kaiuk Khan.'

Talleyman watched the farewells. He pondered a possible solution to a problem. When he got aboard again, he ordered,

'Bring Garvey out of the forepeak.'

The Marine looked pale, anxious. He stood in front of Talleyman on the quarterdeck, a semicircle of seamen and Marines around. Talleyman told him,

'You know that I ought to have had you hanged on the spot. I decided that it would be more appropriate to have you hauled back to Britain to stand a proper trial. But that would bring disgrace on your corps.' He looked round at the seamen and marines. 'Men, Francis Garvey, late of the Royal Marines, is now about to desert.' He had expected a murmur of mixed agreement and dissent, but he was surprised to hear the men cheer. 'Corporal Egan has separated your own property from the Queen's. You may not take the Queen's coat to draw further shame on us. You may take an extra shirt and your furs. Mr Biddell will pay you, in gold, up to the day of your crime. You are not going ashore in the ice, friendless. The people who brought Mr Esteron back will take you in. They live in

286

the same way as the tinkers of Ireland. Go out, Francis Garvey, and be a tinker.'

The men cheered again, but Garvey spat, first at Talleyman, who dodged it, and then, more daring, on the quarterdeck.

'Throw me to the heathen savages, will you then, Thomas Talleyman? I will come back to haunt you yet, and bring your house down in the shame.'

4

They were there, all the officers and the mates, in the wardroom. Orton was in his cabin, singing in a high voice, wordlessly. Esteron ignored him, and was ready to answer, he said, rational question. Talleyman asked,

'Did you find Shamyl?'

'Let us say, I did what I was sent to do.'

'So you did not reach him?'

'It was not entirely necessary. He did not need to receive my goods in person. My munnish friends took me to a place agreed, near Bokhara. There were some of Shamyl's people there, Chechens, and others, different nations. We came to an amicable agreement. Some had weapons, some had gold, some had both, in proportion to their capability for causing harm to the Tsar. Shamyl's ambassadors, of course, got the major part. I kept a little of the gold to pay my passage home. I was confident that you would wait for me, even though I was a little later than expected. I broke my left leg, you see, and we had to come on slowly. Then the snows came up with us, and we hid in a village they made on the spot, of willow withies and yak skins. If Kaiuk would wait there for me, in the snow, I knew that you too would wait. I was not entirely a beggar among them since I had bought a horse and sold it back.'

'What news of the war?' Talleyman asked.

'News? Hardly any. That there is a war and that it has something to do with the Tsar wanting to go on a pilgrimage to India, on that the tribes are in general agreed. There has been a great battle between the Russians and the English at Erzurum or Kars, there are some doubts which, but it has drawn Russians down along the coast road into Turkey where it is easy to ambush their columns and steal horses and powder. Apart from that, there are tales of another battle somewhere further north, outside a great city, Kiev or Minsk or Perm, these being cities the people of this place have heard of. Perhaps even Moscow, they say.'

'Sebastopol,' said the Chaplain.

'Very likely. They say that the two sons of the Tsar fought there, and struck many strokes of valour, but were borne away by their fleeing comrades, leaving the field to the Franks or the English: accounts differ. And even more recently, they say – '

'Who are "they"?' the Surgeon asked.

'They are the wanderers, Turkomen and Lapps and others who scavenge these snowfields for anything that will keep their animals alive. They also had tales of a great battle in the north, perhaps at Archangel, where thousands of the Russians were killed and the rest retreated to the south-west, dying in the snow as they went, and leaving untold booty behind them of woollen clothes and muskets and mirrors, and meat for the wolves.'

'There was such a battle,' Talleyman told him. 'We fought it.'

'A few broadsides, and a regiment gave in and came to us for leave to depart,' boasted Cricklade. 'I, with my little gun, I killed Tsar Robin.'

'But there is also a tale,' Esteron warned them, 'of a great army of English horsemen swept away and

288

scattered by a single discharge of Russian guns. And, lately, a rumour that the Tsar is dead. But there have also been rumours that Queen Victoria is dead, and the King of Prussia, and that Napoleon Bonaparte has returned to the walls of Moscow and fallen there in battle. Kutusov too has returned in one-eyed glory, walking in the night before the walls of Warsaw.'

'There *has* been a battle at Sebastopol,' Dincombe observed mildly, 'and there were some of our cavalry regiments there which suffered badly.'

'I will jest, like Pilate,' Esteron answered appropriately. 'Yet strange things have happened in the heavens. There has been snow in Krim, a depth not seen in a hundred years, vast storms at sea and such ice no man may walk. And up here, we are told, the winter has been warm and unseasonably mild, and the snow scanty and rare.'

'Are you trying to tell us something?' asked Longville.

'In a few words, yes. In a day or two the surface ice will begin to feel mushy underfoot. In a week, a lookout in your tops will be able to see gleams of water among the icefloes to the north.'

Talleyman looked at Craddock.

'What's the coal state?'

'Moderate.'

'Why only that?'

'Consumption on number two. Otherwise we'd have all frozen.'

'I know that.'

'And we haven't been able to coal for six weeks, with the coal dump frozen.'

'Frozen or not, we'll have to coal before the ice gets too mushy to bear it.'

'With bunkers full,' Craddock calculated, 'we'll have about fourteen days. Less if we need full power to push through floating ice. Sacks in the orlop, and we ought to make home. 'What about the frozen dump?'

'Blast it!' Talleyman looked at Esteron. 'Didn't blast

289

before. Might attract attention.' He remembered that this was a stupid reason, now, after they had fired half a dozen broadsides and been attacked by a regiment. He ordered, 'Coaling parties at first light. Weather permitting.' He caught Longville's eye. 'Any comment, Mr First Lieutenant?'

'Weather all right. No snow, I could smell it coming, no snow now for four or five days. But I don't much like the idea of going all the way under steam, ice or no ice.'

'Right. Pass the word to Mr Wasely to make up blasting charges and fuses. Bo'sun to send up topmasts and topsail yards, bend on courses and topsails. Captain Fincham – '

'Sah!'

'Section of Marines first ashore on that side.'

'Sah!'

'Is anything happening?' asked Orton, emerging. 'I overslept. Sorry. I say, Thacker, that tonic you make up isn't as strong as the one I brought with me. I'll be glad to see Dr Wormset again.'

'I have advice, gentlemen.' Talleyman sounded weary, Dincombe thought; for the first time he is looking weary. 'Invite Mr Esteron to dine in the wardroom. Then he can tell Mr Orton strange tales.'

'"The ear of man hath not seen, nor the eye of man smelt, all the terrors and dangers I have undergone,"' said Esteron, 'and Orton can have enough wonders to fill his speeches, and the Chaplain enough to make his sermons at least interesting. I also have new recipes for Nussey.'

'For myself,' said Talleyman, 'for once I shall go to bed. Early.'

I need the rest, he thought. I have done all that was required of me. I have held this ship and this crew here in the ice for a whole winter. Now we can go home, take the news, share the rewards, and sorrow for Only.

5

On the second day of coaling, Talleyman went ashore. Esteron asked him why. Esteron was in what had been his cabin on the way out, lying in a cot.

'Keep off it,' Thacker had told him. 'As you say, not much of a break, and you can get around, just, with a broken left fibula if the tibia is whole, but it pains you to put weight on it, and it won't heal like that. If you don't want a limp for the rest of your life, then stay on your back for a couple of weeks.' So Esteron lay there, in his cot, with the door open and a small iron stove, watching what went on in the chartroom. He enjoyed the sight of Longville, harassed, fumbling with papers while Talleyman looked over his shoulder. Sometimes, Talleyman would come in to Esteron's cabin and close the door.

'Tomorrow morning,' Talleyman said.

'Why?'

'I have been here five months. I have been ashore once. To meet you.'

'Twice. You saw me off.'

'So I feel like a run ashore. Collingwood stayed at sea for four years, they say, after Trafalgar.'

'Don't you trust Fincham with the working party?'

'I've seen more of the world than he has. Can you hear the lower deck?'

'Singing? I thought that was what you all did in the long winter evenings.'

'Not like that.'

Esteron listened.

'I see what you mean. Where did they get it?'

'Not in the ship. I have asked Biddell. He lives in

terror. He thinks the ratings may get at the rum. He might have to pay for what they drink. Besides this is the first time.'

'Flog the first three that have drink on their breath. I thought that was the universal naval remedy.'

'I can't. Only had two men flogged. Ordinary seamen, ten-year men. For buggery. But I can't. Because of Cricklade.'

'On the bottle, is he? I thought so. Bad?'

'He's always fit to stand his watch. He began when the cold came in, to keep himself warm. Just a tot of brandy when he came in off watch. Then he began to keep a flask in his pocket, just a heartener when he was on deck now and then. I could stop that: I threatened to search him whenever he came on deck. Me or Longville. In private. After the change, it was worse. I talked to him. Mr Wasely preached to him. Mr Dincombe prayed for him. Publicly. No good.'

'Where does he get it from?'

'He won't say. I know he brought six cases of brandy aboard at Portsmouth. Only found out and told him to get rid of it in Dundee. He hid it all in very curious places around the ship. I've found three bottles.'

'I'll see what I can do. And Orton?'

'Oh, he's really ill. All right after his daily dose. Up to that, you've seen him. Shakes, dreams, weeps. Tonic's running out. The Surgeon's cut the dose down. So I can only have Orton for one watch a day. Chaplain does his teaching, then locks himself in his cabin. And prays, loud. Gunner does the same. Surgeon's moved his cot into the sick bay. When he's awake, he goes round the ship to find things to try his carbolic acid on. Cuts, grazes, ingrown toenails, ruptures, sore throats. Nearly killed seven men. Worse than the coast.'

'Sounds like up country in the Madras Presidency. What about a game of chess before you turn in?'

6

Talleyman went ashore with the first party. He accompanied Mr Wasely and three armourers and another blasting charge, Fincham and three Marines. Yesterday there had been twenty Marines, but nothing had happened; so today these were only a couple of sentries and the rest could take their turn in hauling coal in the ship. The first coal-cutting party would come in half an hour with their hastily made sledges.

'Feels slushy underfoot,' Talleyman remarked to Fincham.

'It'll hold,' the Marine told him.

'It looks nasty up there.' Talleyman looked up at the gathering cloud. 'I'd have said snow. Longville says no.'

'We'll get a move on just in case.'

'Do so. If the ice breaks before we are finished, we can use boats. A blizzard will stop work altogether.'

While the armourers laid their charges at one end of the long mound of coal, Talleyman climbed to the top at the other end. Nearest was the church, where the two coffins lay, Sladen's and Madden's. Beyond that, the empty warehouse where the furs had been kept. Strewn over nearly a mile of snow were the dozen or so huts. The snow around the coal mound was trampled, cut up, stained with coal dust. From this area, a couple of hundred yards each way, a man could easily slip off unnoticed. One man at a time, pleading a call of nature, vanishing among the snow hummocks. Fincham was calling to him.

'We're going to fire the charge.'

Talleyman came down on to the trampled snow, made his way in a wide throw around the working area.

When Fincham blew his whistle, Talleyman crouched and heard a satisfyingly low and dull thud. The end of the coal dump cracked in a dozen lines and there were little avalanches. The cutting party were halfway across the ice, with their sledges.

He went on with his survey. Fincham was finishing his roll call. Talleyman waved to him. It was not as easy as he thought to find a trail of foot prints from the coal dump to any of the houses. There had been no snow in the night, but the wind had kept up. Talleyman went out, about two hundred yards, choosing his direction at random. There was a house, a shack, a shed here, logs with a thatch roof rotten and green. There might be something here, the snow in the lee of the hut seemed to have been disturbed. He found a door, a broken padlock. Talleyman pushed open the door and looked inside.

This was it. There was a pile of empty bottles by the door, and a damp bed. Across the one room was a counter. On the counter and on the shelves behind it were full bottles, about forty of them. Talleyman opened one, sniffed at it. He went back outside, and fired his pistol in the air to attract attention. By waves and gesticulation, and by pointing, he managed to have the Gunner and his armourers come over to him through the snow.

'Going back to the ship, Mr Wasely? Take these with you. Thirty-seven bottles. Hand them over to Mr Biddell.' He looked directly at the armourers. 'I found this myself. I wonder what else there is.' He left them to their work, bringing out the bottles. He had reloaded the empty chamber of his pistol.

The next shed was empty, at least for these purposes. No bottles, only on the long low counter a bowl with needles, three or four pairs of scissors, odds and ends of cloth, a ready made shirt on a hook. The little Jewish tailor we saw first, thought Talleyman: I suppose he would call me a Shamyl.

The third hut – to reach this he had to cast round a short way – was further from the shore. Ah, here it was. Thank God the sailors hadn't found this. Half a dozen bottles each for them, and a couple of huge casks. There was no way that all this could be got back into *Flamingo*, and it could not be left here. Only one thing. Smash a half-dozen bottles, soak the usual mound of bedding, let it run over the tops of the casks. Pull down handfuls of thatch from the roof, soak it in the vodka, and light it with a lucifer. Then throw the torch into the puddles of spirit, and stand back.

The hut went up with a whoosh. It couldn't have burnt better, Talleyman thought, if he'd sprinkled the whole place with loose powder. A great pillar of smoke went up, and then began to drift eastward before the rising wind. Talleyman floundered around to the east. He could see *Flamingo*, and there was no doubt that someone was watching him through a telescope, outlined against the snow. He waved his arms to show he was still safe, and felt the snow on his face.

Before Talleyman had taken a dozen paces back towards the dump, the snow was whirling around him, the wind was pushing him this way and that. He cursed Longville for his certainty about the snow, and then himself for listening to Longville. It was probably different in China. Somewhere far away he could hear the hooter from *Flamingo*. The moisture was icing up his beard, his lips were stiff. He pulled his hood closer about his face, and realized he could no longer hear the hooter. Which way was it? The wind was gusting about from one direction to another, the soft snow was up to his knees, he found it impossible to walk in a straight line. He had lost his direction.

Talleyman pushed on straight forward. But was straight forward now what it had been half an hour ago? He thought he was going uphill, turned round and walked the other way, but surely this was uphill too. He slid on ice, and fell to one side. Then he realized that he had not fallen to the ground, but was leaning against something, surely not a wall? No, it was a tree trunk: but there were no trees here, the only wood seemed to be in the sides of the shacks.

Yes, it was true, he could see the pattern of the snow. He was standing against the wall of a house, a hut, a shack. He felt his way around the wall, going always to his right. His hands found something hard in the wall, something shaped, sticking out. He had lost his left glove, he could tell it was iron. A latch? He was dizzy with the cold. Yes, there was a line, a seam almost, in the wood, vertical. His hood had slipped back, the ice was forming on his eyebrows, would soon clot his eyelashes, fill his eyes, hold them open as he lay dead. Out of the dizziness of cold, a thought came to him. He lost his right glove too. He felt into his pocket. He had hold of his pistol, the lanyard was round his neck, but he had to twist it round his wrist too. With his Deane and Adams in his right hand, wondering if he had the strength to cock the hammer, he groped further, the first metal must have been a hinge, he felt with his left hand to a latch. With the edge of his left hand, he knocked the latch up, and fell sideways though the door that opened under his weight. He caught at the door jamb so as to keep upright.

Yes, he was in a house, a room at least. The ice melted quickly off his eyebrows. There was a man sitting looking at him, a pistol in his hand. The two pistols pointed at each other. Two Deanes thought Talleyman, I'm not Swift, he must be. The seated man said, sharply, in English,

'Shut the door!'

Talleyman moved across, reached behind him, shut the door, kept out the blizzard. The room was warm. There was a charcoal brazier in the middle of the floor, with a pot on it. He peered through the steam at the other man, and said, grasping something,

'You're the storekeeper. You speak English.'

'I speak German with my parents, Russian to the servants and to nobles, English with my nurse, French with my governness. I am Dushan Rakoff. My father is Baron Rakoff.'

'My name is Thomas Talleyman.'

'So I see.' The other pistol jerked a little. Talleyman asked him,

'And the star?'

'Not a star. I know what you mean, but if you look at it properly, you see that it is our family arms, a crab. *Rako* is the Russian for a crab, you know. You see the claws?'

It was an effort, but Talleyman did not look. He said,

'Be careful with the pistol. I have adjusted it. Put a new spring in. Other things. It is very easy on the trigger.'

'I know. And the butt, too, you have altered that to give a better grip.'

'I have big hands.'

'So have I, and I suppose like you I chose this over the Colt for that very reason.'

'Obviously.'

Talleyman watched the Russian, watched his hand. He felt the revolver heavy on his wrist, but he was determined he would not be the first to put a weapon down. It was, as he had guessed, the Russian who said,

'Let us sit like gentlemen.' He began to move his pistol hand outward from his body, both the muzzle and his eyes tracking Talleyman, who followed suit. Finally, the two pistols were down on the table top, at arm's length from their owners. Rakoff brought his hands back to the centre of the table, and Talleyman did the same.

'The snow,' said the Russian, 'looks to be set for an hour or two. I was about to have my dinner. Will you join me?'

'What is it?' It may be his ration for a week.

'Beetroot and barley soup, a Russian delicacy, or so the peasants tell me.'

'I can add to the feast.' Talleyman moved his hand cautiously towards the pocket of his pea jacket, and brought out a packet of ship's biscuits, then a tin of corned beef, and a packet of portable soup, ox-tail he was glad to see for his digestion's sake. 'Shall I drop them in?'

'Not the biscuits, if you please. And if you are thirsty after your exertions, I can let you have some vodka. A spirit produced locally, but many find it palatable.'

Especially matelots who cannot buy their brandy from the mess, thought Talleyman. He fumbled in his other pocket, and said,

'I can make an exchange. I do not know if you have heard of a foreign spirit called Cognac.'

'For a moment,' said Rakoff, 'I was afraid you would offer me rum.'

'Officers and gentlemen,' said Talleyman, 'do not drink rum.' Not unless the officer is named Cricklade, and he will drink the stuff they make in the South Seas, old women chewing the roots and spitting them into a bowl to ferment. If he could find yeast, he might try that with ships' biscuits. He brought out his clasp-knife and opened the tin, scraping out the beef, fat and all, into the bubbling pot, and the tablet of portable soup for good measure. By the look of it, the pot had been bubbling, on and off, for most of the winter, never quite emptied, and was like to keep on until Heptagesima Tuesday. But all the time, he kept his eye on his revolver – whose revolver? – and his hand within reach of it, and Rakoff watched him watching. The Russian stood.

'That will be fit to eat in ten minutes or so.'

He stepped away from the table, from the pistols, and walked to a tall cupboard. The door was hinged to conceal the contents as he groped inside, brought out two tin bowls, two spoons, a couple of enamelled cups.

'The landlord has not provided the most lavish appointments, but at least my nanny taught me to keep things clean. I do not want to have a stomach ache up here.'

He's got more than a stomach ache, Talleyman thought. Black bloodmarks under the skin, the breath stinking, the gums swollen, and his nose has been bleeding. He's probably getting tired early, needs more sleep. If I can wait him out. . . if he's alone. . .

If I can keep him alone, thought Rakoff. He's been trudging about in the snow, he must be half beat. It's warm in here, a heavy meal, enough vodka, perhaps it may turn him sleepy, careless. I may persuade him I'm harmless, that I've given up. Perhaps, perhaps. . . But they'll be looking for him. Indeed, I have caught a bear.

Talleyman asked, casually as if it hardly mattered,

'How goes the war?'

'The war? The Austrians have not declared war yet, and I think that we will wait for them to move before we strike.'

'But the war, the war between yourselves and Britain and France? Is it still going on?'

'Oh, yes, and the King of Sardinia has joined in. Well, it has not been much of a war. Your people have made raids around our coasts, like this one. At Archangel, in the Baltic, at Petropavlovsk, at Sebastopol. That was the only one which landed in force.'

'A dozen regiments.'

'Perhaps. They landed at Eupatoria, and left the Turks to face the great battle on the Danube.'

'You evacuated the Principalities.'

'Poof! We can be back across the Danube in a week. Your troops marched round Sebastopol, to the south, and our armies came down from the Ukraine and sealed them in under the walls of the fortress, so they will never get away.'

'And your fleet? And ours?' Perhaps half of this is true.

'Your fleet would not approach the forts, although they outnumbered our ships by ten to one. That great fortress was built with all its guns facing out to sea, so we sank the ships in the mouth of the harbour, and moved their guns to the south walls. We drew out your cavalry and destroyed it, and then we drove your infantry till they had their backs to the sea.'

None of it true, thought Rakoff, none of it true. He had letters. '...the black day of the Russian Army...two regiments of hussars and four of cossacks fleeing from a handful of madmen in red coats... troopers fighting each other to get over the Traktir bridge...my own men say they will not follow me against the English...' He went on, 'Your fleet brought food and clothes into Balaclava, but it was destroyed by a storm, and the snows came. You would like to spend the last winter in tents without food, in summer uniforms? That is what happened to your Army. Very few remain.'

Talleyman shrugged.

'That happens to armies. You, I suppose, suffered no loss?'

'Oh, very little.' No need to tell the Englishman about the long lines of conscripts marching down the long road through the winter into the Crimea. No need to talk about the mounds of dead in the snow between Kiev and Odessa, about the empty villages, about the estates where there would be no new generation to pay the landlord's rents. No need to talk about the memories. No need.

They ate. He can only eat stew like this, Talleyman thought. Give him a steak to chew and he'd leave his teeth in it. And it would hurt. Nobody who hasn't had scurvy, even only a touch, can understand what it feels like. Talleyman asked,

'So you count this as a raid? Like Sebastopol?'

'Perhaps this you have pushed home with more determination.'

'We had no choice.'

'You still have the same choice. You may surrender whenever you wish.'

'To whom? Your cavalry regiment? That lunatic? He would not have charged a stone fortress like that. What made him think he could charge a ship? We were well protected, we had a battery of guns heavier than anything you would find on shore, we had plenty of ammunition. Why attack us like that?'

Rakoff sat in silence for a while – a minute or two, perhaps, but to both men it seemed like an hour. Then he replied dully,

'We had to. We needed your food.'

'You needed the food?'

'You do not know who we are?' Rakoff sounded incredulous. 'We were not a regiment, with regular supplies, with regular commanders, specific orders. Nobody cared about us, nobody knew. We are. . .were. . . all officers, some sergeants, sent into exile for being unreliable politically. We were ordered to live in this village or that, two or three in a village. I was ordered to live here. Our pay comes, some of us even brought our wives and children here, but we may not move out of the village we are sent to. This is exile to Siberia. Most of us are expected to die here.

'When we heard there was a war, and the English ships were off Murmansk, we put on our uniforms again, and came together at the depot, where we come to report that we are still alive, and draw our pay. We brought what weapons we had. We all knew how to fight, we formed our own regiment, we marched to Murmansk to fight, and fight we did, when you tried to land.

'But before that I was sent here with a few others to watch any attempt to land. There is nowhere else along the coast. I watched you come and go the first time.

301

We thought you would go back, but when you came in again I tried to burn the coal, and then to force you out. I – we failed. I went down to our depot, it is at a place called Vologda, and the Colonel, the man we accepted as our commander, we who were disowned by our own army, he decided we must attack the ship now when you were trapped in the ice.

'We reckoned we had five days' rations, enough to reach Vladi Sever. But we took longer than we had thought, we lost horses, a lot of horses. We did not reach you for eight days, all the food was gone. We had to attack you or starve to death. The Colonel was a cavalryman of the old type, he decided if we charged we could take you by surprise.'.

Talleyman knew the rest. Rakoff understood that. Talleyman would not ask anything more, not on that attack. But he did ask,

'You say you are here. . .almost as a prisoner?'

'I did unreliable things. Before there was any war. . .I subscribed to foreign papers, to the *Illustrated*, for example. I am sent here for taking the *Illustrated*. But my subscription still runs, and the *Illustrated* is still sent on to me. It is several weeks late now, it has to come through Prussia, but here I get it on the shores of the Arctic Ocean. My father sees it comes on. I am really here as a hostage for my father.'

'A hostage?'

'He is a courtier, an official in the Foreign Ministry, or the Finance Ministry, or whatever ministry they need someone with more brains than a Great Russian. He is a Baltic baron from Courland. It is simple: as long as I behave myself here he is trusted and well treated, and leaves Russia on the Tsar's business. He is out of Russia now. As long as he behaves, I am allowed to live in peace here and allowed to have my mails, my hunting weapons, everything, as if I were on my own estate in Courland. It is still snowing.'

'It sounds like it.'

302

'Do you play chess? Perhaps we could have a game while we wait for it to stop.'

'Yes.' Or till something happens, thought Talleyman, to break this deadlock. He watched Rakoff bring out the board, set out the pieces on their squares. Rakoff took the King's Rook's pawn from each side, turned his back on Talleyman while he shook the two men together in his palms. The pistols were in clear view and in easy reach: Talleyman ignored them. He reached out to touch Rakoff's outstretched right fist, took white.

Rakoff poured two more glasses of vodka. Talleyman reflected that he had not tasted anything quite like this since he had shared his brother-in-law's poteen in Eyories, only Lawrence was not his brother-in-law then. He wondered how good this Russian was. They said you played only as well as your opponent would let you. Hardly anyone in the wardroom or the gun room knew much more than the moves. With no good players to test himself against, Talleyman was afraid his game had gone off.

You always began with this, he reminded himself. Pawn to King's 4. Rakoff considered a long time. Come on, Talleyman thought, move *your* King's pawn to its fourth. It's the way to start. Rakoff was considering. Which was Talleyman asking for? King's Knight's Game? Allgaier's gambit? The English seemed overfond of the Sicilian opening, Staunton had used it when he had played him in London at the St George's. Pawn to Queen's Bishop 4.

Talleyman stared. The proper reply was a mirror of his opening move. Oh, well, this must be the way they played in Russia. Let's mirror him. Pawn to my King's Bishop 4. Good enough, thought Rakoff, he's accepting the Sicilian. My Queen's Knight to Queen's Bishop 3.

Talleyman looked in surprise. He had not seen this before. But then, he had not seen any fresh move very often for most people he had played with, like Harriet or Biddell, he had taught the game to. He echoed

303

King's Knight to King's Bishop 3. Let him think about that.

Rakoff thought, quite a time. He considered each of three possible moves, extrapolated each a dozen moves into the future, seeing how each demanded a set move from White, how each of his counters imposed without choice new moves. He made his own choice, at last answered with pawn to King's 3.

Talleyman asked,

'Why do you stay here?'

'I told you, I must. I have been sent here, into internal exile.'

'But there is no prison, no guards, no warders. If all you must do is to report and draw your pay – when? Once a month, once a quarter, once a year?'

'Six months.'

'It would be easy. Start just after pay day, ride south and west, jump a ship that comes in for the furs, steal a boat yourself if you can sail, and make west, across Finland into Sweden. No one would miss you.'

'I cannot.'

Rakoff made a move carefully, calculating ahead. Talleyman replied after a moment. Rakoff was puzzled. What is this Englishman thinking about? What is his plan? Never the expected move, never a basis for my own plan. It is almost as if he is moving at random.

It was almost at random. Talleyman was irked, four moves on each side, and not a single man taken yet. Ah, there was a chance. My Bishop can take his Knight, there. Damn, I didn't see that, he had his pawn there to protect the Knight, there goes my Bishop, right let's move this pawn, at least it's safe. The wind has changed. The Russian hasn't noticed that. A little while ago while I was talking, I heard the saluting gun, very faint, not much more than a pop. But they must have been firing it at ten-minute intervals as soon as the snow came down. I couldn't hear it before, but now the wind must have come round. If I talk I may stop him hearing the next one.

'I suppose you hope that if you fight well here, if you can prevent us landing again, or keep us from moving out, they will release you? A medal from the Tsar, perhaps?' The Ruskies, so I hear, set a lot of store by medals, they have a lot of them, wear them all the time – that was the gun, a little louder. Well, he may be an infantry officer and a rich man and hunt elk but he is not a man for the weather. He does not smell it, like Longville.

Rakoff was irritated at Talleyman talking while they played, and he made his next move before he answered.

'The Tsar will never hear of this, or give any medals. He has cast us off, and nobody on the staff will bother to notice us. We are abandoned.'

'But the staff remembered all of you well enough to send you to defend Murmansk.'

'The staff did not send us. We came, we heard Russia was in danger. The Tsar, the government, have forgotten us. We came together to defend Russia.'

There was something the Chaplain had heard the cavalrymen say, half of them dead, the rest dying, now of wounds, later of starvation, and they knew it. They had said, for Russia, not for the Romanoffs. There were more than ten minutes gone, and no gun sounded. This must mean that the snow had stopped. Hello, he's castled. I know it's legal but I've not seen anyone do it before, I thought it only happened in the chess column in the *Illustrated*. I suppose I'd better do it, too. Just let me get that pawn out of the way in the next move.

Rakoff wearily shook his head. What would the Englishman do next? What can I do next? Try pawn to Queen's 4. It offers him the pawn, but I can probably begin to develop properly then.

Talleyman moved at once. I'll bring that knight forward. Oh, damnation, I missed that I ought to have taken that pawn. Oh, never mind. So, the snow's stopped, and they've stopped firing a gun for direction. Now, if I were Longville, what would I do? Or, more to the point, what will Fincham do? Longville was right, the weather is changing. The snow was different when it came, big wet blobs.

The game went on. Talleyman listened. He pressed his argument. 'But you could get abroad easily. You would be welcome in a lot of places. Are you afraid for your father?'

'My father does not matter. When I was sent here, he was in a situation of some delicacy. But that was three years ago. Now there is a war, he is in a position of strength. He is a courtier, and an official. The point is that he is one of the few men in Russia who understands money and the money market, and who is not a Jew. He is safe now, and he thinks I am safe.'

'Safe? Because you cannot go to the war?'

'True.'

They played. Rakoff seemed disturbed. The game was now more to Talleyman's liking, men were taken, there was less of this stupid struggling for position. Bishop took pawn. Bishop took Knight. Pawn took Bishop. Pawn took pawn took pawn. Talleyman listened. That Rakoff was listening too he took for granted. He was wrong. Rakoff was not listening to the outside world, he was playing chess. He felt his game was disturbed by the need to listen.

'You can escape even now.'

'Escape?'

'Escape from this imprisonment. Exile if you like. We have steam up. By now. We will sail as soon as the ice is thin enough.'

Talleyman had never taken a pawn en passant. He had heard of it, and now there was a pawn offered. He took it.

'You could sail with us. Come back to England. I offer you hospitality.' Were there noises outside, feet shuffling over snow? Was there breathing?

Rakoff heard the words, saw white pawn take black Knight. He cried,

'Do not tempt me! How could I ever leave Russia? How desert Mother Russia? Tsar or Republic, how could I leave Russia?'

He saw the chance through his tears, black Rook to take white Queen. He acted. And then he looked ahead three moves, and saw what this led to. He cursed. Talleyman looked puzzled, did what he could in revenge, took the black Queens's Rook. And the door opened.

Talleyman snatched for the pistol at his right hand. Rakoff brought up his boots, kicked the table at Talleyman, and jumped back. There were figures in the door, men in furs, unrecognizable. Someone let off a shot. Talleyman had fallen back under the table. Rakoff fired his pistol at random, at no target, only to make smoke and give him time, now to pull the cupboard forward and let him through the other door, behind it. The falling cupboard struck Talleyman as he tried to rise, knocked him sideways on top of the brazier. He felt the fire bite into his left hand, and yelled, pushed harder against the burning cupboard.

Talleyman thought, after all this, after all this, to be killed over a chess board, burnt, crippled, scarred. The cupboard was pulled away, hard hands tugged him to his feet and rushed him through the door. Now he could tell who they were. The men he expected – Fincham, Egan, Hanlon, Smales, Parkes, Calne, were around him, the track of their snowshoes led away, melting now under the weather. It was not snow now that fell on his face, but water, the blessed rain driving hard into his skin.

'You were quiet,' he said stupidly. Fincham laughed.

'Calne stalks deer, and Parkes is a poacher. The rest of us followed. Back to the ship, hurry. We can sail in an hour.'

'How did you find me?' There was a Marine holding

Talleyman under each arm, half carrying him along.

'We knew where we saw you last, when the snow come down. When it slacked, we came to the nearest house you had on your sketch.'

They were, somehow, on the quarterdeck, Talleyman could not remember how, and he was being hustled into the wardroom. Biddell was holding for him a cup of – quarter rum, quarter sugar, quarter coffee, quarter what? Longville was asking,

'Permission to prepare to sail, sir? Mr Craddock says we can steam in one hour.'

'Yes, yes, we must go. But first – Mr Biddell? Have we good stocks of beef? Can we spare three days' ration for one man? And, more important, a half gallon jar of lime juice? A party quickly to build a . . . a snow castle over them, the height of a man.'

Talleyman could feel his left hand burning still. It was the worst he had ever had. And the other quarter in the mug, now he knew: it was opium.

VII

The Agapanthus Club

1

Talleyman brought Dincombe into the Agapanthus Club at about midday. He had taken a cab from the railway, after coming up from Portsmouth. In the main room they found Orton sitting at a table.

'Is this your breakfast or your lunch?' Talleyman asked.

'I'm not sure. I've been to a doctor today, and I don't know if he left me on my hips or my heels. You know, I've been six full days ashore without a drop of my tonic, knowingly. I think it had better have been lunch. I have a guest coming.'

'I'm putting up Dincombe for this place,' said Talleyman. 'You won't blackball him, will you?'

'No, nor will anybody else. I'll get Craddock to come and talk to him. How was Biddell when you last saw him?'

'He's nearly finished the paying off. He was having another attack. Not bad. But he thinks he's had enough of the sea. He was talking of becoming an attorney. My brother is an attorney. I thought I would try and arrange for articles. Surprise him.'

'Don't bother,' Orton said airily. 'I've talked already to a firm who do a lot of the briefing for my chambers. It's all arranged. And you, Chaplain, I suppose you've gone back to your college as though nothing had happened. Anyone notice you'd been away?'

'I'm not staying in Cambridge. I have a friend, a Doctor Williams of King's, who is professor of Hebrew at a college in Wales, somewhere, where, he says, they take ploughboys who speak no English to teach them enough Latin to be curates in the hills. He has

311

persuaded the head of the college, Dean Llewellyn Llewellin, to offer me a post: professor of mathematics and Church history. I have accepted for three years. I will, of course, retain my fellowship at St Tibb's.'

'And the income?' asked Orton.

'Oh, yes, and the stipend.'

'That's the fellow,' Orton applauded. 'Ah, here is my guest.'

'Good heavens!' said Dincombe, and then inwardly scolded himself for such profanity. 'It's Moulton, and his fur coat.'

Moulton came to attention.

'The ship, suh, is decommissioned. The whaler men have taken their fur coats back to Dundee to find new ships, and the ten-year men are selling theirs around the shops of Southsea. The going rate, depending on fur and condition, is anything from twenty to fifty pounds. More than they would have got as prize money.'

'Where is Calne?'

'He has gone back to Dundee to redeem our sextants and watches.'

'How did you decide who went?' asked Orton.

'We played poker for the two tickets.'

'You resorted to chance?' asked Dincombe.

'Poker, suh, when Ah plays it, is no game of chance. Ah tol' th' portah hyah, suh, that Ah wus an ensahn, and he showed a remarkable ability to believe the impossible.'

'You are staying here?' asked Dincombe.

'I have called on the American minister, and I find I am required to return to Washington. I have left the legation to apply for a medal on my behalf, if there is one, and to send it on.'

'There's a new medal,' said Orton. 'Going to call it the cross of the Order of Victoria, or something like that. You might put in for that, too. Novelty value in your service. Just get a senior officer's signature, I believe.'

312

'Are you applying for it, sir?'

'No, don't think so. It's being given to all ranks, private soldiers and up. No rarity value with us, more distinctive not to have it than to have it.'

'A bit more distinctive,' said Talleyman. 'I've seen the draft regulations. It can be given – one only – to a ship. The Captain wears it.'

'So you could put in for it.'

'No. Only is to get it.'

'But Only is dead,' said Dincombe. 'We all saw him walk off into the snow.'

'The Russians took him,' said Talleyman. 'They held him all winter in Petersburg. They are exchanging him.'

'You mean he might walk in here any moment?'

'No. Not walk. He had frostbite. That is how the Ruskies took him. He has lost most of each foot. Is a medal a fair exchange?'

'So he got maimed feet out of the war,' said Orton, 'and two medals. The seamen got their fur coats, and their medals. The officers only got their medals, if they ever come – we had to pay for our fur coats, Moulton, Pusser's prices. What else? What else did you get out of it, Chaplain?'

'I got a lot,' said Dincombe. 'I have three things on my study walls. A Russian painting of the Virgin. A discharge certificate, saying that I am an AB, and able to hand, reef, steer and use the belaying pin, signed by every seaman and Marine. When we sailed, you will remember we had twenty men who signed their articles with a cross: every man signed my papers with his name, and read what he was signing. Craddock's young men took a sword that was left after the charge, and they have made a small ploughshare out of it.'

'And anything else?' asked Moulton.

'Discontent,' said Dincombe. 'Discontent with only knowing one kind of man, I have talents, and knowledge. I believe that by accepting Dean Llewellin's offer

313

I can use them. I can educate clergy in the term, and in the vacation I can work in some parish among the colliers. After three years, we will see.'

'You grew up,' said Moulton. 'We watched it. When you came into the ship, we on the lower deck called you "the curate". At the end, we addressed you as "Vicar". In these new plans, sir, are you still taking Mr Kingsley's advice?'

'That dreadful man,' said Dincombe with energy. 'Did you see in print what he wrote to someone in a letter? He said something like, "what would I not give for an hour's skirmishing in the Sebastopol ditches, followed by ten minutes of butt-and-bayonet as a bonne bouche". Oh, that man! He has never seen a fight, never seen blood, never felt pain, has never *done* anything! Oh, I pray every day – '

'For peace?' asked Orton.

'No. I pray every day that the time will come when no man ever needs to climb a mast in a storm to carry wasteful trifles across the sea.'

Orton was silent a moment. Then he said cheerfully,

'What's up with you, Tal? You're being a Craddock, not saying a word. Are you going to hit somebody?'

'I am worried,' said Talleyman. 'I may hit someone. I gave the ship back to her owners, Gunner and Boatswain and Carpenter. I have sent telegrams to my home and to my father's – no, my family's house in London. There have been no answers. I went to Bedford Square on my way here. The house is shut up. There was only a housekeeper. She did not know me. She told me my brother is abroad. She could tell me no more.'

At Fen Dilney, the postman knew quite well that the Dower House was shut up and empty. He saw no point in walking an extra twenty minutes each way with post no one would open. He therefore put all the Dower House post and telegrams in a separate box to deliver all in one batch when the house was lived in again. Harriet had seen in *The Times* that *Flamingo* was home. She had had no word from Thomas here where she lived now, in the Manor House.

The four at the Agapanthus Club were preparing to leave, standing in the hall outside the Secretary's office.

'Would you like to join, then, Chaplain?' Orton asked. 'Friendly Club, mostly officers. I'll put your name down, now. This is Mr Bolton, the Secretary. Probably the last man here who really remembers the old *Agapanthus*.'

'I was in her, and I saw her go,' said Bolton. He thought this a good berth, after a life as a Purser. 'I was a Pusser's assistant, as low as you can go, I was fourteen. She was on fire from end to end of the main deck. The Captain had the wheel and the First Lieutenant and the Bo'sun were at the headsheets, keeping her sailing towards the French, and the rest of us was jumping off the back end, like fleas off a drowning dog. And then she went. Poof!'

'Let me put his name down. There are a couple of other clergy, old chaplains. I'll pass the word, you'll not be blackballed,' Orton went on. 'You too, Moulton? Perhaps we could spend an hour now in the card room. There are some members who would be pleased to teach you an English game called Brag. But we *are* select, you know. Tal's brother tried to join last year, but he was blackballed, wasn't he, Tal?'

'I,' said Talleyman with some satisfaction, 'passed the word.'

Then,

'Wait,' said Talleyman. 'I think you have something else from this voyage. A gift from the gun room officers. I was asked to bring it up for you.'

He pressed a book, wrapped, into Dincombe's hands. By the time the Chaplain looked up again, he had disappeared. Dincombe unwrapped it, and laughed, loud and long and in a way most unsuitable for a clergyman. It was a new copy of H. H. Fincham's *A History of Naval Architecture*.

315

2

It was early in the day. Talleyman sat in the train between Peterborough and King's Cross. He could feel the weight of his Deane and Adams in the inside breast pocket of his morning coat. His revolver, or Rakoff's, it did not matter. He had done some machining on the ship, brought the grip nearer to his ideal. He had fired fifty rounds the day before, to get used to the new balance, a matter of pennyweights in difference. He could now get a six-inch group at thirty yards.

All five chambers were loaded. He had polished the bullets till they shone, at least, like silver. The caps were still in their box in his pocket. He proposed to kill someone before the day was out. His brother, or Philip Suttle, or perhaps some stranger, but someone.

At King's Cross, by chance, he bumped into Longville.

'What are you doing here?' Longville was in civilian clothes, of course, but somewhat shabby. His top hat was greened, in a telltale way, with salt spray. He answered,

'I was inquiring for trains to Scotland. There is someone in Edinburgh who may offer me a ship: or a first mate's berth.'

'Who gave you that black eye?'

'Orton. Outside the Agapanthus.'

'Not in it, thank God. Why?'

'He said he'd do it to anybody who's been dealing in opium.'

'Well,' said Talleyman, 'you were in *Waterwitch*, you know. That's the reputation.'

316

'The reputation is justified. What else would you do in China in a ship as fast as that, and too small to carry a worthwhile cargo? But at least it wasn't slaving.'

'No. At least it wasn't slaving.' An idea struck Talleyman. He had got on the train, as he had moved for the last two days, in a white-hot fury, hardly able to think. But, now, he was beginning to reflect, to form a plan of campaign. 'Are you doing anything today?'

'No, only trudging to ship owners.'

'Meet me in the Club. About one o'clock.' There might be advantage in having a second, or at least a witness, who will be neutral. No one would accuse Longville of favouring me.

He looked at his watch. There were still twenty minutes. The sky was grey, but there was no real threat of rain, nor any rain last night. It would be easy to step between the piles of horse dung before the crossing sweepers cleared them. He need not take a cab, he could walk down to the Bedford Square House. It would give him time to think. Outside the station, the noise changed. The hissing of the engines and the crashing of shunting gave way to the roar of a myriad iron-tyred wheels, the clatter of thousands of iron-shod hooves. All London ran on iron. That was the greatest difference from the ship, from the creak of the wooden hull, that and the angry shouting of five million greedy people, not the whispering of two hundred orderly sailors. But the very noise would shut out the rest of the world, would let him think better than he could in silence. Think: and remember.

3

Talleyman had come home to the Manor House toward the end of the afternoon. He knew by now most of what had happened since he sailed, at least Barnet's version as he was rattled from the station. He knew now how his father had died, how Harriet had faced the great horse, faced him down without so much as a whip in her hands and saved the groom's life. He knew that after the funeral, some time after the funeral, his brother had taken her to foreign parts to cheer her up, shutting up the Dower House, leaving the boys with Arabella.

'But she knew you was coming back, sir, she was set on it, when there was lots around these parts, and in Lunnon too that thought you was all gone, and the Ruskies not bothering to tell us. Or lost you was in the ice like poor Admiral Franklin, and never to be seen no more. But she said you was coming back in the spring, and there was no cause for her to stay here in the grumps and dress all in black if she could be going abroad, to Paris and to Brugg and all the gay places. And she knew you wouldn't mind, and you could afford it now with the old master gone and half the money in the world in your pockets. And it was two days ago she come home and anxious to see you if ever you came home alive and looking well as a bumble bee in August.'

'Stop here!' Talleyman got down from the trap. Yes, the bailiff had finished it off, got this part of the fen drained and ploughed. There were men moving methodically along the furrows, planting potatoes. By hand? There must be some way of doing it by machine. Like steam ploughing, he would have that under way

318

by the next spring. He had the drawings all ready, made up in the ship, in the ice, painstakingly laid out on elephant sheets by the light of an oil lamp. Only to get Hurrels to do the casting, and ask Craddock to recommend some bright young man to superintend the setting up. Or, rather, do the setting up for he would superintend it himself. He might even be able to have the potato picking done by machine. He asked Barnet,

'Gypsies?'

'No, sir, them's Irish. They comes around in gangs, and a terrible nuisance they are, too, sir, stealing hens and going for the girls, and I don't suppose they've ever seen a potato before, sir.'

They came to the front of the Manor House. Talley-man asked,

'When did they shoot Emperor?' They could not have kept the horse, not after what it had done. It had killed a man, it would have had to be shot. And yet... it had been a good horse, one he and his father had gone to buy together. It was the first thing for years he and his father had done together. For once they had agreed, without discussion, let alone argument. They had, Talleyman thought, begun after all to come together. Yet it had killed his father and it would have to die. Had they shot it here, he wanted to know, and buried it somewhere on the farm, or had they sent Emperor to a knacker's yard, to feed hounds? ... Or poor sailors? Barnet answered,

'Oh, no, sir. The missus, your missus, she wouldn't let them shoot 'un. She said that 'e were a brute beast that knew not bit nor bridle and had no understanding but would fall upon thee with no intent of evil. And she said that they should shoot her first, or that they should wait for you to shoot 'un, and wait for you they decided to do and she still rode 'un round the farm and the park every day till she went away though she didn't hunt him because them around was too afeared to have 'un out on the hunt, and she were riding him yesterday the day after she came home, and she did have 'un over the jumps in the paddock all yesterday morning, and in the afternoon she did have 'un all round the farm and all over the hedges, even the highest ones, and again this morning all the morning as if she were trying to set 'un at a hedge that were too high for 'un and she couldn't find none nor even a hedge he hadn't the stomach for. But she didn't come out this afternoon at all.'

They were at a halt now. The footmen came out to bring in the cases, but Talleyman carried his canvas bag in himself.

Arabella was there to meet him. She had the two boys with her. Talleyman bent to them. He rummaged in the bag and brought out his presents.

'Look, here are Russian hats made of fur. These are what the Russian soldiers wear. And I've worn one, too.'

He tried to put the hats on the boys' heads. Alfred cowered away, began to cry, and then as Talleyman persevered he started to scream as loud as his two years would let him.

Arabella put out her hand, and he clung to it. Edward looked gravely at his father. He did not cry, he just shook, shrank away.

Arabella said,

'Let them have time to get used to you.'

'Nine months,' Talleyman agreed. 'At their age an immense time, a quarter of their lives. And I have a new face, my nose pushed the other way. Does it become me?'

He turned his face one way and another. He's trying to make me laugh, thought Arabella, the way he used to do when we were both little children, before he went into *Argyle*. She tried to oblige, said to Edward,

'Look at daddy! Look at the funny face he's making!' Highly useful, she thought, now Edward's crying too. Oh, what a happy return, who'd bother with a husband and children if this is what happens? Her brother asked,

320

'But where is Harriet?'

'She is a little unwell. Only a little, but she has had a tiring week, all that travelling. She went to bed after her luncheon. I have told Emily to take her up a pot of tea and help her to wash and wake herself. She will be down directly.'

4

Harriet was indeed unwell. She was sunk in despair. She had been sick again, not merely in the morning, but after the midday meal, although it was nothing but a trifle of cold ham and hot potatoes. The gin and water had not done it, and the slippery elm had not done it, and the olive oil had not done it, and the hot baths had not done it, and the dose that Marie-Claire had produced, smelling of foxgloves and juniper, had not done it. And the riding had not done it. The riding had done nothing.

She had hoped for something from the jumps, the high jumps and the shocks of landing. She might even have hoped for a fall, for a bad fall and for being rolled on. Surely that would have done it, would have brought it on. At the worst, she might have died. And then nobody would have known. But the great horse kept on jumping, kept on running, and nothing came of it. She had even, down in the paddock, shucked off her wraparound skirt and in her winter under trousers, black leather, had straddled the beast bareback. It was useful to have that excuse, that she wanted to try him bareback, at least it would be respectable, she would have no trouble even if she were thrown. But, curse it, she found herself clinging to him as if she were glued and she could not let herself be thrown. That was a sign, for sure, that she was born to be a rider, and here was a whole season's hunting she had missed again and heaven knew if she would ever have another, if she would ever even have a house of her own again or keep her children, for he was sure to want to take them away and brand her as an evil woman and a bad mother for ever. And here he was now in the house and asking for her and for God's sake there was no facing him, and the thought made her sick again, genuinely sick.

But by six o'clock she was well enough to come down to dine, and she worked hard at showing her pleasure at having him with her again and feeling him hold her. And that joy was as real as her sickness. It was all a strange mixture of true feeling and dissembling that even she could not disentangle. And she felt Tom kiss her, and she kissed him back with passion as she had never kissed him before. But there, he was too full of himself to notice.

'And that is the tale,' he told the two women. 'We went into the ice where few have been, and we stayed on the Russian coast for the whole winter. We were a thorn in their flesh. They sent a regiment against us.' There was no point in telling them what Rakoff had said. 'We must have cost the Tsar God knows how much in money and men, just us two hundred or so, not to talk of what Esteron did. We must have him here.'

'Will they want you to go back to sea?' asked Arabella.

'I don't think so, not in this war.'

'Have you plenty of pictures? Will they be published?'

'I have, but I don't think they will be printed.'

He had been to see his friend at the *Illustrated*, and been told,

'There's no market. Nobody wants to see this any more. As far as our readers are concerned, this war took place in the Crimea and nowhere else. What have you got? Sailors in beards with icicles on them, fields of snow, guns going off, cavalry charging. We have carried nothing else since September. Now we hardly

322

print any at all. The readers are tired of the war, they take it for granted. They are more interested in the Empress Eugenie's gowns. Besides, the war will peter out soon.'

'Peter out?'

'We are running out of men. Look, Tal, have you forgotten that there was a famine in Ireland? Ireland had a third of the population of the Kingdom, and almost all our soldiers come from Ireland. But we lost over half the population in Ireland, and that means nearly a fifth of the population of the Kingdom. Didn't you notice that Portsmouth is garrisoned by militia? Every regular soldier we have is at the Russian war, and there is no one else to send. The French have run out of money. They are sending plenty of troops, and so are the Italians, but they have to beg us to let them have ammunition and food. We are paying for the war, and the French abuse us for not fighting it. But the Russians can keep on for ever. They have plenty of men, and they have the money. They have just negotiated a loan of fifty million in Brazil and can go on as long as they like.'

Talleyman shrugged that off. He told his wife and his sister,

'Oh, we did splendidly in the ship. We ate like fighting cocks, and we all got fat as you, Harriet. You've put on half a stone at least over the winter. But we ate so much we could have satisfied Fat Jack Pither.' Did well. We only lost four men dead and one deserted. But there was frostbite and there were burns. There were hernias from lifting sacks and waterbutts and hands caught by running ropes and feet the guns had run over. Thacker had 173 names on his treatment lists by the end of the voyage. There were twenty-five or so who would never go to sea again, and at least a dozen who would always be unfit for hard work. But no scurvy. No mutiny, unless you counted Garvey, only three or four men knifed of bludgeoned in fights. A very happy

323

cruise all in all. Probably the last cruise of the old Navy. The next time he would go to sea, if he ever did, they'd all be ten-year men, going to the ship they were sent to, not to a ship they had picked, and knowing that after this voyage there would be yet another commission.

'But yourself,' asked Arabella, 'were you hurt at all?'

'Oh, no, nothing to mention,' he told them. 'Only my nose. The Surgeon reset it straight.' And the burns, and the bayonet through his armpit, not much of a scar to show. I wonder if it will twinge in the rain. Mark of a veteran, to wince and say, oh it's my old wound. 'But Harriet, you haven't said a word. Nothing about what you saw and heard in Bruges. Or why you went. I suppose that Richard will tell me all that. Perhaps you don't want to bore Arabella. You must have told Arabella all about it. We don't want to bore her.'

Oh, if I could tell you, Harriet, if only I could tell you, I have so much to tell you. Being presented to the Empress in Paris, that lovely woman with her great eyes and so much prettier and smarter than the dowry Victoria I was presented to so soon after we were married. And the streets of Bruges under the snow and so full of people, and the Christmas tree on the tower of the town hall and the carillons playing, and going to Brussels for the Shrove Tuesday feasts and to that ball there and being presented to the Crown Prince called Leopold, such a pretty name and him a big strong young fellow and so good-looking, and he seemed quite taken and talked to me such a long space and said he hoped I would get my husband to bring me back to Brussels for the season and the other big balls, and if it meant I would miss some of the hunting then sure he could give me hunting himself and not only after tame foxes but after stags just like they do in Devon, and perhaps after wild boars and strange savage creatures they are and so dangerous to come on if they are hurt. Or perhaps, he said, in Paris, if ever I were in Paris he would be glad

324

to see us there. And riding through the snow in Baron Krabbe's troika as he called it, or in his sleigh with its bells under the stars and the clear winter moon with the trees shining with the ice stretching their boughs down and all crisp and crackling, or riding in the spring with Mr Strand and his strange saddle with the silver bells on it that he said he got in Mexico, and how he was in Mexico when he was a Brazilian and how he spoke English to well but so strangely accented he never quite explained. But he had given her those turquoises set in plates of silver to make a collar that went around her neck and halfway down to her waist and quite covered her bust, and Lord Dunscore leaning on his two sticks had said she could not go to a Royal ball without good jewels for the honour of Britain and for the Queen, and she couldn't give a straw for the stuffy Queen but the diamonds were worth wearing, all his wife's so he had to have them back afterwards which was a pity but he did let her keep that smallest necklace, and she could wear that to things like hunt balls, and sure that ball in Brussels was worth twenty of the balls she had been to in Ireland and even better than the one the Blazers gave up there in the north, and she would have been a great sensation there if she had had the bracelets that Baron Krabbe gave her with the tourmalines and garnets and what she had thought were emeralds but he had said nonsense, and they weren't set in gold, he had told her, but really it was copper with some gold mixed in to give it a shine and a colour in case it looked like brass.

And all the things she could have told Tom that had happened, with him out there in the ice and fighting, and nearly dead of cold and burnt all over his poor hands and his face hit and his nose pushed to the side and sure wouldn't his catarrh be worse now in the winter, and coming home and never a word about it in *The Times* or in the *Illustrated* and nobody wanting to take his drawings and no promotion and no prize money and wasn't it to be Captain he deserved, and at least couldn't they make him a Commander with the gold lace on his hat when he went to the Lord Lieutenant's receptions, and perhaps no medal and how long would the medal take to come when the war wasn't even over yet and sometimes it took years and years. And Harriet in her mind went through all the things she would like to tell Tom, and all so she need not think of why it was she could not tell Tom.

Talleyman took his brandy into the study, old Josiah's study. Arabella had had a fire lit there, and lamps set for him. Sometimes, Talleyman thought, he'd rather have Arabella than most of the First Lieutenants or Pursers he had known. He opened the great docket that Richard had arranged for him, old Josiah's will and the deed to land and property. He could understand the accounts of a ship, he could set a course, find his position with sun shots and star charts and tables of deviation, so surely he could make sense of these papers. And he could not.

After midnight, Talleyman came to bed, to the room where the candle still burnt. Harriet was sitting up, staring into space. This was the bedroom, the very bed, that old Josiah had used. Arabella had given it to him as the head of the family, the householder, only now he wasn't sure he deserved it on those grounds. He washed in his dressing room, got into his nightshirt, still strange to be wearing night clothes and not lie down half dressed for the deck. He came into the bedroom and, idly, opened the nearest wardrobe door, to be sure that Arabella had taken the old man's things out. His fingers met the sable cloak, sank deep, and he started a little, thought that there was not a man in *Flamingo* but could tell what that was, could not value it. He asked,

'What is this?'

'Oh, it is . . . it is . . .something from Bruges. Richard . . . Richard said furs would be needed, that it would be paid for out of the transaction. I do not know what

326

transaction, it must be something that would show our dignity . . .'

She tailed off. Tom was getting into bed, sliding his arms around her. And in another voice, he said,

'And what is this?'

Harriet screamed . . . and screamed . . . and screamed.

5

All that he remembered, walking to the big house in Bedford Square. Through all the new streets laid out in squares and straight lines, all over the Russell land. He reached the house, and rang. There was a butler here today to answer the door, signs of life in the hall, as if a staff had been got together now that Richard was home from foreign parts. Old Josiah had taken the house ten years ago. The first butler, Holmes, had stayed for six years, and then died of falling down stairs, either of a stroke, or of drink. After that there seemed to have been a butler a year. Talleyman merely said,

'I have come to see Mr Talleyman, junior.'

'Your name, sir?' How could the man know him?

'I am Mr Talleyman senior.' He had never said that before. It did him good, he needed something to do him good.

Richard had taken over the room which had been their father's study. Once it had been a barren office out of place here, drifted from some abandoned counting house. Now it was thickly carpeted, the walls papered ornately, pictures on the wall, silver candelabra, a big mahogany desk, chairs and a sideboard to match. No sign of papers, law books, anything that would suit an attorney with wide interests. Tom Talleyman sat opposite his brother, sipped the Madeira he was offered, exchanged conventional inquiries into health. Then Talleyman said, bluntly,

'I have come about the will.'

'I had not imagined otherwise. Have you read it?'

'I worked on it all day yesterday. Who drew it up?'

'Fogg.'

'You had no hand in it?'

'As a legatee it would have been most improper.'

'Yes. That is why I asked.'

'So?'

'I am sure that the will does not say what I construe it to say.'

'If you do not believe your interpretation, then it is probable that your interpretation is right.'

'I can take it to my own lawyer for an interpretation, or even go back to Fogg himself.'

'Fogg drew up the will as we instructed him.'

'We?'

'You do not think that our father would have embarked on a document as important as this without some advice from me? He was dealing with a complex affair, a matter of several hundred thousands of pounds. Not with small potatoes.'

'Thank you.'

'I was the only one who knew what was going on almost as well as he did. Besides, the will was intended to stand unaltered for some years. The new bill, the Limited Liabilities Act as it will be in a few weeks when it is passed, changes the whole structure of our business. You noted that the bill concerned a number of companies.'

'I tried to count. I traced twenty-seven.'

'You missed two. All these will change from ordinary joint stock companies the day the Act comes in.'

'Limited liability – is that not a device for making cheating easier?'

'It may do that.'

'You hope?' This, thought Richard, is like a nightmare version of a clients' meeting. He answered,

'Broadly speaking under the old law, if we were partners, on paper, but you had put neither money or work into the enterprise, only your name to a piece of paper, then if I failed and I were a man of straw, then you would be liable to the full extent of your property to make good the losses. Under the new measure, you would be liable only to the extent to which you had pledged yourself at the outset. I have spent the last year turning those twenty-nine partnerships into companies with limited liability. And after that – our father had a great scheme in mind, and all I did I did under his direction. It would, he thought, take ten years. At the end of that time, we would have no control, no interest, in making things, in doing things, only in making money. Bankers, you may say, with specialized interests, lending money on the making of things. Under that you must see the will.'

'But under the will, as far as I can see, I get nothing. Not even my farm.'

'You will get your farm more surely than you would like.'

'Explain it.'

'The Manor House, the Dower House and all the Fen Dilney estate, they come to you, but not absolutely. They come in entail. You may farm them, improve them, enjoy the income, but you may not sell them. They are yours in entail, they must be left undiminished, to your eldest son.'

'And otherwise?'

I told you, each of the twenty-nine companies, the boilerworks, the two foundries, others you will not have heard of, like Dunscore's bank, into each of these we, as the legatees, have put more than half the capital. When the bill goes through, we will, as a family, have more than fifty per cent of the shares. But we, the

329

legatees, are left shares in another limited company, which exists merely to hold the shares in the other companies. In this company, you are left forty per cent of the shares, Arabella twenty per cent, myself forty per cent. But the profits of this last company will not necessarily be paid out. For ten years, our father laid down, the profits must be ploughed back. Except that each of us may be allowed such moneys as the controller of the company may think necessary to keep up our positions in society.

'Which means, my dear brother, that you are left what profits you can make from the farms. Otherwise, for every penny you need, you must come to me and ask. And make out a case.'

'So I understood.'

'After ten years from our father's death, we may meet and revise the constitution of the company.'

'What were you doing in Bruges?'

'Working. For our company. We used the facilities of our company, Dunscore's Bank, to persuade various city interests to underwrite a loan to finance the Newfoundland–Chihuahua railroad. Half was underwritten in London, the rest in France. We did not need to call on the underwriters, the full loan was raised in Brazil. We collected our commission, a quarter of a million pounds.'

'How much?'

'The loan was for twenty-five million.'

'But – you intend to back a railway from Newfoundland to Mexico?'

'There will be no railway.' Richard leaned back, poured more Madeira. Our commission will be used, through other limited companies, to make other operations possible.'

'Then who will that loan go to?'

'To the Tsar.'

Talleyman went rigid. He reminded himself that he was here to find things out, not to explode. 'I would remind you that we are at war with the Tsar and I have been at sea for nine months fighting the Russians.'

'Yes, it is all the fault of that stupid Trading with the Enemy Act. But, my dear Tom, you see you did not fight for nothing. We were moderate. Half a million will stick to the fingers of the French and English collaborators in this. A million at least will stay with the man who actually found the money, selling small bonds.'

'Mr Strand?'

'Indeed. At least as much with the Russian gentleman who negotiated the loan, Baron Krabbe.'

'I have seen his arms on a bracelet. Emeralds, set in solid gold.'

'Oh, Harriet, yes. She deserved all she was given, she worked very hard as our hostess.'

'And a cloak of sables, worth at least a thousand pounds?'

'A charming gesture. And Dunscore was very kind. He lent her some of his wife's diamonds to go to the Mardi Gras ball in Brussels, a tiara, a shoulder knot, two rings, luckily the right size, bracelets, a necklace. Of course, he took them all back, except the smallest, the necklace. You should have seen her, Tom, she looked magnificent. I think it was the sight of her that brought Krabbe down. He agreed to my terms.'

'Your terms?'

'I held the loan in my fingers. I let it go through for a consideration.'

'What?'

'I now have the coal concessions for nearly half of Russia. At least *our* company has.'

'We are going to cut coal for the Tsar?'

'We are going to sell the concessions.'

Oh but he is smooth, thought Talleyman, he is too smooth. I have seen smooth men like this before, playing lightly with other people's lives. He asked,

'So you took Harriet to help in this work – for our company?' He fidgeted with his fingers at the open breast of his coat.

'For the company – for you, for us all, for her children.'

'For *her* children?'

Richard held the recharged glass of Madeira to his lips.

'Yes, for her children. As well as for sables, emeralds, diamonds. . . .'

'And so . . .' Talleyman searched for the most direct word, for something to break the smooth surface . . . 'you know she is pregnant.'

The glass smashed on the desk top, the wine puddled and poured, dripped over the edge to the carpet. Richard's jaw dropped slack, he stuttered in his throat. Nobody could act like that, thought Talleyman, nobody could pretend to this extent of surprise, of shock, even.

'It can't be.'

'It is true.'

'You surely don't accuse me?'

'No, it was not you. But you were responsible.'

'Responsible?'

'You took her to Bruges. It was your place to watch her, to look after her, to protect her. Did you not know already how foolish she is? I married a fool, Richard, and last night I realized it. And I thought every one else knew but me. She lives in a world of her own, she acts without forethought. If you stood her on the middle of Westminster Bridge, she would find a way to fall off. And you took her, *her*, to Bruges, left her to herself with unlimited credit, virtually unsupervised credit. And with these men. Dunscore, the strange Mr Strand, the Russian baron. One part of his family was trying to kill me, while he was . . . was it him? Or Dunscore, a man infamous throughout Europe, a man even more depraved than was his brother?'

'Dunscore,' said Richard coldly, 'is past all that. Besides he was more interested in boys.'

'That leaves only one.'

Richard now really raised his mental eyebrows. If one, why not many? He attempted to bring some realism into the discussion.

'What are we going to do? If you like, I will consult Dr Wormset, the young Dr Wormset, not old Dr Wormset, or the new Doctor Wormset. These things can be arranged. And there is very little danger.'

'No, no. I cannot have that. There is always danger. A great deal of danger. And Harriet would not have that.' But Harriet, he thought, would surely have it. She had been jumping Emperor. Yesterday she had fallen down stairs, and not by accident. He could not risk Harriet, what would he do without her? All these parsons prated about forgiveness. Dincombe even. How could they know what forgiveness cost? But something must be done, he could not sit here, talk with this desk-riding worm, and do nothing. He said urgently,

'Paper!'

Richard passed him a sheet of paper, watched the pencil come as ever out of the stuffed pocket, tried to see discreetly whether Tom was drawing or writing, failed. His brother folded the sheet, said, again urgently,

'Wax!'

The paper was sealed. Talleyman went out into the hallway, said something, hardly heard through the open door, to the butler. He returned, said,

'Well, that makes life all the easier. If it is life. I may soon need a lawyer. I will find my own.'

Without any other farewell, without shaking hands, he went out. Richard took paper and pen and ink, and wrote furiously. He rang the bell. From the inner depths of the house three clerks appeared. He told the senior,

'You will go at once to Leadenhall Street. You will ask to see Mr Pearson, and hand him this, in person. Do not entrust it to anyone else to deliver, wait while he reads it. Tell him that he may expect me at three o'clock this afternoon, by which time I expect much to be done. Tell him also that it was by my instructions you say this.'

'And us, sir?' asked one of the other clerks.

'Why, back to your desks, in the main office. The event for which I required you did not occur.'

As they went out, the butler entered.

'I beg your pardon, sir, but I thought you ought to know. Your last visitor. . .'

'My elder brother, Poole, as much your employer as I am, and do not forget it.'

'No, sir. Well, sir, I thought you ought to be told, he had a pistol in his hand, sir, in the hall, as he was leaving. A revolving pistol, sir.'

'He is a Naval officer, Poole, and used to weapons.'

'Yes, sir. He was putting the . . .the caps on the cylinders.'

Richard came alert. Tom had been in a fury, that cold undemonstrative fury that Richard remembered from childhood, that others remembered, Pither and Partridge, only Partridge was dead, Langer and Delauney and Superintendent Trant. He asked, now, awake to danger,

'My brother sent a message. Who to?'

'Oh, yes sir, he ordered that a footman take a message to Lord Denain, at once, sir, by a cab. He said you would pay for the cab, "out of the company", sir, whatever that meant.'

Richard knew what it meant. All of his life he lived in the state which came so rarely to Tom, an icy glaze over his needs, his wants, his triumphs and despairs. Now, for once, he entered the state in which Tom lived almost all the time, a driving fury. Only one thing was uncertain.

'Where did he go? Mr Talleyman *senior*?'

'He asked for a cab, sir. I found one at once. He told the man to take him to the Agapanthus Club.'

'I will join him. Call *me* a cab!'

6

Talleyman got out of his cab at the Agapanthus Club. He paid the cabbie, went in, and hung up his hat. Mr Bolton looked out of the office as Talleyman passed, and called,

'My felicitations, commander.'

It seemed Talleyman did not hear him. Bolton returned to his reading of the Admiralty promotion list, men who had been elevated for services in the current war, underlining the names of members of the club.

Philip Suttle, Lord Denain, was already in the great common room of the club. The buffet was laid at the inner end of the room. Before six o'clock in the evening, members might help themselves free, if only they bought something to drink; most favoured beer. After six o'clock, dinner was served in the dining room beyond, and that was really expensive. As a result, the company tended to vary from time to time in the day.

But, Philip saw, it was the usual crowd for that time of the day. A couple of dozen men, all respectably dressed, although some were shabbier than others. In the corner, Only sat in what was to be come his usual corner, his walking sticks at the sides of his chair. Philip remembered him vaguely, someone he had met once in Ireland. He did not know the young man talking to him, smooth-faced with yellow hair and a scar through it.

He saw Talleyman come in, and stood to greet him. But carefully: he had seen that light in Talleyman's eyes before.

'Why, Tal, will you have a drink with me?'

Unexpectedly, the young man with the yellow hair interposed, in an unfamiliar accent,

'Mr Talleyman's drink is already ordered, and paid for.'

Philip looked around. The room was unusually silent, and everybody was looking at him. And at Talleyman. He knew hardly anybody here: it was clear that everybody knew Talleyman.

'I think, my lord,' said Talleyman, 'we have things to discuss. Shall we go into a private room?'

'Why so formal? I am sure there is nothing that we have to talk about that requires a private room.'

'I would advise it.'

'Surely we are among friends. We are all members of this club.'

'If you must. In public. You may disgrace yourself.'

'Disgrace myself? That is a strange phrase, Tal old man.' Philip genuinely had not the slightest idea of what this was about, why he had received that note, written in terms of urgency. 'What does it mean?'

'If you must, here, then listen.' Talleyman was breaking one of the strictest rules of the club. He did not care, he knew he did not care, he did not understand why he did not care. He was seeing the whole world plain, the old glass wall was dissolving like a layer of varnish. Seven years' scorn and resentment were scraping the view clear. 'It is a matter of wives, yours and mine.'

'If our wives quarrel, what is it to us?' Philip looked around him. The men's faces were as blank and impartial as the faces of the portraits on the walls.

'First, you took from me the woman I loved, the woman I wanted for my wife, and married her instead of me. You dazzled her with a title.'

336

'I had no idea Jane had any liking for you. You have not spoken ten words to her in any year since we were married.'

'And do you not understand what that has cost me?' It might be dirty linen, Talleyman thought, but I must speak now, I have bottled this up for seven years. 'Now you take Harriet from me, too.'

'Harriet was anybody's for the taking. Mine especially. If anybody was dazzled by a tittle. . .' Philip let the words dwindle away.

'Yet she was all I had, the poor man's lamb.'

'Lamb, sheep. . .' Philip was past caring what he said. Looking in for a moment from the door, Mr Bolton reflected that this would be another day to go down in the annals of the club, the unwritten annals, like the night of the Reform Bill when the Whig members were thrown out through the front window.

'I will have satisfaction.' For this moment, Talleyman was the more in control. 'You may choose the weapons. I am sure that there is somebody somewhere who will be your second. And wherever you choose. On your land or on mine, or even in the Park. . .'

'I am sure there are women in the Park who will give you ample satisfaction,' said Philip. And at that moment he realized he had gone too far. He saw Talleyman's hand move to his breast pocket, the revolver come out, someone – he thought it was Mallow – making a charge at Talleyman, he heard the shot like thunder in the high room. He choked in the white smoke and fell.

'Christ, it's double action,' shouted Moulton, and moved as Talleyman brought the pistol up. But it was Only's stick which came, straight as a javelin, as a belaying pin, to strike Talleyman's wrist and send the shot up past his ear.

Richard Talleyman was rushing into the club from which he had been blackballed. Moulton had Talleyman by the shoulders. Dr Wormset, the new Dr Wormset, was already kneeling by Lord Denain. Mr Bolton

337

watched as Talleyman was hustled from the room, half
dazed, into a waiting cab. He said to the constable,

'No, you may not enter without a warrant. This is a
private club. I do not see how you can have reason
to suspect any crime has been committed here. Many
of our members are young officers, they have been
experimenting with a new form of gunpowder. You
have no cause to enter.'

He returned to his office, and continued the writing
of a letter. He had looked forward to writing this for
some years:

> ... having mentioned a lady's name in the club, and
> caused thereby a fracas during which fire arms were
> discharged, the Committee have been unanimous in
> deciding that you should be requested to remove
> your name from the books of the Club, forthwith.

> I remain, my Lord, your most obedient servant. . . .

7

'Why?' Richard demanded. 'Why, and in public in the
club, surrounded by men who knew you, who knew
you both? True,' he added as the thought struck him,
'in front of men who will not talk of it.'

'It was the entail,' said Talleyman. 'I thought the
entail would see my sons safe. At least they would not
starve. And if I killed Philip Suttle first, my honour
would be safe.'

'You want to be him who died a'Thursday? What
came into you?'

'You must remember,' said Dincombe from a corner,
'that he has been under a strain that you cannot even
imagine. He has been the whole winter in the ice, he has

carried all two hundred of us on his shoulders through frost and fire and blood. If any man has a right to be mad, he has. What will happen now? Will Lord Denain prosecute for yesterday's assault?'

Richard shrugged.

'If Lord Denain prosecutes, there are twenty members who will swear they saw Denain shoot himself. But if there is a prosecution, this will all come out.' All the business of Bruges, not only what Harriet did there, but also what I was doing there, and Dunscore. There will be the scandal of the century. 'He will remember that affair all his life, he had his collarbone broken, and it is likely he will never again be able to lift his hand above his shoulder. He may want to have you prosecuted in the courts, or he may want to sue for damages. If he does, then I will break him. I have him in my debt, he no longer has a penny except by my favour. If he does sue, I will have him out on the street a beggar, with no roof to his head.'

'I cannot have that. Think of Jane.'

'Do not think of Jane. Think of Harriet. We have to find a way of saving her honour as well as yours. The only way to do that is to have you both out of the country for a considerable time, a few years. When you return, who is going to remember dates?'

'Abroad? As a pensioner?'

'No. While you lay here yesterday full of opium – that was young Dr Wormset, not new Dr Wormset – I went first to the East India Company, and then to the Admiralty and to the House, and backwards and forwards. I have made arrangements.'

'India?'

'The Company will today offer you an appointment in their sea service. *Flamingo* has quietly been returned to those who paid for her. She is needed in India, and must go with a cargo as soon as she is out of the dockyard again. They think about three weeks. You will be in command.'

'I am not senior enough. I am only a Lieutenant.'

'This is not the Navy. If you are worried, I may be able to arrange that you are made up to commander on the half-pay list.' It will be months before he is calm enough to go back to the Gazette, to the lists, to compare lists, to find that he has already been promoted for merit. By then he will be at sea, or in India. So long as he is out of the country, and settled there. 'You will have command pay and table money from John Company. As well as that we must arrange that you receive each month out of our family funds, to begin with, at least the equivalent of your full pay as a commander. That will make you a man of substance in India. They say living is cheap there.'

'But. . . Harriet?'

'I have arranged a passage for her next month in an Indiaman to Bombay. As your wife, she too is a person of importance. She will have her own stateroom, and she can take her own maid. And she will have company, for there is a lady going out, a Miss Henry, to stay with her sister, a Mrs Hodson, one of John Company's military officers.' Hodson, Talleyman thought, a fine fellow, none of his friends liked him. He asked,

'And the boys? With her?'

'Oh, good heavens, no. India is no place for toddlers like that. They will have to stay. They will be quite safe with Arabella.'

'For three years?'

'Only three years.' Three years will be enough time to start. Scandal or no, I would have had to arrange something like this. With Arabella, I can do what I wish in our company. But if Tom stays, then, well, he was always Arabella's favourite, she would vote against me as he ordered. And in three years, not only will it be too late to change: there will be no scandal. Of English children born in India, there aren't one in ten who live to the age of one. When they return, who will remember dates?

'With Arabella?'

'You know how much she loves them, how much they love her.' Probably, they know her better than they do their mother. 'I will, of course, be their legal guardian – '

'No.' Talleyman tried to take a decision, be more than a cipher. 'Not you. Dincombe, my good fellow, will you act as their guardian?'

Let him have that, thought Richard. A clergyman, eminently suitable, unworldly, a bit of a milksop, I'm convinced. Putty in my hands.

'And the land? The estate?'

'Well, that is yours, you can either put in a bailiff or rent it. In any case, it will suffice to support the boys till you come back.' If you ever come back, but there, if he has survived five years in West Africa, he's bound to survive India. 'I suppose you will want to get back to Fen Dilney this afternoon, tell Harriet.'

'No.' On this, Talleyman was firm. 'If I see the land again, I will never go. I must make the break now, without time to repent. Arabella must tell Harriet, tell her everything. I must get to the ship.' I must go back to work, to the regular routine, get her ready to sail, even man her? – even appoint, perhaps, my own First Lieutenant, or First Mate, or whatever the John Company phrase is. I have ruined my life. I must not think of it, not blame Harriet. I must get to sea.

8

Captain Paxton Only hobbled on his two sticks into the presence of the Queen. He received from her hands his Crimean Medal, and the Cross for his valour in maintaining his ship deep in enemy territory throughout

341

the winter, and for destroying a regiment of Russian cavalry.

Biddell settled down to his law books. Orton began to make himself a reputation. Dincombe learnt a nimbler language by the waters of Teify. They met occasionally at the Agapanthus Club. Mr Bolton happily amended his membership list.

Moulton and Calne found a ship for Baltimore. Parks, Silverwright and Sterling went back to the depot hulk. Smales returned to a whaler, Nussey to his pots and pans.

Harriet, pregnant, appreciated her stateroom on the Indiaman. She thought that sailors lived very well indeed on suety puddings and duffs and lobscouse, all of which she had heard of.

Albert and Edward were happy with their Aunt Arabella. They hardly noticed when their parents came to say goodbye: separately.

Commander Talleyman stood out to sea in *Flamingo*, with Longville as his First Mate, and in the lower deck a cargo too important to be trusted to any other ship, fifty thousand of the new Enfield rifles: and twenty cartridges per weapon, ready greased.

And across the wastes of Tartary, Marine Garvey brought steadily south a heart of hate.